WORD MADE FLESH

WORD MADE FLESH

JACK O'CONNELL

Perennial

An Imprint of HarperCollins*Publishers*

Epigraph on p. vii from Paul Auster, CITY OF GLASS (Los Angeles: Sun & Moon Press, 1985). © Paul Auster, 1985. Reprinted by permission of the publisher.

A hardcover edition of this book was published by HarperFlamingo, an imprint of HarperCollins Publishers, in 1999.

HarperCollins books may be purchased for educational, business, or sales promotional use. For information please write: Special Markets Department, HarperCollins Publishers Inc., 10 East 53rd Street, New York, NY 10022.

First Perennial edition published 2000.

Designed by Laura Lindgren

The Library of Congress has catalogued the hardcover edition as follows:
O'Connell, Jack.
      Word made flesh / Jack O'Connell. —1st ed.
         p. cm.
     ISBN 0-06-019209-7
     I. Title
   PS3565.C526W67   1999
   813'.54—dc21   98-41174

ISBN 0-06-109722-5 (pbk.)

00 01 02 03 04 ❖/RRD 10 9 8 7 6 5 4 3 2 1

To Claire Teresita

Adam's one task in the Garden had been to invent language, to give each creature and thing its name. In that state of innocence, his tongue had gone straight to the quick of the world. His words had not been merely appended to the things he saw, they had revealed their essence, had literally brought them to life. A thing and its name were interchangeable. After the fall, this was no longer true. Names became detached things; words devolved into a collection of arbitrary signs; language had been severed from God. The story of the Garden, therefore, records not only the fall of man, but the fall of language.

—Paul Auster
City of Glass

You are hearing the screams of a small, fat man. This will be your last opportunity to turn away. The noise should end presently. At the very least the sound will be diminished, transformed into something you might find somewhat more acceptable. The ghost of the scream. There may even be a moment or two of silence—the time between the man's realization of what is about to happen to him and his realization that there is absolutely nothing he can do to prevent it from happening.

I refuse to accept blame for what you are witnessing. This is not my fault. To some degree, we all have to admit, Leo Tani put himself in this situation. He knew full well the hazards of his particular occupation and he did not behave prudently. Had he never heard the advice, Act reverently when sojourning in a foreign land?

You will argue, at some future date, that the 'Shank has long resided in the city. That he has made the city his home since his arrival, from Turin, in the midst of his extended and overheated puberty. I would only answer that this is one more rumor we will never see confirmed, a statement without evidence to prove its truth, repeated for so long that we accept it at face value. But you should know, better than most, that no one can make this city his home. We remain transients here even if we never leave. And strangers to each other forever.

If you move to the left, you should be able to see them preparing. Don't be ashamed. It is nothing but human to be fascinated by ritual. Please try to relax. In days to come you may wish to castigate yourself over your passivity. But this is a futile and regressive response to a new form of knowledge. You were simply curious and since when has this been a crime? Isn't wisdom born of curiosity, the inherent need to watch and to listen and thus, to know? Isn't this the nature of the witness?

I hope you have the generosity to admit that there is a kind of beauty in the ritual. A perverse grace, I will grant you, but still. My advice would be to look for the significance of each small gesture. These signals tend to coalesce, to bind together in the end and reveal a larger and deeper pattern. Notice, for instance, that they use Leo's own silk monogrammed show handkerchief as the blindfold. Try to remember, if you can make it out in this light, the color of the masking tape they use to secure the cotton wadding in his mouth.

I have no way of knowing if you are a religious individual. I cannot say that I care either way. But as you watch them now, stripping the 'Shank of his fine clothing, do you think of some historical precedent? Or can you not move past what you imagine to be going through Leo's mind? Let me assure you he is mistaken. The violation you are about to behold is something so much greater than a common rape. It is an outrage against the entire corporal world. Do you think I am being flamboyant?

That is Gallzo you are smelling. A liquor produced in a particularly arid region of the Middle East. Derived from the roots of the hyssop reed. It is an acquired taste. I will tell you a small secret: each barrel is flavored with a drop of urine from the honey buzzard. Have you ever had the pleasure? It is known to be one of Tani's greatest indulgences. You might take heed of the fact that none of them guzzle. One reverent sip. And then the remains of the bottle are poured over the victim's naked expanse. A bit closer you would hear the small splash, the liquid bouncing off his girth, running down the skin, off the body and finally into the cinder bed beneath their feet. Through this century of ash and into the dry earth itself.

Like a trip to the River Jordan. The action has that kind of power. You might expect a black dove to appear up here in the balcony with us, the flutter of the wings somehow worse than Leo's muted cries. Do you believe the alcohol will cause the burn to be even more intense? Or will the 'Shank be unconscious by then, the body fallen to shock, the victim unable to observe what you will remember forever?

I suppose there is a lesson here for every businessman—be careful what you bring to market. And isn't that what we all are in the end? Businessmen. Merchants. Entrepreneurs of one sort or another.

The bread crusts on the floor? Most likely they were left by the tinker children. By all accounts, this train station is their home. I see by your face that you distrust this myth as well, but I can attest to its veracity. They are not nearly as feral as the common wisdom would have you believe. They are extremely crafty in their own way, but, of course, they lack your years of experience and the formal training of a rational mind. This is why you are the witness and the tinkers have abandoned their refuge for the night.

Excuse me, look closely now. They are readying their tools. I only wish you could hold the blades yourself. It would make the event so much more palpable for you.

They still produce their cutlery by hand, in the manner of the ancients, particularly the Greeks. Though it is said they have acquiesced to the use of stainless steel rather than bronze. They employ the techniques perfected in Solingen. They are not dilettantes—none may use the blade who do not craft the blade. Beginning to end. They refine their own steel in individual clay crucibles, forge the blade with hammer and anvil and grinding wheel, endlessly polish until the motion of the soft rub becomes a kind of trance-making prayer. I once heard they used a roue of their own blood and bile as the cutting fluid. But you know how these types of legend can take on a life of their own. The same source swore to me that they must single-handedly, and in an elaborately orchestrated fashion, kill the beast chosen to provide the handle of horn or bone or tusk. Elsewhere I heard that every hilt is made of mother-of-pearl. Who are we to believe?

It takes years to complete a single scalpel in this manner, but the instrument will last a lifetime. Or, perhaps, several lifetimes, if you follow my meaning. After the winter of glazing comes the spring of buffing. And after the summer of mirror satining, we are to understand, a name that will never be spoken is finally etched into the blade.

Now, please, pay attention—here is the first incision. There may be a spurt of—yes, there it is, did you catch it? You see, they start at the base of the neck, very careful to avoid the arterial network. They want Leo alive throughout the entire procedure, if possible. They believe it keeps the tissue more vibrant and supple in its afterlife.

I have no way of knowing how much background you have in human anatomy. And certainly I don't wish to interfere with your observing. It is just that I personally find the integumentary system so fascinating. Both in the area of its organic nature, the beautiful complexity of its layering, and in the fact of its existence as an ecosystem itself, the housing it provides to that microscopic, parasitic world we ignore every day.

I see you flinch. And we are only at the beginning. But you did not close your eyes and that will make all the difference. It bothers you, I suppose, that Leo is still conscious. The way his head attempts to jerk back and forth within the confines of their hands. You imagine him choking as the wadding works its way deeper down his trachea. Try to think of Mr. Tani as more object than person. This has worked for others in the past.

Now this is the ventral incision. They will make a clean cut from the center of the chest downward to the anus. You are terrified of viewing a castration, I understand. But this is not their purpose. You have to trust them at some point, my friend. It is true they have no use for the genitalia. But their intention is not one of sadism.

You see here the natural genius of the body, how the ribs prevent them from cutting too deeply. And I want you to take special notice, this is surely of some importance, that they refuse to use anything resembling forceps. They peel back and hold the tissue with their own fingers. They have developed a highly refined strength and precision in this area.

Is the skin more blue than you would have imagined? Can you see clearly enough? Perhaps it is the contrast with the intense redness of the muscles below. Such great care they take as they move down through the abdominal wall. The concentration at this point is enormous. If they pierce through into the intestinal cavity everything could be ruined. They are very concerned with hygiene, have strict mores regarding purification.

You would never know how wildly the body should naturally be flailing at this point. The holders secure their grip so rigidly. If not for the bulging eyes and the well-muffled, but still audible scream you would have no indication of Leo's discomfort. Surely he is working his way toward shock as we watch. The brain may begin shutting down consciousness at any time now. I would not be surprised if they decide to wait before rolling the body—

No, I am mistaken. They will take a moment to resecure their hold once he is in place on his stomach. There, now you are seeing the beginning of the dorsal incision, there along the center of the back, from the shoulders down to the rectum. Watch as they lift the tissue back, so careful to control the rate of force, the pressure constant, pulling the layers away from the meat beneath, see the cartilage resist then finally give way, fall back to the body. You might expect some tearing, and I am told it does happen on occasion, when the subject suffers from some epidermal disease. Apparently the 'Shank is in fine condition.

They seem to be after as large and continuous a sheet of tissue as they can extract. They do not like patchwork. At this stage, a scissors would make their job much easier, but again who can argue with ceremony? They will cut the flesh at the hip area and they may find it necessary to pop the leg out of the hip socket. For your sake I hope this is not the—

Again, I apologize. You would think Leo was beyond the capability of a scream of this magnitude. We never know how much strength and tenacity an individual possesses, do we? They will work their fingers under the skin here. The region of the tailbone proves very stubborn for some reason. At times they find it necessary to remove the legs entirely. This is a long and tedious exercise without the luxury of technology. Do our doctors fully appreciate the benefits of the high-speed bone saw? I wonder at times.

Those hooks and chains? This means we are entering the final stages. They will truss the body—yes, you see, lancing the main hook through the jaw and then hauling upward on the chains until fully suspended above the rock. An old and decrepit building like this, the approach gives you pause. But those beams survived the '53 quake and I doubt even Tani can pull them down.

The way the body hangs, certainly life is now gone. Does it make the watching easier?

Gravity offers some assistance at this point. They move downward, faster now, the sheets of skin resembling, at times, small sails. Any one of them can manage this stage of the paring, but for the close work along the skull, only the most dexterous among them will be allowed to cut. The muscles at the base of the ears are small but particularly strong. And an apprentice will often make his first mistake at this exact point. Right there, around the eyelids. The lips are cut free and, though never collected with the rest of the tissue, neither are they discarded. I have no idea what use they could be.

That cloud? They are dusting the tissue with powdered borax. It makes the going somewhat easier and it begins the preservation process immediately. I am told you can also use cornmeal in a pinch.

This is distressing, I agree. Something about that final series of yanks to pull the entire jacket free.

I thought for sure you would look away. I suppose you've surprised us both.

They will do the curing elsewhere. A tedious procedure involving noniodized salt and formaldehyde as well as a mothproofing solvent and grain alcohol. But, believe me, with a gourmand like Leo Tani, it is the degreasing that will take the most time. All the cheesy fat of his robust appetites. That he was not a moderate man is self-evident. Look at him hanging there. Look at that world beneath the skin, the subterranean detail. Think of it as pure structure. Such intricacy.

You may despise them and fear them, but you must allow some degree of esteem for their talent. They are more force than creature, wouldn't you agree? My God, look at the skill, the undiluted confidence with which they work, the instinctual grace. They are the surgeons of history. The pathologists of our shared memory. The skivers of our race dream. Some part of you can't help but respect the genius of their craft, that level of intensity and shapeliness that elevates their practice into art. Admit that much to me. Be honest, at least with yourself. And understand that this respect cannot help but grow. Into admiration. And imitation. And ultimately, as the past has shown us so well and so thoroughly, into love.

Do not speak—I know what the question is. You are curious as to what happens to the epidermis itself, yes? You see them collecting it in the burlap sacks and you wonder what use it could possibly have. But everything has a use. I was hoping I could expect more from you. I must confess a small disappointment. Wouldn't you agree that we invent the usage? Isn't this what we have always done?

Even the tidying-up work is a solemn responsibility.

You are disgusted with the way they clean their tools? But I assure you, in their tradition the saliva itself is thought to hold many purging and strengthening properties.

As to Tani, the corpse will be left hanging. As a sign, I suppose. Eventually, inevitably, it will become one more dark myth from the belly of Gompers Station. Though the blood loss was spectacular, I believe the death certificate will make mention of absolute trauma. By the time the remains are found, by the train bulls or by the scavengers, a multitude of parasites will have swarmed to the open meat, drawn by the immediate initiation of decay; a veritable legion of vampiric organisms will have massed upon the bare altar of the 'Shank's subcutaneous corpus. They will give nothing. They will only take. Because they can do nothing else. Because that is the nature they were born with. There was a saying back in Shinar—

I'm sorry, but they appear to have spotted you.

No, there is nothing you can do.

You may know other ways out of the station, but sooner or later they will find you.

You have been the witness.

That was your choice.

You were warned at the very beginning.

1

Someone must have been telling lies about me is all Gilrein can think as they squeeze open his mouth and lay the barrel of the Glock on his tongue. Softly, as if it were a communion wafer.

The tall one with the ludicrous overbite asks again, "Where is the package?" the voice accented and a little phlegmy.

The one with the face made of burn scars and the eye that won't close drives a fist into Gilrein's stomach and they all lurch away from the wall for a second, then they push Gilrein back against the bricks, drive the gun farther back toward the tonsils until the choking starts.

"Where is the package?"

Gilrein tries to shake his head, to indicate a lack of understanding, but they won't let him. He forces his eyes to stay open and sees the two men look at each other. The tall one tightens his grip on Gilrein's throat and the other nods and steps away.

A blast comes from the mouth of the alley, and all three look and in the lights from the Checker they see a silhouetted figure extending a shotgun in their direction.

A voice yells, "Blumfeld, Raban, let him go now."

Blumfeld and Raban glance at each other as Gilrein tries to suppress a gagging sound. Then the Glock is pulled out of the mouth and the tall one backhands him across the cheek and says, "This is not over."

The two of them walk out of the alley as Gilrein lets himself slide down the wall onto his ass and begin to vomit. His eyes are pressed closed and he's seeing bright flashes of light and there's an awful pain flowing through his temples, a building pressure that feels like it may never stop increasing. He makes himself hunch onto all fours and when his stomach empties, he tries to calm his breathing.

Finally, he's aware of the hand on his shoulder and he lets it guide him back to the wall. He wipes at his mouth with his forearm, takes some deep breaths. The intensity of the pain begins to diminish slightly. He lets his head come up and opens his eyes.

There's a face half hidden in shadow and when the voice comes—"C'mon now, Gilly, you're okay"—he realizes it's Bobby Oster.

He tries to speak and Oster shakes him off. The savior is down on one knee with the Ithaca pump resting on his shoulder as if he'd just completed some kind of urban cattle drive.

Oster moves into a sitting position next to Gilrein, his back against the alley wall. Pockets of steam gust around them and in the distance a stew of sounds becomes audible—sirens, horns, the bleak purr of machinery.

"Blumfeld was the one with the Glock," Oster says. "Raban's his creature. They're both meatboys for August Kroger."

Gilrein tries to focus on his breathing, but he knows that as the shock dies out, the reality of the beating is going to arrive. In the kidneys and the stomach and in the groin.

"How bad did it get," Oster asks, "before I got here?"

Gilrein attempts the first words and stops before the tongue can deliver.

Oster stands up and says, "Can you walk?"

Gilrein nods without looking at him.

"We'll take your car," Oster says, reaching down, softly grabbing a forearm and pulling Gilrein up to standing. "You're going to be okay, Gilly."

Oster wheels the Checker up onto the interstate. Gilrein lets his head lean against the passenger window and in the reflection cast by the passing halogen lamps, he can see both eyes already starting to swell up. The inside of his mouth is cut and his tongue pokes at the pulp and initiates a flow of blood and a burning like a bee sting.

"You still keep a bottle in the glove box?"

Gilrein shifts to face the driver and says, "What were you doing there?"

"Looks like I was saving your ass."

Gilrein pops the glove box, pulls out a new pint of Buber Gold, and cracks the seal.

Oster says, "Just rinse and spit."

Gilrein cranks the window with one hand, takes a small draw from the bottle, and braces for the pain. It's a goddamn inferno and he holds it for a second, then gets his head out the window and swallows and tears come to his eyes.

"You lose any teeth?"

Gilrein takes a breath and wipes a hand over his face.

The highway is deserted. It's still four or five hours until dawn. The air feels winter-cold for mid-April. A few drops of rain pock the windshield and then stop.

Oster runs a hand around the steering wheel and says, "I'd forgotten how sweet these babies are to drive."

They pass a chrome-strangled low rider pulled into the breakdown lane, a couple of kids sitting on its roof. There's half a moon showing in the west. Gilrein puts the cap back on the pint and stows it.

"What were you doing there, Bobby?"

Oster gives a smile, shakes his head just a bit.

"You always were a grateful little mother, weren't you, Gilly?"

"Where are we going?"

"Promise you one thing, Gilly," as he takes an offramp. "My boys will find those bastards. And you'll get first chance to stomp some Maisel ass. How's that sound?"

Gilrein looks out the window and sits up in the seat, his heart punching.

"Where the hell are we going, Oster?" even though he knows.

The Checker slows, cruises toward the end of Bigelow Street, past the long-empty industrial park. They swing right onto Rome Avenue and the road narrows and after about a quarter mile the vacant lots on either side turn into a scraggly wood, nothing clean nor remotely majestic about it, just a lot of scrub and weed and gnarled, petrifying trees killed off by a century of toxic waste.

Gilrein turns and stares at Oster and says, "You should've just let them shoot me, you son of a bitch."

Oster bears left when the road forks and turns to gravel.

"It's just a place," he says. "It's just a goddamned building. It can't hurt you, all right? We're safe here."

The Checker rolls to a stop in a makeshift parking lot filled with a selection of perfectly restored muscle cars. Beyond the lot is a miniature trailer park, a couple aisles of shabby, dented-up RVs and campers on cinder blocks. And beyond the trailers is the place Gilrein never thought he'd see again. Kapernaum Printing & Binding.

It's an enormous three-story mill, a classic old-time factory out of the heart of the industrial age, all worn-down red brick and age-darkened mortar, smokestacks and concrete loading aprons and double steel doors. The front face of the mill runs about a hundred yards and is fitted with boxy windows lined with black wrought-iron bars and sealed with gray wire mesh. The entry is an expansive granite archway with the name KAPERNAUM carved into the stonework in huge, fat block lettering.

"I won't make you go in," Oster says.

"Like hell you won't," Gilrein answers.

Oster kills the engine and they sit quiet and stare past the trailers at the factory. And though Gilrein knows there is no way to stop it from happening, he actually tries to think of something else for a minute, to focus on his wounds or the taste of the steel of the Glock in his mouth or the voice that phoned in tonight's call. But within seconds, staring at the printworks, staring at the section to the left where the bricks degenerate into unrecognizable shards and continue, after all this time, to lie in a sloping pile of rubble, all he can see is Ceil's prone body being pulled from the wreckage by the EMTs, the whole thing lit by the dozens of revolving lights from the cruisers and fire teams and ambulances, the way her bloodied arm dropped off the stretcher and Lacazze stepped forward and tucked it back under the blanket. The way the stink of the smoke and chemicals billowed out of the factory a full hour later and everyone—Petrashevski from bomb squad and Chief Bendix and Inspector Lacazze and even Oster— kept wiping at their eyes as they walked. And the lines that kept forming at the ambulances for hits off the oxygen tanks. But most of all, Gilrein remembers Ceil's face when they finally let him look. Just Ceil's beautiful face, somehow, impossibly, untouched by the concussion of the blast that lacerated her body, stroked red and blue by cruiser light.

"Would it make any difference," Oster asks, his voice odd and soft now, "if I told you the boys would all like to see you again?"

They both know it's a lie.

"Old times' sake," Oster says. "Brother officers."

Gilrein pulls in a trembling breath and manages to say, "You miserable bastard."

"This miserable bastard just saved your lousy ass, Gilly," almost yelling, then getting hold of himself, bringing it back down to friendly and quiet. "It's just a building, all right? It's been empty for ten years and it's been ruined for the past three. We just took it over, okay? Christ's sake, it's just a building." A pause and then, voice even lower, "You ever think it might do you some good to—"

"Don't even say it."

Oster nods, holds up both hands, lets some time pass.

"We've got to talk, Gilrein. There's some things I've got to ask you and there's some things you've got to ask me. So let's just do it."

"And if I refuse?"

Oster smiles, pats his shoulder.

"Then I put you out of your misery."

Gilrein stares at him, pushes open the door, and says, "Could've been anyplace else."

Oster shrugs and says, "No, Gilly. It just couldn't."

2

Oster presses a bell and in a minute there's the sound of dead bolts sliding out of the loading apron and into the hollow of the door. Then the panel rolls up on its tracks and they step into a dim concrete foyer filled with stale beer smell, cigar smoke, dim lights, and a faint trace of country and western music.

Just inside the foyer, set up like a reception desk, is a short section of industrial conveyor belt. Behind the desk, perched on a fold-out aluminum step stool, is a young cop named Danny Walden. He's dressed in jeans and a red corduroy shirt and he sports a sparser version of Oster's mustache.

Walden nods to Oster, smiles at Gilrein and says, "Been a hell of a long time."

Oster hands over the Ithaca, which Danny mounts on a wall rack. Then Oster takes his department .38 from a hip holster and puts it on the desk, followed by a Heritage .25 that he pulls from an ankle rig. He straightens up, puts a hand on Gilrein's shoulder and says, "A brother officer just got the shit kicked out of him by a couple of Kroger's assholes. What do you think about that, Danno?"

Walden puts the handguns into a file cabinet behind him, shakes his head and says, "I think that's something we're going to have to look into."

Oster extends his hand to Gilrein's far shoulder and starts to pull him down a short, fat corridor and deeper into the factory. Walden calls from behind, "It's good to see you, Gilrein."

Oster is wearing steel-toe engineer's boots and there's an echo as the heels slap the floor. They take a left down a longer but narrower corridor and the sound of the music gets louder.

"Wait till you see what we've done to this place," Oster says. "I mean the damage was unbelievable. The rear of the building is still demolished. Looks like a quarry back there. But, you know, who needs it? There's still plenty of room."

They come to a set of swinging double doors painted pumpkin orange. From his coat pocket, Oster pulls a thumb breaker that he's modified into a key chain. He unlocks the doors and opens them, steps through into the main work loft of the printing mill.

He says, "Welcome to the Houdini Lounge."

The place is lit by a few dozen fluorescent fixtures hidden behind an enormous American flag suspended from the ceiling. The oil-scarred concrete floor is squared by high brick walls. One wall houses a bank of small windows, but the majority of them have been boarded over, giving the whole room a sickly, claustrophobic air. The loft is part frat house, part pool hall, and part old-time garage all rolled into one gritty, sweaty package. There's a makeshift plywood stage at the close end of the room and a chunky stripper is trying to perform to a Waylon Jennings tune off a flashing Wurlitzer juke. There are folding felt-topped card tables clustered beyond the stage, and a half-dozen poker sessions are in progress inside blue clouds of smoke. One full wall is blocked off by an endless bar made of cherry-stained plywood. The front face of the bar is bedecked with aluminum beer cans. There are no stools; everyone stands or leans. Spray-painted across the length of the wall behind the bar, in a loopy kind of child's attempt at a cursive scrawl, are the words PEOPLE DISAPPEAR.

There's a clutter of rec room games—Ping-Pong, air hockey, pinball—seemingly plunked down with little thought given to traffic patterns or the necessity of unrestricted arm movement. An extensive Universal weight-lifting system is parked beside two large-screen televisions that sit side by side. One screen is showing dim images of a boxing match to a group of men crammed onto a green Naugahyde couch. The other is beaming a grainy black-and-white skin flick to a group of men crammed onto a matching red couch. Both couches are spilling a coarse, gray-colored stuffing from split seams.

Gilrein can put a name to half the faces in the room. The other half are familiar, like younger siblings of people he might have known at one time. The stripper is the only woman in the place. Everyone else is a cop.

Oster stands with his hands on his hips surveying the scene. He turns to Gilrein and says, "Bet it makes you miss it."

"Miss it?"

"The camaraderie. You know, being on the job."

Gilrein says, "I'm really starting to stiffen up here."

Oster nods, concerned and brotherly. "C'mon upstairs. We'll get you fixed up. You're going to be okay, Gilly."

They make their way through the room, Gilrein's name being called out over and over, long-neck beer bottles lifted toward him, hands clapping down on his bruised back. At the far end of the hall he follows Oster up a set of stairs to a large office lit by candles and smelling of harsh incense. The room is outfitted with a wooden desk, a leather couch, and what looks like a padded hospital gurney. Hanging in a corner is a heavy bag for boxing workouts. And reclining on the couch is a small, elderly woman dressed in what, at first, looks like an old nun's habit.

Oster snaps on a wall light and says in a loud voice, "Wake up, Mrs. Bloch."

He closes the office door and adds, "Couple of Light White Sparks for my friend and me, if it isn't too much trouble."

Mrs. Bloch goes to the desk, opens a drawer, and removes a label-less bottle and two clear plastic tumblers.

"Da ist nein eis," she says in a thick, dry accent, maybe Eastern European. "Der ma'jine brook e'gein."

And that's when Gilrein notices her face. Mrs. Bloch has no eyes. Or rather, where her eyes should be are two flaps of skin bulging from below the forehead to above the cheekbones. It's as if two smooth tumors have grown over the eyes like fat pancakes. It's possible the skin was grafted onto the face for some unknown but horrible medical reason. The skin is just slightly darker than the rest of the face, but there's no evidence of any stitching or scarring where it melds into the original tissue.

Gilrein stares down at the floor and Mrs. Bloch comes to him and hands him his drink, then goes back to the desk, opens a new drawer and takes out a small case, about the size and shape of a cigar box, but covered in deep blue felt. She opens the top of the box back on its hinges, puts her hands inside and fiddles with something.

There are two large plate glass windows cut into the long walls of the office and facing each other. The inner window looks down over the club below. Oster moves in front of it, sheds his leather jacket and drops it on the couch, then starts to unbutton his shirt.

He turns to Gilrein suddenly and says, "I'm sorry, have a seat."

Gilrein walks to the opposite end of the couch and sits down slowly. He takes a sip from the tumbler and tastes something like rum but with an additional medicine flavor.

Oster puts a foot up on the couch cushion and begins to unlace his boot.

"You were driving for Leonardo Tani tonight, weren't you, Gilly?"

Gilrein's stomach churns. He lets out some air, wonders if there's a bathroom anywhere nearby. He says, "You're the only one who ever called me Gilly."

Oster kicks free the boot and goes to work on its mate.

"Not the first time you were Tani's hack-boy. Breaks my god-damn heart, Gilly."

Gilrein sits up, hunches over his knees even though it seems to hurt more.

"I'm a cabdriver," he says. "I got a livery medallion. I pay the city a fortune for the privilege of driving its citizens around town. That's what I do for a living."

"You are a goddamn cop," Oster yells, then quiets. "And god-damn cops don't haul goddamn piglets like Tani around the god-damn city."

Gilrein takes a long pull of his drink, wonders if Oster would stop him if he just tried to walk out. He goes for a low voice but it just comes out weak.

"First of all, I haven't been a cop for a long time now. Unless Bendix has been misplacing my check every week for the past three years—"

"It doesn't work that way, Gilly," Oster says and moves to the desk to pick up his drink. "It's like being a priest. You can't just walk away. It marks your soul forever."

"And second," Gilrein says as if he hasn't been interrupted, "Leo Tani is a passenger like any other. He pays me my fare and tells me where to take him. It's none of my business what he does once he gets there."

"Is that right?" Oster says softly, then turns and moves to the far side of the desk. He slides open the middle drawer, pulls out a manila folder, walks back to Gilrein, and tosses it into his lap.

Against his better judgment, Gilrein opens the file and stares down at an eight-by-ten black-and-white photograph in sharp focus that shows a human body bound, gagged, hanging by chains from a steel beam. And skinned of any trace of epidermal tissue. The photo is slick to the touch and has a waxy chemical smell that says it's not long out of the bath.

"Leonardo 'Vealshank' Tani," Oster says, "a.k.a Italo Sciasci, a.k.a. Oreste Calvina, a.k.a. Rollo Griswold . . ."

"Oh, Jesus," Gilrein says.

"How many times did you take him down when you were working fraud?"

Gilrein doesn't answer, just closes the folder.

"How many of your passengers end up like this, Gilly?"

"You whack him, Oster?" in an even voice.

Oster picks up his drink and raises it toward the couch.

"I whacked him, Gilly, there wouldn't be any photos, would there?"

"The 'Shank was just a goddamn fence. All he tried to do was keep everybody happy."

"Yeah, well, looks like he dropped the ball sometime last night, doesn't it?"

"He moved merchandise for people. What the Christ did he do?"

"You're asking me?" Oster says. "You're the one who spent the night driving his fat carcass around town."

"Did Kroger do this? Is that why you were in the alley?"

Oster gives an exaggerated shrug, picks up his drink, moves to the gurney and strips off his clothes, dropping them on the floor. Gilrein sees a multicolored field of lines, different lengths and widths, that stretch from Oster's shoulders down to his ass.

Mrs. Bloch moves around the desk, picks up the clothes, folds them against her body and places them in a neat pile on the desktop. Then she goes back to her felt-covered box and withdraws a cinched bag made of black fabric, maybe satin. She tugs open the drawstring and extracts a set of silver needles. She reaches back into the box and takes out a small glass jar.

Oster hops up onto the table and stretches out on his stomach, turns his head so he faces Gilrein.

"I hope you don't mind if Mrs. B works while we talk," he says. "If we miss a night, she loses a little continuity."

Gilrein knows Oster wants to hear the question and so he stays silent, forces his host to say, "You got any tattoos, Gilly?"

Mrs. Bloch gathers her instruments and moves over to Oster. She puts her back to Gilrein so he can't see exactly what she's doing, but she starts to work on the area of the unmarked buttocks.

"Mrs. B is the best. No shit. Blind or no, you *cannot* find a better skin artist on this coast. She says you feel the design with the fingers, isn't that right, Mrs. B? Spent some time in Tokyo. Worked on some Yakuza meat, honest to God. Big dragons and flowers. All that symbol shit. Goddamn samurai, you know?"

A new wave of nausea coasts through Gilrein. He turns sideways on the couch, looks out the window down on the main hall below, watches as the stripper puts on a terry-cloth robe and joins one of the couch gangs to study how Filipino bantamweights beat the life out of each other.

"I'm getting the whole body done," Oster says, folding his arms on the table and resting his head on top. "You ready for this, Gilly? It's going to be a map of Quinsigamond. The whole town. I'll be a walking goddamn road map. Can't wait for the first time somebody asks me directions."

He tries to look back behind him and Mrs. Bloch barks, "Stei steel."

Oster stifles a laugh and says, "She's working on Bangkok Park as we speak. Bangkok on my ass. I love this."

Gilrein finishes his Spark, gets up off the couch, moves to the desk, and takes the bottle. He stares out the rear window onto the demolished half of the factory, heaps of broken brick and twisted metal and charred wood everywhere. It looks like someone has brought in a bulldozer and tried to organize the destruction into grids, pushed mountains of debris to the sides and created an open central crater before giving up any hope of restoring anything resembling order.

"Why'd you bring me here?" he asks.

There's a couple seconds of quiet. Voices downstairs explode into whoops and cheering.

"I know it's horrible, Gilly," Oster says. "I've never been married, but I know it's got to be killing you. You know, we all loved Ceil. Ceil was the best."

"We all loved Ceil," Gilrein repeats and brings the bottle to his lips.

"But it's just a building, all right? And it's the only place you're going to be safe for a while."

Gilrein swallows. "Safe from Kroger, maybe. But what about you and the rest of the boys?"

"Oh, that's not nice at all, Gilly. That's out of line. That's just goddamn outrageous. A fellow officer—"

"People disappear," Gilrein says, quoting the graffiti behind the bar, "right, Oster? Isn't that still the motto of the Magicians?"

"I can't believe what I'm hearing here, from a brother officer—"

"I'm just an independent hack-boy who drives piglets like Leo Tani on their mob errands."

Oster says, "You're all turned around, Gilrein."

And Mrs. Bloch says, "Du stei steel," and swats his buttocks.

"What were you doing in the alley, Sergeant?"

"Saving your lousy ass," Oster says. "For all the good it's going to do you."

Gilrein walks over to the gurney, stands so that Oster has to twist his neck to see him.

"I didn't want anything to do with the Magicians when I was a cop. I sure as hell don't want anything to do with you scumbags now."

Mrs. Bloch breaks off from inking an alleyway in Little Asia, folds her arms and waits for her canvas to explode.

Oster just stares up, then smiles, rests his head back down onto his arms and closes his eyes as if to nap.

Gilrein moves for the office door, taking the bottle of Light White Spark with him.

"You know what, Gilly?" Oster says, and Gilrein stops in the doorway. "I think the wrong cop died when this place blew to hell."

3

Otto Langer, the eldest of Quin-
sigamond's last independent cabdrivers, steers his hack into the
curbstone of Dunot Boulevard and waits for his fare to climb
inside. He does not activate his meter, but reaches instead for the
small vial of tranquilizers that rests precariously on the dash-
board, Otto's version of a St. Christopher statuette or lucky pair of
fuzzy dice. He spills one of the tiny blue pills into his palm and
lifts his hand into the air for the man settling into the backseat to
observe.

"I wanted you to see," Otto says, nervous and distracted. "I
have been very conscientious since the last incident. I am doing
much better, Doctor. I am feeling like a new man."

As always, there's no reply from the rear of the cab, not a
grunt of acknowledgment. Otto understands that this is not rude-
ness per se, but a simple fact of the new methodology. And so he
pulls out into Dunot and drives toward downtown without any
specific destination in mind. He would feel so much better, could
speak with much more clarity, he's sure, if he had Zwack beside
him, buckled in and riding shotgun, as they say. But it is another

of the Inspector's rules that the dummy remain locked in the trunk.

"I had another Gilrein dream last night, Doctor. Excuse, but *Doctor*—I have been meaning to ask, this is acceptable to you? A man with so many titles. It is hard to know which to use. Herr Doctor? Herr Inspector? Perhaps even Father Emil? Of course, I mean no disrespect . . ."

A pause, waiting for reassurance even though he knows it will not come. He turns onto Monaldi Way, notes that he's low on gas, and feels his stomach tighten. Otto's cab is a restored Bogomil Supreme, the limited edition that came with the sunroof and the tail fins. He'd love to crack open the roof right now. It's an unusually cool night and he could use the air, but his passenger would have a fit and Otto can't risk alienating the man right now. Progress could be just around the corner, a time when the nightmares and the migraines will finally cease.

"In the dream," plunging back in, "Gilrein was again dressed in the Censor's uniform, but he was not holding the knife this time. In fact, I had the distinct impression that he had misplaced the knife. I thought you might find this significant. You understand, I am not attempting to tell you your work. After all, you are the doctor. And I must stress, once again, how much I appreciate your efforts on my behalf. I still wish you would accept some form of payment."

The passenger shifts in the enormity of the taxi's backseat.

"Yes, of course, I realize the conditions of your arrangement with the facility. I researched the term—*pro bono*. But you must allow me to say, it's only my opinion of course, the word of an ignorant droshky driver, but the people at the Toth, perhaps they do not realize the treasure they have in such an associate? Again, it is none of my business."

The passenger gives out a dry cough. Otto flinches and the Bogomil jerks a bit and crosses the center line. He rights the hack as an oncoming motorcycle is forced to skid wide. The biker gives him the finger and a chorus of unintelligible obscenity.

"Forgive me, Doctor. The pills sometimes affect my concentration. And without sleep, well, you can imagine. I have a love-hate relationship with the night shift, Doctor. We avoid the traffic, but there is sometimes a loneliness in the empty streets, you understand? It is a different city at night. All cities are different in the night, yes? And yet, the night is an opportunity. I see things that I would never see in the day. I am witness to a parade of nocturnal oddities. Some of the spectacles are mundane, events that could happen in the glare of the noon hour. But seen at night, they are changed somehow. They take on a new significance. They leave a very different taste. Let me give you an example. Last week, over on French Hill, I saw a dog that had been hit by a car. Killed. A large dog. Enormous. A mastiff, I believe. This is the breed, yes? There was a small girl kneeling by the body of the animal. Just a child. All alone. No more than seven or eight years old, if I am any judge. Dressed in a nightgown. The girl was howling. Crying and shrieking and moaning in a way that I have heard referred to as *keening*. I am almost certain this was the term. I am sure this sound was what it meant. She was on her knees, bent over the carcass of the beast, her arms trying to lift the dead weight of the thing.

"Now you would ask, why did I not stop and help the girl, console the poor child? And that question, Doctor, excuse, would show your ignorance of the taxi business and the night shift. You do not get out of your cab. You are only safe inside of your cab.

"Another time, last winter, I was circling the rotary at Bishop Square and I looked up to the roof of the old train station and at the very top was an enormous burning cross. It looked as if it had been constructed out of two gargantuan telephone poles. And it was blazing. A genuine inferno. I pulled up next to the front steps where a woman was holding a camera, taking pictures of the flaming cross. I rolled down my window and she yelled to me that she was from *The Spy*, though I had not asked. I nodded to her and drove on. I checked the paper for the next week, but there were no pictures of this curiosity.

"Do you begin to understand why I both love and, at the same time, hate my job, Doctor?

"There was a night last month. I had just dropped a fare at Camp Litzmann, a warehouse in German Town that sometimes serves as an after-hours club. I was winding my way back to the Visitation when I made a foolish turn down one of the service alleys of the textile park. The price I pay for seeking a shortcut, I know. My way was immediately blocked by a small crowd and they swarmed around me before I could shift into reverse. They were waving money at me, their hands stuffed with bills of every denomination and many countries of origin. I almost panicked, was ready to mow them down before I realized they meant me no harm. They were all locked in a mass gambling frenzy. A man like yourself, Doctor, a counselor, a healer of the mind, surely you know how frightening this kind of mob can initially seem. I shook my head at them as they pounded on my window and in the middle of my protests a space opened before me and I was able to see, for a moment or two, the nature of the sport upon which they wagered. There were two men facing one another within the confines of a chalk circle. They were stripped to the waist. They were connected, one to the other, by a long stretch of rope, the kind of taut, white rope used in the making of drying lines for clothing. The rope was tied at each ankle. It allowed them, at their farthest distance, to reach opposite curves of the chalk circle. They were chasing each other, perpetually maneuvering to intercept one another. And they were both bearing enormous machetes in one hand. A moment after I understood what was happening, one of the players charged his opponent. And in the instant they passed each other, the blade was thrust and found its mark, sliced into the unfortunate combatant and came close to severing his arm from his shoulder.

"I sometimes think that just seeing these things is like having a curse put on my head. Do you agree, Doctor?"

They slow to a stop at a red light and the passenger ignites one of his cigars, a signal that he will not tolerate much more digression.

"Yes, of course, Inspector, I'm wasting your valuable time. I apologize for the foolish ramblings of an old man. I would ask you remember that, even after all these years, the English is a second language to me. It never comes as easily as my native tongue. Gilrein and Miss Jocasta, they grow so impatient with me at times.

"But where were we last night? Where did we leave off? I know I had come to speak of the July Sweep. As I always do. Everything leads to the Sweep and the Orders of Erasure. This should not surprise though, should it, Doctor? Surely I'm not the only Maisel Jew to obsess on this particular topic? If only I could explain it in the words of my people. It would all be so much more vivid. It would bring the event to life. I know, with as much force of certainty as I know my name, that I could not bear to live through the ordeal again. I no longer have this type of strength. There are times, when I wake from one of the nightmares and I am bathed in the sweat and the tears and the heart is doing things that it should not do, there are times when I wish I could give this burden to someone else. Hand it away. No matter what the consequences. No matter what this would mean regarding the kind of man I have become.

"I wish on those occasions that I could restage every heinous instant of that night in July, replay it right here on the streets of my new home, for everyone to see and hear and smell, replay it until they could never forget what they had witnessed. No matter how hard they tried.

"For if you yourself, Doctor, yes, even so fine a man as yourself, of great strength and character and learning, if you were to look out that window there, if you were to turn your head and witness what took place in Maisel, in the Schiller Ghetto on the night of the July Sweep, it would never leave you, Doctor. It would change you permanently.

"The best I can do for you, however, is simply tell the story."

Without any warning, Otto jerks the taxi into a U-turn and his passenger loses his balance and pitches into the door. Otto offers no explanation or apology.

"You must understand, Herr Doctor, what I need to tell you is that to this day, my homeland, the cursed city of my birth, is alive inside of me. This is how I feel day and night. This is what I live with. The waters of the Zevlika rushing through my veins. The portals of the hunger tower sitting behind my eyes. My brain is nothing but the street of my youth, the cul-de-sac of the Ezzenes.

"Maisel is the most superstitious city on the earth, Doctor. You must know some of our legends—the water spirits of the River Z. The headless Templar. The alchemist Mladtus who was pulled through the floorboards of his house straight into hell. Yes, you have heard the tales? In your own youth, perhaps? Ghost stories told in the dark by overexcited children? Allow me now to tell you a new story, Doctor. One to put the old myths in perspective."

I was not always a cabdriver, Inspector. Does this surprise you? Back in Maisel, I was a biloquist. A common street performer. What you would call a ventriloquist. For the most part, I was self-taught. In my early youth I had studied the ghetto clowns who worked in Old Loew Square. My father had died before my birth. We lived with my mother's family in the Schiller Ghetto. Before coming to Quinsigamond, I lived all of my life in the Schiller. So it is as something of an expert that I tell you that of all the Jews in all of Old Bohemia, the Schiller Jews were, perhaps, the poorest. And the most despised. You have heard something, no doubt, about the decade of pogroms in Maisel? Most of those attacks were on the Schiller Ghetto.

My people could be called neither Orthodox nor Reformed. We were more of a sect set apart, looked upon suspiciously, at times, even by the larger Jewish community. Or is this just an old man's paranoia? If so, Doctor, I feel I have earned it. We were called the Ezzenes. We were, by and large, all progeny of the Hasidim of Maccabean times. Perhaps the best way to explain, to define, our specific bond would be to say that we built our lives around a

basic, unshakable cosmology which involved a complicated tradition of gnostic belief that one day God would
speak to us directly. No more need for prophets nor
dreams nor glossolalia. From God's lips to our ears in a
language we would both share. Over generations this
dogma became mingled with an intense respect for the
liberty and dignity and imagination of all peoples, a code
of what you might call inalienable rights, as well as a
strict, intractable adherence to a unilateral pacifism.

The Schiller was the heart, and, I am forced to add, the
soul, of the entire Jewish Quarter of Maisel. It was simply
a complex of adjoining tenements on a small spit of an
alley—a dead end, you would say—off Namesti Avenue.
There were thirteen rickety buildings in all and they
formed a kind of horseshoe at the end of the alley, six
buildings on either side of the street and one long, narrow, bridging unit at the far end. I had a friend, a very
funny young man and, I will admit, something of a troublemaker. He called this building *the pelvis*. Do you
understand? The way it was positioned, joining one side
of the street to the other. Such a character. He lived in the
bridging building. As did I. The entire complex backed up
to the banks of the Zevlika River and each spring there was
a dreadful problem with the water rats and other vermin.
Understand that the buildings were quite old and of ques-
tionable construction. They were continually undergoing
repair, but all of these measures were just temporary
stopgaps in the general decay of the structures.

As you might imagine, each family within our community crammed as many people as possible into their small
home. We slept five and six to a bed. And that was if you
were fortunate enough to have drawn a bedroom. We
slumbered in kitchens and lavatories, on couches and in
chairs—I had a cousin, Jaromir was his name, famous for
being able to find an uncrowded corner and slip into a

restful doze while standing up. *Like a horse,* we would laugh. And, to be honest, some of the men did take to calling him pony-boy. But it was always used in an affectionate way. Never cruelly or without warmth.

There was often a shortage of food. This should not surprise you. You are familiar, I am sure, a man of your intelligence and curiosity could not help but be familiar, with the story of the Maisel blockades and the rationing. It is something you always come close to being accustomed to, the stomach always churning. The slow fatigue of the long-hungry.

But know that there were fine times as well. We were, in every regard, a community like any other and closer than most. I have always felt the cliché to be true—suffering binds people more tightly than joy. Even a righteous joy. We made our world within the Schiller. We had our own small customs and habits. As if we were, indeed, a larger family. A tenacious clan cleaving together in too small a space. We kept our own markets on Schiller. Our own butcher shop, of course. There was a small school for the young children. More of a nursery perhaps, but they were taught the old fables. When there was paper and ink, we even printed a small weekly news sheet. In our own tongue, of course. If you can believe me, there was even a library. It is true. I am in a position to know. Better than any other, I assure you. We were poor, but never ignorant. There was no illiteracy that I knew of. At least not among the men. We came to think of ourselves as separate even from the other Jews of the Quarter. And I have often wondered if this is not at least part of the sin we were punished for. For there must have been a sin. It is unthinkable to accept what happened without an impetus. Without a logic, however abstract, somewhere deep in the mind of God. Ah, I see your face. You seem surprised that I use the word. Surely, you've heard me use it before? My stories about the Independents' Collective and our battle against the Red and the Black? No? I am sure I must have.

In any event, you are familiar with the July Sweep, Doctor? I am quite sure it was reported even here in Quinsigamond. The pogrom to end all pogroms, yes? Some dramatic phrase like this? They must have interrupted your soap operas and football games to mention the July Sweep? There must have been notice in the World Digest section of *The Spy*? A paragraph at least?

Even Hermann Kinsky lost family to the Sweep. Even one as connected and feared as Kinsky was vulnerable to this particular purge. Can you imagine, sir, if the shadow of the Sweep could penetrate into the armor of a mythical animal like Kinsky, what it could do to the people of the Schiller? I have heard it asked—never here, not in this city. Who beyond a refugee would give this much thought to the whole affair?—*Was there no indication of what was coming?* Yes, of course, there was indication. We talked for weeks of nothing else. The street attacks were increasing daily. And the brutality of those attacks likewise escalated. Our merchants had their shanties set ablaze, first in the middle of the night and later, as the spring progressed, in broad daylight, with customers in the midst of transaction, children around their feet. Our old men were pulled from the steps of the temple as they exited, knocked to the ground and dragged through the square, spit upon, kicked and whipped and cracked with the nightsticks. The attackers were young men like many of your associates, Doctor. I mean no insult. I simply mean to describe, you understand, their age, their bachelorhood. And many of them were known to be from the government police. They did not wear their uniforms. At first. For a time, the attempt was made to give the impression that these attacks were independent actions. Unsanctioned. Officially disapproved of.

In fact, the attacks were just a prelude. Just a cheap coming attraction for the main event.

The night of the July Sweep was a stifling one, airless from dawn. Most of my people could not sleep. They sat on their stoops, wilted and fatigued, waiting for the heat to break, hoping for a reprieve from the oppressiveness of the humidity.

What they received instead was a visit from Satan himself. Leading a convoy whose purpose the average man or woman, even those of the most depraved nature, could not imagine.

The brigade was actually something of a ragtag troupe. I have heard they were all volunteers and I tend to believe this. It is rumored that they had a communal nickname, that they called themselves the Reapers. Like a sports team or a fraternal order. They came in a variety of utility vehicles borrowed from the city garage. Some even drove jeeps and motor scooters privately stolen just for the occasion. None of the young men or women wore their badges that night, though each carried their government-issued machine pistols.

There is a myth that the Reapers assembled in some secluded corner of Devetsil Park prior to the raid, that they performed some sort of bonding ritual to strengthen them for what was to come. I have heard it said that they liberated an infant lamb from one of the farms out beyond the Polish Quarter and formed a circle around the mewing and terrified animal and slaughtered it, gutted the quaking newborn from throat to entrails. That each soldier took a bite of the steaming heart and passed it down the line. I have also heard a version of this story in which the sacrificial victim was a newly born baby, a human child, just hours old and spirited out of the convent at St. Wenceslas Abbey. I mention these tales for your consideration, Inspector. You are the man obsessed with puzzles and myths. For myself, I only know that the Reapers were first spotted that evening already on the march, snaking their way toward the fifth district under cover of the over-heated night.

The rear of their cavalcade was brought up by an ancient, paint-spattered flatbed truck carrying as much cyclone fencing as could be strapped upon its apron. And the very last float in the parade was the crown jewel of the procession, so large and beautiful, in fact, that it looked like it could not have belonged with such a shabby convoy as preceded it.

Tell me, Inspector, how do I describe for you what has come, inevitably, to be the central monstrosity of our hideous myth? How do I make it both technically accu-rate, conveying the *fact* of the machine—the truth of its existence in this world, that it was born of etchings and blueprints and the draftsman's toil, that it was con-structed from prefabricated metals, assembled by men in greasy coveralls, that it was powered by the common internal combustion engine and that it fed on diesel fuel, that it operated with the same grinding noise, belched the same noxious exhaust as any piece of heavy industrial equipment—how do I tell you this and, at the same time, express to you what that fact *signifies*, the enormity of this creature's monstrousness, how its purpose that night in July elevated it to something greater than a machine, larger than a piece of equipment, made it into a steel metaphor, transformed it into the demon which had been waiting for us since the expulsion from the garden?

As always, we start with a name. There is no existence without the naming. To name is to create. So let us bring the demon to life once again, Doctor. The machine was called the Pulpmeister. I am not being humorous. I am not being perverse. Though I can see where you might think so. No, this is the truth. The Pulpmeister. Were you

to obtain one of the catalogs routinely mailed to the larger
lumber corporations, you would find an entire section
devoted to all makes and models of this beast. At heart, it
was nothing but an industrial tree shredder that had been
wildly enlarged and customized. This was, ostensibly, the
machine's only purpose, the on-site pulping of raw wood.
I am told there are sales films in which the larger models
are shown to transform enormous sections of fallen redwood forests into mountains of soft, sandy powder. No
doubt you have seen tiny versions of this particular piece
of equipment. Last August, after that particularly costly
windstorm, the city had the machines everywhere. You
could find them on every avenue where a tree had suc-
cumbed or a large branch broken away. Surely you have
seen the public arborists in their deep green jumpsuits,
their yellow helmets and their heavy gloves, parking their
pet monster in the street, proudly setting up their orange
cones supposedly to ward off traffic, though I tend to
think that the purpose of the cones is actually to draw the
attention of the passersby—*look at our machine, look
closely at our obliterating devil, see the teeth, see the
speed with which it can make nothing out of something.*

But just in case you are ignorant of the beast, Doctor, I
will play Jonah for you and describe my monster. First let
me say, the shredder which came to visit the Schiller that
night was very likely the largest that has ever been constructed. And this is what leads the professional theorists
to their refrain of full governmental knowledge and consent. For who, the reasoning goes, could have ordered the
customized construction of such a monstrosity but the
Ministry of Public Works itself? No fanatical death squad
operating on its own could have afforded such a luxurious
and opulent tool.

Something about the thing itself was decadent. Something about its very design seemed to send a message.

There is, I believe, a saying in this country about using a Howitzer to kill a housefly. At first I believed that was the case in the July Sweep. A matter of overkill. The inevitable result when zealous despisement breeds with an insane egotism. But later, thinking about the use of the machine, thinking about the process, the particular way the disappearance was performed, no, Doctor, there was more to it. There was a brilliance behind the manuever. Because one of the simplest lessons of history is that slaughter alone is not enough. Even in the case of the most brutal and inclusive slaughter. No, Doctor. One must wipe out all trace of the despised. One must obliterate the remains. One must make any and all evidence vanish in such an absolute way that you are left free to begin denying that the despised ever existed in the first place.

For a time, you may have to argue with the memories of the neighbors. But if you are obsessive enough, meticulous enough, even memory can be manipulated in the end. If you eradicate until there is nothing left to eradicate, there will be nothing for the cantankerous to point to. And even reasonable men and women will come to accept your version of the truth.

The passenger places a hand lightly on Otto's shoulder.

"Is our time up already?" Otto asks. "So soon? But I have not even begun, Doctor."

The hand is removed.

"Very well then. You are the boss, as they say."

The passenger secures the high buttons on the collar of his tunic and raps on the window to signal that Otto should pull over. Otto steers the cab to the curb, doesn't bother to shift into park. The passenger exits the taxi without payment or goodbye and disappears down an alley into one of the labyrinths of Bangkok Park.

4

Gilrein steers the Checker down Rome Avenue with one hand, tilts the bottle of Spark with the other. The hooch will cut into the real pain until tomorrow, then he'll have to scrounge for some Demerol down at the Visitation. Worse comes to worst, he'll head into Little Asia and pay retail to one of the storefront healers.

He aims for downtown and tries to put the past twelve hours into some kind of logical order. Things happen for a reason. Effect follows cause. As Ceil used to say, *Nothing is as random as it appears.*

But Ceil is in the family plot three years now, buried next to Gilrein's mother and father, an American flag folded into a stiff triangle of allegiance and cradled into what's left of her arms like some surrogate for the child they never had.

At nine o'clock tonight, Gilrein was lying on his bed in the hayloft at Wormland, reading a page in one of Ceil's books on Klaus Klamm for the third time, writing useless questions in a spiral notebook and thinking about having a nightcap. When the phone rang it was Leo Tani, calling, as always, from Huie Tang's

Visitation Diner. Twenty minutes later, Gilrein picked Tani up and was told to head for Gompers Station.

What would Ceil think of it?

Back when he was on the job, Gilrein rode Tani's chubby ass as if he were God's own cop, a plague designed specifically to make life unbearable for a midlevel fence with an insatiable appetite for the veal at Fiorello's. Now he plays chauffeur to the 'Shank, hauling him from exchange to exchange and always pocketing the overgenerous tip.

Tonight was a standard drive—Tani climbed in the Checker dressed in one of his dozens of silk Michelozzi suits, smelling of musk and hazelnut and playing hail-fellow-well-met like a manic campaigner who's just seen a big drop in the polls.

Leo the 'Shank loved to talk as much as he loved to eat and he had Gilrein circle the city for a half hour while he spieled, telling blue jokes, running down the backroom gossip from City Hall, mourning in a low, priestly voice, another rumor of death from St. Leon's Grippe. And, once again, relaying his ambitions to one day write his memoirs. *The whole freaking story, my friend, names and all.* Leo seemed to love the word *memoir,* as if the sound of it alone conveyed the grandiosity of his life in *the business.*

When the hour came round, Gilrein was directed to Gompers Station. He wheeled the taxi off-street and crossed into the train yards, where a rupture seems to perpetually sprout in the chain-link fencing, then rolled into hiding behind a line of wheel-less boxcars and cut the engine. Tani adjusted his tie—red silk with baby calves patterned in white—pushed his hair back on his skull with two flat palms and told Gilrein he'd be back in fifteen minutes. Then Tani walked into the abandoned train station as if he was entering some embassy with news that could sink or save a nation.

He emerged before Gilrein could finish a single page of Klamm. Leo looked a good deal worse for the wear, his tie loosened, a film of sweat on forehead and upper lip.

He settled into the backseat, gestured with his head and said, "Let me tell you, Gilrein, there's no talking to some people."

The Checker deposited Leo in front of Mano Nero down on the far end of San Remo Avenue. Leo handed a fifty over the seat top and said, "You want to join me? I'm taking a goddamn bath in Gallzo."

Gilrein begged off and headed for the all-night library branch at Sebond Square, found it closed without explanation. He thought about sampling some cuy at the Floating Kitchen, then realized he hadn't yet heard of the restaurant's current location. He even considered heading back to Wormland and going another round with Klamm, but he felt infected by Tani's cloud of failure, gave up on the idea and changed direction.

So he settled for coffee in the rear booth at the Visitation, waited for his fellow indie hacks to show. Around midnight, Huie Tang took away Gilrein's empty mug and said there was a fare waiting down on Voegelin for a lift. Recently, the two corporate fleets that dominate the cab trade in Quinsigamond—Red Rover Cab and Bunny Blackman's Taxi & Limousine—stopped going into Bangkok Park after dark. That leaves all the Park calls to the last three independent taxis in town. For the indies, servicing Bangkok, day or night, is less a case of pride or stubbornness and much more something closer to existential disregard. At least it is for Gilrein. Though he's never consciously admitted it to himself, every night run in Bangkok is a possible ticket to join Ceil. And, being a Catholic, it's his only alternative to waiting out this lifetime.

Still, death is one thing and robbery another. And that's why he continues to keep his service revolver mounted under the dash, the chamber fully loaded.

Gilrein headed for Voegelin. As always, the radio was tuned to the Canal Zone station whose playlist was limited to the recordings of Imogene Wedgewood. "Drunk on India Ink" was oozing through the cab as he pulled up to what should have been the right number, but instead was only the mouth to an unlit alleyway. As he reached under his seat to grab his street guide, the Checker door was pulled open and the meatboys hauled him into the alley before he could get hold of his piece.

The only thing he took away from the beating were these erupting bruises and the question, *Where is the package?*

Leo Tani hadn't been carrying any package when he got in the cab. He didn't have a package when he came out of Gompers.

But if Oster was right and the meatboys really did belong to August Kroger, there was only one thing the package in question could contain.

Huie Tang is a poor relation to the notorious Tang Family of Little Asia. Lately, the Tangs have ascended to neighborhood mayor status after the instability caused by the death of the legendary Dr. Cheng. Some years back Huie Tang had a falling out with his cousin Jimmy and lost his position supervising all the domino parlors of Chin Avenue. Something about a skim job that couldn't be laid off on the underlings. For months Huie tried to wheedle his way back into the good graces of the clan, but when even Auntie Rose stopped speaking to him, he knew he was on his own.

Ashamed, he went to work managing Fritz Henry's All-Night Diner and by the end of his first year he bought the lunch car, the restaurant license, and the extortion agreement with the health inspector. Now Huie's plan is to use the diner as the cornerstone, the first step in challenging his ex-family and becoming a serious rival to his ungrateful cousin.

But slinging hash is a tough way to start unseating a mob dynasty, and until last month, Huie was starting to lose heart. It was the end of March and the diner was empty except for the one regular who took all his meals there—Father Clement, a senile Jesuit from St. Ignatius College. Huie had just served the old priest some grouper lo mein, then, on his way back to scrub the grill, he casually, absentmindedly, turned on the radio to WQSG and the local news hour. The diner filled up with an advertisement for a free introductory session of the Camisard Institute of

Speed Reading Course at the Armory. And at some point in the midst of the announcer's hyperbole, just after the voice on the radio promised astounding comprehension and increased recollection, Father Clement went crazy. He leapt up onto his table, sending fish and noodles to the floor. He began to wave his arms and scream out in a high-pitched cackle, stomping his sandal-clad feet, pointing furiously toward the radio with a dripping fork.

"Can't you hear it?" he finally managed to ask as Huie reached under the register for the lead-filled baseball bat he kept handy for various security purposes.

But before bunting the priest into some degree of control, Huie allowed himself to ask, "Hear what?"

The question stopped Father C in midfit. He ceased flailing and stared at the diner owner, then cocked his head toward the radio and after a moment of intently, maybe desperately listening to what, to Huie Tang, sounded exactly like any other Loftus Funeral Home ad, the priest's eyes closed up and he said, "It seems I'm to be the interpreter." And then, "Come here, my son."

It has been said around the rice carts of Little Asia that no one possesses quite the combination of cynicism and impatience of Huie Tang. But on that afternoon in his empty and failing diner, there was an authority in Father Clement's voice that convinced the transgressor and exile to drop his cudgel and sit down in the priest's booth. And for the next half hour, with no customers to interrupt them, Father Clement revealed to his first listener that Yahweh had spoken. That God had decided, for reasons that would soon be made clear, to use the radio advertisements as the vehicles for his messages. That the shouted promises and treacly jingles and earnest testimonials to products and services of every brand and stripe were nothing but the sacred dialect of the Almighty himself.

"With your radio," Father Clement proclaimed to the bewildered counterman, "and my translation, we will show this city the way to salvation."

And before Huie's eyes, his only regular customer was trans-formed from a lost soul waiting out his last days into a crusader born again with the fervor of the raving mystic. In Huie Tang's diner the priest had found a new Pentecost, a fresh take on Shavuot and Whitsunday.

By the end of the first week, Huie, at first curious and amused, was so exasperated by the nonstop, instantaneous interpretations that he was ready to evict his sole patron, to call the police and the mental health agencies. Until Father Clement started bringing in the pilgrims. They came, both male and female, in all ages and creeds and ethnic makeups. And they came with money in their pockets. They ordered breakfast, lunch and dinner and they never noticed when the prices on the blackboard menu skyrocketed 50 percent.

Father Clement installed himself permanently in the booth opposite the radio. He ate and slept in the diner around the clock and took to standing on his seat and preaching apocalyptic rants for all customers, believers and nonbelievers alike. Within a month, Huie had a line out the door. He brought in a painter, changed the name on the lunch car to the Visitation Diner, altered the culinary selections to include Our Father's Recipe Hash and Revelation Stew. One night at two A.M., in the midst of hearing the options that came with the Last Blueplate Supper Special, Gilrein had to tell the restaurateur to calm down.

But the pilgrims' gain is the independent cabdrivers' loss. What was once a quiet hangout to juice up on cheap coffee and swap horror stories about who had the worst fare of the night has turned into a hysterical circus, with patrons speaking in tongues and hustlers in the parking lot selling Day-Glo crucifixes out the back of their vans.

The indie cabbies are nothing if not stubborn. They refuse to relinquish their reserved booth no matter how much they're offered. And they won't give up the business phone mounted at their table even though Huie, uproariously drunk on greed and good fortune, has jacked their rental fee twice already.

■ ■ ■

Gilrein parks the Checker next to the Buick of a guy who has set
up shop renting a Polaroid camera to pilgrims who want to have
their picture taken in front of the lunch car. It's the same clown
who, last week, was hawking a trunkful of polyester undershirts
emblazoned with

MY GIRLFRIEND HEARD THE WORD OF GOD

AND ALL I GOT

WAS THIS LOUSY T-SHIRT.

He pushes through the crowd and into the diner, tries to make
for the cabbies' booth, but Father Clement grabs an arm, pulls
himself up until their faces are almost touching and says, "You too
can be saved, my son."

Gilrein shakes loose and says, "Where were you an hour ago,
Father?"

He wonders if the priest remembers him from the days when
they were both at St. Ignatius. He also wonders if it's possible he's
the only one who smells the bourbon on the old man.

Huie Tang is perched on his stool in front of the register ring-
ing up a souvenir Visitation baseball cap and ordering around his
newly hired trio of waitresses.

Huie yells, "What happened to you?"

"Another bad fare," Gilrein answers and shoves back to the
corner booth where Jocasta Duval is counting their night's
receipts, and their shared dispatcher, the legless Mojo Bettman,
is finishing up a plate of Redemption Rings, a deep-fried melange
of compressed and coiled onion and fish by-products.

Jocasta puts down her roll of cash and says, "Not again?"

Gilrein slides in next to her and nods affirmation.

"How many were there?" in her sweet Senegalese accent.

"More than enough," Gilrein answers and tries to flag down a
waitress for a coffee.

Bettman puts a hand to his left temple and says, "There goes
the streak. We were coming up on how many weeks?"

"Sorry to mess up our safety record."

"You get yourself looked at?" Jocasta asks.

"Yeah," Gilrein says, "just what I want to do, sit in the E.R. up at General until next Thursday."

"We need to rethink our policy again. This is becoming more than ridiculous."

"Bullshit," Bettman snaps. "We bend on this, we might as well just hand our medallions to the fleets. Couple years, there'll be one goddamn cab company left in America. That's our choice, take it or leave it."

Jocasta gives a glance that shuts up the dispatcher and turns to Gilrein. "You want me to take you up to General? I know an intern."

Gilrein shakes her off and Mojo says, "How did it go down?"

"Same as it always goes down," Gilrein lies. "I made a judgment call and it was the wrong one."

"Man or a woman?" Bettman asks.

"One of each," Gilrein lies. "I got two blocks down Voegelin and I felt the piece at my neck—"

"I've been telling you you've got to get the fencing fixed," from Jocasta.

"You resisted?" from Bettman, eyes raised in rebuke.

"I handed over my roll. They pulled me out anyway and went to town."

"Bastards," Mojo says.

"I'll be fine," Gilrein says. "Few painkillers and some sleep."

"Anything I can do?" Jocasta says, and Gilrein seizes on it.

"Matter of fact, Jo, there is one thing."

She gestures toward him with her chin.

Gilrein tries for a smile and says, "If you could tell me where I could find Wylie."

"Oh, for God's sake, mister," Mojo says. "Stop it right now."

Gilrein ignores him and says, "C'mon, Jo. I just need to talk to her. Five minutes. Just a phone number."

Bettman looks from Jocasta to Gilrein and says, "You know the woman doesn't want to see you, my friend."

Gilrein is about to get upset when Jocasta says, "I drove her last night."

"She called for an indie?" Mojo says. "How'd she know she wouldn't get . . ." and leaves the last word unspoken.

"Where was she?" Gilrein asks, trying and failing to sound relaxed.

"It was a flag-down. I was cruising the Zone. Guy she was with waved me over. They get in, I turn around, you know, *Wylie, what a surprise*."

"The guy?" Gilrein asks.

Jocasta sighs. "You really want to do this to yourself? You've had a pretty awful night already."

"C'mon, Jo."

"All right. Hispanic guy with a trimmed beard. Wore a Hawaiian shirt—"

She doesn't have to finish. Gilrein is already out of the booth and heading for the exit, wiping away the holy water that the pilgrims throw at him. And pushing aside Father Clement as the Jesuit yells, "Salvation is yours for the asking."

5

While it is not a requirement for admittance, if you plan on visiting the Last Man Supper Club in Little Asia on karaoke night, it might be a good idea to brush up on your knowledge of pop standards. In a place where every possible human activity seems to have an analogous ritual, you can't be too overprepared. Don't imagine you'll be carried out to the delivery platform and stomped by some Tang Family goons if you blow a line of, say, "Book of Love" when the microphone finally gets passed your way. But the name of the tune in any Tang establishment is respect. And on any given Thursday evening in the Last Man, respect might be measured by the extent of your familiarity with the poetry of teenage heartbreak.

It's not that August Kroger is oblivious to the mores of this part of town. He's transacted business along the Little Asia border long enough to pick up the required smattering of totems and taboos. And he's at least an instinctual enough creature to sense the weight of Family power emanating from every doorway under Tang protection. It's just that as a would-be neighborhood mayor, Kroger feels he can't grovel, that the need for respect is a given, but groveling will come back to haunt you, plant an image that will one day undo every inch of bloody progress you've worked so hard to attain. And surely, for an independent businessman like August K, born into the sobering history of Old Bohemia, memorizing the chorus of "Big Girls Don't Cry" must be considered in the realm of the grovel.

His personal assistant, however, would probably see things in a different light, but she's too fresh in her career to have gained the confidence required to argue with the boss. Even in her current condition, halfway to sloshed on a house drink called a Cranberry Morpheme. For all intents and purposes, Wylie Brown was hired by Kroger as his archivist and librarian, overseer of his magnificent collection of rare books and decorative papers. To her surprise and confusion she was promoted, just this morning, to the somewhat more vague position of general secretary.

Is Wylie aware that her advancement is really the result of Kroger's newly discovered lust? It's unlikely, given August's unilaterally stoic facade, the unflinching mask and imperturbable body language he perfected back in his native land. But if she has qualms about her new duties pulling her away from the heaven of Kroger's immense penthouse library and into mob bars like this one, the pay raise and the bonus of a rare Brockden first edition— *In the Beginning Was the Worm: Selected Dream Journals*—were compensation enough to buy her acquiescence.

The evening, however, is to have a dual purpose, which August failed to explain on the way over, taking up more than his fair share of the back of the Bamberg, letting his thigh brush up against Wylie's and slapping driver Raban across the back of the skull when he missed the turnoff to Chin Avenue. Certainly, the night is to be a celebration of Ms. Brown's first step up the Kroger Family ladder. But while they're celebrating with the best dim sum in town, why not have a friendly chat with Jimmy Tang himself? Jimmy, the Tong King of the moment, might just be interested in an Asian-backed knockover of Hermann Kinsky. Kinsky, the neighborhood mayor of the Bohemian Wing, is the closest thing Kroger has to a boss, and that humiliating fact alone is motivation enough to risk all the uncertainties involved in throwing an allegiance across ethnic lines.

Which is why August is currently feeling so distracted, trying hard to listen to the object of his most innovative fantasies discuss her doctoral thesis, while at the same time keeping an eye out for the arrival of Jimmy the Tiger and his ever-present flock of meatboys. What's making concentration even harder is the troupe of drunken Japanese business jocks wrapped around the bar, smashed on sake and the day's trading at the gray marketplace, already engaging in a little push and shove as they vie for the microphone and attempt to will their way past the haze of the booze and the genetics of their native tongue just to croon a verse of "Love Letters in the Sand."

Kroger watches the bizboys with a mixture of contempt and envy. He knows they're Tang employees like everyone else in the club, the linked synapses of Jimmy's personal brain trust. Though they dress and act in rigid imitation of the ziabatsu warriors back home, the particular conglomerate they work for, while perhaps technically no darker than its legal, government-sanctioned cousins, still does business in the shadows and, at the moment anyway, still tends to rely on payroll assassins a bit more than tax attorneys. These are Tang's money movers, born savvy in the ways of numbers, markets, and the valuation of goods. They spend their days with a telephone implanted in their ear, a cryptic balance sheet just below their fingers. In the course of a weekend they change opium capital into real estate capital, real estate capital into livestock capital, livestock capital into munitions capital, and, very likely, munitions capital back into the milk of the poppy. They could quote the price of yen against the deutsche mark in a coma. They wash Jimmy's profits in the Caribbean Basin, stockpile them over in the Pacific Rim. And though each, as a servant of the Tang Family, necessarily carries a gun, they leave the blood and guts work to the meatboys and the new generation of street samurai.

Kroger and Wylie are mounted on the last two stools of a bar made from a circular block of lucite filled with one-spot butterfly fish and an occasional specially bred miniature octopus. Wylie wanted a booth, but August needs to keep an eye on all entrances and exits, especially given the fact he's forced by protocol and common sense to walk softly into the kingdom of Tang, sans weaponry or his two favorite lackeys. But Raban and Blumfeld have other, more pressing duties tonight. And besides, being alone with *the librarian*, as he still enjoys calling her, is a burden he can learn to love.

"The interesting thing about karaoke," Wylie is saying, raising her voice just a bit to pull back the boss's wandering eyes, "is that its popularity in America coincides with the moment the Asian corporations bought up all the rights to the standard playlists. It's a brilliant maneuver. You create the demand for your back product."

August picks her hand up off the table and caresses it, trying to stay just this side of fatherly. "Your compulsion to analyze is, forgive me, Ms. Brown, simply adorable."

Wylie is uncomfortable with both the gesture and the sentiment, but she reminds herself she's dealing with the product of a foreign culture. So he's coming on a little too strong tonight, the guy's got a library that could rival the Library of Congress. With a love of books that pure and strong, he can't be all bad. And her recent experience with men makes her savor a bit of harmless admiration. So for tonight, anyway, she's ready to toss back a few drinks and say to hell with being a guardian against objectification.

"Myself," Kroger says, hesitantly releasing the hand, "I tend to look at things much more simplistically. I am a bottom-line mentality. Go with what works, jettison what does not."

Wylie raises her drink to him and says, not without humor, "You're the boss."

August turns to look toward the restaurant entrance and says quietly, "So I am."

Fukiyama, the ancient Japanese maître d', tired of and not understanding the constant inspection, attempts to stare Kroger down and ends up nervously resorting his menus and table diagrams. August turns back to the bar and says, "But this is your night, not mine. You were telling me about Brockden's demise, I believe."

To say that Wylie Brown has sacrificed her young life to the memory of a two-hundred-year-old schizophrenic murderer might be overstating the case. To say that the life of Edgar Carwin Brockden has been Wylie's single, abiding fixation since she first heard about the Minster of Wormland at the age of fourteen might not.

Born in Mettingen, Pennsylvania, in the time of a disgraced president, Wylie relished the kind of idyllic childhood that can lead to a fuzzy bitterness when the balance of one's existence proves less serene or fulfilling. But when she found herself unable to sleep one night a week after her first, long-delayed menstruation, and uncharacteristically turned on the television set in her parents' modest ranch house to witness an embarrassingly shabby, Z-budget retelling of the Brockden saga, complete with once-noble Shakespearean lead reduced by alcoholism and serial divorces to perform in creature features and, ultimately, domestic wine commercials, Wylie's fate was forever altered.

Hollywood may have played fast and loose and cheaply with the tale of the most famous colonial familicide, but neither the bad dialogue nor the cornball farmhouse sets could dull the central intensity of the story for this young and deeply impressionable girl. And when the credits rolled and the television was reduced back to reruns of *Boston Blackie*, Wylie Brown knew she had found her calling.

She took down her bedroom posters of koala bears and boy singers and replaced them with maps of a New England factory city called Quinsigamond. She put her boxes of jigsaw puzzles in the cellar and had her library card relaminated. And she struggled through all four of the outdated, spine-broken, and historically suspect biographies of E. C. Brockden that were available at that time. The idea of a person being driven mad by his love of language and books was something she needed desperately to understand for reasons that did not become evident until years later.

In the meantime, she pursued this new obsession with a passion that argued against her tender age and made her parents wonder where they had failed and why their daughter had to become the oddball of the neighborhood. For her part, Wylie was already beyond their bourgeois controls. She had embarked on an intellectual and spiritual journey, intent on solving an esoteric mystery that had confounded scholars for generations: what happened to Edgar Carwin Brockden and why did he slaughter his family?

Compulsion eventually brought Wylie to the promised land of Quinsigamond straight out of the Streeter School with a newly minted Ph.D. She'd done her undergrad work at the University of Pennsylvania, where she impressed the grant officers enough to get a full boat to the Streeter. She'd spent the last five years studying the spectrum of the book arts at a variety of institutions around the globe, loving Iowa City and later, Florence, where she conquered all aspects of restoration and preservation, aggravated by Manhattan where she vanquished the complexities of book appraisal, finance, and risk management, and ending up, inevitably, here in Q-town, a Southwick Fellow at the Center for Historical Bibliography. It was a sweet package that any book maven would swoon over: all-access status to the Center's holdings, housing in the adjoining Southwick Manse, a more than generous living stipend, and the surety that at the end of her research she could just about name her position at any public or private repository on the planet.

But the only place Wylie Brown was interested in going was the City of Words, which she sometimes calls the City of Worms, also known as Brockden Farm, a place where tragedy and madness had once played themselves out in a linguistic nightmare that resonates to this day.

■ ■ ■

"The obsession with the worms came *after* he arrived in America," Wylie explains to her employer. "I'm sure of it. The researchers who point to the Roscommon Journals are reading in. They see what they want to see. You have to be hard-nosed in this area."

"I can imagine," Kroger responds, spooning some Crab Rangoon onto his secretary's plate and wondering what this young woman might look like spread naked on the floor of his library.

"You can't explain away the fact that this specific breed of worm did not exist in Ireland," Wylie says, as always getting a little too excited about her topic. "Brockden couldn't have had contact until the family was established here in the States."

Trouble flares at the other end of the bar. Word has come down that the city's finest car thieves are playing a session of Shock the Monkey down on Eldridge Ave and some of the bizboys have whipped out their cell phones and are barking orders to their street bankers, arguing the odds, laying down wagers that could bankrupt a small municipality. Problem is, the phones are wreaking havoc with the karaoke machine and for a couple of these boys, who've waited all week for the one moment when they can shut down interest rates and carrying costs and focus solely on the lyrics to "Mack the Knife," that's just unacceptable.

But before any Hong Kong silk can be torn, order is restored as Canton Mia, the barkeep, who is known by all to have Tang's ear and, possibly, some measure of his heart, hammers the ceremonial gong that sits next to her cash register and delivers a quiet, sisterly edict—karaoke will carry the night. The cell phones are slipped back inside jacket pockets and the offending gamblers buy a round of Kamikazes for the whole group.

And everyone's happy again except for August Kroger. He's never been good at waiting and when the waiting occurs in the context of a foreign culture, his anxiety is tweaked a notch forward by this discomforting sense of *otherness* all around him. One would think this would have branded him a disastrous candidate for immigration, but Kroger has found America anything but unfamiliar. In the ways that count, Quinsigamond is the most natural milieu in which August Kroger will ever exist.

"The central mystery to me," Wylie Brown says, emphasizing the *me*, and pausing to chug down a generous wallop of Cranberry Morpheme, "isn't how, exactly, the murders took place, but what was going through Brockden's mind, what exactly pushed him beyond the brink."

"Will we ever really know?" Kroger asks, trying for polite and managing only indulgent.

"I don't mean to be egotistical," Wylie says, having difficulty spearing a collection of sesame-fried sprouts, "but I swear I'm on the verge. You spend this many years studying another life . . . I don't know, you begin to think in the same patterns, your brain starts to move in the same orbit as that of your subject."

"That," August says, surprised to find himself intrigued, "sounds dangerous."

"Dangerous?" Wylie says, considering his meaning, suddenly a little dizzy. "You mean because of the murders? Because of what happened to the family in the end?"

Kroger shrugs and leans across the table to wipe yellow sauce off her chin with his napkin.

He says, "What is the saying about looking too deeply into the eyes of a monster?"

It's a mistake. Wylie reacts as if she's been personally insulted.

"This is exactly the kind of preconceived prejudice I have to continually fight—"

"Please, Ms. Brown, I meant no—"

"The general public's ignorance of the man. That willful simplicity about a very complicated and little-known series of events—"

"All I was saying—"

"All those nasty limericks and folk songs."

> *Edgar Brockden took a knife*
> *And carved his children and his wife—*

"Please, Ms. Brown, Wylie—"

All because God whispered terms

—louding up now, enough volume to steal the attention of the rest of the bar—

Of worship through his friends the worms.

"Is there a problem here?"

And though Kroger looks up hoping to find the maître d', he knows even before he turns that the question has been asked by the king of Little Asia, Jimmy the Tiger Tang.

August looks from Tang to Wylie and back to Tang, then says, "No problem at all, sir. We were just enjoying the delights of your wonderful establishment."

"So there is no problem?"

Before Kroger can answer, Wylie, more drunk now than she realizes and staring down at her plate, says, "The crab is a little chewy."

August Kroger cringes. At this moment, he would like to travel back in time five minutes and crush his beautiful secretary's windpipe. But Jimmy Tang, five and a half feet of pure class when it comes to even inebriated women, says, "In that case, my profuse apologies. We will do better next time, I assure you."

Kroger's shoulders release. He takes a breath, extends a hand toward his host and says, "Allow me to introduce—"

"I know who you are," Tang says, sliding onto the stool next to Wylie, smiling at her like some high school romantic, "and I know why you are here."

Kroger is thrown for a loss. Does Jimmy intend to discuss an overthrow right here in public? Granted it's his domain, but there are ways to do these things and surely, in a manner this delicate, some privacy is in order.

"I want to thank you for taking the meeting, Mr. Tang. I know our relationship will be—"

"Mr. Kroger," Tang says, an edge placed purposefully in the voice, "you haven't introduced me to your associate."

"My associate?" It takes Kroger a second to understand that Jimmy is referring to Wylie Brown. "My associate, yes, of course, Ms. Brown, Miss Wylie Brown, my personal assistant."

Tang bows his head in Wylie's direction and she gives a moderate bow back, still sulking over what she sees as the attack on her life's obsession.

"I hope you haven't been waiting too long," Tang says.

"We were enjoying the festivities," Kroger assures him and motions to a skinny young man with an embarrassing attempt at a goatee, the cigarette in his hand more prop than addiction, putting a wealth of emotion behind "A Big Hunk o' Love."

"I'm glad to hear that," Tang says, and he sounds sincere. "Because, you know, I am a creature of ritual. And before I even discuss business, I like to know who I'm spending my time with."

Kroger is lost but tries to cover.

"A wise habit," he says. "A prudent way to proceed."

"I'm glad you agree," Tang says as Mia takes the microphone away from the singing bizboy in midsentence and brings it to her boss along with a steaming bowl of green tea. Tang takes the microphone and smiles at Wylie, then turns and hands the mike to Kroger, asking, "What would be your favorite song?"

Kroger stares at the Tiger and says, "Excuse me?"

"I'm sure we have it," Jimmy says. "We've got all the oldies. An outstanding selection. All standards."

"Mr. Tang, I'm not sure—"

"You look like a doo-wop kind of fellow," Tang says, squinting, trying to size up the Bohemian intruder. "What do you think, fellas?"

The money weasels fall all over themselves trying to agree with their superior.

"But I could be wrong. Are you more Motown? Surf music? We've even got a few country-and-western chestnuts. That Mr. Hank Williams, he was a talented man."

"Mr. Tang," Kroger fumbles, "I don't, that is, I'm not a . . ."

"Is there a problem, Mr. Kroger?" the tone suddenly colder, Tang beginning to let his annoyance show. Kroger has only so much time to allow himself to be embarrassed and belittled.

"Because, as I'm sure you are aware, I'm an exceedingly busy man. And in agreeing to take a meeting with you I not only had to rearrange my schedule. I had to risk offending Hermann Kinsky. So I hope you won't disappoint me, Mr. Kroger. I hope we can all be friends here. I would very much like to get to know you better"—the head turning for another smile at Wylie—"but when in Little Asia, I would expect you to honor the customs of my land."

Even in her drunken state, Wylie wonders exactly when karaoke became an honored cultural tradition.

"I mean no disrespect, Mr. Tang," August says, peripherally noticing a handful of the Tiger's street muscle file into the bar, their leathers and tattoos silencing the bizboys and turning what was a second ago just a kernel of tension into the full-blown ache of a room about to be filled with consequential violence. "It is simply that I am not familiar with this type of . . . that is, I simply don't know any of these songs."

"I find that hard to believe, August," use of the first name at this stage not at all a good sign for Kroger. "Everyone knows these songs. They're universal."

"I'm not exposed to very much popular entertainment. I don't get out very much."

"I'm asking you to try, August. I'm asking you to pick up the microphone and give us a verse or two. That's all."

"If I had some time to prepare—"

"What is the goddamn problem here? A child could do this, August," as the meatboys approach and stand behind Kroger with their arms folded across their chests and their sunglasses covering their eyes. "I just want to hear you sing. Are you telling me this is too much to ask?"

"Perhaps tonight wasn't a good time—"

"Pick up the microphone and pick a song, August," Tang

yelling now, a few of the bizboys slipping out of the lounge. "Let me hear you, right now."

There's a long second of anticipation until Wylie grabs the microphone, saying, "Oh, for God's sake," and climbing up until she's seated on the teak top of the bar. She looks down at Mia and yells, "Give me 'Klaus, Baby,'" the Imogene Wedgewood tribute to everyone's favorite German linguist. Mia punches up the instrumental and the Tiger is at once enthralled. And as the sultry music of piano and bass fills up the Last Man, Wylie Brown spreads herself out, reclines along the length of the bartop, and begins to belt out

> *Write down your love*
> *and pass me the note*
> *Write down your love*
> *that I'll own the quote*
> *make it true, make it real*
> *let me know, let me feel*
> *Klaus, Baby,*
> *Write down your love*

She works it for all it's worth, momentarily turning even the gang meat into something close to lovestruck.

By the second verse, she owns the lounge, caressing and manipulating a tune that both August Kroger and Jimmy Tang, from this day forward, will come to think of as *our song*. But what neither man will ever know is that, as her eyes close and head falls back and the tips of her fingers run provocatively down her neck toward her cleavage, a genuine torch song goddess, Wylie Brown is singing not to her boss and not to the neighborhood mayor of Little Asia, but rather, to a delusional heretic and murderer who's been dead for over a century.

6

If you want information on the rare-book trade in Quinsigamond, there are any number of people you could go see, including Gilrein's ex-lover, Wylie Brown. If you want information about the *stolen* rare-book trade, then Rudy Perez is the only man in town. The Text Shoppe is a trashy little place down on the corner of Eldridge and Waldstein, a cellar hole that takes in water every spring. Gilrein visited the place more than once when he was working out of bunko.

And now, sitting in the Checker a block down Eldridge, he thinks of those days with a detachment that he neither understands nor wishes to understand. The memories are as clear as a familiar movie, as sharp as his vision in this instant through the windshield of the cab. But it's as if it were some clone of himself shoving open the door of the Text Shoppe, flashing the badge and hoping, just a little, that Rudy would run so he could knock the little shyster to the floor, maybe throw an elbow or two and rip one of those pathetic floral shirts the dealer insisted on wearing. Let the word get back to Oster and his boys that Gilrein was capable of his own heat.

But being a hard-ass has never come naturally to Gilrein. The best he ever managed was to walk up and down the aisles, his shoulders knocking stack after stack of manuscripts and magazines and binders into a snow cover of paper all over the greasy linoleum.

"You call this a roust?" Perez would say, nonplussed, squinting and scratching at his beard. "You're a nuisance, not a threat. Nobody ever tell you the difference?"

Ostensibly, the Text Shoppe is an eccentric secondhand bookstore. That's how the joint is listed in the Yellow Pages directory and that's what it says on Perez's business cards. And Perez may well spend a quarter of his working hours hustling a mishmash of rare first editions and worn-out pulp novels and limited-series broadsides that only twelve people in the world can decipher. But where Perez really makes his true coin is in the murky side of the business, the gray margin of pirated collectibles and bootleg variants, the world where copyright law gets interpreted at the most liberal end of the spectrum. Remember that beyond the usual run of specialty collectors there are half a dozen colleges in this city. And if their curators and librarians aren't too curious as to the source of the materials Perez can provide, then the only specifics left to discuss are financial.

When you walk into the Shoppe, you think you've stumbled upon the final yard sale of a very sloppy paper hoarder. While it might be overstating the case to say that Perez's emporium perpetually looks like a bomb has just gone off, the fact is nothing seems very organized and everything seems shabby and dog-eared.

Perez operates out of the basement of his old brownstone on the periphery of downtown. Gilrein is no book expert, but he can't believe a cellar is the best place to store paper products, especially if the bulk of them are old and fragile. The back of the basement houses the building's original furnace, and once a puff-back put Perez out of business for six months. There's a washer-and-dryer setup next to the furnace and Perez has been known to change a load of his Hawaiian shirts in the middle of a transaction.

The floor of the shop is poured concrete covered by a roll of scavenged linoleum that doesn't quite make it to the walls. The walls are unfinished, rough stone painted white, with the paint peeling everywhere in big circular patches. One side of the store is filled with narrow aisles of mismatched filing cabinets, both metal and wooden, the metal units usually some shade of green and often dented in a place that makes the drawers hard to open. The opposite side of the basement is lined with plywood shelving crammed with used books for sale. And in between the file cabinets and the shelves are redwood picnic tables used as display space and featuring review copies and limited editions, small press runs and foreign titles. Above the tables are lines of strung wire running front to rear, and clothespinned to the wires are assortments of typewritten manuscripts, some of them autographed, hanging like yesterday's wash or the butcher's display of salamis.

Usually Perez sits on a stool behind the front counter reading stock through ancient bifocals, his hands never far from the little .32 he keeps tucked inside his ankle boot. He'll nod to browsers when they enter and he'll respond if they ask him a question, but other than that he'll remain silent and work on an air of suspicion, peering up repeatedly at the customer over his tortoise rims until the patron is subliminally forced to either make a purchase or leave.

Perez doesn't have any great love for unknown browsers anyway. He knows his customer base. His clients all have their own unique and unspoken protocol for barter. Perez knows their areas of interest by heart. He can sense when they're branching out and when they're looking to unload some items and free up a little cash. The colleges are hesitant to leave their wrought-iron-and-ivy enclosures, but still, on principle, Perez makes them come to him. St. Ignatius is always on the prowl for stolen missives from any of the vaults of Rome. Every spring, Jonas Hall University is interested in Freud juvenilia. Come fall, they're salivating for the "lost" notebooks of an early rocketry pioneer. And last year, Perez

unloaded a cache of love letters from the city's school superinten-
dent to a variety of sixteen-year-old coeds. The buyer was the
State Teachers College, and it paid through the nose.

Over the years, Perez has put together some deals that belie his
shabby little workstation. He was an essential player in the auction
of Levasque's last and supposedly nonexistent novel. He grabbed a
percentage of the take on the sale of the suicide note by that beloved
of depressive feminist poets everywhere, Janine McBell. And
though he never actually handled the artifact itself, he arranged for
the shipping of the rarest Quatrich volume of all, *Con Crete Crib*, a
book that could be physically taken apart and reassembled into an
unknown number of tremendously intricate labyrinths.

All of this without any major legal consequence, beyond the
original deportation and lifetime banishment from his native
Puerto Rico. So he'll miss springtime in Luquillo; life is a trade-off.

There have been a few scrapes here and there. Detective
Gilrein did manage to nail Perez a few times. Nothing spectacular—a bootleg draft of a book of poems by someone named Quinn,
a stash of letters written by a forgotten novelist that had been
missing from a university library in Iowa for a decade. Perez
always made bail by suppertime and nothing ever went before a
judge, but being a pain in the ass had to count for something,
didn't it?

Rudy Perez turns the corner of Waldstein, fishing in his pockets
as he walks and finally pulling free a huge set of keys on some
kind of fur-covered fob. Gilrein gets out of the cab and tries to be
casual jogging across the street through traffic. Perez climbs down
the five stairs and is stepping into the store when Gilrein reaches
the brownstone and, without a word of warning, leaps the stairs
and shoves the dealer into a table that overturns and spills its display to the floor.

Perez yells as he rolls onto his behind and pulls his .32 out of
an ankle boot crafted from some kind of animal skin and dyed
kelly green.

Gilrein's got his own .38 leveled down on Perez and Perez yells, "Jesus Christ, it's you."

They both stare at each other as the moment diffuses, and then Perez gives a forced laugh and reboots his pistol.

"What?" he says. "You don't knock no more?"

"Got to talk to you, Rudy."

Perez gestures to the mess they've made.

"You got to talk to me, *coño*? What, you don't have a phone? Look at this place. Take your Prozac today, officer?"

Perez stands up and they both start to put the display table back in order.

"I'm not on the job anymore," Gilrein says as he picks up a cardboard, hand-lettered sign that reads EPHEMERA AND ODDMENTS.

"Tha's right," Perez says gleefully. "You some low-rent cab-boy these days. I feel for you, Gilrein. My heart breaking from it all."

"Don't be a dick, Rudy, okay? I still got friends—"

"Hey, Gilrein"—gloves off now—"you don't got no friends, okay? You never had no friends, all right? Your wife, she had the friends. Christ sake, *I* had more weight with the boys in blue than you did."

"Good to know you haven't changed."

"Just so we understan' each other, *cabron*."

"Don't call me names, Rudy. It'll just piss me off."

"You're the one jumps down on me. I di'n't come to your taxi an' mess you up."

As a wedding gift, someone, maybe Zarelli from narcotics, gave Gilrein and Ceil a set of matching his-and-hers blackjacks. An elaborate and overpriced joke at a time when they really could've used a new microwave oven. Gilrein wishes he could remember what he did with them. He'd love to sap Perez across the belly right now, follow up with a couple of shots to the back of the head, ring his bell till he never said the word *chico* again.

Perez moves behind the sales counter and starts shuffling papers. Gilrein stands in place and looks around the Text Shoppe.

He takes in some air and gets that same smell, something like old glue and hay and wet suede and maybe just a little sewage.

"So," he says, "you still scouting for St. Ignatius these days?"

Perez looks up, scratches his beard. "Wha's a cab-drivin' fool like you care who I trade with?"

"You're going to be a hump about this?"

"Someone knocks me down, trashes my store, that puts me in a bad mood all day, cab-boy."

"You know, Rudy, savvy businessman like you, I'd think you'd know when there might be some coin involved in a discussion."

Perez stares at him, picks up a pencil, and taps on the counter.

"Tell you how savvy I am, mister taxicab, mister I stop for any scumwad whistles my way. I learned long time back, you don't piss on tomorrow's dollar for today's nickel."

"Where the Christ did you learn English?"

"Cab-boy, you flatter me so much, I'm going to close down the shop and take you to breakfast. Tell you everything you want to know."

"Let's skip breakfast and instead we can go down the Manetti Home. Pay our last respects to Leo Tani."

Perez looks up but keeps his mouth shut.

It's Gilrein's only chip so he plays it all the way, looks around the shop and in a low voice asks, "You wouldn't have a Mass card lying around here?"

"Tani's dead?" Perez says and Gilrein gives a single nod.

Technically, Leo and Perez were business rivals. But where Tani's merchandise varied from month to month and client to client, Perez stayed in the specialty line. Gilrein knows that now and again the two men broke bread together down on San Remo Avenue and that more than once they made a mutual profit off a joint transaction.

"Leo Tani was trussed up like a pig inside Gompers," Gilrein says, watching Perez study his face. "Somebody peeled all the skin off his body. You imagine that, Rudy? Can you get a picture of that?"

"Holy mother . . ." Perez begins and lets the sentence fade.

Gilrein walks to the counter and comes close to Perez's face. "I heard," he says, "he was sniffing around for August Kroger."

He waits a beat, then adds, "What did you hear, Rudy?"

Perez starts to shake his head, but there's no joke and no insult. He simply says, "I don't know shit, Gilrein."

"If the 'Shank was working for Kroger," Gilrein says, "we both know it was a book. And we both know that means at some point he gave you a call."

"I knew this was going to be a bad day," Perez says.

"Rudy, there are always two ways to do this. First way is, you tell me everything you know about Leo Tani and August Kroger and what business they might have had cooking."

"What's plan B?"

"Plan B is I come back here tonight with a gas can and a butane lighter."

"That's pathetic, Gilrein. Tell me something I can at least pretend to believe."

"Listen, Rudy, understand something. You don't know me anymore, okay? You haven't known me for three years now—"

"You grow some balls in the interim?"

"You might have this dump insured," Gilrein says, straining to keep an even voice, "but I'm pretty sure none of the real stuff, none of the bootlegs or the hot property, would be listed on your policy. Would it, Rudy?"

"Gilrein," Perez says, "you know the San Remo boys still look out for me, huh? You know I go fifteen percent a month to avoid threats like this."

"You don't know me anymore, asshole. I don't give a pig's bladder about your San Remo thugs."

"You be a dead man before the last fire team pulled away, Gilrein."

"You do what you want, Rudy," Gilrein says. "Because I sure as hell will."

Perez stares at him, then shakes his head and says, "Your wife, she'd be rolling in her grave."

Gilrein nods.

"All right," Perez says. "It's not much but you can have it. A new book came onto the market. Something from out of town. Eastern Europe. Old Bohemia. More than one party is interested."

"Kroger and who else?"

"Don't know, but the product originated in Maisel, so who you think?"

"You're trying to say Hermann K?"

Perez nods.

"But Kinsky's no collector. Bastard's never read a book in his goddamn life."

"First of all," Perez says, "collectors aren't always readers. Second, just 'cause he wants it doesn't mean he wants it for himself. Man's the neighborhood mayor for the Bohemians. His people wanted it, Kinsky would do what he could."

"What kind of book is it?"

"I've heard a lot of rumors. None of them scratch my butt, you know?"

Gilrein takes a deep breath and says, "Okay, Rudy, this has been a good start. Now one last piece of business and I'm out of your life."

"Don't make promises you won't keep."

"It's about Wylie. And where I can find her."

"Oh no, shit, Gilrein, c'mon," Perez whines, shaking his head. "This is pathetic. Don't do this. You embarrassing both of us."

"A phone number or an address. Then I'm gone."

"I don't step in boy-girl fights. This ain't dignified, *hermano.*"

"It's business. She'll understand. Let's go."

Perez puts a flat hand on his own chest and says, "She may understand. But I don' think her boss would be too excited, you know?"

Gilrein looks at Perez and says, "Her boss? What are you talking about?"

And Perez realizes he's made a huge mistake, that as bad as the morning has been already, it's about to get worse.

"I wish I could help you," he tries, feeble and distracted. "If I knew where—"

"Cut the bullshit," Gilrein yells. What little play there had been is now immediately sucked out of the exchange. "I know you were with Wylie last night."

Perez shakes his head, conscious now of just how tightly wound up the cab-boy is, of the bruises on the taxi driver's face. He stares at Gilrein, frantic for a way to end the dialogue.

"She's working for Kroger," he says, spilling it all at once, opting for the truth in a moment of fright and weakness.

The sentence has an effect on Gilrein exactly the opposite of what Perez was hoping for.

"You lying sack of shit," Gilrein says.

And then he does what he's never done before. He throws the first punch, connects under the chin and sends Perez reeling back into the plywood shelving. The dealer falls to the floor and reams of paper tumble down on top of him. Gilrein leaps the counter as Perez pulls his piece again, but this time Gilrein stomps his wrist and Perez screams and the gun comes loose. Gilrein kicks him in the ribs, kicks down on a kneecap, pulls Perez to his feet, and then sails him into a glass case filled with oversized Bibles. The case topples and shatters and blood starts flowing from Perez's cheek.

Gilrein comes down with a knee into his chest. Perez tries to roll and Gilrein drives a foot into his stomach. Perez loses his air, hunches into a fetal tuck, one arm up waving, trying to signal surrender.

Then Gilrein takes a step back and as the adrenaline recedes, he realizes what he's done. His own body is throbbing and he goes down on his knees, gets his hands under Perez's arms and helps him into sitting.

"Jesus Christ," Perez's rasping.

"I'm sorry" is all Gilrein can say. "You okay?"

Perez shifts and cradles his wrist, tears in his eyes, sniffing in blood and mucus, trying still to get a good draw of breath.

"What the hell happened to you?" he whispers.

Gilrein needs to get outside now. He reaches into his pocket, takes out a fold of bills and, without looking at it, lays it on the floor next to Perez.

Neither threatening nor pleasing, but in an overly controlled voice, Gilrein says, "You call Wylie. You tell her to meet me at the greenhouse. You tell her it's an emergency."

Perez clears his throat and says, "You out of your mind, Gilrein. You can't do this. You ain't no cop no more."

Gilrein gets up and goes to the door. Without turning back he says, "I don't want to come back here, Rudy. You make sure Wylie gets my message."

7

Moving down Granada Street, walking faster than his age and condition should allow, the Inspector has a moment of mild satori, understands in a flash of enlightenment that what he is feeling is a common but overwhelming fear. It is not an emotion with which he has had a great deal of experience and there is no way to tell whether it has been triggered by his suspicions regarding the status of his health or his exposure to the ravings of the old cabdriver, the ever-expanding myth he has come to think of as Otto's Tale. As if it were already a long-held oral tradition. The kind of story that over time transforms itself into the best definition of a race of people.

He hates the old cabdriver and he hates the myth he is forcing himself to endure, several times a week, as a kind of penance. He is beginning to believe the old man's insane story is the very thing that is making him sick. As if the story could be a virus or an infection. But the truth is, the fear currently flooding his body—the elevated heart rate, the shortness of breath, the tidal perspiration—probably has more to do with finding himself visible and vulnerable on a street filled with people he has spent a brief career terrorizing.

He stops for a moment beneath a shattered streetlamp and reaches into the breast pocket of his tunic, withdraws a crumpled scrap of paper that bears a name and a location. He stares at the paper as he catches his breath, then throws the scrap away, lets the wind carry it south, and moves around the corner onto Voegelin where a krewe of Bedoya's whores are waiting to ambush him.

They descend like overly perfumed locust, propositioning him bilingually in a chorus of lewd suggestion. He pushes away what hands he can, lets the rest pull money from his pants pocket.

"Célibe, célibe," he cries. *"Soy un hombre de Dios."*

The women, and the few transvestite moles, get a great kick out of this, and Voegelin fills for a block with the cackle of junkie laughter. But the Inspector's pleas work after all. These are merchants who will accept amusement if it's the only currency offered and in a moment they've turned their hive-attention to a pair of stretch limousines rounding the corner and rolling to a stop for some appraisal and bartering.

Technically, the Inspector has told the whores the truth, a kind of Jesuitical veracity. But though he has not known a woman sexually in over forty years, he has given himself away in what he considers a more intimate manner, a consummation more perfect in its carnal purity, a union still unbridled if not physically erotic.

Her mind and her soul belonged only to me, he thinks as he scans the storefronts of Latino Town looking for a meat dealership called Brasilia Beef. It's a stale mantra, an old balm that he uses out of habit, a justification that he can't seem to stop employing, though it has never assuaged even a portion of his loss or lessened the burden of his many transgressions. *All you had was her body, Gilrein.*

He spots the beef shop and makes his way down the adjoining alley. At the far end is the promised Chevy van, twenty years old and perched on concrete blocks, painted a dull pumpkin orange but for the front end, which is charred black from a long-ago fire-bombing. On the side of the van, in faded but still-legible glitter paint, reads the pronouncement DAMASCUS OR BUST. The Inspector approaches the rear double doors with little caution. If it's filled with his old enemies, he decides, their attack could only be called an act of mercy at this late hour.

He gives a weak knock on a spray-painted window, hears some movement inside, and the doors swing open to reveal an emaci-ated individual dressed head to toe in filthy denim. It's impossible to estimate this man's age. He's missing full tufts of hair as if his skull has sported some analog to canine mange. He's also missing half a dozen teeth and the ones left rooted are all variations on a caramel tone. His face is death-camp gaunt and zombie white but his neck features some sort of raw, scarlet rash that glistens a bit before disappearing down into his mechanic's coveralls.

"Can I help you?" he says, and though his voice is choked with the ongoing paranoia of a lifelong methedrine shooter, there's the definite ghost of a French accent.

The Inspector sighs and looks down at the ground, wondering why he's come. He looks up and says, "Are you Mr. Clairvaux?"

"You here to be tested?"

The Inspector nods, unfastens several buttons on the tunic, reaches to an interior pocket and withdraws a bill so old and thin it resembles tissue paper.

Mr. Clairvaux takes the money, shoves it up a sleeve and offers a shaking hand to his newest client. The Inspector ignores the assistance and pulls himself inside the van, secures the doors behind him without being asked. The interior is dark and musty. The floor is covered by a multicolored shag rug, white and orange with flecks of brown and crusty in spots. The rug, in turn, is cov-ered with heaps of what appears to be medical equipment—loose syringes, drug vials, tongue depressors—tangled indiscriminately with typical junkie refuse—old potato-chip bags, discarded cloth-ing, crinkled balls of dollar bills. The walls are lined with used and split mattresses, a cheap attempt at soundproofing. The Inspector forces himself into a sitting position, legs folded painfully into a broken lotus. There's a heavy smell, something like a mix of garbage and sweet incense. He glances toward the front of the van where the bench seat has been removed. There's no steering wheel. The cab has been transformed into something resembling the nest of an enormous and slovenly bird. Door to door is packed with an eclectic and copious pile of trash—plastic wrappings and soda bottles, yellowed newspapers and orange peels, rubber tubing, bubble-gum cards, corroded battery casing. And there's a low-grade rustling sound emanating from the nest's interior. As if a small creature is buried in its core and has found a way to move through this maze of debris but never to exit.

"So you think you got the Grippe," Mr. Clairvaux asks, not a question, simply words to fill the air as he lights a flame in a Sterno rig, then slides a series of IV needles out of his coverall pocket and into a dented coffee can resting on a cake rack above the burner.

"That's what I'm here to find out," the Inspector says, losing enough control so that he peeks into the coffee can and, seeing the bubbling green solution within, catching the aroma of sour wash water, immediately regrets it.

"You can call me Armand," the doctor says, friendly now, his version of a bedside manner. "How'd you find out about me?"

The Inspector can't help but smile.

"Your reputation is widespread," he says as the tester wipes his nose absentmindedly on his sleeve and pokes at his makeshift sterilizer with a snapped-off car antenna.

Armand nods as if he couldn't care less about the response and picks up a package of store-bought cupcakes from the floor of the van. He tears open the package with his teeth and extracts a pastry, takes an enormous bite, smearing his face with chocolate and a dab of marshmallow.

After a moment, and as if realizing for the first time that there's someone sitting opposite him, Mr. Clairvaux holds the half-eaten cupcake in the air and says, "Want some?"

The Inspector shakes his head *no*, looks down at his aching and trembling hands and can't keep himself from inquiring, one more time, where it was he went so utterly wrong.

The smart money has always said that, had he wanted it, Emil Lacazze could have taken the chief's commission. The smart money may well be right. But that doesn't mean it knows anything more than anyone else about what is true and what is false within the many legends regarding the man whom everyone, whether fellow officer, politician, gangster, or Jesuit, has come to know simply as the Inspector, as if there were no others.

You would think that Gilrein would know more of the rumors than anyone else and that he might even be able to confirm or deny some percentage. After all, he was Ceil's husband and from the time Lacazze was given the Dunot precinct house, Ceil was the only detective to meet the unknown qualifications for serving on the Inspector's fully autonomous squad.

In this regard, however, Ceil kept Gilrein as much in the dark as the rest of the force. Most of the old bastards, who'd seen everything and then an encore, said that even Chief Bendix himself wasn't aware of half the operations Lacazze was running out of Dunot. But, like everything else, that was before the Rome Avenue Raid. Before Ceil's death and the Inspector's tremendous fall from grace.

Ironically, Gilrein had heard Lacazze's name years before he actually met the man, long before the Inspector even was the Inspector, before Emil the Proud, as the Trinity secretly called him, had been stripped of his soutane and his beads and marched out the front gates of St. Ignatius, a traitor to the black robe, a turncoat shaken from the folds of the Society of Jesus itself.

Lacking spousal affirmation, the version of the legend Gilrein chose to believe went something like this: Emil Lacazze was born in the rear of Hotel Dieu Nunnery, or "the night convent," as it was more commonly known, a specialty brothel on the west side of Paris. His mother was a profoundly beautiful call girl who was murdered while Lacazze was still an infant. Though it was never confirmed, his father was said to be a lecturer at the Sorbonne, a famed French cryptographer who was rumored, when the mood and the price moved him, to consult with assorted ministries around the planet during various political tumults. The child never met the father, however, and was raised by Maria LaMonk, his mother's madame, with assistance from the ladies of the house. It was said he was so adored by the women of Hotel Dieu that he caused more than a few vicious rivalries that lasted to the grave.

When the boy's extraordinary intellectual capabilities became apparent in his youth, Madame LaMonk made the heartbreaking decision, for the good of her charge and over the vehement protests of her minions, to place the boy in L'Abbaye de Hanxleden, whose seminarians in those days were among the nunnery's best customers.

Though Lacazze sorely missed his home among the sisters of mercy, he adapted well to the abbey and was soon recognized as a prodigy of varying media. By his teen years he mastered Thomistic theology alongside quantum physics, and the black robes of Hanxleden split into a multitude of factions, each of whom thought they had divine knowledge as to the appropriate life course for the boy. This bickering, it is said, often incidentally, may have been what triggered Lacazze's first experiments with laudanum, and, subsequently, his periodic and tumultuous struggles with a variety of opium-based addictions. It has also been noted that this was likely the start of his passion for those seven-inch, purple-banded Magdalena cigars that the Society had shipped in straight from the El Laguito rolling house of Havana.

Eventually, sometime during a stormy adolescence that saw him flee the abbey more than once and take refuge among the branchés of Rue de Lombards, Lacazze fell into his natural passion—linguistics, tempered and guided by deep and broad readings in cultural anthropology. When he published a highly controversial treatise on a linguistic theory of criminality in the

notorious journal *Conspirateur*, the word came down, possibly
from as high as the Father General, to move the young man safely
to the confines of research and mediation in the murky cellars of
a Rome the general public would never see. Here he spent innu-
merable hours in the bowels of the Registra Vaticana, possibly
even in these early years already beginning to formulate what
came to be known, across a broad spectrum of not always sympathetic disciplines, as Lacazze's Methodology.

Mr. Clairvaux finishes his cupcake and methodically sucks the
last traces of goo from his fingers. Then he looks the Inspector up
and down and says, "We all set here?"

The Inspector says, "You tell me."

Getting down on hands and knees, Mr. Clairvaux begins
searching the van until he comes up with a single work mitt, a
worn and filthy canvas gardening glove decorated with a floral
design. He makes a show out of fitting the glove onto his right
hand, then fishes inside the bubbling soup of the coffee can and
withdraws a needle. It looks more like a knitting tool than a surgi-
cal instrument. It's at least five inches long and its width
increases up the barrel. Steam is coming off the steel and boiling
liquid is dripping onto the floor.

"We'll give it a second to cool," Mr. Clairvaux explains.

"How thoughtful of you," the Inspector says, and the words
come out more sarcastic than he'd intended.

"You do know this is a fairly painful procedure?"

"I'll survive."

"You've never been tested before, have you?" with the smile of
a man who truly enjoys his work.

"I've never had the pleasure."

"The pleasure," Mr. Clairvaux repeats, holding the needle up
near his head and snapping a finger at it to flick away some of the
cleansing solution. "Well, I'm probably the best street tester in
the city, but I've had people jump out of the van with the first
prick."

"I'm sure I'll control myself," the Inspector says, wishing they could begin in silence.

"It's just that the tongue is a very sensitive organ. Lot of nerves in there, you know. You ever burn it really badly? The pain lasts a while."

"How quickly will you have the results?"

Mr. Clairvaux shrugs and slips a precautionary mask over his mouth which gives his face the appearance of a starving albino pig.

"Give me three to five days and—" He breaks off and says, "Christ, I almost forgot," then crawls to a corner of the van and rummages through a pile of trash, repositioning cotton swabs and pornographic magazines and mismatched tennis shoes until he discovers and pulls free what he's looking for. He shuffles back to position holding a pair of handcuffs and says, "If you'd just slide these on, we can get started."

The Inspector stares at the manacles. They're not police issue. Probably imported.

"No one said anything about handcuffs," he says, but Mr. Clairvaux goes into a furious head-shaking spasm.

"No cuffs, no test. House rule. No exceptions."

"But I—"

"Look, I've had people go crazy in the middle of the proce-dure, all right? Had a woman bite straight into my shoulder. Now, luckily she wasn't a carrier. But I won't take that chance again. So if you want me to check you out, kneel down, sit back on your ankles, and lock the bracelets in place."

The Inspector considers calling the whole thing off, then takes the cuffs, fastens his left wrist, fumbles a bit but manages to secure the right.

Mr. Clairvaux inspects and says, "Thank you. I wish it wasn't necessary but you have to understand. This is a very unorthodox practice. I never know who is coming through that door."

The Inspector nods, closes his eyes, tries to concentrate on past history. Then he opens his mouth as wide as he can.

■ ■ ■

Upon taking his initial vows of the Society of Jesus, Emil Lacazze
was dispatched on his virgin mission and began traveling to the
more remote island tribes around the globe. Armed with only his
rigorous intellect and a beautiful but rugged Nagra tape recorder,
he was charged with developing a study of myth stories and rituals
in the native tongue of each culture under investigation. But
halfway through his assignment—lodged at St. Leon's Parish in
the heart of the Palmer Peninsula, and in the middle of recording
the startling sounds of a village folk chant that depicted the
raunchy intricacies of a particular breed of penguin's mating
dance—Lacazze received word he was being redeployed to America. And so he came to reside in the comfortable if less challenging confines of St. Ignatius College in Quinsigamond, where his
miles of audio tape were to be transcribed, analyzed, and archived.

Disappointed but surprisingly obedient, Lacazze shouldered
his new duties as special-collections curator in the Horwedel
Library. Paradoxically, it is at this juncture, when the story trans-
ports to a local milieu, that the rumors mutate and become hazy.
According to some accounts, upon his arrival at St. Ignatius,
Lacazze developed an obsessive interest in administrative power.
Over time, some would say this interest became pathological.
Other, more reasoned sources claim that Lacazze was simply a convenient scapegoat, that he threw his meager support to the wrong
side in a vicious coup to unseat the Trinity, the trio of Jesuit fathers
that jointly presided over the college. Whichever the actual case, the
results were the same—the Trinity slapped down the insurrection
with their standard and brutally effective talent for suppression. In
a post-midnight purge, Lacazze quite literally found himself out on
his ass, thrown roughly into the backseat of a chauffeured Rolls
Royce Silver Spur alongside his prepacked black duffel bag, wondering in four languages how he could have been so mistaken.

The beauty of the purge became evident later, when it was
understood that simultaneously across town at police headquarters, the commissioner's office was having its own family squab-

ble. A power climber named Waldegrave, who'd been promoted too far and fast up to Internal Affairs detail, began nosing into a series of alleged ties strung awkwardly between the department, City Hall, various neighborhood mayors, and even St. Ignatius College. Before the stupid bastard could write the first page of his IA briefing notes, one of Chief Bendix's shadow creatures from Bangkok set up a classic prisoner swap. As if delineated by the semiotics of some edgy cold war spy movie, representatives from the blue shirts and the black robes met at a designated early-morning hour in a gritty chamber inside Gompers Station. The Jesuits took Waldegrave back up the hill with them. And the department was handed Emil Lacazze.

"Just what we need," Chief Bendix is supposed to have remarked, "a horny smart guy in a black suit. Does anyone know, can he type?"

Rarely if ever in the whole of his wildly blessed career had Bendix ever been more off the mark. After the prisoner swap it was assumed that Father Lacazze would hang on till pension time as a pathetically overqualified file clerk and substitute secretary, rotating forever between traffic reports and the dispatch desk, maybe cataloging over in the evidence locker, a position that sometimes utilized competent spelling skills.

But Lacazze had learned a dear lesson at St. Ignatius concerning the ways and means of power grabs. He courted the chief like an obsessed lover and offered his unique intelligence at the department's disposal round the clock, playing Joseph to Bendix's pharaoh. Even a bloody hack like the old chief soon came to see what a natural resource Lacazze could be, and Lacazze was made the chief's aide-de-camp, advising on everything from restructuring mob payments to improving public relations. As his fortunes rose, Lacazze's position and title and duties became vague and finally unknown. He was seen as a one-man think tank, a policy interpreter who never revealed his own opinion, a close reader of the daily zeitgeist and a compromise broker whose commission of privilege went unspoken. If, in the beginning, he was a

conduit of varying power bases, in the end he became an entity
unto himself, a force that orbited the common arrays of rank and
influence and took from each what he needed. A free agent of
sorts, he turned himself into the department's Rasputin, until no
one really knew who, if anyone, he reported to.

He can feel the tester's breath on his face. Can smell sugar and
bong water.

Mr. Clairvaux's fingers come to the sides of the mouth, push
in and dimple the cheeks, as he says, "Whatever happens for the
next few minutes, try to continue breathing regularly."

The Inspector feels the needle penetrating the tongue, piercing the mucous membrane, exploding through the sea of epithe-
lial cells and forcing, cutting its way into the networks of striated
muscles, ripping through fat and nicking its way past salivary
glands, inexorably rooting toward a place just short of the hyoid
bone.

It begins as the bite of a viper, the fang piercing into the soft
meat of the tongue like a fat razor. Then it changes to an insect
sting. From an enormous and hideous wasp, a wasp mutated to
the size of a falcon. And then the sting grows into a burn. As if the
tongue has been taken from the head and pinned to the red heating coil of an electric stove. As if it has been swaddled in jellied
gasoline the way you might engulf a frankfurter in ketchup.

This is a different kind of pain, rarer than one can imagine,
working its way, in a geometric progression, to some level of torture without demarcation. This pain breeds, births smaller versions of itself and dispatches them downward to the heart and to
the groin on their own missions of agony, but never diminishes at
the source. And when the distress can't seem to grow any worse, it
finds brand-new planes of excruciation to colonize.

His resolve vanishes and the Inspector begins to scream.

Emil Lacazze's unique status was cemented into unheard-of enti-
tlement when he was allowed to annex the ancient, abandoned,

and vermin-ridden station house on Dunot Boulevard, at the
border of Bangkok Park. With funds left uninked in the line items
of the police budget, he turned it into his own home and office.
He set up a single room as living quarters on the second floor, a
spartan studio more suited to a cloistered Trappist than a once-
worldly Jesuit.

Downstairs, in the former precinct commander's office, he
invented a chamber that was part analyst's study, part priest's
confessional, and part inquisitor's sweatbox. Lacazze kept a
generic gunmetal desk in the center of the room. Behind the desk
was a slat-back schoolmaster's chair on rollers and behind the
chair a wood-frame, grammar-school-style chalkboard that could
pivot on a center axle and swing wholly over to its opposite side.
In front of the desk was a small shoe-fitting stool, a low, vinyl-
covered seat attached to an angled rubber pedestal that slanted to
the floor. The walls of the room were left bare, in places showing
cracked horsehair plaster, but the floor was littered with reams of
stacked notepaper, all of it filled with what was either Lacazze's
illegible handwriting or some sort of idiosyncratic shorthand or
code. Many of these piles reached two feet high and were
weighted in place by a variety of red-painted wooden apples fitted
with rawhide wicks for stems.

But the strangeness of the office was just a minor aberration
compared with the eccentricity of the Inspector himself. There
was the anachronistic dress uniform he insisted on wearing—a
stiff, double-breasted, high-collar garment with garish brass
fittings that the rest of the department had abandoned a generation ago. And the small, rimless green spectacles that he favored
even inside and at night. The rust-colored Magdalena cigars he
chronically fingered and pointed with. And the tiny, pink plastic
hearing aid always secured behind his left ear with a coiled tail
that snaked down his over-starched collar and, in fact, was connected not to any sound enhancing device but to a miniature
tape machine that was forever playing loops of interrogation
sessions.

With his image and his office established, Lacazze began to choose what he hoped would be a very select cadre of officers whom he planned to train in his unique and complex systems of analysis to be part of what he christened, not without a trace of humor, the Eschatology Squad. The exact purpose of this unit was left undefined to all but the Inspector. The most he would tell Bendix was that the E Squad would assist him in *implementing the Methodology.*

This begged the question, in the Chief's vernacular, "What in the name of sweet Jesus is the Methodology?"

And Lacazze was forced to sigh with the long-felt futility inherent in explaining his theories to deficient intellects.

Lacazze's Methodology was a radical and multifaceted system of critical inquiry, he explained to Bendix's already deaf ears and glazed eyes. The system could be utilized in any number of problem resolution capacities, but, surprisingly, it was in the old-fashioned logic-driven art of criminal investigation that it now seemed ideally, perhaps organically suited. Would it be overstating the case to say that Lacazze's Methodology, when used correctly, would possibly prove to be the most effective interrogation technique in the history of criminal pursuit?

Lacazze didn't think so. And on an apprehensive nod from Chief Bendix, the new baron of 33 Dunot Boulevard began putting his squad together. A small sampling of possible recruits was given a test—brought into the precinct house and left in a small, windowless room, barren but for dozens of radios tuned to various stations. After a time, Lacazze would question the applicants as to how many sounds they were able to isolate. This questioning could be either gruff or good-natured and might or might not take place over a game of chess. In some cases, Lacazze, without explanation, would begin speaking in another langauge. In others, he might suddenly break off any queries regarding noise differentiation and begin probing, with deeply embarrassing questions, into the candidate's sexual history. There was one rumor that he requested a certain narcotics officer remove all her clothes and waltz with him.

No one understood the scoring method of these screenings, but the results were disheartening as to the viability of the project: out of two dozen officers tested, only Detective Ceil Gilrein managed to fulfill the opaque specifications.

The question might be asked, did Ceil ever come to fully understand the nature of Lacazze's Methodology? Before her death, Gilrein ached to know. It was never quite that he wanted his wife to pass on her information, to make the apprentice betray the mentor. It wasn't a matter of desiring the arcana itself, but more a question of simply knowing Ceil as fully and deeply as possible.

After Ceil was killed, it occurred to Gilrein, just once, to dig out some of her casebooks, read through her field notes and see if they revealed some hidden side of the woman. But he could never bring himself to do it. Somehow looking at Ceil's notebooks would be risking a pain that he knew could go deeper into him than even the fact of her death. The thought of her handwriting on the white page, like some lingering aftereffect of a life that was no longer, would be a measurement of the immensity of his loss, a signal of a forfeiture too enormous to sanely bear.

What he had, couldn't avoid, were memories of conversational scraps, the kind of verbal minutiae that becomes a binding force in marriage, husband-and-wife noise, some of which contained incomplete and not always logical recollections of those rare occasions when Ceil let down her guard and discussed her work with the Inspector. Gilrein had never been able to think of what his wife did in terms as common as work. In his mind it was more like a mission of alchemy, a calling to a mystery religion that was cloaked by curtains of fear and superstition.

Ceil spoke of how Lacazze often stayed up all night in his office after an interrogation, writing incessantly on his blackboard, chalk dust everywhere, like some crazed researcher working on a millennial breakthrough, symbol after symbol, some looking vaguely recognizable, like letters of the alphabet that were in midprocess of mutating into something else. By dawn, when Ceil arrived,

Lacazze's hands might be trembling like a reprobate caught at the height of his DTs. The Inspector would have to swill a load of laudanum for breakfast, then bring himself back to competence with a dose of Bangkok street speed. But when it came time for the next interrogation, Lacazze would transform himself into nothing short of Quinsigamond's own grand inquisitor, his uniform impeccable and his eyes unblinking behind his mod glasses.

The suspect would always be brought to Dunot by one of the more roguish night-duty rookies. The prisoner would be manacled to the shoe-fitting stool and then left alone with Lacazze. Ceil remained close by in the cavernous squad room, in case of the unlikely event that the Inspector needed some assistance. Lacazze would commence scribbling on the blackboard, ignoring the suspect's always worried pleas for explanations and attorneys. At some inner-designated moment, the Inspector would flip the blackboard to reveal the reverse side was a mirror, and not an ordinary mirror but one that magnifies and bends as well as reflects. Then the lights in the room would be lowered as the Inspector lit a fat, squat liturgical candle inscribed with Latin—VERBUM INCARNATUM EST—and placed it atop a pedestal, directly behind the suspect's head, composed of dozens of enormous spine-broken dictionaries. On the desk between them, Lacazze placed his own red, bejeweled chalice from his days as a Jesuit. The chalice was filled with what the Inspector referred to as Spanish sherry. "In case you get thirsty," he would mumble to the prisoner, indicating the cup. Finally, Lacazze would ease into the seat behind his desk, elevated above the level of the suspect's eyes, and the pair would spend some tense moments staring at each other. Behind Lacazze, the suspect couldn't help but start to glance at his own enlarged and warped image made even stranger by the glow of candlelight from behind his head.

And then Inspector Lacazze would launch into a series of rapid-fire word associations, throwing out, void of any instruction, every known part of speech, but after a time honing in mainly on the verbs—*want, push, take, use, will, kill, run, hide, wait*—until the suspect finally caught on and began to reply, often in the hope that cooperation would end these proceedings sooner rather than later.

Lacazze dealt with all manner of alleged transgressors—dealers, extortionists, arsonists, rapists, murderers. From simple but annoyingly persistent pickpockets up to sociopathic and wildly dangerous, most would say unredeemable, serial criminals, abusers and killers and roving, conscience-deficient madmen whose only motivation left in this life was to be the initiator of widespread chaos and terror.

The Inspector handled them all the same. "The criminal bends to the Methodology and not the other way around," he once told Ceil, then added, "though I must say, I love the schizophrenics the best. Their language is not only unique to themselves. It is also chronically shifting, changing even as it is born."

There is no way to know the exact schematics of how Lacazze determined guilt and innocence, motivation and mechanics. He would word-associate with the suspect until the handcuffed detainee was ready to drop. The Inspector never flagged. His ability to go hour after hour without food or sleep or break from the procedure was close to frightening. More than one interview produced confessions without the need for analysis, the criminal breaking down and explicating all from the sheer pressure of verbal bombardment. This, invariably, was disappointing to Lacazze, left him depressed, as if he'd been cheated of a promised reward at the end of exhaustive labor. Because it was the analysis that gave him his juice. The criminal and the crime, at that stage, were almost incidental. It was in enacting the system he had spent the bulk of his life constructing and tinkering with that he received the majority of his meaning.

The analysis consisted of tedious hours, sometimes days, of listening. Simply turning on the pink earpiece and activating the tape player and settling into a state of being whose sole activity was focusing in, deeper and deeper, on the sounds of the preceding interrogation. Lacazze would walk through the necessities of life—the breathing and eating and evacuating—as if they were secondary and annoying endeavors. All the while he would be locked into another realm, a dimension comprised solely of sound, the noise of words traded back and forth like Ping-Pong balls. The Inspector's voice, followed by the suspect's voice, followed by the Inspector's voice, until the two voices became one unit, a note that would in time give up its secrets and reveal the nature of the mind of the accused.

And eventually, after hours of relistening to sound after sound, replayed over and over, looping around the same track, gutturals and dentals and moans void of significance whispering endlessly into his ear, Inspector Lacazze would feel the pressurized rush of an approaching epiphany. His concentration at this point would reach its maximum expanse and finally, he'd feel a burst of cold pain across his forehead, as if he'd bitten into a block of ice, and his vision would fade out for just an instant, an ache would course through his body from groin up through stomach and into his chest, the analytical climax that would become manifest in the birth of the solution, the big bang, the second coming of truth. The answer would congeal, birth itself into the world of Lacazze's consciousness. And he would turn off the tape player, remove the hearing aid, call Ceil into his office and reveal the *what*, the *how*, and even the *why* of the suspect and his particular crime. What happened to the criminal at this point could not have mattered less to Lacazze. His part in the drama was over. The guilty party could be executed or unconditionally pardoned for all the Inspector cared. From Lacazze's perspective, the only interesting aspect of the case was concluded. As much as it was genesis, each epiphany was also a small death. Invariably, each conclusive solution brought about an interval period of intractable depression that lasted until the next, seemingly inscrutable suspect was led down to Dunot Boulevard.

The needle begins to withdraw, the retreat as fierce as the insertion.

The Inspector quiets and opens his flooded eyes in time to see Mr. Clairvaux hoist the instrument to his nose and sniff it like a dog on a chase.

"Is anything ever as bad as we fear?" Armand asks, grabbing a rag from a rear pocket and handing it to his patient.

The Inspector looks down at a threadbare Rorschach of stains and realizes it is actually the remnant of what was once a pair of boxer shorts. He shakes his head and extends his hands to indicate that he wants the cuffs unlocked.

Mr. Clairvaux complies and the Inspector immediately throws open the van doors and jumps down into the alley, both hands covering his mouth.

As the patient breaks into a stumbling run toward the street, Armand Clairvaux is forced to yell his prescriptions out into the world.

"Get some ice on that as soon as possible," he hollers. "You'll be able to talk again in an hour or so."

8

Wormland Farm sits out on the northern border of the city where the elevation makes winter come a little earlier and last a little longer. The official name of the estate is Brockden Farm, after the founder, E. C. Brockden, but to the consternation of the historical commission, everyone knows it simply as Wormland.

Edgar Carwin Brockden was one of Quinsigamond's original legends, the myth by which all of the city's future mayhem could be measured. By all remaining accounts, he was a brilliant but unstable man with an unhealthy passion for language, books, gnostic tradition, and, later, parasitology. He was born in Ireland to a rare family of shepherds that had escaped the charisma of Saint Patrick and vehemently, if covertly, maintained their pagan ways over generations. Edgar, the eldest son, born of vigorous intellect and natural enthusiasm, nevertheless came to either disappoint or horrify his parents, depending on which account you read, by claiming a devout belief in monotheism at some point during adolescence. Refusing at the age of sixteen to participate in the rituals of the equinox, Edgar was banished from the family and so began a series of wanderings about which we can only speculate.

In one of the first biographies, Dunlap's *The Heretic*, we learn that Brockden, though unrepentant regarding his belief in a Judeo-Christian God, retained his clan's obsession with the mystic and occultist traditions. Clark's detailed *Tongues of Fire and Madness* suggests that young Brockden's "missing years" were spent traveling around the Far and Middle East where he began in earnest collecting a variety of fabled, esoteric, and some might say, diabolic texts. But there is no direct evidence of his whereabouts until his arrival in Quinsigamond with his common-law wife, Lucy, heiress to the Courtland Publishing fortune and daughter of the famed vermesophile, Cecil Stritch.

Brockden moved his clan to New England at the turn of the eighteenth century and it was here that he came to feel his true life began, came to believe there was something in the earth itself that clarified and unified his many obscure theories and grounded them in the flesh. Finding Boston already too settled for his notions of a new and unspoiled Eden, he pushed westward and, for "a pittance and a promise," as one commemorating folk song later put it, Brockden purchased just shy of fifty acres of stony land from a Packachoag chief named King Mab. And on this plot Brockden set out to make concrete his peculiar, and finally tragic, vision. He founded his own sect, and though the entire congregation was limited to his small family, he named them anew as *Babelonians*. Their place of worship would be the farmhouse, which Brockden called, perhaps, as Grabo suggests, more in mockery of than tribute to St. Augustine, the City of Words.

The structure was designed by Brockden with the aid of a mysterious Italian named Santarcangelo. It almost resembles a storybook castle replete with peaks and spires and featuring a stone tower rising out of its center. The tower consists of a series of floors, one spiraling into the next and each level housing an esoteric library, the fruits, presumably, of Brockden's early years of traveling and collecting.

Using Lucy's dowry, Brockden spared no expense importing workmen and materials into this neverland. His wife and two children, Theo and Sophia, survived a trio of spirit-breaking winters in a one-room shelter until the family manse was constructed. Upon completion, their suffering appeared to prove worthwhile, because as far away as Gloucester and New Bedford, people spoke of the paradise that Edgar Brockden had forged in the middle of the heathen wood.

But just three years later, this City of Words was deserted, the culmination of the tragedies that stubbornly rained down upon the Brockden clan until the patriarch was pushed beyond his breaking point. Now the place is just Wormland. And to Gilrein, it is home.

Or, rather, the small section of barn loft where he keeps a bed and a child's dresser is the closest thing to a home as he's likely to get in the foreseeable future. And this haven exists only through the good graces of Frankie and Anna Loftus.

He parks the Checker in the barn and climbs up the ladder to the loft. It's a modest setup, wood-plank floor and walls, slanted dormer ceiling, a roughed-in bath. But it's clean and it's quiet and that's all he wants to allow himself these days. He strips off his clothes and moves into the bathroom, running a hand over his bruises as he goes. In the center of the room there's a porcelain tub with claw feet. He turns on the radio, and the air fills with Imogene Wedgewood singing, in her Creole-accented French, "Last Chapter (in This Sad Book of Love)," then he starts the hot water and climbs inside, lays his head back over the curl of the edge and stares out the window into the distant cluster of dead apple trees just barely tipped inside the borders of his vision.

Frank and Anna Loftus are the only people left that Gilrein can call friends. The other indie hacks are his associates, colleagues he values and trusts. But when Ceil was killed and Gilrein fell apart, it was Frankie and Anna who brought him to Wormland and saved his life. He hopes he never comes to hate them for this act of compassion.

Frankie Loftus is the son of Willy "The Mortician" Loftus, the neighborhood mayor of the Irish Acre. Frankie and Gilrein met when both were students at St. Ignatius College. Frankie's family duties at the time involved running the Castlebar Road Boys, the family's street muscle, a real beer-and-speed crowd that was usually reliable for battering each other instead of their rival gangs. It made for a ludicrous and often schizophrenic existence that found Frankie spending mornings at lectures on Thomas Aquinas and evenings trying to keep up with the CRB ass-kicking parties down in Bangkok.

"Honest to God, Gilrein," Frankie used to say to his friend, "I don't know if I'm supposed to be Stephen Dedalus or Sonny freakin' Corleone."

Frankie's real passion was for pop culture in all its cheesy forms, but he never spurned the fat scratch that the mob world provided. He learned to put up with the contradictions of his life and eventually found a way to see an ongoing and ever-expanding humor in his dual existence.

Today, everyone forgets that Anna Coleman wasn't a local girl. She came to St. Ignatius out of Galloway, north of Boston. Galloway, like Quinsigamond, was a factory town whose massive textile mills on the banks of the Passaconnaway attracted the first hordes of European peasantry to crash the industrial revolution. Anna was the daughter of a one-time boxer—cum—railroad cop and a registered nurse, the youngest of one of those teeming Irish broods that took over an entire tenement and made its walls swell to bulging with offspring.

It was probably clear, right then on that first night, when Loftus and Gilrein, both wildly drunk and pissing next to the Jesuit cemetery at dawn, bumped into Anna Coleman, studying century-old tombstones, that somebody was bound to get hurt. To this day, Frankie will claim that he saw Anna first. But all Gilrein can remember is zipping up the fly of his jeans and turning around to see this stunning young woman, backlit by the rising sun, peering at him from behind a faded slab of marble.

What she was doing in the cemetery is now a matter of debate, though it likely involved a study of missionary martyrs. What's more certain is that Frankie paid the check for the endless break-fast the trio went on to share at the Miss Q Diner down by the rail lot. And by the time the boys argued over who would leave the tip, it was apparent something had begun.

There were a few sweet years there, the three of them insepa-rable and probably a little giddy with the *Jules and Jim* allusion, insulated in the way only college brats can be and living out of Frankie's well-stocked wallet. They took the requisite road trips and stayed up all night arguing about French pedants, pop music, and how many people Frankie's dad might have whacked. They gnawed pizza crusts and worried over what kind of pesticide might be coating their dope, scrounged the Ziesing Ave book shops for old Levasque paperbacks and spent countless days sealed in movie theaters. And if, at some point, Gilrein began to sense he was becoming the useless third wheel, it wasn't long before the Transubstantiation Scandal and his subsequent dis-missal from St. Iggy.

Frankie and Anna married the week following graduation. After much internal debate, Gilrein showed up at the ceremony, late and feeling sorry for himself, finally drinking so much at the reception that, unbeknownst to the bride and groom, one of the Mortician's meatboys, an enormous and legendary ex-cop named Toomey, but more commonly known as the Antichrist, escorted him out the rear doors of the Hibernian Social Hall and dismissed him from the affair with a good-old-boy joke whose punchline was *Jaysus, I thought that was your teeth chattering.*

Gilrein stayed away, did his year of sorrows down the Canal Zone bars among the hopelessly affected young artists until he was so disgusted by artifice of any type that he put down the bottle and chose the only career he felt capable of—bunko cop. He kept occasional tabs on his old friends through the humps in the Organized Crime Unit, found out the couple had used the Mortician's substantial wedding present to buy and restore Wormland Farm. Everyone in the department was more than suspicious when word came that the newlyweds were turning Wormland into a nonprofit corporation called Sanctuary Ltd. Half the cops in OC were betting on a new smuggling line. The other half were split between money laundering and some kind of narcotics stratagem. But after countless wiretaps and stakeouts and the shakedown of every mick informant in town, the enterprise, unbelievably, proved legitimate.

According to the intelligence profiles that Gilrein sometimes secreted home at night, Anna had begun traveling the globe on the Mortician's nickel, figuring there was a way to wash blood money clean. Using her father-in-law's connections with the other neighborhood mayors, Anna slipped into a series of similarly blighted holes that the planet's bureaucrats called refugee camps, shanty towns, tent cities, anything but what they were—a particular circle of hell reserved for that most viciously and relentlessly exploited form of chattel in human history, the innocent child.

With equal parts bribery and physical threat, the latter backed up by certain signs and signals known only to the local mob bosses and political hatchet boys, Anna began bringing the orphaned and the starving and the abused back to Quinsigamond with her. By the time Gilrein made plainclothes detective, Wormland Farm was filled with children of every size and hue. By the time Gilrein met Ceil, Anna had decided to expand the parameters of her mission to include adult casualties of political torture, souls victimized in ways unconceived by even the better-than-average imagination. By the time Gilrein and Ceil got married, Anna was in a Central American jungle getting hustled, for the first time, out of a big chunk of the Mortician's cash by a death-squad cop who failed to turn over the prisoner they'd negotiated for.

And when Ceil was killed in the Rome Avenue raid, Gilrein was brought to Sanctuary by Frankie and Anna Loftus, a victim, though he couldn't have known it at the time, of Quinsigamond's own, uniquely twisted brand of political terrorism.

Gilrein agreed, by lack of argument, to stay a month. In his numbness, the time mutated into three years. His leave of absence from the force segued into an inevitable resignation. It was as if he was replaying his postgrad lost year down in the Zone, only this time the performance had been restaged from indulgent melodrama into a kind of endless, absurdist, horrific opera, a surreal fable of meaningless loss whose Greek chorus was played by a multicultural crop of children heard only, always, from a distance. Gilrein never learned whether the children had been cautioned to stay away from him or simply sensed the barrier of gloomy emptiness he emitted like organ music, perpetually warning of the madman hidden around the corner.

He couldn't bear to live in the main house. Anna came up with the barn-loft alternative. They never talked about Ceil's death, never discussed the raid and what went wrong, as if to bring up the subject, voice it, give it sound and attendant meaning, would be to make Ceil die once again. Gilrein spent his first season at Wormland walking the orchards daily, trying but never managing to lose himself in the gnarled maze of lifeless fruit trees.

Until that Friday when Frankie came to the barn and yelled up to the loft asking for some help with the furnace. Gilrein tried to shake him off, swearing ignorance regarding the mysteries of plumbing and heating. But Frankie wouldn't listen and Gilrein ended up following him through the weaving jogs of the farmhouse and down the foolishly steep stairs into the basement. It was pouring that day, as it had for most of the previous week, and the cellar seemed even more dank and oppressive than usual. Anna had bundled the kids up and taken the whole lot to a story hour at the public library, so the unnatural quiet of the farm accentuated the standard undercurrent of timber and joist groan that the stress of mismatched carpentry work had engendered over the years.

They wound their way toward the farthest rear reaches of the basement, came to a stop at an industrial-size oil burner looking like a horrible, grease-scarred green oven salvaged from some long-abandoned detention camp.

"So what's wrong with it?" Gilrein asked, immediately abandoning hope in the face of dozens of unlabeled valves, half of which were dripping rust-colored water. Frankie had enough money to heat the place with uranium if he wanted, so why didn't he just phone up a repairman?

"Not a damn thing," Frankie's voice holding that barely repressed burden of restrained glee that in college had been, if not endearing, then at least pardonable, and now was just taxing on the patience.

"So what are we doing down here?"

By way of answer, Frankie led the way past the furnace and oil tanks to a narrow plywood door held closed with a padlock. He fished a key from his pocket, popped the lock, threw open the door, and stepped aside to reveal a closet housing nothing but stale air.

Gilrein stared at him. Frankie took a silver penlight from a rear pocket, snapped it on, and shined it at the closet floor. Set into the concrete was what looked like a municipal manhole cover. It was made of tarnished brass, maybe two feet in diameter, and in its center was a recessed bolt with an inlaid, swing-up handle below it. Gilrein got down on one knee, brushed away a thin cover of dirt. Above the bolt was some sort of design cut into the plate—something like a snake spiraling up out of the center of an open book. Below the bolt was an inscription.

"It says," Frankie answered without being asked, "*Liber Vermiculosus Vertit.*"

Then he kneeled down next to Gilrein and began to unscrew the bolt. His face was apparent even in shadow, spreading into childish smile.

"You'll get a little dirty," he said, "but it's worth it."

■　■　■

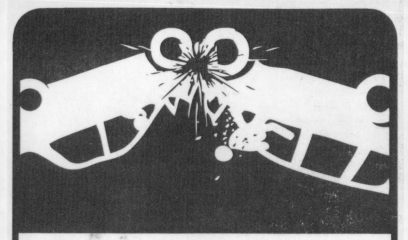

The best drunk drivers in the nation have gathered at the U.S. Capitol for a race to the Pacific Ocean. They have talent. They have ambition. They have breathalyzers in their cars that will shut off the engine if the driver's blood alcohol content drops below .16. The flag drops at the height of rush hour.

After a fifty-car pileup at the starting line and dozens of major accidents on the streets of D.C., only six cars make it out of the city. Second-string stockcar drivers, German Kung Fu masters, forgotten Soviet sleeper agents, frat boys, an unemployed sommelier, and a washed-up 80s pop star battle it out in this grueling, action-packed race. Facing overwhelming obstacles and outrageous intoxication, the racers battle the police, AA sponsors, each other, and themselves for the grand prize of one million dollars and a free liver transplant.

From the most sardonic voice in modern fiction, comes a debaucherous action-comedy in the form of a bizarro *Cannonball Run*.

Gilrein pulls the plug in the tub and sits still until all the water drains away. Then he climbs out, towels off, throws on some clean clothes and runs to the main house before he can debate the consequences of what he's about to do.

The entire Loftus clan is currently in Miravago, ostensibly touring an obscure Inca ruin near the mouth of the Urubango River, but in reality bartering for the freedom of a nun, a Sister of Torment and Agony, who has been alternately captured, raped, tortured, and released by both rebel and governmental forces in a kind of round robin of philosophical sadism.

Unlocking the rear door, Gilrein lets himself into the massive kitchen, all wainscoting and ceiling timbers, overstuffed rockers and a central table so large and heavy you could park a car on it. He knows this is where the family tends to congregate and Anna once remarked, without any sign of mockery, that this was where the bulk of healing at Sanctuary took place. Gilrein wouldn't know—he's never eaten a meal here.

He quickly unbolts the cellar door and makes his way down into the basement, grabbing a flashlight off the first stair. He moves past the furnace and the oil tanks, comes to the closet and opens it. He unbolts the manhole cover and opens the lid, then lowers himself down into the earth, into the burrow where Edgar Brockden tripped over the line that separates the sane from the demented. The chamber where this new Eden was transformed into Gehenna.

The box is down here somewhere. He just needs to get his bearings. He sets off along a random corridor and begins taking turns based on instinct more than memory. He gets lost a half-dozen times but manages to find his way back to the starting point and try again. And finally, just before giving up and acknowledging that this is probably not a smart thing to do, he comes to the section he's been seeking, the place where someone, possibly Brockden himself, graffitied the floor with the words THE SPIRIT GIVES UTTERANCE.

Gilrein goes down to his knees and begins to push books off the shelf closest to the ground, lighting up title after title until he comes to a series of books that have no title, a trio of odd-sized, ramskin-bound notebooks, imported from France, affixed with ridiculous taxes and tariffs. And filled with the handwriting of Gilrein's dead wife, Ceil.

Three years ago, when he squirreled the notebooks down here, he believed he could never bring himself to either read them or destroy them. Now, he folds himself into a sitting position, fixes the flashlight into the crook of his neck, and opens to page one.

9

Field Notes: A Book of Evidence & Conjecture

A. From the files of the E Squad: For your eyes
   only. The names have not been changed. Only
   abbreviated. And as we all know, there are
   no innocents.
      The tyranny of the notebook. The
   compulsion to record. The burden just seeing
   it. Witnessing its existence. Its
   extravagance—do I really need to import this
   exact brand from that tiny papetier on Rue
   de l'Ancienne Comédie? Did an animal have to
   give its life, its shell, its dignity, so
   that I might bind the words of my petty ego?
      The notebook has become fetish object. It
   has taken on an aura, become magnetic,
   possibly radioactive. Perhaps it has become
   sentient without me consciously knowing it.

It is an infection. It is a virus. It is a
disease and a weakness. It is the
manifestation of the paralife. Which becomes
the antilife. You can choose one or the
other, life or antilife, but you cannot
choose both. You either live or you record
the living. You either exist or reflect the
existence. Your days will become material.
Your years will become fodder. The love you
could have cherished becomes something to be
described, to be transformed into graphical
representation.

This act, this heinous process, is a
cannibalism of the worst variety. It is
vampiric in the most infantile and anal
sense. It is insidious in the degree of its
addictive qualities. And, do not be fooled,
do not believe the lies—there is no antidote
beyond death.

Which begs the question: To whom am I
writing? Who is it that I'm willing to bite
and infect? To whom would I allow such
intimacy?

Allow me to clarify by starting again.

B. My Dear Love:

If you are reading this, then it seems all
of my suspicions have been proven true. And
if that's the case, what good will this
notebook do me? Better that I should use
this time and ink to write down all those
things that I could not tell you.

I know that, at times, you have doubted my
love. But I'm not sure what I could have
done to give you definitive proof of my

affection and my commitment. You were the
original skeptic, could have given the
Apostle Thomas a run for the honor. And this
is not just my opinion, like so much else
that will come to clutter this notebook. The
folks at St. Iggy's would have to concur.
(But, trust me, I'll come back to the
Transubstantiation Scandal.)

I have doubts of my own, love, but none
of them involve you. I have come to wonder
exactly what I have done to myself in
joining the Eschatology Squad, in working
day after day in such close proximity to
the Inspector. My brain has changed.
Nothing I can define for you, no specific
symptoms I can inventory and cross-
reference. Just this feeling. As if I have
burned a crucial bridge. As if I have
exchanged a vital faith for something dark
and mephitic.

Tonight, I sit at our kitchen table in
the perfect bungalow where we came to make
a life. You are asleep in the bedroom. The
sound of your dreamlife makes me hate this
insomnia even more. I'm sipping from a
glass of Gallzo. Poured from a labelless
bottle I keep hidden in the hall closet. A
gift from an informant. One more thing that
I've kept from you. And now, the first of
my many confessions to follow. Such a
bitter drink. But you can develop a taste
for anything.

Would you wake if I turned on the radio? I
need some Imogene right now. I would like to
fill the next page with sketches, blueprints

for the Church of Wedgewood. You promised we
would build it together and I will hold you
to your word.

But I won't draw any blueprints tonight.
Instead, I will sketch my doubts.

C. Please understand that it is impossible to
write about the Inspector without writing
about the Methodology. They are fully
intertwined at this point. It would be like
trying to write about Gautama without
mentioning Buddhism. Encapsulating Moses
without mentioning the Commandments. Jesus
without the Last Supper. It can be done but
more is lost than gained.

The Inspector is in a delicate position.
The position of all progenitors. The burden
of being the Papa. He forms the Eschatology
Squad to pass on his legacy, his gospel, his
essence to be left behind. He forms the E
Squad out of fear of death. But to remain
after he's gone means he must give up his
essence. And this is his strength. This is
all he has.

He wants to give me the Methodology. But
he wants to hold it back as well. To hand
over the secrets of the Methodology would
certainly be a little death for him. Sampson
losing his hair. And so he moves forward and
back, undecided, provoked to inform,
determined to obfuscate. Our ritual dance
each day inside the Dunot is a decidedly
kinky version of sex. (I know he desires me
on this level as well.) Which one of us is
the more maddening tease?

Emil may be the most self-deluded man I
have ever known. It's as if his brilliance has
made him an idiot in this singular regard. As
if this were the specific price to pay the
devil. He tries to get me to read Mallarmé.
Leaves books on my desk each night. *Les Noces
d'Hérodiade*, *Mystère*, and *A Tomb for Anatole*
(the Benjamin Wilson translation). Specific
pieces bookmarked with the bands from his
Magdalenas. (This, knowing I am in the grip
of Klaus Klamm.) He worships Heidegger like a
son, hating him, and not knowing he hates
him, without rejecting any of the teachings,
imprinted by the Papa, played like a puppet,
wanting only to be an individual, to be
unique. He imagines the Methodology will be
the tool to cut the strings he cannot see but
forever feels, hooked into his skin, pulling
him through the world.

And now I see I cannot accept the
parameters of the Master's lesson plan. I
will never agree to such an infantile
arrangement. He should have realized this
about me. His interviewing process should
have revealed this: the only candidates who
should qualify for the Eschatology Squad
should be those who could unravel the
Methodology without the teacher.

So I do what I am trained to do.

I am a detective.

I investigate.

I uncover clues and tease out their
meanings.

He'd be mortified and perhaps even
frightened—does he get frightened? Is this

technically the correct word?—by what I've
uncovered already. I know that before the
black robes put the kibosh on him, he'd
managed to publish a trio of highly
controversial essays in the cutting-edge
quarterlies. All of these journals have
ceased to exist. But Leo Tani managed to
locate the Inspector's first breakthrough.
(What will I owe the 'Shank for this
errand?)

In a pretentious and precious little rag
called *Minotaur* I found the article "Look
Who's Talking: The Hypernarrative Evolution
of Pagan Liturgies" by E. Lacazze. The piece
is too dense and full of itself for useful
summary but it has Emil's proverbial
fingerprints all over it—sanctimonious,
petulant, esoteric, pun-laden, self-serving,
bursting with neologisms and the sense of
the author's uncontainable ego.

Tell me, reader, what does a responsible
person do when they start to suspect a truth
they do not wish to know?

10

It's not so much that Otto Langer places any credence in the childish superstitions attached to Wormland Farm. It's that he dislikes coming this close to Gilrein's temporary home. Langer can control himself in Gilrein's presence inside the neutral confines of the Visitation Diner. But who knows what might occur were the two cabbies to come face-to-face in the shadow of these gloomy woods?

Still, the Inspector has indicated that this is an essential element of the therapy, and who is Langer to disagree with his last possible savior? He pulls the taxi to a stop where a pine tree has been savaged by lightning and the priest appears out of shadow, pulls open the rear door and climbs in.

The momentary glow of the dome light illuminates the interior of the cab and the Inspector can't help but see Zwack the dummy, Langer's ventriloquial figure, belted into the front seat next to its master. This is a clear violation of the Inspector's prescription. The dummy is to be locked in the trunk at all times. But Langer feels he can no longer tell the story without the presence of his oldest companion. And what good is the therapy without the story?

"And how are we tonight?" Langer says and smiles into the rearview.

"I was thinking, wondering really, if perhaps you might like a donut? A nice donut, or maybe a cruller? I know of a place, open all night, everything quite fresh. I could run in, leave the motor idling. You could lock the doors."

There's no response from the backseat.

Langer nods and shrugs.

"I just thought I might ask. I feel as if I have been a poor host."

The Inspector leans forward and puts a hand on the security divider and Langer actually trembles a bit.

"So, no donuts," Langer says. "Not even a bearclaw?"

The passenger tilts his head forward and raises his eyebrows.

"It is a kind of pastry, you know?" Langer says. "It is not important. Sometimes the sayings, the bits of slang, they can be quite eccentric. I remember when I arrived in the city. The first time I heard the phrase *cat got your tongue*, I was mortified."

The Inspector shifts in the seat and tugs at the hem of his tunic. He lets himself sink back and sideways into a corner, folds his arms across his chest as if he were lazing before a fireplace in a remote country home, waiting for the elderly patriarch of a large clan to continue a holiday fable, something that would act as a bridge between the waking and the sleeping lives.

Langer knows this is another sign. So he turns up the heater a notch and clears his throat, glances at his passenger in the mirror one last time and begins to speak in a lower and more formal voice, saying, "So you wish to know about the Censor?"

There are those who would tell you that the Censor rode to the Sweep sitting on the shredder itself, perched atop the stomach of the thing, his legs and arms wrapped around the inverted rectum of the satyr. In point of fact, it seems much more likely that he rode inside a dilapidated Cathar pickup truck whose doors bore the words

OFFICIAL VEHICLE
MAISEL DEPARTMENT OF SEWER ROOTING
THIS TRUCK STOPS AT ALL REFUSE CHECKPOINTS

and the ornate seal of the city. More likely that as the brigade made its way, as silently as possible, down Namesti Avenue, the Censor of Maisel, a bourgeois and a bureaucrat from all we can gather, was bouncing over the cobblestones of the fifth district toward the heart of the ghetto, his stomach much too distraught from lack of sleep and his newfound authority to possibly feast on the hot flesh and blood of lamb or human.

When they arrived at Schiller Avenue, the Reapers began to maneuver the Obliterator into place until it came to rest exactly dead-center in the mouth of the street. Some say the machine was as large as a house itself, but let us face facts—it had to, at very least, be small enough to fit through the lanes that lead to the Schiller. And remember that Maisel is a very old city, not known for the enormity of its avenues. Let us say, then, for the sake of creating an image for you, that it was, perhaps, larger than the average cement mixer but much smaller than any of the tenements in the ghetto. It was bulky and angled and painted the color of rust. It sported stenciled lettering here and there, the words DANGER and WARNING in a faded green. It moved on rotors like a tank. Its rear end was composed of a compressor with metal, snakelike coils spiraling from port to port and funnels, mufflers, gauges, exhaust flutes. Extending toward us from the compressor was a vault, a multichambered middle compartment, what some have called the stomach of the beast. Rising out of the top of this midsection, angled backward, was an enormous chute, an upward sloping head, smooth and glossy like the skull of a sea serpent and culminating in a window which could vomit out an endless jet of microscopic, masticated dust. And finally, the most important component, at the front of the machine, facing, always, its helpless prey, the head, the mouth, the jaws into which an entire tree could be fed like a snake into the gob of a mongoose. The mouth was a tremendous window, a boxlike rectangle, as large, I would guess, as a commercial movie screen. Large enough to run from curbstone to curbstone, effectively blocking the only exit out of Schiller Avenue.

Recessed several feet within the mouth of the machine were the teeth. This is not an appropriate description of the eviscerating mechanism, however. In fact, there were two industrial beaters, enormous revolving drums, like the enlarged steel rolling pins of some demonic, cannibal baker. The drums were fitted with alternating rows of meticulously honed blades and hooks and when engaged they would spin at a tremendously fast rate of speed, instantly pulverizing, atomizing anything fed into the mouth and pulling all remaining minutiae into the belly of the shredder, where jets of gas-fed flames and an acid bath incinerated debris into lighter-than-air ash. Finally, mounted on either side of the mouth were the hydraulic winches, the lips of the dragon.

Can you begin to picture it, Father? Does an image begin to form in your mind?

Near the entrance to the ghetto, the handful of Ezzenes still awake and seated on our stoops, trying to ignore the humid air playing on the skin like fat, slow flies, looked toward this visitation and then looked to one another for explanation, and, finding none, looked back to the machine, this mutant steel calf, this industrial Trojan horse. Some must have known, must have sensed in the intestines, that a decree had been issued. And, as always, it was read to us by a lackey in leather boots and, always, a jaunty cap on his head decorated with a symbol of the authority which the state had vested in the man. He stood

in front of all his hardware, dwarfed by this host of inele-
gant metal, the city trucks so mismatched and bulky they
seemed to be frightening and at the same time, equally
comical. Cartoon terrors. And the man, the soldier, a petty
bureaucrat elevated to warrior by the gutless sadism of
more powerful bureaucrats, he appeared comical as well, a
vision from the children's funny papers given flesh and
noise. Much later, the rumors spread as to the man's identity. There was a school of researchers who felt the soldier
was a reservist, a dim scapegoat with little understanding
of the mission he would be leading. Other, more pragmatic
scholars argued that the military protocol of Old Bohemia
did not allow for this, that the individual who stood that
twilight before the small brigade would have more reason-
ably been, at very least, a lieutenant colonel. Today, if you
linger in Boz Lustig's tavern, sooner rather than later, you
will hear one of our people launch into a discussion of the
July Sweep, with the kind of fervor available only to those
who were not there, who did not witness the act nor the
aftermath, the type of secondary testifier who will never let
his outrage affect his appetite or his sleep. And in the
course of this discussion, when attention is turned to the
individual who read us the decree that ignited the Erasure,
they will call him Meyrink. Meyrink, the Censor of Maisel.
I do not know where they came across this name. I only
know that at this late date it appears to be fixed in time and
that it is some sort of joke whose meaning and humor will
always elude me.

We stared at this thin, forgettable man holding the
silver clipboard. Stared as if this was the transfiguration
we had waited thousands of years to receive. And a communal realization broke through the crowd that this
vision was not the long-promised redemption from per-
secution, but the climax of our centuries of fear and
betrayal.

Now some will tell you, with absolute certainty, that had we chosen to run at that first moment, instead of standing to listen to our own death sentence, then more of us might have survived. I can only assure you that the people who spout this nonsense never stood in the nauseating heat of the Schiller that night. Never faced down, for the last time, the persistent nightmare of our birthright. Whether the machine began to feast before we listened or after would have made no difference. The results would have been the same.

We watched as Censor Meyrink popped a whistle between his lips and trilled a signal to his staff of sulky young troopers. The squads jumped down from their trucks and scooters and, in teams of twos and threes, dispatched to every front stoop on Schiller until they'd formed a full circle around the avenue. Then, with their guns held at chest level, they began kicking in the nearest tenement doors with their black boots. The visitors stormed into every apartment and woke the residents with orders screamed in a guttural, disgusted bark. When we did not move quickly enough, they would grab us by our hair or our necks and begin to haul us, push and shove us, out the doors and into the street. The elders infuriated them with a lack of speed and understanding and the state's bullies threw the aged to the floor, kicked and stomped the fragile and decaying bones of our parents and, on one or two occasions, simply took possession of an old Jew's body, one thug taking the arms and another the legs, and heaved the patriarch like a sack of spoiled, vermin-ridden grain into the road. They made sure to rip open the nightshirts of our young women, fondling them, groping and laughing as they forced the girls into the avenue. They took a special pleasure in terrifying the children, stooping to shout into their ears that the young ones had been very naughty and now their mothers and fathers must suffer for the children's sins.

When the community was assembled in the street, packed together like carp in the fishmonger's barrel, everything suddenly grew quiet and Censor Meyrink stepped farther into the road, his boot heels ticking on the cobblestone. He positioned himself in front of the shredding machine and waited until convinced that all eyes were upon him. Then he took his silver clipboard from under his arm and read to us the Orders of Erasure.

The Bogomil rolls out of the cavern of the downtown financial strip, the small cluster of midget skyscrapers, a lane of flat-faced, reflecting cubes that will one day tell future architects and archaeologists that this was the valley where imagination came to die. Langer exits the shadow of the First Apostle Bank & Trust and the Inspector watches through the safety divider and the windshield to find the outline of Gompers Station.

During every drive, they end up, at some point, circling Gompers, and the Inspector wonders if a time will come when the cabdriver will confess the nature of his compulsive attraction to the decrepit train hall. Its hold on him is self-evident. The story slows and Langer's voice drops toward a whisper. The speed of the taxi decreases to a crawl and the old man stares out at the building as they wind their way round a 360-degree panorama of obsolescence and decay. Always the same route, a slow and rigid circle around Gompers and then back off into random parts of the city, the speed of both the cab and the story instantly restored to normal.

Technically, the charge leveled against us, the whole community, every baby in the Schiller, even those still asleep in the womb, was the study and dissemination of subversive texts. To the best of my reasoning, back when I used to dwell on minutiae of this sort, back when this kind of obsessive and futile detail would plague me for weeks on end, I would assume by *subversive texts* the Censor was referring to the nihilistic pamphlets distributed by a small clique of adolescents in the Schiller, among them Fritzi and Kolo who lived with their mother above Loisitschek's butcher shop. But at times I have also wondered if they could have been referring to that circle of old men, amateur cabalists, hobbyists of the mystical, who spent the last of their days in the back of the Kokoschka bathhouse, exchanging angry commentary on *The Fecundation of the Soul*.

I ask you, does it really matter? What is the difference between foolish young boys overheated with the first bloom of the darker philosophies and foolish old men enjoying the mysterious algebras of other worlds beyond our own? Both are to be pitied and, to a point, indulged, for one group may learn from their excesses and the other is past the point of being a danger to anyone.

Up until this juncture, the subversive-text provision was an ancient and seldom-prosecuted statute of the old ecclesiastical courts of Maisel. But it had been subsumed into the secular charter under the definitions of treason. And as a treasonous offense, of course, it was punishable by death, to be administered in a manner acceptable to the Magistrates. If there had been some sort of court trial, no one from the Schiller had been invited to it. And the Capital Fires a year later destroyed whatever documentation might have been found.

Still, that night in July, there was no mention made of treason nor of a death sentence. The Orders of Erasure appeared to be a mundane warrant that authorized the search, seizure, and destruction of any and all radical materials circulating throughout the Ezzenes community of Schiller Avenue. But do you haul the largest eviscerator in Old Bohemia to a tiny ghetto in the middle of the night just for a common search and confiscation detail? Whose sense of the dramatic is so inflamed?

I ask you, Doctor, what should we make of the Ezzenes'
capacity for naïveté? We thought they were going to throw
our *books* into the dragon's mouth.

But at some point, as Meyrink read the Orders, perhaps
at some preunderstood moment, some sentence or word
sounding a silent alarm, the Reapers, as if animated by an
electrical shock, ran for the flatbed truck and began to
offload the rolled bundles of cyclone fencing. You know
the type of fencing I am referring to? You must know. For
another of the great ironies of the Sweep, this one unique
to me, is that the fencing was manufactured here in Quinsigamond. I am not joking. Produced right here in our
city. Black Rose Wire and Cable Company. Down on
Terezin. A family concern, I understand. Very much a
quality product, the wire so fine and yet so unbreakable,
so malleable and yet always razor sharp.

The community as a whole was attempting to listen to
the legalese and babble being proclaimed much too fast by
Meyrink and at the same time trying to watch as the
unmarked soldiers wrapped us in the fencing. They ran
down the length of the avenue, unspooling the taut rolls of
chicken wire the way you would unfurl a flag, past Haus
Reuben, Haus Simeon, and on, separating the people
from their homes, making the corner at Haus Levi, and
returning toward the front of the alley and the patiently
waiting monster. We thought they were fencing us *out* of
our homes. That they would search each apartment for the
mythical subversive tracts and, in the bargain, help themselves to whatever humble trinkets they might find. At
worst, some of the pessimists believed we were finally
being relocated, that the city was taking our street by emi-
nent domain and shipping us to a place even more
removed and destitute.

And yet, if this was to be the case, why the need for the
expurgating machine? Did none of us look beyond the

Censor at the hardware flanking him and wonder why they had gone to the bother of hauling this demon through the sickeningly hot night in order to threaten a roadful of pacifist Jews?

It was only after Meyrink spit out his last words— something about "the security and sovereignty of Old Bohemia"—and clapped the clipboard under his arm and did an awkward goose step past the shredder, outside the net of fencing, that our panic began to simmer.

And when the Reapers hooked the free ends of the fence to the winches and turned them on and the fencing immediately began to retract, to condense, to roll itself up upon the drums, to pull inward and force the entire community in upon itself, this was when the panic exploded into full boil, into hysteria and the madness of primal, undiluted terror.

As the motors of the shredding machine were switched on and the grinding of the various movable parts began to mix with the screams of the crowd, the outer edge of my people began to feel the first sting of the wire, the thin steel strips cutting into their faces, their arms and legs and backs and bellies and genitals. There was nowhere to run. Nowhere to go. We were trapped within the net of the fence. And the net was closing in on itself. We were mashed one against the other. And the horrific chaos within the web was growing more atrocious with each passing instant.

Can you imagine, Inspector, what the next three hours were like? That is how long we agree it took to complete the Erasure. Can you imagine what took place within the corral in that time? Within the minds of the trapped, clawing at sky and ground and lattice to get free? Clawing finally at one another out of desperation and even out of basic physics, out of the way the body was being manipulated by the force of the wire net pulling forward, pulling inevitably toward the mouth of the eviscerating beast.

Immediately, in the first seconds of constriction, some made the mistake of trying to climb up the fence. But they were betrayed by the flexibility of the construct. And even if the makeshift netting instantly began to bend back down on top of them, this did not stop the Reapers from firing a spray of artillery at the would-be escapees. It was like a fishbowl. There was literally no place to hide. Boys and girls climbed up their fathers' backs and shoulders, trying to jump, to heave themselves over the barbed top of the fence, only to be shot by the State's marksmen. One young mother simply gathered her infant into her chest and squatted down in the midst of the tumult until she disappeared under the cover of swarming bodies.

Contrary to what you sometimes hear from witnesses of sudden calamities and unexpected holocausts—car crashes, gasoline fires, earthquakes, this kind of thing— there was no slowed-down rhythm to the events of the next several minutes. There was no music hidden within the mix of the screams and the shouting and the sound of rifle discharge and the underlying purr of the Obliterator. There was no seemingly choreographed dance taking place in the heart of the instantly convulsing street, bodies smashing up against bodies in a thousand desperate and futile attempts at escape, people falling at different speeds, in different directions, like icons of a children's game suddenly knocked from a table.

When you hear the word *chaos*, what does it summon in your mind? Do you call up some clinical, perhaps mathematical, definition of disorder? An elaborate lack of categorization? The mundane clutter of a sloppy room? Let me give you something better, or, at very least, something more vivid, meatier. My gift to you. From this day forward, think instead of a thousand panicking individuals, packed into square yards of street space, in the stillness of a humid July night, bodies pushing against each other in a discordant sway. Now picture this scene placed under an additional amount of pressure, as if some essential measure of oxygen was forced out the skin of the atmosphere and escaped into the cold void of space and was replaced by a denser, more oppressive substance, a previously unknown element that felt exactly like the palm of God breaking through the sky to crush his people into the ground, but slowly, with all the time and restraint available to an omnipotent entity. I am trying to make you feel how it felt that night, in that place. I am trying, knowing, from the start, that this is an impossible task. I say *imagine*, but somehow I need you to do more than imagine. I need you to put yourself there, in the Schiller, in the street, trapped up against other bodies, a small sea of bodies, no passageways out, no lane that will lead you to safety. I use this word—*imagine*—as if it were a kind of miraculous prayer, some type of witch's incantation. As if it has a power that we both know it does not. It is a word. Nothing more. It cannot do what it is not made to do.

Isn't this tragic, Father? Have you never felt this was a tragic thing? That all we have between us is langauge. And it is never enough. Never. Not once. Not for one precious instant. And we go on anyway. Every moment. Acting as if it *is* enough.

Imagine, I say, the sound of the shredder's engine igniting, the rumble that reverberated from the mouth of the Schiller down to the face of the bridging tenement and echoed back to wash over us. Imagine knowing, in that instant, what would follow—the immediate panic, the trampling, the sound of a chorus of gunfire erupting, the sound of 206 thousand bones being ground into pulp.

Let me attempt to do the impossible now. Let me try to explain the unexplainable. To give an image to the unthinkable.

One night, years ago, when I first came to Quinsigamond, when the plague of the insomnia and the migraines
was only just beginning and I had not yet found a way to
drive the taxi while afflicted, I chanced to turn on the
television that Gilrein had given to me. It was four o'clock
in the morning and I came across a documentary—I
assume it was a documentary—in black and white and at
times out of focus, as if the camera had been hidden for
some reason. The pictures showed a series of dead horses,
all of them hung, suspended by the neck, from enormous
steel hooks, the hooks, in turn, mounted inside a conveying belt. And the belt moving toward a slaughtering station, a white-tiled room, a laboratory of infinite
efficiency, the product of much study and brilliant analysis where an automated series of coordinated band saws
and guillotines and rotary blades and serrated grinding
wheels would converge on the line of dead animals and
the most appropriate tool would be instantly matched to
the correct part of the horse's anatomy. And in a matter of
minutes, the animal would be perfectly rendered into a
kind of mealy silt to be packaged as dog food.

I watched these pictures. I was paralysed. In a fever
state. Incapable of turning off the television. And yet
unable to make my eyes close.

I want you to understand, Doctor—those pictures were
but a silhouette of what took place in the Schiller Ghetto
on that night in July.

The bodies fell, piling up higher and even buried near
the bottom, even in the midst of the screaming and the
confusion now pushed up to insanity, one could smell the
stink of diesel and blood and excrement as the shredder
began to feed on this ant-heap of writhing flesh.

The ones closest to the mouth of the expurgator were, of
course, the first to be hauled inside. It is said—though how
anyone would know remains unexplained—that Rabbi

Gruen was the initial victim to be erased. He entered the mouth of the beast headfirst. The spinning hooks pierced his skull instantly and pulled the whole of the body inward, where the first of the whirling razors began to transform our rabbi into an unsolvable jigsaw puzzle. The flesh of Gruen was yanked forward and devoured by orbiting shards of honed steel. The very substance of his corporeal being was . . .

What words shall we use, my friend? *Disassembled? Disassociated? Decompiled?* Are any of them useful in the least? Is there another that might serve us better?

Once tiny enough to pass the gullet of the demon, the remains were then spit into the acid and brimstone of its stomach. Broken down with flame and chemical. Artificially evaporated into common dust and blown out the anus of the gorgon. Into the humidity-choked air to settle between the cobbles of Namesti Avenue. Obliterated? Annihilated?

Erased.

And the rest followed. Man and woman. Child and adult. The Ezzenes were sucked like porridge into the yap of the State's mascot. I would have thought the screams would reach the farthest edges of the city.

But no one came to the see the reason for our cries. No one came to witness the Erasure of the Schiller. And now I'm forced to ask you, my Inspector, since there is no one left to ask—what did they think the next day, the next week, the next time they passed our street and we were no longer present? What did they tell themselves about where we had gone?

11

The orchards cover a couple of acres of land north of the Wormland farmhouse and run adjacent to the borders of the state reservoir. They were planted by Brockden during his first season in Quinsigamond, but they suffered from some unnamed blight before the initial harvest and never managed to take hold. The trees are all dead and desiccated now, but if you make it all the way through a sometimes dissolving path, you come to a sudden clearing, a small valley, in the center of which is the remains of a greenhouse. It wasn't a large structure, and after decades left untended and vulnerable to storms and wandering vandals, most of the glass panes are shattered and the foundation has even sunk a bit deeper into the earth than originally intended. Inside, what's left of the clay pots and planters, fertilizers and hand tools and petrified bulbs, still sits under a frozen shower of glass shards and twisted, hanging steel frames.

Wylie and Gilrein used to come here last year, hike through the orchard and end up inside the hothouse, studying the remains like unschooled archaeologists trying to find clues to a lost culture through its botany habits. They spent a week once trying to clean out debris, thinking they could transform the place into a hidden retreat and going so far as to carry a secondhand powder-blue love seat over their heads and through the orchards, placing it finally in a corner of the hothouse swept almost free of glass. They had scavenged it from a local Salvation Army store and it had brass studs scrolled along its rim. At some point Wylie brought a tasseled quilt embroidered with a generic pastoral scene—some wild-haired maiden on her back in a meadow, lost in the reading of a tiny book—and draped it over the love seat to hide the torn fabric and bulging stuffing. And more than one night they spent riding each other in the greenhouse, wondering if their choked-off cries frightened any of the native wildlife.

"Gilrein," he hears and flinches, his own name once again sounding like the start of an attack.

But when he turns, there she is, dressed in clothes—jeans, oversized sweater—he no longer recognizes.

"Wylie," he says, the name coming out strange, sounding like an anachronistic curse.

She steps through what was once a doorway and is now just an oddly angled portal.

"I got a phone call from Rudy Perez," she says. "He didn't make a lot of sense."

"You know Perez," Gilrein says, studying her face, and upset but not at all surprised by how nervous he is, "totally uncomfortable when he's got to handle the truth."

Wylie smiles and says, "Good thing it doesn't happen that often."

She walks over to him, leans in, and kisses him on the cheek, sisterly, warm but setting up the correct distance right at the start.

Gilrein runs a hand through his hair.

"Jesus, Wylie," he says, "couldn't you have made yourself ugly or something?"

She gives up that laugh, the chin shooting out at him slightly. She says, "I could say the same thing, you know."

"No," shaking his head, but keeping everything friendly, "no you can't. Those are the rules. The walker doesn't get to carry the torch for the walkee. It would screw up all those pop songs."

"Yeah," she says, voice soft, restrained. "I guess so."

And then back to business. Gilrein has always attributed her ability to instantly screw down her emotions to some kind of inherent, maybe genetic coolness just under the surface of her skin.

She says, "I can't believe Rudy Perez rang me up because he was so concerned about affairs of the heart."

He can match her, he lies to himself. He can keep the whole thing on some kind of professional, detached plane, just two bureaucrats swapping information. Two adults involved in a short business discussion whose protocol leaves nothing at stake.

"Perez tried to tell me you were working for August Kroger," with maybe just a little exaggerated disbelief in the voice. He'll need practice.

Wylie turns sideways, rests half of her behind on the edge of the love seat.

"And why would that be any of your business?" But she's missing her mark as well, getting overly defensive too soon.

"Hey, Wylie," he says, all of a sudden completely unsure of just how to play this, "look at me, for Christ's sake. We don't have to be this way with each other, do we?"

"Look, Gilrein, I told you, what, six months ago, that we couldn't talk to each other at all. That's the only way to do this—"

"Have I called you? Have I come by the Center?"

"—I get this call from Perez saying you've gone crazy or something. Saying you threatened to burn down the Shoppe and you were serious. He says you beat him up."

"Screw Perez, okay?"

"What's going on?"

"You don't want to see me, why'd you come down here, Wylie?"

"I don't want to do this, Gilrein. I can't do this, all right? I'm feeling a little hungover right now, okay?"

"Just answer the question and then go if you want, okay? Just tell me, Perez is lying, right? You've got nothing to do with August Kroger, right?"

They stare at each other. Gilrein watches the way her hand toys with a tassel on the quilt.

Finally she says, "The fellowship was running out. I hadn't finished the book. I didn't have any money."

"Jesus Christ" is all he can manage.

"It's just a stupid job, Gilrein," her voice getting louder and tighter.

"August fucking Kroger. I don't believe this."

"It's a job. In my field. Okay, all right. I need to stay in town. Until the book is done. You don't have any—"

"You couldn't teach?" knowing it's exactly the wrong thing even as he says it.

"I'm not a teacher," the studied accenting of the last word carrying the perfect resentment, "I'm a researcher."

"Could've just sold your ass down in Bangkok, you know," getting nastier than he'd feared. "Some people love that clinical look. And real blonds are at a premium on Chin Avenue."

"You bastard," glad to hear it because he knows he deserves it.

"What do you want from me, Wylie, huh? You remember who I am?"

"Yeah, I remember who you are—"

"August Kroger, for Christ sake," sputtering, not at all sure how to convey his sense of outrage and bottomless disappointment. "You leave the Center to go to work for a filthy little gangster like Kroger."

"Mr. Kroger has never been arrested—"

"*Mister* Kroger," yelling now, "*Mister* Kroger. I don't believe this. I was a cop for a long time, Wylie. I knew what Kroger ate for dinner before you even heard his name."

"He's a major collector," she says, trying to go back to a measured tone no matter how unlikely the chance. "He's got a stunning library. And he's not some poseur. He knows his material. He understands what he's buying."

"You don't want to hear it, do you?" Gilrein says, as if he's just figured something out. "That's it, right? You already know the bulk of it and you don't care."

"Is this where you judge me, Gilrein? Is this the part where you tell me how disappointed you are in me?"

"He's filthy, Wylie. Worse than you've allowed yourself to imagine. He's not a neighborhood mayor, you know. He's lying if he's told you otherwise. He doesn't take care of his people. He doesn't have any people. He's just a mob rat who read some books."

"Look, Gilrein, I've got nothing to do with his business affairs—"

"Business affairs," the words bursting out of his mouth.

"I'm the curator," she says. "I've got complete autonomy. I run his library. Period. I've got a budget and a general mission. I go through the catalogs. I attend the auctions. I contact the dealers. I acquire and I inventory and I restore."

He shakes his head and blinks like he's just emerged from a murky pool of water.

"It really doesn't bother you that this guy is a killer. A goddamn down-in-the-slime bad guy."

She exhales melodramatically and says, "It's good to know you haven't lost that paranoia I used to love."

It hurts because, in the larger scheme of things, it's true.

"Wylie," he says, "take a look at this," and he starts to peel his shirt up off his chest. She gets alarmed, gets up off the love seat and takes a step back but then sees the run of blue and purple bruises along his ribs.

"Oh my God," she says, her head bending forward to study the contusions as if they were a map to the library of Alexandria.

"What—" she begins.

And he snaps, "August Kroger did this to me."

She squints up at him, her head still bent level with his torso, her eyes showing either confusion or doubt. Then she confirms that it's doubt by straightening and nodding and gathering herself together for a final goodbye to an ex-lover gone crazy with rejection.

But before she can speak he says, "You ever meet his goons?"

She stares at him.

"Guy named Raban," he says. "And a guy named Blumfeld."

He watches the recognition turn her around, put their entire encounter, instantly, into a brand-new framework.

"So you know them."

"They did this?" pointing to his midsection.

"Grabbed me in an alley off Voegelin."

"But why?" suddenly wondering, he can tell, if it has something to do with her.

"That," he says, "is why I went to see Rudy Perez."

"I don't understand," she says, sitting again.

He lowers his shirt, folds his arms.

"They think I've got something that *Mister* Kroger wants," wishing but unable to avoid the sarcasm.

"A book?"

"It's Kroger. What do you think?"

"You're sure it was—"

"Look, Wylie, just tell me if he's been expecting something new. Was there something coming into the city that he had his eye on? Something Leo Tani might've had a hand in moving?"

She looks past him, her head shaking slowly. "There's nothing. If there was, I'd be the buyer. I'd have set up the transaction. I swear, if Kroger had a purchase in mind, I'd know about it."

"Have there been any brokers calling—"

He breaks off and looks outside, about five feet beyond the greenhouse, and sees a dog standing rigid, staring back at him. Gilrein is no dog expert, but it looks like a Rottweiler, stocky with short black fur and tan markings on the face and snout. Wylie turns and sees it, then looks back to Gilrein.

The animal carries a sense of foreboding with it, a vibration of purposeful menace. There's no play in its body, no sense of random wandering. Its tongue is tucked and sealed in its mouth, its ears look brittle and taut. It stands motionless, doesn't nose the ground, doesn't give any sign of distraction from bird noise or a scent in the breeze.

The closest neighbor is half a mile away and Gilrein knows they don't own any dogs. He squats down slowly, picks up a rock from a mound of silt and rubble.

"I think maybe we should walk back to your car," he says, and without responding, Wylie steps next to him and takes hold of his arm.

They exit the greenhouse and start to walk slowly toward the path into the orchards. The dog moves up behind them, keeping an even five feet or so between them.

"I hate dogs" is all Wylie says and it comes out in a tight whisper.

Gilrein keeps the rock in his right hand, but when they reach the tree line and see the second Rottweiler he knows what he needs is his gun. Unfortunately, it's sitting in the drawer of the nightstand next to the bed. The second dog drops into place on Wylie's left and keeps perfect pace with them. Wylie's grip on Gilrein's arm tightens up, but he tries to keep their steps even and deliberate. The animals could just be someone's demented choice of a hunting dog, some idiot with a rifle who wandered into the bird sanctuary to knock down some protected fowl and managed to get lost in the wood. But though they appear well trained and cared for, the dogs have no collars or tags.

When the path forks right, a third dog is waiting, sitting patiently on its haunches, inanimate as a piece of sculpture until they pass and it falls into a trot on Gilrein's right. The dogs don't acknowledge each other. It's as if they've been bred only to anticipate Gilrein's intentions and match his movements.

"What do we do?" Wylie's voice in a tone he can't ever remember hearing before. He can feel her straining to pick up speed, and he tries to pull her back, stay at a level march. So far, all threat has been implied. But then they come to the small slope that leads to the rear yard of the farmhouse. And at the bottom of the hill is another Rottweiler in the center of the path.

Gilrein stops and the dogs follow suit simultaneously, turning into pieces of bristly stone. It's as if he can feel their joints tightening, ready for the spring. As if he can sense the run of salivation increasing over their gums and teeth and in their throats.

He looks out, scans the spread of forest that breaks right and left to either side of the pathway. And his eyes start to pick out the rest of them. He counts four more, off the path, guarding the periphery, staring back at him through the brush, waiting to see his next move.

"Oh, Jesus," Wylie says, the voice fighting the burn of tears already in her throat, panic coming off her skin like heat.

The dog blocking the way forward seems to lean toward them. Gilrein slowly raises his throwing arm. The animal pulls back the rubbery folds of its mouth, reveals the teeth and lets an almost inaudible growl emerge from low in the throat. It's a sound Gilrein has heard before and never forgotten, a noise that guards the scrap pounds around the edge of the city. The feral voice of the alleys that back the noodle joints in Little Asia. And it means that in a matter of seconds, this animal is going to launch itself on top of them and tear into their flesh.

The surrounding dogs modify their posture and join into the chorus. Wylie is hugging into him, trembling into his arm, something like a horrible, muted keening seeping out of her own throat.

And Wylie's cry is the thing that launches him into motion. He pitches his rock like a bullet into the blocking dog's head and runs, pulling Wylie down the slope and breaking off the path and toward the clearing. He's got the momentum of the hill, but it's not enough. The pack converges, snapping at his legs and ass and arms. Wylie breaks from him, runs to the left. The dogs ignore her and form a circle around Gilrein, charging in, their heads swinging, teeth tearing and snapping in air. Gilrein grabs a fallen branch, swings it like a baseball bat, everything he's got, connects with a head, breaking something, the dog falling to the ground in a pile, not even time for the roar to turn to yelp.

He's hit from behind. He manages to roll as he goes down, but the dog jumps onto his chest and makes a swipe at his throat. He gets his arm up in time to block the teeth.

And then there's a gunshot and the dogs freeze, begin to retreat, back off several feet and hover until a whistle sounds and they bolt in full gallop in the direction of the house.

Gilrein starts to get up, but has to lean back down on a forearm, take a breath to keep his stomach under control. He looks to the tree line and sees a figure approaching, shotgun up on the shoulder. Gilrein gets to his feet, ready to charge the stupid bastard, coldcock him before the idiot can explain. But as he takes a step forward, he realizes the shotgun is being leveled at him.

And the face behind it belongs to August Kroger's meatboy Blumfeld.

12

Who can explain this city? Whose job or duty would this be? Everyone draws his own map. And this is probably as it should be. Think about the physiognomy of the streets. They seem to exist to be pure spectacle. Absolute form and accidental function.

Understand that while a currently fashionable breed of critic defines the standard metropolitan nexus as "faceless," the city of Quinsigamond is the antithesis of this. It is a burg too intensely *there* for its own good. Unlike some urban districts that seem to lack a center, Quinsigamond's center appears, always, to be everywhere at once, radiating a malignant intensity that, for reasons not readily manifest and despite our best intentions, can never be dissipated into something harmless. It's as if the closed-down factories that built and grew this town were still operating on some hidden and secret level, pumping out a new kind of toxin, an unsensed but fully noxious pollutant determined to change us all in unknown ways.

The stretch of land beyond the Bohemian Wing, however, is another story. This sprawl of half-destroyed warehouses and dilapidated garages, junked cars and unlicensed scrap yards and fire-humiliated tenements, is a semiotic blanket of emptiness, lacking even the smallest trace amount of self-knowledge. And perhaps that's what makes it the perfect location for August Kroger's headquarters.

Kroger's castle, the hub of his burgeoning little dominion, lies at the end of Heronvolk Road, across the intersection of Diskant Way, down where the Wing begins to segue into that no-man's-land of ethnic confusion, that mayorless pocket of disorder, that one of the more cheeky anthropologists at the J Street School for Social Research has dubbed the Vacuum. It's an odd and mysterious tract that, for reasons no one can firmly defend, has never become a solidly identifiable neighborhood. As if, for a century now, the block has chronically emitted a warning vibration, a strong and clear sense of bad juju, scaring away every newly immigrated tribe that considered colonization.

But August Kroger has never been bothered by superstition any more than by ideas of racial allegiance. He'll play by the rules of social tradition as long as they are to his benefit. And then he'll find a way to improvise. He was not always such a bold personality. In his youth, back in Maisel, he was known as a shy boy, of indistinct character, the type of child who, it is always assumed, will naturally blend into the weave of the workaday world, will never cause a problem but will never proffer a solution, a gray entity who should, in all likelihood, slouch through a lifetime, head bowed down and voice unheard.

At some point in his maturation, August Kroger threw off the mantle of pervasive mediocrity and willed himself, unequivocally and without the possibility of regression, into a player, a bold man who could make things happen to others. This is the reason he can never be happy running a handful of lucrative franchises for the Bohemian king, Hermann Kinsky. Kroger cannot view himself as handmaid to another. It's a state of being that says the world holds no logic or meaning. It's perverse and totally unacceptable. And so he is perpetually engaged these days in the perilous task of stockpiling enough money, reputation, and connections to topple Kinsky and become mayor to the Bohemians, taking his seat among the businessmen who truly run this city.

The standard method by which a hyperambitious underling advances to the almost mythical realm of the neighborhood mayor would be to feign unilateral allegiance to the king while secretly expanding and fortifying his own troop of do-or-die meatboys until the hour is judged ripe for a victorious coup. Timing is essential and acting ability is enormously helpful. But while every overthrow attempt in Quinsigamond's history has been inevitably bloody and confusing, such actions have always transpired wholly within the folds of the tribal family.

Leave it to August Kroger to annihilate tradition and barter for outside support, spit on honor and leverage his dreams with some extra-Bohemian backing.

Kroger operates a half-dozen low-rent storefronts in the Vacuum, some legitimate, like the newspaper kiosks in Guttwetter Alley, some not so, like the copy shop on Zuhorn that is actually in the business of counterfeiting inoculation papers. But August's only showpiece, the first jewel in his imagined post-Kinsky empire and the base from which he will launch himself into mayoral status, is the Bardo Tissuefable Press, his shockingly successful publishing concern. This privately held corporation is housed in the remnants of the old Bardo Knitting Works, a textile mill that went under decades ago, but in its heyday helped make Gianni "The Peach" Bardo neighborhood mayor to the first generation of Italians down on San Remo Ave.

Architecturally, the Bardo is a product of the short-lived Vagabond School, an amalgam of crackpot theories that resulted in a handful of similar monstrosities speckled across the rust belt. The Bardo, like the others, is an opaque, dull pile of unshapely but imposing bricks, sculpted from the start to look as if they had fallen from the heavens in a random pattern. Kroger held on to the mill's original name and has been restoring the mammoth factory from the top down so that while his penthouse apartment and library are opulent to a degree that encroaches on the decadent, his street-level sweatshop remains as primitive and filthy as it was at its Depression-era worst. The place would give an OSHA inspector a new lesson in outrage, could make some of the piecemeal slave camps of China or Honduras look like a worker's Eden.

All of the labor force toiling in the Bardo is imported. The bulk of it is under the age of consent. Kroger traffics mainly in comic books, what his distributors and marketing people vehemently insist on calling *graphic narrative*. While the stock in trade may seem fully legal if somewhat less than respectable, the fact is that Kroger is a down and dirty pirate. He hires ignorant and poverty-blighted prodigies to draw and ink knockoffs of popular original comic books from the U.S.A. Then he exports the plagiarized fables globally.

His child artists are kept like veal in chicken-wire pens, boxlike cells crammed with stool, drawing table, and first-rate pencils and watercolors. It's rumored that the more escape-prone talent is ankle-chained to the easels. The kids put in twelve-hour days, as August's forewoman has discovered that a longer shift makes the work suffer. And Kroger has rules about upholding standards. He'll chew out your heart before he'll pay a cartoonist a licensing fee, but his forgeries are the best on the market. And though he has little respect for the medium, wouldn't, in fact, be caught reading a single page of his own product, the dingy hallways of the Bardo are decorated with both stolen original prints and their BTP imitations, hung side by side, examples of the quality inherent in a Kroger operation, daring the rare visitor to just try and choose the progenitor.

Kroger has men and women in the field around the globe, individuals he calls talent scouts but who are, more truthfully, art pimps and procurers. They wander through the fellahin ghettos of the planet, meandering around cities like São Paulo and Port-au-Prince, Kuala Lumpur and East St. Louis, basically any ravaged environs where one might find hordes of youths abandoned and left to fend for themselves. The procurers then make their presence known, handing out candy and colored pencils, dressed in clothing that gives tantalizing hints about a place where God goes to party and only the willfully doomed starve to death. Kroger's deputies roam through the rice kitchens and public parks, leach onto the migrant carnivals and underpass campgrounds, cruise the municipal aqueducts where the nomads sometimes bathe. And quickly they insinuate themselves into the life of the disinherited child. The pimps enact a near-perfect routine, inspecting the arts and crafts displays for sale at tourist junctions, browsing the graffitied tunnels of subways, even studying sand etchings in the mud banks of the waste dumps, always keeping the eye peeled for that one child born with the gift of graphical representation. The rest is an easy ride to commission, the promise of life west or north, the transplantation to the heart of a myth named America.

And so they are brought to Quinsigamond and life on Heronvolk Road, life in one of Kroger's art pens in the dim recess of the Bardo. He houses his urchin workers in a basement dormitory that consists of triple-stacked bunk beds and a single toilet with a penchant for overflowing. He feeds them according to their weekly production: *Little Li doesn't finish inking the latest issue of* Ignatius in the Tenderloin, *Little Li goes to bed hungry on Friday night.*

Kroger does not often visit the drawing pens, probably due to the preponderance of mites, lice, scabies, and other parasitic dermatological afflictions rampant among the newest of the indentured artists. August has an excessive, perhaps pathological fear of such infestations. It might be regarded as his greatest weakness, and, oddly, it is a neurosis that developed fairly late in life. He has his charges sprayed down with a homemade insecticide twice a month and forbids them use of the elevator, keeps them confined exclusively to the dormitory and the drawing pens, but this doesn't prevent him, at night, from dreaming of blind, hairless, wormlike vermin twisting their way into the pores of his body and creating a teeming community, a culture of instinctual sucking and burrowing, just under the surface of his skin. He inevitably wakes screaming. And sometimes he has scratched at his arms so badly that he's woken to sheets stained with his own blood.

And now the scratching is advancing into the waking hours, into moments of previously uncharacteristic daydreaming, like this moment, as he peers down into Heronvolk from the perch of his top-floor office, as he watches the taxi-boy being pulled indelicately from the Bamberg by the two foot soldiers. He smiles and slips a finger inside his shirt, the nail scraping rapidly above the navel, and studies Raban's method of escorting prisoners, the almost constant poking and prodding and nudging and slapping and kicking and shoving. Kroger steps away from the smoked window and wonders if Raban was as surly before the Capital Fires. Did his disfigurement trigger an additional gulf of rage that gets released in the course of his nightly duties? The would-be mayor debates the question as he paces the room and begins a series of finger-limbering exercises that his father taught him long ago.

The one with the burn-deformed face shoves Gilrein through the door as it's opened by a preadolescent girl dressed in worn shorts and an extra-large T-shirt that reads ST. IGNATIUS INQUISITORS. The girl has a smudge of charcoal on her cheek and deep circles under her eyes. The meatboys ignore her and move inside.

Gilrein blinks to help his eyes adjust to the light change. The room is enormous, a factory loft of oil-stained concrete floors and high brick walls all sporting lengthy cracks. The general lighting is dim and yellow, a line of low-watt bulbs glowing from tin fixtures high on the walls, but this is augmented by a series of white-blue high-intensity lamps glaring from each side of a wide center aisle.

Kroger's animals pull Gilrein down the aisle toward an open freight elevator shaft at the far end of the loft. He looks from side to side as he walks and is horrified to witness something resembling a dingy human zoo, a shabby industrial terrarium filled with children, row after row of boxes, cells, pens, tiny symmetrical stockades separated one from the next by brittle fencing and an occasional sheet of nicked-up plywood. Each pen is chained closed and inside Gilrein can glimpse youngsters seated behind tables and easels working with pencils and pens and paintbrushes under harsh desk lamps.

As he passes, many of the children rush to their doors and peer out at him but no one says a word. There are no voices. There is no din of heavy labor, just the sound of the visitors' feet tapping off the concrete.

They stop in front of the lift and Blumfeld, the creature with the elaborate overbite, presses for the platform. There's an awful metal whine and then a three-quarter cage starts to descend through the ceiling. Gilrein weighs the possibility of a run against both the likelihood of success and the amount of joy his two captors earned from his previous beating. He decides to be conservative, turns his head to the side and locks eyes with a young boy, maybe twelve years old, Asian and suffering from a forehead full of eczema. The kid is kneeling, turned around on top of a bar stool, facing away from his drawing board and hunched forward to peer through the fencing.

"Jiang," a soft and thickly accented voice says, "geet bahk tu vek."

Gilrein turns and looks across the aisle to the drawing pen opposite Jiang's. And is stunned to see Mrs. Bloch, the woman from the Houdini Lounge, Oster's blind tattoo artist. Her face is pointed in his direction and he can see the sick-making pancake tumors in place of her eyes.

Then a bell sounds and the open cage touches down on the factory floor. The meatboys each take one of Gilrein's arms and yank him onto the metal apron. One of them grabs a free-hanging electrical cord, presses a button on the end, and the entire elevator jerks in place and starts to rise. It's a slow ascent and while the goons stare at their feet, Gilrein studies a framed print mounted on the wire mesh of the left side of the cage. It's a blow-up of the cover from this month's issue of the Bardo title *Alice Through the Attic Glass*. Apparently a thriller comic, the painting depicts a dark-eyed girl, partially obscured by shadow, reacting in what appears to be shock or horror to something she's witnessing from behind the drapes of her window.

The platform reaches its zenith, creaks to a stop in front of a set of glossy walnut doors. There's a long wait until they slide open, then Blumfeld and Raban hustle Gilrein inside the penthouse, pull him through an enormous and ornate foyer, down a dimly lit corridor covered in flock wallpaper, and into a large den rimmed with walls of wood shelving that hold uniform rows of thousands of leather-bound books. At the far end of the room is a podium desk, a little like a scaled-down judge's bench. Behind the desk, bent over an open volume, sits August Kroger.

He doesn't look much like the pictures Gilrein has seen, but then it's been three years since he was privy to OCU files and most of those prints were surveillance shots taken from a distance. The old man looks leaner than Gilrein would have guessed. He's got a huge forehead and his hair is razor cut, close to the scalp. His ears are oversized and pink, but his cheeks are gray and droopy and lined. The eyes are close-set and squinty, covered by rimless oval glasses that are attached to a thin silver chain which drapes around his neck. But all the facial features are just gravy to the clipped rectangle of mustache that may, despite its brevity, be sporting a coat of wax.

Kroger is dressed in a pricey-looking black suit with a minimal gray pinstripe. The shirt is white, rigidly starched, the kind with those odd, rounded-off collar points. He's wearing a maroon silk tie splashed with a pattern of what look like tiny white polka dots, but are, in fact, the letters of an obsolete Slavic dialect.

The meatboys deposit Gilrein in front of the desk, then move to the far end of the room and sit simultaneously at opposite ends of a dark paisley couch. There's a straight-backed wooden chair facing the desk, but Gilrein stays on his feet. A few seconds go by. The sound of a clock ticking can be heard from somewhere in the den.

Kroger holds a flat hand up above his head as if calming a crowd, peers down closer to the book, and breathes deeply through a clogged nose. Finally, he lifts his head, stares across the desk at Gilrein, and slaps the book closed.

"I detest multiple points of view," Kroger says.

Gilrein nods and says, "Did you bring me here for some book chat?"

"In a manner of speaking," in a phlegmy voice layered with an accent, something Germanic perhaps. "You, Mister Taxi Driver, are in danger."

"And you," Gilrein responds, "are a little sewer rat that should've been stepped on a long time ago."

He hears one of the meatboys rise, probably Raban, and then just as quickly sit back down as Kroger waves away the assistance.

"You know me, Mr. Gilrein?"

"I know all about you, asshole."

"Such as?"

"Such as you were a low-rent errand boy from Old Bohemia who never had the balls to put together his own crew back in Maisel."

"Such vicious rumors."

"When you finally annoyed the local tyrants back home, you were lucky enough to be able to buy deportation. You ended up in Q-town a decade ago and weaseled your way into enough franchises to buy this firetrap."

"You don't like my home?"—mock offended. "I thought I'd assimilated so well."

"Must really burn your ass that you'll never be neighborhood mayor for the Wing. I just don't know why Hermann Kinsky didn't whack you already."

"Hermann and I," in a voice that suggests he finds Gilrein's insults amusing, "have an understanding."

"Well, Kinsky's like that. He'll tolerate anybody as long as they're a useful tool. But after that he reaches for the piano wire."

Kroger nods and pushes out his bottom lip. "Hermann is an impetuous man." A pause, a look down at the table. "Anything else you'd like to add?"

Without hesitation, Gilrein says, "You're a book freak."

Kroger leans back in his chair.

"A book freak," he repeats. "That is wonderful. I love it. Just marvelous. Most people call up that tired old pejorative—*biblio-maniac*. I find it so cliché, don't you think?"

Gilrein steps forward, braces his hands against the edge of the desk and leans on his forearms. He waits until the air between them is thick and then, in a low voice that someone else might take for respect, he says, "The one thing every gangboy in this town knows is that you don't dick around with a cop unless you're doing business together."

"But then," Kroger says, "you are not with the police anymore, isn't that right?"

"Hey, moron, doesn't make any difference."

"I am afraid I will have to disagree with you, my friend."

He gets up from the desk and moves around it until he's facing Gilrein. Raban comes off the couch and plays valet, helping the boss shirk out of his suit coat. Kroger starts to unbutton his shirt cuffs.

"I'm not quite the fool you wish to paint me," he says, beginning to fold the cuffs back on themselves. "I've asked around the city. I've spoken to people both inside City Hall and above City Hall. I've confirmed and reconfirmed your status in this matter."

"And what," Gilrein grudgingly has to ask, "is this matter?"

"I believe you may have something that belongs to me."

Gilrein shakes his head. "Like I tried to tell these shitheads the other night, you're mistaken. You've gotten hold of some bad information."

Kroger pulls down the corners of his mouth and shakes his head. He looks like someone's deranged grandfather. He turns to the couch and signals for his vermin to approach, then goes to work on his other shirt cuff as Blumfeld and Raban cross the room, take hold of Gilrein and force him into the visitor's chair.

He doesn't resist. He looks up at Kroger and says, "You know, it's never the big guys who give you the problems. Never the Kinskys. Never Willy Loftus or Reverend James. It's always some little low-end cheesehead who can't get a handle on how the city is played."

"Have you eaten anything recently?" Kroger asks, doing the friendly country doctor as he puts a rubbery bib-apron on over his head. "Say in the past three to six hours?"

"My people will feed your heart to the dogs, you stupid bastard."

"I only ask," Kroger continues as Raban pulls Gilrein's arms behind the chair and handcuffs the wrists together, "because it *can* be a problem. Every now and then, you'll hear of a case of asphyxiation. Choking on the vomit, you understand."

Now Gilrein starts to struggle and Blumfeld immediately puts a brutal choke hold on him, one fat arm wrapped tight around the throat, the other bound in the opposite direction across the forehead. And when Gilrein hears him suck in a deep breath, he becomes convinced that this animal is about to snap his neck, to just twist and squeeze and shove until all those small, fragile bones at the rear base of the head begin to tear free from one another.

Gilrein tries to throw himself forward to the floor, but he can't move. Kroger steps in front of him, leans in, squinting, pulls a piece of lint or a thread from the front of Gilrein's flannel shirt, brings it up close to the eyes and examines it.

"My father," Kroger says, casual voice, fingering the fabric like a soft jewel, "was a tailor. Back in Maisel. A very skilled craftsman."

Raban moves across the room, opens a closet, returns a second later carrying a brown leather satchel that in places has been worn toward a milk white. It resembles a doctor's bag, with a flat bottom and a brass latch. Kroger takes the satchel, places it on the desk, releases the latch and bends open the hinges. He dips a hand inside the bag and begins to fish around.

"I spent a great deal of time in my father's shop. As any boy would."

Gilrein can smell a musklike cologne coming off of Blumfeld.

"My father hoped I would follow in his footsteps, of course. And I did learn the trade. I would help him during the busy season. I became very proficient with the needle and the thread."

And he pulls a fat spool of heavy black fiber from the bag and sets it down. It looks like twine or a ridiculously thick suture.

"It is interesting, yes? You, Mr. Gilrein, have chosen to pursue the family business, am I correct? Your father was also a chauffeur, true?"

Blumfeld lets out a laugh without releasing any pressure from his hold. Kroger loves the response and he jerks back a little, looks around to Raban, lets out his own laugh, too loud and self-conscious. Then he shakes his head, dips back into the bag and pulls out a small, flat case, like an undersized billfold, crafted in what looks like the same soft leather as the satchel. There's a zipper stitched around the edge of the wallet and Kroger begins to unfasten it as he speaks.

"To this day, Mr. Gilrein, I regret that I had to disappoint my father. I could not fulfill his wishes. It was not meant to be. My interests lay elsewhere, as they say." He gestures to the room around him. "I loved the books. Maisel was a town quite rich in literature. The libraries and the book dens. The merchant carts filled with the old volumes. Sold by the kilo, if you can believe it"—a pause, as if remembering something, then, just as suddenly, back to business. "When my father passed away, the tailor shop closed its doors. But this bag"—touching the satchel gently, looking down on it and smiling—"is testament to his memory. The tools of his trade."

Kroger makes a job out of removing a large ruby ring from his left hand and depositing it in his pants pocket.

"When I left my homeland, I had to depart quickly. But I could not leave my father's bag behind. Whenever I take it out, as I have now, it brings him back to me. Do you know what I'm trying to say, Mr. Gilrein? I take out my papa's tools and I'm transported back to Maisel. The Maisel of my youth. Which, of course, is long gone. The smell of the tailor shop. The steam from the presses mixing with the cut leather and the cabbage stew mother would send . . ."

He drifts off for a second, then, "I can almost taste it now, yes, Blumfeld?"

Blumfeld shakes his head enthusiastically and Gilrein's windpipe blocks off for just a moment.

Kroger opens the wallet and reveals a display of silver sewing needles, a dozen or more, all held in a line of increasing size by securing loops. He pulls a midsize needle free, holds it up slightly above his head and studies it as if inspecting a diamond or a photographic negative.

"Zamarelli needles," Kroger says, "and quite hard to come by in those difficult years. Nothing but the finest tools for Father. My mother, she would shake her head. We ate radish soup three nights a week, but father had to have the Zamarelli."

"I think," he says softly, maybe to himself, "this one will do nicely."

And Gilrein tries once again to break free, fall to the floor, do anything but sit here and allow the realization of what's about to happen to him. It's useless. His movements only cause Blumfeld to tighten his grip.

Through clenched jaws, Gilrein manages to say, "You're making a mistake."

But Kroger is already threading the suture through the eye of his needle.

"Mr. Gilrein," he says, "the beauty of dealing with someone as insignificant as yourself is that I can't make a mistake. There is nothing to be lost. You are no longer a policeman. You have no family. No powerful friends. You live in a barn, for God's sake. An attic dweller. You don't exist beyond your pathetic role as a driver. A deliveryman. Even your passengers forget you the moment they step out of the taxi. You are a shadow, Mr. Gilrein. I can do anything I want to you. And no one will care."

He comes to stand directly in front of Gilrein, the needle and the spool of thread cupped in the palm of his hand, held out before him like an offering.

"I am going to ask you a final time. You have taken something which belongs to me. I intend to locate it. Now, Mr. Gilrein, you can either help me in this matter or you can waste my time. But if you do not answer me right now, right at this moment, I am going to be forced to teach you a very dear lesson."

He lifts the threaded needle up to his mouth, dips the point just inside his lips and moistens the tip, withdraws the needle and lowers it down toward Gilrein's face, as if it were a minuscule chalice.

"Do you have anything to tell me, Mr. Gilrein?"

Blumfeld loosens the choke. Gilrein sucks in air and frantically starts to shake his head, yelling, "I don't know anything."

Kroger closes his eyes briefly to indicate his disappointment, then looks to Blumfeld and nods. Blumfeld resecures his vise-hold on Gilrein's head.

Kroger steps forward, runs a thumb over Gilrein's lips and then his eyelids, saying, "As you see nothing, it appears you have no use for the eyes. And as you have nothing to tell me, it seems to me, you have no use for the mouth."

Gilrein tries to scream but it's as if his head is frozen in a block of ice. With one hand Kroger grabs the front of Gilrein's face between the expanse of his thumb and forefinger, then, with his other hand, he takes the sewing needle and punctures the bottom lip at the right-hand corner and as blood begins to flow down the chin, the needle and its attendant thread are forced through the upper lip, which likewise begins to bleed.

"The eyes will be much worse," Kroger says, calmly. "There's no comparison. The lips are supple, plenty of give. But the eyelid, acht, you need to be extremely careful."

Very likely, the process takes several minutes. But Gilrein's perception is skewed from the moment the tip of the needle pierces the skin just below the rim of the lip. What he's aware of through it all is the pain, the blood, the seizing up of the stomach, the tremblings and hidden conniptions exploding in pockets throughout the entire body, their epicenter located, it seems, one moment at the base of the jaw, perhaps half an inch below the earlobe, and the next moment in his temples, where he can feel his pulse revving beyond panic.

And there's the strain in Blumfeld's arms and chest as they struggle to prevent even the slightest movement. There's the smell of Kroger's breath—something like mustard or a strong, overripe cheese. There's the sound, somewhere beyond it all, of movement and, at one point, maybe laughter.

The needle slides in and up, through the soft tissue of lip, breaking blood vessels and igniting a warm flow of liquid down the chin, off the chin and down onto the front of the shirt. The needle slides in again, through the upper, matching lip, pulling the suture along behind, binding the folds of pink flesh together, closing the aperture of the mouth, sealing the wound that holds the tongue, the muscle of speech, the organ of taste. The needle changes direction, follows the lead of Kroger's hand, reverses course and now comes downward toward earth, back through virgin skin, cinching the hole at the base of the face, the repository of noise, the church of oral language.

And as the needle moves through its design, across the track of the mouth, left to right as well as up and down, Gilrein becomes aware that Kroger is making a humming noise, is murmuring the sound of some familiar song, as if he were back in Maisel, back in his father's tailor shop, working on nothing more than the mundane cut of a new summer suit.

Then, at some point, it is done. Kroger leans his head back slightly without moving the rest of his body, studying the quality of his work. Pleased with the outcome, he brings his face forward, this time all the way to Gilrein's cheek until Gilrein thinks the old man is going to kiss him. Instead, Kroger takes the finishing end of his thread between his teeth and bites it loose from the spool, which he repockets.

He stands, takes a step backward, places a fist on his left hip, brings his right index finger up to his face and scratches at his chin, then extends the arm down and runs the finger along the black tracks of the new stitching, blood swamping his finger, which he wipes on the front of Gilrein's shirt.

Kroger nods to Blumfeld while still staring at the craftsmanship. Blumfeld releases his choke on Gilrein who sinks down in the chair, tries to swallow and fights a new, rising fear as the reality of his inability to spit out the blood pooling in his mouth dawns on him. He does the only thing he can do. He swallows all the heavy liquid collecting in the gully around his tongue and uses all his concentration to ward away a gag reflex. He starts to try to pull his lips apart and knows immediately he'll rip them to shreds sooner than he'll tear the fibers holding them together.

He looks up at Kroger, who has taken his glasses off and is polishing them with his handkerchief. "After all these years," he says, almost dreamily, to the room in general. "Father would be so proud."

Blumfeld's hands come to rest lightly on Gilrein's shoulders.

"I am going to need your complete attention now, Mr. Gilrein," Kroger says, wiping the needle clean and securing it back in the case. "Please, try not to fade on me. I know this is difficult, but I'm sure you are up to it."

He takes a much smaller needle from the case, studies it as he takes a second spool of thread from the satchel. This spool is much smaller and the fiber is shaded a deep red, almost a maroon.

To Blumfeld, in a more casual voice, Kroger says, "Father used to tell me, 'The smaller the needle, the greater the skill of the craftsman.' And I remember a saying among his fellow tailors— 'He could stitch the anus of a church mouse.' Of course, it was more lyrical in the mother tongue. Still," now to Gilrein, in a louder voice, "wouldn't that be an awful proposition, my friend?"

A volley of laughter from Raban at the other end of the room.

Kroger sets to threading the second needle.

"I am going to ask you again. One last attempt. In all fair-
ness," squatting down until he's at eye level with Gilrein, "it is
known that you were a chauffeur for Leo Tani. And it is known
that on the last night of Mr. Tani's life, you drove him to and from
a meeting at Gompers Station. You were very likely the last person
in the city to see Mr. Tani alive."

Kroger brings a thumb up to his mouth and gives it a swipe
with his tongue, then extends it to Gilrein's left eye and brushes
at the eyelid as if clearing away a smudge on a canvas.

"Leo Tani," he continues, "was negotiating the sale of an
extremely rare and valuable book. Mr. Tani had received an enormous amount of money from me in exchange for this book."

A nod to Blumfeld. The vise-choke is reapplied around
Gilrein's head. Gilrein bucks up and Blumfeld applies most of his
weight, forcing Gilrein back into the chair. Gilrein tries to speak,
manages a series of garbled noises, muffled and blunted by his
sealed mouth.

Kroger, smiling, brings the needle up to the left eye, maybe an
eighth of an inch from the pupil itself. Gilrein closes his lid,
pulling on the muscles as hard as he can.

"Not too much contraction," Kroger warns. "We don't want to
puncture the eyeball itself."

Gilrein feels a single, sharp prick around the corner of his
eye, just a poke, retracted immediately.

"Now, Mr. Gilrein," Kroger says, "I'm going to ask you what
happened to my book. And if you tell me, we will be done with our
work for the day."

Gilrein keeps his eyes closed, but he can feel and smell the
breath again, impacting on the center of his face. Another quick,
light jab of the needle, but this one closer to the eyeball and this
one drawing a run of blood.

"Where is my book, Mr. Gilrein?"

The words *I don't know* explode in a stunted, softened scream
inside his mouth, in the newly sealed interior, all nasal, undiffer-
entiated, close to meaningless anywhere but in his brain. But he

yells them anyway, over and over, until he becomes aware of the laughter, the sound of all three of them laughing, the noise of their amusement overlapping and blending into a chorus of pathetic and overdone tittering.

He opens his eyes, sees Kroger shaking his head, feels Blumfeld's arms trembling with something like glee.

Kroger breaks away from the joy of his meatboys, cocks his head to the side, and says, "Ignorance is not always bliss, is it Mr. Gilrein?"

Then he turns to Raban and says, "He knows nothing. Take him away from me."

And as Blumfeld unlocks the handcuffs and starts to haul Gilrein out of the chair, Kroger adds, "And give him a pair of scissors for his troubles."

13

They dump Gilrein on the corner of Dunot Boulevard. They don't bother to stop the car, just slow to a roll, throw open the back door, and heave him into the street, where he lies motionless until the Bamberg turns the corner. He anticipates a gunshot, though there's no logic to his expectation. If the meatboys were going to kill him, they would have done it elsewhere and lost the body in the Benchley River or up at Gomi Scrap & Salvage.

Gilrein manages to get up on all fours, then slowly climbs to his feet. He needs to get to a hospital, to get the sutures removed and his mouth checked out. He tries to remember if this is Dr. Z's night at the free clinic. Dr. Z is the favored physician of every cop in town, known for his willingness to lose paperwork and his liberal attitude regarding the keys to the clinic pharmacy. Gilrein is fairly sure that the doc will handle this odd emergency with the speed and discretion it deserves, even though the patient is no longer on the job.

He moves to the curbstone and sits down for a minute to think. He hangs his head, stares down at the gutter between his knees, breathes through the nose and touches his lips, pulls his fingers away immediately at the sting and draws a fresh run of blood. He takes a handkerchief from a pocket and presses it over his mouth.

When he looks up, he realizes that the building opposite him is 33 Dunot, one of the oldest precinct houses in Quinsigamond, officially closed down for years now, but still owned and maintained by the city. There's a light glowing somewhere on the first floor and through one of the narrow front windows that bows out toward the sidewalk, Gilrein can see that he's being watched.

The figure behind the window suddenly stands and begins to signal to Gilrein, motioning for him to come inside. And Gilrein understands, in spite of his wounds and the cumulative effects of the past twenty-four hours, that August Kroger had him dumped here on purpose, a message, a vivid little epistle for the proprietor of the Dunot Precinct House.

He gets up and starts to cross the street, staring at the details of the building and remembering all the hours he spent idling in the car outside, waiting for his wife to finally exit her office and join him, never telling him very much about the events of her shift. And never once confiding anything revelatory about her shift commander, her boss and mentor, the man behind the window now waving slowly out at Gilrein, Emil Lacazze.

There was a time when there appeared to be no case that Inspector Lacazze could not unravel using his Methodology. During his first season of total autonomy he began to accumulate successes like a mad and compulsive collector. Word started to spread through Bangkok Park, horrible, whispered fables about the voodoo cop, the mojo bull, the dark priest with his candle and his mirror, his sweet wine and terrifying eyes, and, worst of all, his voice, this noise that came out of his throat in a bark and jumped inside of you, broke into your head, found a way inside your brain no matter what you did and repeated word after word after word until you were ready to chew your own arms out of the cuffs and run into the night, screaming like the devil had his hands around your heart.

Because of her proximity to Lacazze, Ceil couldn't help picking up her own, somewhat smaller reputation as the mysterious woman behind the black-magic lawman, a Cassandra with gun and badge whose scrubbed beauty only made her more of an enigma. The Grenada Street Popes called her La Bruja Blanca, while the Tonton Loas christened her La Putain du Prêtre. And, though Gilrein never knew it, even Willy Loftus's Castlebar Road Boys spent more than one drunken sunrise both fantasizing and fearing an imagined Q & A session with the Rose of Dunot. At the height of Lacazze's ascendance, the neighborhood mayors began to debate, first separately and then in tandem, whether this new force of nature eroding their landscapes of graft and vice shouldn't perhaps be either co-opted or eliminated. As always, the first choice was to send in a shooter or two. How hard could this guy be to whack, living all alone down in this empty station house, insultingly over the rim of their mutual borders?

Peker the Turk, in his usual showboat manner, offered to shoulder the contract personally. Paco Iguaran and Willy Loftus disagreed, both seeing the possibility of enormous and diverse profits if the Inspector could be negotiated into retiring from the department and consulting for the other side.

Ultimately, however, the debate proved moot. Within a year of commandeering the precinct house and establishing the Eschatology Squad, Inspector Lacazze came to dance with the entity that would not only prove his equal, but when all was said and done, confirm its superiority.

Lacazze welcomes Gilrein as if they were old friends who've been separated too long by cruel circumstance. He actually greets the taxi driver in the doorway with a weak bear hug, then steps backward, keeping the hands on Gilrein's shoulders, inspecting Kroger's handiwork on the lips with a shake of the head and the sad but not really surprised *tsk*ing sound of a disappointed schoolteacher.

The Inspector steers Gilrein by the elbow, moving him through the squad room, a little too fast past Ceil's old desk, and into Lacazze's office, the Methodology chamber. The room is dim and stale, musty and outrageously cluttered. But this isn't what strikes Gilrein as he's eased down into position atop the shoe-fitting stool. It's the simple fact of seeing it all in person, witnessing what, until now, he'd only imagined based on bits and pieces pulled from conversations with his wife. All of the components he'd amassed are present—the blackboard, the stacks of notes held down by wooden apple paperweights, the liturgical candle and the chalice on the desk, the fun-house mirror on the far wall—but none of the chamber's furnishings match up to their imagined corollaries. Everything's off at least a little, larger or smaller or in a different place.

Even the Inspector's voice, mumbling as he rummages in a bottom desk drawer, has a different timber to it. These words— *miserable bastards . . . where did I put it*—have a higher pitch, a different rhythm to the prosody, than Gilrein had ever allowed for.

But when Lacazze straightens up, holding a straight razor and a pair of tweezers, all of Gilrein's comparisons vanish. And as the ex-priest approaches the ex-cop holding the instruments out as if they were sacramental material, Gilrein starts to wonder if his visit to August Kroger was only a prelude to an even worse experience.

To this day, no one can tell you much of substance about the Tung. *The Spy* has always enjoyed classifying them as terrorists, but this implies a traditionally political agenda. It is probably more useful to simply label them anarchists of their own peculiar bent. It is unclear whether they emigrated to the city from elsewhere or were born natives, brewed in that murky cauldron of the Canal Zone where the brutal thuggery of Bangkok Park meets the philosophical abstractions of the intellectual underworld. Federal Intelligence had nothing on them, had never even heard of the name before, but promised to open a file at once. The usual known associates of the various fringe subcultures were mute on this new animal and Lacazze thought their silence was born of ignorance rather than fear. It appeared as though the Tung had sprung fresh and whole from the rectum of the city, without heritage or history, a virgin beast that would make up its destiny as it went along.

The stated goal of the Tung, however, was easily and bluntly understood—the eradication of all written (what they insisted on calling *artificial*) language. The final "linguistic solipsists," as Lacazze came to define them, the Tung believed that written language completely and totally determined reality. Consequently, the act of "mass-producing texts" was the ultimate imperialistic action. And as such, of course, had to be stopped at any and all costs. Toward this end they announced a reign of terror upon "the metaphors of the graphic state," trumpeting plans to bomb printing plants, newspaper offices, publishing houses, and various other pawns of the "scripted world."

Because of their absolute aversion to written language, all of this propaganda was delivered to the police and the media by way of unsuspecting messengers, usually children of the streets, the tinkers and travelers, the gypsy kids and abandoned urchins from the Bangkok area, promised food and trinkets if they could memorize a speech and spit it back to the "ink-drugged pigs of aggression." Questioning the children proved futile. They were all so ragged and hungry and intent on completing their job that they could supply nothing of value regarding their employers.

Chief Bendix was inclined to believe this Tung was one more prank from the artistes of Rimbaud Way, the half-baked product of some new phalanx of performance artists or conceptual philosophers/comedians. Inspector Lacazze disagreed and the task of hunting down and—if they existed and were an actual threat—destroying the Tung was naturally dumped in his lap. It seemed like the kind of chore he was born into the world to perform. And he did put all of his efforts into the assignment. The department's urban assault squad and tactical support units were put at his disposal, just in case. But Lacazze made it clear from the start that Ceil would be his point man.

The seriousness of the Tung's threats was confirmed when a *Spy* columnist named Harrison, arriving back to his desk after a bourbon and pretzel lunch at the Valhalla, discovered a ticking shoebox, wrapped in brown paper and conspicuously void of any address, sitting atop his computer monitor. The bomb squad disarmed a plastique cocktail that could have blown the scribe and most the city room out of the *Spy* building and over the City Hall common in an amalgamated cloud of shared bone and ash.

From that moment on, anyone with any connection to establishments that trafficked in printing, from corner photocopying shops to the chain bookstores, was flinching in his sleep. A member of the board of directors of the public library phoned Bendix at midnight to ask if he should take that long-planned trip to the Continent. The Chief said, "Absolutely," and left the phone off the hook. The patriarch of a local ink and stamp mill indignantly announced his intention of hiring private security, but sent his kids to the country home just the same. And Inspector Lacazze, with Ceil at his side, ventured out of the Dunot precinct and started haunting the Canal-Bangkok border, silently wondering how you go about interrogating a suspect that you can't seem to find.

Lacazze was able to score a lucky break when a Tung messenger, an eight-year-old Romanian refugee with a cleft palate—the anarchists' definition of humor, he supposed—was unable to repeat his assigned speech to the police, but did manage to give a detailed if agonized description of his employer to a sketch artist.

The rendering didn't ring any bells at the station, but Lacazze and company took it to the streets. It was actually Ceil who secured an ID from the junkie desk clerk of the Hotel Adrianople. For a palmed baggie of Burmese smack, the weasel remembered renting a weekly to the guy in the picture. And from there information began to fall like dominoes. They picked up names and descriptions and locations, ran them all down and came up with a Moscow-born lounge singer named Sonia Gorinski, currently booked in a two-week engagement at the Yusupov Garden Room.

They took Gorinski down in the middle of her second set to the catcalls of an audience drunk on generic vodka and bad romance. They drove the suspect through every red light in the Zone and locked her up with Lacazze in the interrogation chamber at Dunot.

The woman was a tougher nut than anyone who'd yet graced the shoe-fitting stool. Lacazze didn't start to sweat until a full twelve hours had gone by and Sonia G hadn't provided him with a pitcherful of spit. Even when she did respond to the word association, the Inspector could tell her answers were carefully chosen and not at all pertinent to the hidden vault of her subconscious. He couldn't find the rhythm that had always come so easily, couldn't establish the natural vibration of dominance and control that used to roll out of his throat effortlessly. It was as if the power of his personality, of his very presence, that had come to live in this room and permeate the air with the force of his will, had suddenly and inexplicably begun to dissipate and vent itself through the cracks in the wall.

Ceil paced the squad room, trying not to hear the desperate noises of approaching failure from inside the interrogation chamber, keeping Bendix's front men at bay. At one point she heard glass break and was shaken by the Inspector howling, top of his lungs, "Illumination! The word is illumination! Answer me, goddamn you!"

For thirty hours the session continued until, with Bendix on his way to call the whole thing off, Lacazze emerged from the chamber for a glass of water, looking like a man ready to recline on his deathbed. And in that moment, watching Lacazze lean against the watercooler, too exhausted to stand erect, swallowing his last hit of crank and splashing at his already moist eyes, Ceil snapped and walked passed her incredulous boss into the Methodology chamber, locking the door behind her. No one has any idea what caused this breech of procedure. Ceil herself didn't know if it was the imminent failure of her mentor or the suddenly uncertain future of her Dunot precinct sanctuary—or maybe it was just a simple lack of sleep and too much bad coffee. But as Lacazze pounded on the wall of the interrogation room, screaming, "You'll ruin everything," Ceil pulled her Colt Python from a hip holster, grabbed a shocked Sonia Gorinski by her slender throat, forced the barrel of the gun past Gorinski's teeth and, in a level but adamant voice, promised the singer she had crooned her final cabaret if she didn't speak quickly and honestly.

In minutes, Ceil emerged from Lacazze's office, unable to look at the Inspector but holding out to him, with fingers stained by spilled ink, a piece of scrap paper with the words

Kapernaum Printing & Binding
Rome Avenue

written in angry, nib-snapping block letters.

"Don't worry, young man," Lacazze says as Gilrein pulls away from the extended razor, "on my Antarctic mission I was the closest thing the village had to a medic. I picked up quite a bit of experience."

Gilrein braces himself by grabbing the chrome tubing that rims the stool. The Inspector goes to work like an emergency room pro, slicing each minute track of suture without nicking the lips, using the tweezer to pull the fiber back through the soft tissue, releasing the mouth back into its functional state.

And though there's a sense of burning that refuses to stop increasing, it isn't quite a matter of pain anymore. Gilrein feels distanced somehow from his corporal self, as if this sudden and unplanned proximity to the place that was once his wife's secret world, the womb in which she and her mentor worked the linguistic equivalent of alchemical reactions, had pushed him outside of his own skin, had made him a ghost to the flesh of reality.

He feels as if he's sitting in a place of death. The precinct house is a mausoleum, like the Kapernaum mill. It has no electricity. No heat. No running water. And yet Lacazze continues to live here. The way a ghost would. Walking through empty rooms, floors littered, completely covered, with papers that no longer matter, hearing and disregarding the rats in the walls.

"We're going to have to control this bleeding," the Inspector says, in his ghost voice, this cross between Popeye the Sailor and John the Baptist on his last day in the desert. This is the sound that captivated Ceil? This is the noise that kept her entranced, prevented her from giving herself up to her husband?

This vibration, croaking, "I have a special balm that should help."

Ceil sent a waiting EMT into the chamber to uncuff and tend to an unconscious Sonia Gorinski, then followed the Inspector outside and into the back of Bendix's sedan. They led a convoy of prowl cars and two tactical vans south to the far side of the city, off the secondary road and into one of the zoning board's no-man's-lands that was part rural farm tract and part aborted industrial park.

Ceil hadn't gotten much for her efforts. She couldn't tell them the size of the Tung or the names of its leaders or what kind of firepower they might be holding. All she had was that for the past two or three weeks, the Tung had been holing up in the old Kapernaum mill and that Gorinski was to have rendezvoused with them tonight.

Ceil was uncomfortable with the information. The Tung using an abandoned bindery as their crib was too beautifully ironic for such a self-righteous crew. But the Dunot precinct autonomy was on the line, so she volunteered to play advance scout and enter the factory in the guise of the revolutionary torch singer. Then she kept her mouth shut through the rest of the sirenless race to the end of Rome Avenue.

The Kapernaum plant had been out of business for over a decade and perpetually for sale since the day the owners shut the doors. According to the various brokers who had handled the property, its main problem was location. Miles from civilization, it sat like a forgotten brick crypt in a clearing beyond the birch forest that served, in the warm weather months, as a little-used campground.

Bendix radioed for his forces to halt and fan at the tree line. Tactical went to work and organized the prowl bulls into support units, threading teams through the woods until they'd secured a perimeter around the factory.

On the jog to the building's main entrance, with her Python drawn and pointing skyward, her movement announced by leaf crunch and lit by a close-to-full moon, Ceil tried to focus and push away the question of the last time she'd called Gilrein.

Lacazze kept watch over her through a night-vision scope and when she reached the mill doors, he gave word to start closing in the circle. The plan was a little too straightforward. The Inspector, still shaken from his encounter with the lounge singer, warned that these were full-blown pros inside the bindery, fanatics with training and the best weaponry of all—a willingness to die for a cause. For the first time in years, Bendix disagreed with the former Jesuit. The Chief still made the Tung for one more pack of ego-crazed, Canal Zone, boho smart-asses who'd gone around the bend sniffing psychotropic poppers along with their street theories. He made it clear that the last thing he needed was a firefight and a federal inquiry into why his SWAT boys unloaded a year's worth of rhino bullets picking off a clique of untenured philosophy professors and a handful of their groupie undergrads. "Can you imagine the press nightmare?" he said. "I'd be seeing flashbulbs for the rest of my short career."

Ceil rang the visitor's bell four short chimes, as Gorinski had instructed, then backed around the corner and sited on the doors ready for an ambush. In a few minutes, a young man, who in shadow resembled Farley Granger, poked his head out one of the doors and whispered, "Sonia?"

She flew at him, took him to the ground with her gun to his throat and a hand over his wet mouth. If this moron was their advance security, the Tung was even more bush league than Ben-

dix had predicted. She turned her greeter over to the four shooters who'd advanced from the tree line and made her way inside
and down to the basement, where Gorinski had promised the
group would be gathering.

She found them in a cellar storage vault, all of them seated
around a picnic table, slightly reminiscent of some Last Supper
portrait if that scene had taken place in a fallout shelter and been
commemorated on a black velvet canvas. But instead of tearing at
unleavened bread and passing a clay jug of wine, the Tung was in
the process of mass-assembling pipe bombs.

No one will ever know definitively whether what followed was
accident or intention. Gilrein has always imagined a shaft of light,
though he can't name its source, cutting across Ceil's face as she
pressed her body against a brick support column and edged her
face around its corner. He fantasizes that his wife made eye contact with one of the terrorists, perhaps the insane but charismatic
leader later identified as a retired linguistics professor from MIT
who'd taken to calling himself Blind Homer. Gilrein imagines
that the look that passed between them lingered for a brittle,
elongated second before their mutual screams—Ceil stepping
into shooter's stance, weapon extended, trained on the one who
spotted her, shouting out, identifying herself as police officer and
instructing immediate compliance. And Blind Homer simply
yelling, the shock of discovery triggering his larynx into nonsensical alarm and his hands into a terminal mistake.

Did Ceil know the entire cellar chamber, packed to capacity
with all brand of accelerants and explosives, including some percentage of imported plastique, was about to be detonated? Was
she aware, even for a millisecond, that everything around her, the
entire shadowy but stable physical existence that encapsulated
her, was about to dissolve and be replaced, in the drawing of a
single breath, into her own ground zero, a liquid and shifting
world of immense, unthinkable noise and heat and absolute dis-
ruption, a plane of antistability, a dimension where skin and bone
and even language have no analogous meaning?

Gilrein would like to believe she did not know. There are many nights when he would give the balance of his life just for the certainty that the explosion caught his wife unaware. That Ceil was dead before she knew she was about to die. But he can't achieve this certainty. In fact, it's as if his desire for it brings the opposite result, as if the more he yearns for Ceil's ignorance in the moment before her demise, the more he has to believe that his wife saw the end coming plainly and clearly and without any illusions.

The entire rear of the Kapernaum factory blew outward and collapsed. The roof came down. Glass fragmented into razor-thin shards and the concussion carried them like pollen through the woods. Some of the perimeter cops reported seeing the fabled black-and-orange mushroom cloud, but most were too busy rolling and tucking and covering their skulls with their arms. A hash of debris made of splintered brick and metal and wood was thrown a hundred yards beyond the mill and the roar of the holocaust shattered the eardrums of some of the closest survivors.

The accuracy of the final pathology reports has always been disputed, but lacking a better count, the department files will always report eighteen casualties: thirteen Tung, some of whom will always remain unidentified, and five police officers—Ceil and her back-up unit.

As in most incendiary deaths, the descriptions of Ceil's remains are best left on the loop of magnetic tape that spooled around, almost noiselessly, in the autopsy room of the county morgue and recorded the dispassionate and clinical words of the city's coroner. Gilrein had no need to ask questions when he signed the release form for his wife's dental records.

He was given the leave of absence that evolved into his resignation. He was picked up, not quite catatonic, but surely within the extended family of that diagnosis, by Frankie and Anna Loftus and brought to Wormland Farm, another voiceless body sculpted from the seemingly limitless insanity this world easily and endlessly provides.

The story of the Tung was disseminated briefly beyond the Quinsigamond borders, picked up by several major wire services, but its carnage and senselessness quotient was defeated in just a matter of days by reports of a new and imaginative "genocidal incident" from the heart of a religious war halfway around the globe. Something about children being fed to their initially unknowing and hunger-mad parents.

As for Inspector Lacazze, he instantly but quietly lost his reputation, his funding, and his untouchable status in the moment that the first of the Tung's pipe bombs ignited. No more prisoners were exposed to the Methodology on Dunot Boulevard, and the word went out to the city utilities that they could terminate service to the old precinct house at their convenience.

The Inspector throws the last bloody fragments of suture over his shoulder. Some of them stick to the wall.

Gilrein pulls his lips in, feels himself start to tremble. Lacazze moves to a corner of the room, roots in a pile of trash, eventually withdraws a small, labelless glass jar. He comes back to the shoe-fitting stool, gets down slowly on one knee, and unscrews the jar, filling the office with the smell of sulphur and garlic. He dips two fingers into a chunky gray paste, extracts a generous amount and begins to smear it into his patient's lips, stopping at one point to dip his thumb into his mouth, collect a cover of spittle and mix it with the muddy balm.

"It absorbs very quickly," Lacazze says, "but we're going to need some ice. Let me know when you feel up to walking."

14

There is something slightly phantasmal about Cabaret Vermin. Walking through Ribbentrop Square, you would have no sense of the chic decadence conceived nightly in the cellars below the old Bubben-Krupp Iron Works. But on any given evening, as you sit beneath the low, vaulted ceilings breathing in the nicotine and schnapps, as you listen to piano ballads that make Teutonic myth infectious, your sense of spacial perception can seem to slip just a touch. Patrons report finding themselves unable to keep track of time. Trips to the rest room become perilous due as much to the constant hint of vertigo as to the mazelike floor plan. Sampling the complimentary knockwurst cubes, you find your mouth flooded with the taste of metal and ash.

No one can provide an adequate explanation for the phenomenon, and while some point to the architecture of the basements and others the lack of proper ventilation, owner and host Rikki Tzara will simply shrug off the analysis and say that people come to the Vermin to lose themselves and that process is always a bit dizzying at first.

It's no secret that more than anything else, Tzara wants canonization into the Canal Zone mythos. He yearns nightly to be remembered as one of the era's arbiters of hip, a legend carved along the same lines as Elmore Orzi. And Cabaret Vermin could well be his vehicle for ascension into decadent sainthood. The club has anticathedral possibilities, the way it insinuates itself into the earth, snakes itself underneath the streets of the Zone, weaving and bobbing, rising and falling, tunneling its way into a morass of geometrical confusion, chambers leading into mushroomlike hollows that flow into fishbowl parlors with each little squat café having its own subtle but absolute individuality. The only unifying decor, the single motif that extends from bunker to bunker, is an ongoing tribute to dancer Anita Berber, the once legendary star of the old White Mouse Club in Berlin. Tzara has made Berber into something of a deity and it is said that when he locks up the Cabaret at dawn, his last act is to genuflect before a marble statue of his lascivious goddess, bringing his head down to her cold, bare feet—nails made apple red one night by an impulsive beautician—and repeatedly mumbling the word *Morphium* as he beats his breast.

When you exit the Vermin, you never know what street you're going to arrive upon. Tzara would have you believe he's the only one who can maneuver through the entire club without a map and a trail of bar nuts, and that may well be the case. But it's really Tzara's innate talents as both showman and provocateur that define his character. Dressed each evening in his chartreuse velvet dinner jacket, his remaining hair dyed the color of oxblood and slicked back on his skull with what the waitresses swear is Crisco, Tzara can fondle a microphone stand in a manner that could make the most hardened barkeep at Caesar's Palace phone in sick for a shift or two. Tzara's oiliness knows no limits. Introducing the perennial amateurs of open mike night, the Rikkster will have you believing the King himself has risen from his Memphis grave just to shimmy to a backup band that features the Angel Gabriel blowing "Don't Be Cruel."

And that's not far from the patter he gives as he leads Gilrein and Inspector Lacazze through dense clouds of purple-tinged smoke to a cocktail table adjacent to the lip of the stage. The club is packed and as Gilrein slides into his seat he watches Tzara refuse the Inspector's attempt to palm the host a gratuity. Tzara shakes his head adamantly as he removes a RESERVED sign from the table and begins to snap fingers for a waitress.

"So good to have you back with us, Father," Tzara fawns.

"Please, just call me Emil," the Inspector says.

"As you wish," Tzara replies, bowing slightly and at the same time corralling a spooked young woman dressed in a reflective sequined minidress. "Katrina will see to all of your needs."

Tzara claps a hand on Lacazze's shoulder, then disappears through an archway into the club's next cavern.

Katrina says, "Welcome to Cabaret Vermin. Tonight's special is the Witch's Sabbath."

Gilrein picks up a small, plastic-coated card from the table thinking it's a drink menu. Instead he reads

FIVE SYMPTOMS OF ST. LEON'S GRIPPE
- SWELLING OF THE TONGUE
- CHRONIC DRYNESS OF THE TONGUE
- NUMBNESS OF THE TONGUE
- WEEPING PUSTULES ON THE TONGUE
- MALAPROPISMS

IF YOU HAVE EXPERIENCED ANY OF THE ABOVE PLEASE *DO NOT* BOTHER CONTACTING A REPRESENTATIVE OF THE CITY'S HEALTH SERVICES AS THEY CONTINUE TO DENY THE GRIPPE'S EXISTENCE.

"I'll have a double Siena with an onion," Lacazze says. "And bring my friend—"

"Could you just bring me a bowl of chipped ice?" Gilrein says through fingers dabbing lightly at his lips. It's been less than an hour since the Inspector swathed them with the horrid-smelling mud, but already he can speak again.

Lacazze shakes his head and inclines toward the waitress.

"He'll have a glass of the Spanish sherry."

"Malflores?" Katrina asks.

"The private label," Lacazze whispers and winks.

Katrina departs and the two men stare at each other.

"Have you ever been down below before?" the Inspector asks.

"Never," Gilrein lies.

Ceil brought him to the Vermin once on one of her book hunts. She was supposed to meet with a periodicals dealer who never showed.

"Are you a regular?" Gilrein asks.

Lacazze smiles and shakes his head.

"I know Rikki from the neighborhood. Not a bad sport but just a bit too needy. If you know what I mean."

"I think I can guess."

"So," as the Inspector gets comfortable in his chair and steals a glance around the room, "would you like to tell your brother officer who did this to you?"

"Brother officer?" Gilrein repeats. "Is either one of us still on the job?"

Lacazze bows his head and raises his eyes.

"Technically, and for tax purposes, I'm an independent consultant. But I retain my commission. And all the powers of the badge."

"Well, God and Chief Bendix both work in perverse ways."

Lacazze smiles.

"It's *mysterious*, Mr. Gilrein," he says. "The word is 'mysterious,' not 'perverse.'"

"My mistake."

"And in either case," Lacazze says, "it doesn't ring true coming from your unfortunate lips. I'm sure Ceil told me you were a devout atheist."

"No," Gilrein plays along. "I'm just a cabdriver. I don't spend a lot of time thinking about the esoteric."

"Just as well. Though, to be honest, I really can't make myself care about which systems you do or do not subscribe to, Mr.

Gilrein. Whether you bow down before the classical Western Daddy in the sky or some notion of romantic fate or that old bitch of cruel and random chance, none of it matters to me. But I might enjoy my drink a bit more if we could agree that whatever the agent, it is fortuitous that you and I have been brought together again. Perhaps we should even thank August Kroger."

Katrina arrives with the drinks and places them on the table.

The Inspector raises his glass of Siena and says, "To the men in Ceil's all-too-brief life."

Gilrein doesn't move for a moment. Then he breaks eye contact and touches his bottom lip without flinching. He pulls the fingers away, looks at the smear of tacky blood and residual silt, and says, "Are you trying to bait me, Inspector?"

"Bait you?" Sipping the Siena, he shakes his head and tries to look amused. "Not at all. Just the opposite."

Lacazze pulls down a long drink and rotates his head around his neck as he speaks.

"When I came to this city, I looked out from the hill on my first night and cursed my own particular construct of faith—"

"That's an odd phrasing," Gilrein says.

The interruption seems to focus Lacazze. His voice drops and he says, "Yes," in something of a drawl. "I suppose I've never been able to wear my learning very lightly."

"Hazard of the trade, I guess."

"Which trade are you referring to?" Lacazze asks. "I've had a few."

"Your choice," Gilrein says.

The Inspector tries to shrug but it comes off as a shiver.

"Every profession has its quirks. But my point is that I was wrong to profane my new home. It may not be Paris but it has its own charms. And, more importantly I've found, it appears to be the locus where my most important work is to come together."

"I thought all your important work was behind you, Inspector."

The old priest goes silent for a moment and stares down at his glass.

"That would be a misconception, my son. But it's not your fault. I don't expect you to be familiar with my Methodology. I know Ceil was never comfortable discussing her work at home. She didn't want to burden you."

"My wife was a considerate woman."

"Among other things."

Gilrein lets it go.

"I'm sure I heard the department had abandoned the"—a pause to show a little contempt for the word—"Methodology."

"Oh, Gilrein," the Inspector's voice faux-tired from dealing with deficient minds all his life, "my work for the city was only the lowest function of my system. I'm moving on to the next phase, so to speak. I'm taking my child out of the laboratory and into the street. Where it belongs. Where it can find its own organic ends. We need a new language, Gilrein. Surely, your wife must have shared at least this one secret with you?"

"Like you said, I don't think she wanted to burden me."

The Inspector nods, pulls down his jaw to show his impression of fatherly understanding.

"You have no idea," he says, "how often I wish she was still with us. She's the only witness I would want for what's to come. She's the only one qualified to appreciate where we go next."

"We?"

"The city, Gilrein. Our city, 'these streets of oozing muck,' to quote a poet I once knew. Quinsigamond is where the final battle of the war will be fought."

"The war?" Gilrein repeats.

But the Inspector has moved from conversation to soliloquy.

"Think of all the arrogant, logocentric rationalists before me. I could spit in every one of their enigmatic faces. Reason lovers. With their cannibal picnics and their Japanese fashion shows. Every one with their own metalanguage. Every little bastard promising the Grail, the map out of the darkness. Promising us they could slow down the world, cool down the input, build us a new tongue that would be the universal translator we've lusted after since they built the beautiful tower in Shinar—"

Gilrein says, "Inspector," reasserting his presence just to stop the babble.

Lacazze blinks a few times, sniffs, and stares at his table companion as if one of them has just woken up.

"You brought me here to tell me something."

Lacazze's mouth opens and closes. Gilrein leans in and gets a smell, something close to paint thinner.

"Inspector?"

A deep exhale and then, "I wanted to tell you—"

But Lacazze's words are interrupted by microphone squeal as Rikki Tzara bounds onto the stage, ubiquitous handkerchief at the ready, mopping his brow as if he's just wrapped up a lifetime of telethon appeals.

"Ladies and gentlemen," Tzara says, and waits for some modicum of quiet to fall over the lounge, "as you know, it is the mission of the Cabaret Vermin to discover and encourage new talent wherever we may find it. In constant pursuit of that mission we have established Saturday night here in the Rudi Anhang Room as open mike night to showcase the finest amateur entertainers in our fair city. So without further ado, I'd like to introduce our first act of the evening, a really sweet guy, he's just trying to break into the business, would you give a big, warm Vermin welcome for Shecky Langer."

Otto Langer walks out onstage dressed in a rented tux that's clearly too small for him, carrying Zwack the golem, his ventriloquial dummy. Zwack looks like a cross between the Gothic woodcarving of some nightmare-plagued folk artist and a Raggedy Ann doll that's been dragged through a thousand ghettos in the teeth of a mange-scarred dog. The house lights go down and a classic blue spot comes up and trains itself on a profusely sweating Langer seated on a bar stool, a glass of tap water resting near his feet. For a moment he looks hypnotized by the spotlight, stares into it as if it was a sun about to go nova. Then the drummer cues him with an introductory burst of timpani and Langer snaps out of his trance and nods to the audience. He positions his figure on his lap and uses his free hand to adjust her black-yarn pigtails.

The dummy opens her lipsticked mouth and says, "Take my partner," pauses and deadpans, *"please."*

The audience comes back silent, caught communally wondering if this is one of those ultrahip performance artistes, a socio-cultural commentator playing the part of retro borscht-belt comedian while in actuality holding up a mirror to their hidden bourgeois pretensions.

"That's not nice at all, Zwack," says Langer in a halting, stagey voice as he wags a finger at his wooden cohort. "Now you behave or you go back into the trunk."

Zwack swivels her head and looks out at the crowd.

"You'll have to forgive Shecky," she says. "He just flew in from Maisel and, boy, is his soul tired."

A nervous undercurrent begins to sound and a rimshot only accentuates the discomfort.

"My darling," says Langer, leaning forward and lifting the water glass from the floor, "don't you know any new material? These good people would like something a bit more relevant."

The golem somehow manages to roll her eyes. This actually produces a sympathetic if abbreviated laugh from the crowd.

"Knock knock," the dummy says.

"Who's there?" Langer responds.

"The Censor."

Langer suddenly drops his stage face and stares at the dummy as if the puppet has launched into an improvisation, as if this were not the line they've rehearsed a hundred times. Flustered, Langer makes a production of bringing the water glass to his lips.

"The Censor who?" he asks hesitantly, then tilts his head back and sips from his glass theatrically as Zwack launches into song.

The Censor of Maisel
The Censor of Maisel

Hi ho the derry-oh
I'll send you straight to hell

After a shocked second or two, the crowd begins to shower the duo with a smattering of applause. And of the two performers it's the dummy who seems to respond to the approval, nodding to the room, a sense of confidence installing itself on the pinewood face. The golem rolls with the audience's minuscule endorsement and seems to take over the act.

"There was a young girl from Maisel," she crows,

Whose talent for tales was quite swell.
She built a library
But things got a bit scary
When Meyrink rang the front bell.

Langer gets furious and suddenly it's more difficult to tell if his anger is genuine or part of the stage act.

"Now you stop this nonsense at once," he bellows at the dummy, his face growing flushed. "You perform as you are meant to perform. You will tell the story that these people came to hear."

Zwack the golem stares into her master's face. The partners glare at each other for an uncomfortable parcel of time and the audience begins to get antsy, maybe even a little unnerved.

Finally, Zwack turns her gaze from Langer to the crowd, as if inspecting their worth, as if the wooden dummy were trying to calculate this small mob's value as listeners. Her bottom jaw drops open, then seals closed, then slowly opens again. And a voice emerges. It's neither Langer's voice nor Zwack's, but some other persona utilizing the golem's wooden mouth, some entity possessing the larynx of both performers and uttering a new sound that nobody in the room can possibly ignore.

And the voice says, "This is the story of the girl who disappeared."

15

There was a young woman in our community, really a girl, but quite beautiful and very mature for her age. She was, in fact, only seventeen years old at the time of the July Sweep. She never knew her mother—the woman died of typhus when the daughter was still an infant. The child lived in the attic of Haus Levi with her widower father, who was a kind man but not the best of providers and, to be honest, he had a propensity for the drink. *The creature*, as he sometimes called it. Nevertheless, he loved his daughter with all of his being and he attempted to do his best by her.

The daughter was named Alicia. She learned to read at a very young age. Her father was both amazed and proud of her skill with words and he was known to bring the girl to the neighbors' kitchens after supper and have her perform, reading from the storybooks, the cheap little fable pamphlets and tissue-paper parables that he would purchase with the meager wages he earned as a marginal performer in the Goldfaden Carnival Troupe. The child loved her fairy tales, came to memorize them, so that after a time, she did not even need the books to tell the story. The neighbors in Haus Simeon—Miss Svetla, Mr. and Mrs. Wasserman, the Brezina family—appeared to enjoy these visits and would remark that the child indeed seemed blessed with a natural gift for language and the architecture of the tale.

Alicia's talents blossomed as she grew and her skills were noted and praised by Mrs. Gruen, the teacher at the unchartered and makeshift school that was operated, somewhat clandestinely, in the basement of Haus Zebulun. *I have never seen anything like it,* Mrs. Gruen would croon to the father; *she has been given this blessing for a reason.* And the widower would nod and smile at the honor lavished on his only child. But he could never completely understand the teacher's point. If there were a way that Alicia's talents could secure her escape from the poverty of the Schiller, he couldn't imagine what it was. And if Mrs. Gruen knew of a method by which Alicia could utilize her gifts to flee the privation of her surroundings, then why not come out and announce it instead of hinting at some vague and hidden destiny?

By the time Alicia was a teenager, she was contributing as much to the household support as her father. She took in washing and mending and for a time she held a delivery route for *Der Kehlkopf* in the German Quarter of the city. But the papergirl job kept her out of the Schiller past dusk and with the pogroms increasing at this time, her worried father made her give up the position. Still, these were good years. They ate fairly well and, most important, there was enough money to prevent Alicia from having to take a violet passport, the term, at that time, given to the government license for sanctioned brothel whores. Many of the Schiller girls, upon turning fourteen, were brought to the so-called tailor shops of Kaprova Boulevard for a pitiful bounty that the madams liked to call a dowry. It had been the fate of Alicia's closest friend. The father promised the daughter he would cut off his legs and beg as a cripple before he would allow his angel to dance with the perverts of Kaprova.

In fact, this small family made out comparatively well with daughter laundering and stitching for a growing list of happy customers and father working the circuit of cafés near the university and sometimes near the fountains in the Park of Love, bringing home each night a top hat full of tips which amounted to more than one might think. For a time it was a happy existence, and when they realized they had the resources to actually move out of the attic of the Levi and into more comfortable quarters, they decided that they'd grown to like their room too much to leave it, that it had, in fact, become their home and that it was unlikely they would ever desire another.

Alicia's passion for words and stories and, ultimately, for books did not abate during this period. If anything, it increased. When most of her peers began babbling incessantly about boys and the mysteries of courtship, Alicia found her own interests tending toward the novels she was discovering in the bins of the Wednesday bazaar. On the afternoons that she managed to finish her cleaning early, she would haunt the book stalls near the Teachers' College, searching sometimes an hour or more for the single secondhand, threadbare paperback that she could afford that month. The bane of her life was not the agonies of first-time romance and unrequited puppy love but the unimaginable fact that, due to her race and her sex, her creed and her status in this city, she could not gain entrance to the massive library that sat like a foreboding temple in the central square, holding in its belly half a million books which would never fall under the decoding gaze of her Schiller-born eyes.

Yes, the exclusionary policies of the Maisel Public Library were the wound of Alicia's entire existence. It only hurt more when the father, in one of his periodic binges, would announce that as soon as he won the national lottery he would buy her more books than she could read in a lifetime. The fact that Schiller Jews could not buy lottery tickets seemed to be chronically forgotten when papa was in his cups. But Alicia was as clever as she was persistent, and one night as she finished darning a pair of Mr. Zottman's stockings, it occurred to her that if the people of the Schiller were not allowed into the Maisel Library, perhaps what they needed, what they would learn that they wanted, was a library of their own.

It was the kind of idea that comes in an instant, not the gradual brand of notion that grows to its apogee in measured intervals, but the type of epiphany that lands without warning in the core of the thinker's brain and then takes over like an invading warlord, a ruthless imperialist who will broach nothing but an unconditional surrender of the mind's attention. In the second that Alicia let Mr. Zottman's socks fall from her lap to the floor of the loft, she knew she had found her calling, she knew this idea would possess her until she turned it into a solid and working reality, that it would not leave her alone for a moment, would paw at her like an insatiable, overbearing lover. So she left Haus Levi that second over the slurred but ineffectual protests of her patriarch and began to go door to door up and down the block, attempting, breathlessly, to explain her plan to the community and to solicit donations.

She was somewhat less than successful that first evening. Many people could not comprehend her spiel and shook their heads at her spasmodic talk of turning an entire floor of precious lodging into a lending library. It is true that from this night forward, Alicia's reputation developed from that of a cherished prodigy to an eccentric, possibly even dangerous, dreamer, a young lady who had spent too much time with her head hung over a book and would now bear the consequences of such obsessive behavior for the rest of her days. In the end, she agreed to swallow a spoonful of Mrs. Wenzel's relaxation tonic and walked home more determined than dejected. She pulled her father into his cot to sleep off his day of excess and then she began to rearrange the attic loft, making a pile of expendables that could be trashed and relocating the remaining possessions into a single, crowded corner.

By the time father woke the next morning, Alicia was already out scavenging produce crates at the Hay Market and bargaining wildly in the book stalls of the Bazaar. She returned to the loft dragging her spoils behind her to find her father gesticulating to a small group of Schiller elders, including Rabbi Gruen, in the middle of the near-empty attic, raving with the question of how he could have been robbed by his own people as he slept in the middle of the pilfering. It took a few minutes for Alicia to convince the old men that no robbery had taken place, that she had simply been cleaning and redecorating. It took much longer to explain her plans to her father. He proved less than enthused with the notion of turning his humble room into a public library and used all his energy to dissuade his daughter, even as he helped her carry the stained prune crates, overflowing with the dank aroma of old books, up to the top floor. He told her to use her God-given sense as Alicia stacked the crates one atop the other and attempted to tack them together using their one good saucepan as a makeshift hammer. He pleaded that the community had already spoken and rejected any need for a library as Alicia set to alphabetizing her meager collection of volumes. He warned of the resentment they could incur from this nonsensical venture as the daughter fash-

ioned a piece of discarded plywood and two dented milk
urns into an unlevel desk by the attic's entrance that
would serve both as checkout station and barrier between
library and living quarters.

When Alicia finally stopped moving to survey her work,
her father took her by her wrists, softly, not without love,
and said, "I cannot let you do this, my child."

Alicia pulled a hand free, stroked his face, and in the
same calm but inflexible tone, replied, "You cannot stop
me from doing this, Papa."

The old man knew he was beaten, but struggled out of
habit.

"They do not want a library, Alicia."

"Yes, they do," the daughter said, moving a soup can
full of pencils to her new desk. "They just don't know it
yet."

The comment proved more prescient than possibly
even the girl herself could have known. She hand-printed
a series of posters announcing the opening of the Ezzenes'
Free Lending Library, its location in the attic of Haus Levi
and its hours of operation. In the beginning, her collection of books was meager and somewhat uniform. The
German peddler she'd gotten most of them from seemed
to specialize in either melodramatic love stories or ques-
tionable historical tracts. Alicia's first visitors to the
library were a trio of middle-aged ladies from Haus
Issachar led by the midwife Rosina Waikby. They were
cordial if a bit frosty until one of the group spotted a copy
of Paul de Kock's *Georgette* and remarked, with a bit more
interest than condemnation, that she'd heard it was a very
decadent tale, very Western in its morals and use of epi-
thets. Alicia saw her opportunity and descended upon
these potential readers like a hound on a lame hare. She
scooped up a handful of like-minded Gothics and distributed them to the ladies, pointing out the flamboyant cover

art, always a depiction of an alluring if distressed heroine, struggling, or succumbing, depending on your point of view, in the arms of some picaresque rogue whose pectoral muscles were bursting through his inexplicably shredded pirate blouse.

When Alicia penciled in the return date on the inside of the rear cover of *Barber of Paris*, Mrs. Waikby dropped a coin into the coffee can marked *donations*. The hollow metal echo was the noise of a launching, a departure into a world where books, ideas, and language held the value of currency.

"It was only a bloody half-kreuzer," the father said that night, squeezed under the rafters in the new and more compact dining space.

"No," Alicia said, maybe a bit smug in her delight, "it was more than that. It was the beginning of an endowment."

"Endowment," the father repeated, cutting up a sausage. "Well, just make sure the Zottman's shirts are ready before your meeting with the investment counselor."

Alicia began to find books everywhere. She seemed to develop a kind of instinct, a second sense that led her to uncover troves of stock for the library. The coffee can donations never amounted to very much, but when added to what she could spare from her laundering fees and combined with this knack for tracking down caches of unwanted and discarded and forgotten books, she managed to continually expand the holdings of the attic repository. She entered into negotiations with the barbers of Hahnpasse Row, offering a discount on the cleaning of their hair sheets and shaving towels in return for some of the lurid crime novels that sat in racks for waiting customers. She washed chalkboards down at the university in exchange for the right to pick discarded texts from a variety of disciplines. She even collected the refuse of tear sheets from the Dumpsters behind the city's largest newspaper office, spent hours at a worktable clipping and collating the serialized stories of the rear pages, hardening them with a mixture of paste and soap flakes, and binding them in pressed boards that she made from a mash of fish scales, cinders, rag linen, and starch. These volumes proved more popular than she had expected and after a time the odor from them began to vanish.

As her archives grew, she divided her stacks of produce crates into sections. The wall adjoining the washtubs now housed an array of dog-eared philosophical treatises, while the shelving that ran from the bathroom door to the attic's single window was host to collections of history, science, and mythology. And always, in the midst of the dwelling, swelling to the point of rupture, the wheels creaking under the burden of a weight it was never designed to support, the new-books bin, once a common laundry basket of dingy white canvas stretched over an aluminum frame, the bin was now the repository of each week's new and as yet unsorted volumes. Coming into the attic at night and more than a touch inebriated, the father would inevitably collide with the bin, toppling the cribful of books and cursing Pandora's box.

For every day that ended in disappointment—a trade agreement that fell through, a borrower who confessed to the loss of a long-overdue item—there were just as many delightful surprises. There was Mr. Hulbert of Haus Ephraim who labored nights at the rubberworks and once brought her a genuine, rotating date stamp and a felt ink pad. Old Man Klopstock, who still manned a shovel detail at the city dumping ground, dropped off, one dawn, a cardboard box filled with a Bible, a dictionary, a huge geographical atlas, and an assortment of children's comic books. And the widow Tschamrda, who washed windows at Busson, Mirski & Moult, salvaged the treasure of a multi-volume set of legal statutes—*The Revised Criminal Code of Old Bohemia*—when the firm demanded a fresh edition with bindings that matched the new office decor. The widow rescued the books from the back of a trash hauler and secreted them away in a supply closet, then carried one volume home each night, tucked under the rags in a mopping pail, until she'd reunited the entire set. For her bravery and efforts, Alicia labeled the shelf that housed the statutes the Tschamrda Memorial Law Library.

People started visiting the attic with increasing regularity. And if father groused about the lack of privacy, he was quietly impressed with his offspring's ability to turn a lunatic daydream into a thriving reality. He adjusted to the change in his routine, was able to sit at the dinner table in his undershirt, suspenders hanging to the floor, savoring a pan-fried kidney while to his left a duo of smoke-engulfed old men prowled for a rumored American "cowboy" book and to his right a circle of, to his mind, overly serious young women filled their arms with out-of-date German economics texts. And in time he thought nothing of sitting in the bathtub, soaking behind the thin muslin curtain as the young bachelor Karp, from Haus Manasseh, continued to nervously interrupt a reading and sewing Alicia with made-up questions and inconsequential comments. The young man clearly had a smoldering and ill-disguised passion for the girl. But, as Alicia herself would put it when questioned by her father about settling down and starting a family, "I'm not interested in such things, Papa. I have a higher calling."

"Don't end up alone, like me," the father warned, but he knew, in this area at least, his words held no sway over his daughter.

The library was closed on the night that Censor Meyrink came to visit. Because of the heat, the attic was close to unbearable and many people were doing their reading outside on their stoops. Alicia, however, ignored the airless oppression of the book room and went to work sorting out the latest acquisitions in the new-books bin. From her vantage point before the front window of the loft, she had a sky-view of the whole of the block, could see the convoy of trucks and scooters, could see the shredding machine as it formed a barricade between the Schiller and the outside world. It is not so much that she froze when she realized what was about to happen. It is more that it all happened faster than her ability to analyze and solve the problem. Or, rather, faster than her understanding, in the moments that Meyrink began to read from the Orders of Erasure and the Reapers began to kick open all the doors and haul her neighbors outside, that there was no solution to be found. She spotted three soldiers running toward Haus Levi and, rather than making a conscious choice, gave in to the instinct, born of terror and confusion, that was flooding through her body for the first time.

And she dove into the book-filled laundry bin, squirmed and flailed her way to the bottom, covered herself with books, curled up into the smallest fetal ringlet her body would allow and blanketed herself with a shroud of paper and ink.

Moments later the door to the loft room exploded off its hinges with the kick of a steel-toed boot. This, even though the door had been unlocked. Three barking soldiers, not long past puberty, stormed inside. They spread out like rabid and clumsy street dogs, shoving over shelf after shelf, throwing anything they passed to the floor.

Then one of them yelled, "Tell the Censor we found it," and the three exited the library as quickly as they'd entered.

Alicia waited, unable to move, so far beyond anything she would have previously labeled horror, floating in a jellylike void of paralysis, already on the verge of thinking *I should have let them find me.*

The screaming from the street below came into the attic loft through its only window. And as the screaming grew, Alicia lifted herself, pushed up with her palms, books sliding away like heavy water. She brought her head just above the lip of the bin, looked out the window to see all of Schiller Avenue packed to bursting with its inhabitants. She had the finest view of anyone present that night. A vantage so clear and unobstructed that it combined with the nature of the event itself to create the sense that she was watching a movie. This was how it appeared to transpire—a staged performance crafted by the best in a profession dedicated to agonizingly brutal illusion.

She made herself watch. She forced the eyes to stay open through it all, willed the ears to record every scream. She would not look away. She listened to the man read the Orders of Erasure. She saw the impact of his words on the faces of her neighbors. She watched the cyclone fencing being pulled from the flatbed and unspooled up and down the street. Saw the fencing being connected to the winches of the obliterator and watched the machine roar into life. She watched the penned-in crowd instantly turn into an enormous, flailing beast, crazed with the latest and highest fear, turning against itself, rearing up and striking out and, finding nowhere to run, lashing back in at its own body. She saw the trampling begin. Saw the soldiers climbing up on top of their trucks to get a better position for picking off targets futilely trying to scramble up the metal netting. Watched the teeth and hooks and razors spin into a blur, salivating grease as the monster prepared for its banquet. And she saw the first bodies hauled inside the Pulpmeister.

She was a witness, ladies and gentlemen. She was an attestor. She stayed hidden, but she kept watch, her eyes always just above the rim of the book bin. Never sinking below. She did not allow herself. Would not give herself even this small reprieve as her whole world—the only world she had ever known since birth, the only people she had ever lived with—was summarily destroyed and, literally, shredded into pulp. She was just seventeen years old, ladies and gentlemen. Can you imagine this kind of will at this tender age? This kind of control? Making your eyes and ears bear witness to the slaughter of everything you hold dear? Knowing, instinctually, that this was all you could do and still doing it?

Zwack stares out at the crowd, head pivoting slowly on the neck as she squints through the spotlight trying to see faces. Her wooden lids are unblinking. Finally she asks, "Could any of you ever agree to submit yourself to this kind of test?"

But after a long silence, the only answer comes from Otto Langer. Blinking his eyes as if he's just woken up, his voice now restored to its familiar timber, Otto pulls in a deep and trembling breath and replies, "I could not."

16

Wylie Brown walks deeper into the orchards thinking about the cost of useless knowledge, about the fact that she's one of maybe ten people in the country who understand that the dead apple trees around her are a unique breed, a variety peculiar to this farm, a hybrid created by E. C. Brockden himself, not because he had any particular interest in the husbandry of fruit, but because he was told in a dream that "new apples will be needed to feed the new worms."

And so he invented the Fleshy Red Quince, a dessert fruit that starts out pale yellow like the Maiden Blush but late in maturation develops the scarlet stripes of the Spiced Ox Eye. Not as susceptible to the scab as, say, the American Fall, or as likely to sprout cedar-rust as the York Imperial, Brockden's breed did exhibit a tendency to drop too soon. But what actually brought the fruit to extinction was its penchant for a manner of blight unknown at the time in New England. Brockden's journals debate and ultimately discount the possibility of any form of bitter rot or blister canker or fire taint, but he does make one cryptic mention of a parasite he calls "the worm within the worm."

In any event, Brockden's experiment in horticulture failed as miserably as everything else connected with the farm and today the trees are a forest of lifeless wood, row after row of slowly petrifying sculpture that might be said to depict the results of specialization and compulsion. But right now, for Wylie Brown, the trees are something handy to lean against, a tool for supporting herself as she bends groundward for another bout of vomiting. Regurgitation has always been her leading fear response, but last night's celebratory binge in Little Asia has to be contributory as well. The Rottweilers have been gone for some time and yet she can still feel their predatory intent all around her. And it's this primal anxiety coupled with the depth of her bad judgment that's wreaking havoc on her stomach: she can detail for you the most minute facts about the life of an obscure eighteenth-century philosopher, analyze and interpret those facts into theories that touch on the farthest edges of contemporary theology and linguistics. But she doesn't know enough to stay out of the employ of a deadly Bohemian gangster.

Compulsion really can lead a person to a kind of hysterical blindness.

So August Kroger is everything Gilrein said he was—a filthy little criminal, a mob rat, an amoral machine who regularly engages in kidnapping and murder as easily as he collects rare books and papers. And Wylie has gone to work for him, become his librarian, his personal assistant. It's an old story, really: seduced and corrupted, in the end, by an obsessive love for the text.

The thought triggers her stomach, drives her down on one knee, but before she can release any bile, she takes a deep breath and closes her eyes. And though she knows she should be running to the farmhouse or the main road, phoning the police and telling her story, she finds herself, after a time, getting up and making for the rear of the estate. She moves past the last trees Brockden ever planted, at a time just before his final, apocalyptic episodes. They were the extreme end of his hybridizations and they proved most susceptible to the disease that engendered a kind of spontaneous abortion among the entire fruit crop as it bloomed. Writing about the phenomenon in his journals, Brockden called it "the death in the midst of the birth, the silence in the heart of the word."

She comes to stand in the wrecked portal of the greenhouse studying Brockden's doomed trees, thinking about Edgar's final days, the time of his descent, his free fall into an irreversible madness when the migraines increased in intensity and duration and his tongue developed a painful swelling, when he began to suffer from the nightmares in which hundreds, at times thousands, of tiny, writhing, fat red worms—parasites he termed "new creatures from the other world"—began to twist themselves into specific shapes that, when linked together, Edgar would christen "the divine alphabet, the method by which we will finally talk to the Father."

Wylie starts to feel dizzy and moves to the love seat, bringing up the images of those tiny drawings, the doodles that Brockden made in the margins of his last journal, the squiggles, so tentative, inked with such obvious hesitation, looking in the end like a child's illustration of some imaginary insect.

And she sits down on top of a notebook. A heavy, beautifully bound diary that she immediately takes in both hands, gently, and studies as object, which she opens and stares at without reading the script spread across the face of the page. She lets herself sink down into the love seat and, knowing there will be no turning back, she begins to decode.

     M.

INSTRUCTIONS FOR THE OPERATION AND MAINTENANCE
OF THE NOTEBOOK

     Avoid direct heat and light.

     Store in a cool, dry place.

Wash hands before and after handling.

Caution: pay careful attention to all
margins.

Contains small parts: not recommended for
children under the age of (spiritual)
puberty.

If stalling occurs, jump forward vigorously.

If epidermal irritation occurs, increase
dosage.

Replacement parts may be ordered from
domestic internal departments.

In the event of significance breakdown, shut
off all machinery and vacate the area
immediately.

Excessive exposure to the notebook may cause
assorted irregularities in the dream life.
The manufacturer accepts no responsibility
for any claims of sleep disorder.

Do not operate heavy machinery for a full
week after ingestion of excerpt.

Remember: The various components that
comprise the notebook can be used in any
order and in multiple combinations. Each
section can be viewed as a letter in an
alphabet that is neither divine nor diabolic
but chronically evolutionary. All taxes

```
apply. Do not void where prohibited by law.
Be playful and creative.
```

And now there is no thought of breaking into the farmhouse, of making for the main road and flagging down a car. Now Gilrein's fate is immaterial as the world compresses to fit within the borders of this inscribed page. Wylie is once again hooked, caught in the ceaseless need to scan and unlock meaning. It is irrelevant that she doesn't fully understand what it is she's reading. It is the process that has taken her. As it has since childhood, never letting up; if anything, its intensity increasing with age and the ever-growing capacity for confusion.

She turns to another page, unconcerned about the fact that this hunger will never abate, that she could feed on every book inside Wormland and never be sated, that her body could break up and mutate into a plague of book-eating locusts and the locusts could descend upon the farmhouse, the City of Words, and ravage it, devour every printed surface, strip the pages themselves down to the primary rag fibers of their making and burn them into energy with the secretions of her digestive system. And she would still want more. Would still need to turn one more page, as she does now, and read:

```
N. Lacazze seems to believe that when one
looks at a text to determine its most basic,
literal meaning, one instantly,
unconsciously, falls, cascades, as he says,
into a brainwashed mode, a system of all-
encompassing autohypnosis in which our eyes
scan the graphical symbols and relay those
symbols to the brain, which processes them
and extracts appropriate representation from
a lifelong file of meanings. However, L
contends that this file has been tampered
with, the file room has been broken into,
```

over and over again, throughout the course
of every human life. The file is always a
manipulated and specialized agenda, a kind
of intricate database of propaganda,
compiled over millennia by an elite
consensus.

In other words, according to the
Inspector, there simply is no plain sense of
the text. There is no such thing as literal
meaning. It is not just that decoding text
is subjective, that we bring to the task our
inherent and cumulative lifetime of baggage,
from brain chemistry to our choice of
lovers. No: decoding is subversive. And
totally out of our control.

He stands upon his desk, his legs
straddling the chalice. He says, in a voice
so low I have to strain to hear it (and
that, of course, is exactly the intention),
"Remember this, if nothing else: WE DO NOT
ACT UPON THE TEXT. THE TEXT ACTS UPON US."
So, when we venture into Little Asia and
seat ourselves at the Last Man Supper Club
and open the menu and select "the sweet and
sour ribs" we are not choosing a plate of
small, curved bones swathed in edible flesh
and cut from the torso of a swine,
marinated in corn syrup, brown sugar,
soybean oil, peanut oil, vinegar, pineapple
juice, apricot concentrate, Worcestershire
sauce, xanthan gum, dried red bell pepper,
FD&C red #4 artificial color, and charred
over flame to be served to us as
gastronomic feast. We are doing something
else entirely.

And when I fully unravel both the
Inspector and his Methodology, I will tell
you just what it is that we are doing.

She makes herself look up and take a breath. Was Gilrein
holding this notebook when she first entered the greenhouse? He
was standing when she arrived, positioned here in front of the
love seat. But was there anything in his hands? Since she can't
answer definitively, she turns back to the book.

0. The 'Shank scores for me once again.
What would Gilrein think if he knew I was
doing business with Leo Tani? Surely he'd see
my actions as a betrayal. Even if Tani's help
were essential to an "official" investigation—
and it is not. My research regarding the
Inspector cannot be considered much more than
a hobby at this point—G would have to feel
hurt. Perhaps even emasculated. As if trading
with the 'Shank indicated that I hold my work
not only in greater esteem than my husband's
work, but that I would negate, erase G's work
in order to advance my own.
I met the fat man inside Gompers
yesterday. I don't know why he insists on
transacting in that dank cave but I suspect
he has a weakness for all things dramatic. A
Turin birth will sometimes do this to you.
He wanted five hundred dollars and the
promise that I'd speak to G about looking
the other way for the next month or so.
I offered him two hundred and the
possibility that I'd never tell G that I'd
been propositioned by his least favorite
receiver of stolen property.

```
      We agreed on two-fifty and he handed over
   a sealed plastic bag containing the journal
   Mikrogramme (formerly Minotaur and now
   published by the "Herisau Institute"). I
   politely declined the offer of a Gallzo at
   Fiorello's and made myself wait until Tani
   had exited the station. Then I found a shaft
   of light and sat down right there in Gompers
   and tore open the bag with my teeth. I
   turned to the contents page, ran my finger
   down the list of titles and found what I'd
   been looking for.
      The article was titled "Bite Your Tongue:
   Self-Mutilation and the Loss of Oral
   Tradition." The essayist was listed simply
   as "Lacazze."
      There were no contributor notes.
```

The pages must have belonged to Gilrein's wife Ceil. The *über*-woman. The owner of his heart and his brain, even in her death. And the reason, finally, why he'll never give himself to another. They are Ceil Gilrein's work journals. They have to be. Her field notes. Her dialogue with herself regarding her job, her career, her investigations.

Did Gilrein think they would explain something? Translate the meaning, give him a linguistic key, a Rosetta Stone that would decipher why his wife is dead and why he might as well be?

Wylie flips through the book, picks another page.

```
   that I was a detective.
      I was a superb detective: watchful, quick
   thinking, analytical, innovative.
      But I became something else. Without
   realizing it. Without desiring it. I became
```

a writer. I became a transcriber. I mutated
into a recording machine.

My hubris: I thought I could work in such
isolated spaces with the Inspector and remain
untainted. I thought I could exist in the same
closed hothouse of the Dunot Precinct with L
and remain uninfected. Hadn't I been listening
when my husband relayed his childhood stories
of Father Damien and the lepers?

Edgar Brockden—

And Wylie is stunned by the reference to Brockden, almost
closes the book without finishing the sentence, as if the name
were a curse directed specifically, only, against her. But she
steadies herself and continues.

—thought he could French-kiss the Almighty
and detach himself, intact, to boast of
their passion. An atheist to the bone, the
Inspector thought he would be immune to
Brockden's disease, thought he could turn
the entire system of Language around and
bugger it, make Language his prison bitch,
the slave to his boundless ego.

But in raping the mystery of Language, it
was the Inspector that became impregnated.
And the fetus is a growing monster with
claws that will rend the man from within.

You, who are reading these words,
understand this: you are just as culpable.

And now you are infected as well.

And with these last words Wylie suddenly comes back to herself and realizes that she does not want to read any more of this,
does not want to be in this greenhouse or on this farm.

She wants to simply get her belongings from the Bardo and go away, leave this city that she spent so much of her youth striving toward.

She closes the notebook and places it back on the love seat, exits the greenhouse and begins to run for the main road, surrendering any chance of ever viewing the disclaimer which, scrawled on the inside of the rear cover, in Ceil Gilrein's increasingly illegible handwriting, reads

```
To G. Or to the one who comes eventually to
read the words: Consider that maybe every
one of them is a fiction. Perhaps I've
invented the entire thing. A product of a
raging paranoia that's escalated to
hallucinatory levels. Hold that possibility
as I ask you (and as you ask yourself): Does
this matter?
```

17

Boz Lustig's is a greasy all-night cafeteria in the Bohemian Wing of Bangkok Park. It serves an array of tried and true recipes from the homeland—*fazole na kyselo, kanci*, a slew of *holub* dishes, nothing fancy and everything suspiciously inexpensive. Lustig himself works the steam tables, matching the customers step for step as they point to their selections, his hair-swaddled arms ladling the soupy courses into the slotted plastic trays whose bottoms testify to their black market origins with the stenciled words SPOONER CORRECTIONAL FACILITY.

To step into Lustig's joint is to be assaulted by a combination of aromas not commonly found in American eateries. The uninitiated can sometimes swoon, and though the bulk of Boz's customer base is made up of transplanted Maisel natives, the collegiate art crowd from the Zone will occasionally venture in, charmed by the enormity of the green leather booths and yearning to bask in the accidentally Deco-noir lighting thrown by a dozen bare bulbs that hang from fraying fiber cords in the pressed tin ceiling. Lustig will take the outsiders' money, but he always serves them from the coldest end of the steam pan.

The cafeteria is sandwiched between a Pest-B-Gone extermination franchise and Leppin's Pawnshop, whose proprietor has earned the nickname "Lucky Leppin" by managing to drop a total of five would-be armed robbers in the past year alone. The blood is washed off this particular sidewalk so often that the exterminator gifted Leppin with one of his spare garden hoses.

These days, the cafeteria does its peak business around three in the morning, not because the denizens of the Wing have discovered this is when Boz finally relents and brews fresh kava, but rather because this is the hour that the neighborhood mayor of the Bohemians, Hermann Kinsky, has of late been waking with pangs of postdream hunger and lumbering down from his crib at the Hotel St. Vitus with his trusted business aide and legal advisor, Gustav Weltsch. Hermann has fallen into a habit of enjoying a predawn feast in the largest booth in the establishment as he receives the night owls among his people. Word soon spread that this was prime time to hit Kinsky up for all manner of favors— loans, employment opportunities, housing, sometimes even a good word to his friends on the city council. Insomnia spread too, when it became an unconditional given that if Boz Lustig was serving the boiled hare's tongue stewed in a gillyflower white sauce, Hermann Kinsky was a happy man and consequently intent on lavishing assistance on his less-powerful brethren. Gustav Weltsch would sit perpetually half-asleep over a cinnamon cocoa giving nonstop, yawn-broken warnings that Hermann cheerfully ignored.

But if Kinsky's people still love him like a flesh-and-blood guardian angel, his status among the rest of the city's neighborhood mayors is at its lowest ebb since the day he disembarked from the freighter that brought him to this country. Kinsky has had a bad year. His heir apparent has run off to become a filmmaker and the nephew who ran his street muscle met an unfortunate end. Subsequently, the Gray Roaches, who worked all his filthiest departments, the extortion and the pharmaceuticals, and who served as the Wing's only border patrol, fell into chaos and disbanded. Hermann has been reduced for the past six months to renting the services of a variety of hit-and-run street soldiers from out of town, and it's more than embarrassing for Kinsky to be leasing non-Maisel muscle. It's dangerous in a variety of ways. It sends out a message of instability and weakness. If push comes to shove and another tribe makes an expansion move into the Wing, Hermann can't count on these mercenaries laying down their lives for Bohemian territory. It's the difference between having family and having a labor force. The difference, as always, between love and money.

Gilrein has eaten at Lustig's once before. Ceil took a meeting with Kinsky on Lacazze's behalf and Gilrein tagged along. Kinsky was as polite as his Eastern Euro-peasant ways would allow, as if he needed his pragmatic intelligence to control the reflexive absurdity of discussing business with a woman. And not just a woman but a female *policista. How has this country prospered so,* Hermann wondered, *with such nonsensical ways?*

Gilrein no longer remembers the specifics of that dinner's discussion, as a good deal of it was conducted in a certain pidgin-Slavic ghetto dialect that Ceil had spent weeks practicing. He does recall the amused look on Kinsky's face each time Ceil spoke on behalf of the department as well as the unmitigated heartburn he suffered for close to a week afterward. "I tried to warn you," Ceil said later that night, dispensing a pale green antacid into a table-spoon, "never order the guinea fowl goulash unless your stomach was born in Maisel."

Gilrein enters the cafeteria to the sound of accordion music and the suspicious mass-glance of the diners. He gets in line behind a trio of young men who appear, by their scent and their freshly crimson-stained coveralls, to have just gotten off the night shift at a nearby slaughterhouse. The threesome gesticulate wildly to Boz Lustig, bathed in a perpetual cloud of steam behind the counter, yelling at him, it seems, not to spare the gravy nor short-change them in the area of internal organs. Gilrein takes deep breaths till it's his turn, then signals Lustig for a simple cup of coffee, which the owner retrieves with a maximum of unintelligible grumbling.

Gilrein overpays the man, though it fails to cut the complaining, then takes the coffee mug and moves to the rear of the room where, as he hoped, he finds Hermann Kinsky installed in his reception booth, decked out in his trademark red flannel pajama suit beneath a maroon paisley silk robe, one hand shaking the paw of an elderly and toothless woman, the other shoveling the remains of glazed blood sausage into his mouth. His sidekick Weltsch sits on the opposite side of the table, studying bond prices in the *Wall Street Journal*.

Gilrein approaches and without waiting for an invitation, slides in next to Weltsch, startling the lawyer and spilling just a bit of his cocoa. It's a rude maneuver and not too smart considering Gilrein's noncop status. But he knows from Ceil that Kinsky likes to see someone's stuff up front and he needs to make it clear to Hermann that he's not cowed by a gangster who currently has to rent his street balls.

"Are you the new busboy?" Kinsky says and takes a sip of some kind of liqueur from a short fat water glass. "Have you come to clear my plate?"

Gilrein gives a small smile and a nod.

"You know who I am, Hermann," he says.

Kinsky mimes recognition.

"Of course," he says and licks syrup from all the fingers of his eating hand. "You were the husband of the Inspector's woman."

Gilrein thinks about throwing his coffee in Kinsky's face, but manages to suppress the urge.

"That's right," he says instead, "and you're the little haberdasher who's about to get his ass permanently kicked by the Iguaran Family."

Weltsch looks up from the *Journal* and stares at this intruder, as if trying to determine if the man is clinically insane or just pathetically stupid. Because the fact is that though Kinsky is more than vulnerable to a hit from Latino Town right now, he doesn't need the Gray Roaches to garrote one insulting ex-cop. He could do it right here on the tabletop with the help of Lustig or the slaughterhouse crew. And everyone in the cafeteria down to a man would scream out their pride in their mayor.

It doesn't come to that. Hermann Kinsky almost always wants to hear what a man has to say before he judges whether to preserve or cancel a life. He lets a huge smile come over his jowly face, claps his hands into an explosion over his head, and yells, "Lustig, my friend, becherovka for my guest."

Boz breaks off from the serving line and immediately comes running, plants on the table an unlabeled brown bottle and a mismatched plastic glass that's sporting some kind of crust around its rim. Lustig waits for Kinsky's nod, then jogs away. Weltch pours Gilrein a drink. Gilrein accepts it, lifts his glass toward Kinsky and the two toast one another silently and sip a hootch that goes down like kerosene.

Weltsch, seeing that the threat of violence has been contained for the moment, goes back to the trading news, but says quietly, over the edge of the paper, "His name is Gilrein."

Kinsky absentmindedly stares down at his tray, looking disappointed, and says, "We dined together once," nodding as he remembers the night. "I was very sorry to hear of your wife's demise."

Gilrein accepts the condolences, however graceless, and says, "Ceil thought you were a comer. Out of all the new arrivals, she said the old boys should keep their eyes on you."

It's no secret in Bangkok that, even more than most of the neighborhood mayors, Kinsky is easily flattered. And that flattery can buy you a small piece of his time and maybe even a little advice. But what Gilrein has said is also the truth. Ceil was nothing if not a good judge of the upward mobility of new mobsters in the Park. She saw something in Kinsky that her husband could not. She tried to explain it to him later, after that horrible dinner, back in the darkness of their bedroom, her take on the patterns of

Kinsky's brain, her close reading of the core of this Maisel wise guy: "He may not be as smart as Iguaran or as charismatic as Sylvain or as globally connected as Jimmy Tang, but he's got that pure gangster's soul. He'll end up a real player, like Pecci and Loftus. He's intuitive about the flow of the street. He can feel the natural course of the market. He's got that fundamental ruthlessness, that innate understanding of social Darwinism. I'm telling you, he may have been born and raised in Old Bohemia, but he understands the way America works better than a goddamn pilgrim. He's got the intestines of a down and dirty pomo capitalist. You kill off your enemies and you buy off your friends and when you get your opponent to surrender in the gutter, you kick in his teeth and piss on his head and you take his wallet and his wife. Whatever you can get, whenever you can get it. And the last bastard left standing is king of the hill."

And Gilrein lay there, spooned behind Ceil's body, his face against her head, smelling her hair. And it was as if his wife's voice were coming from someone else, being used by some strange and ambivalent entity, some dark and hidden aspect of God that no one had bothered to explain to him. He tried to hold off a shiver, because it almost sounded like Ceil felt a kind of perverse respect for this monster she was describing, like a confused anthropologist who, miles from home and watching a cannibal feast on his own, couldn't help but smile at the fact that the savage would go to bed with a full stomach.

Gilrein stares at this Maisel cannibal as Kinsky runs a finger around the pool of thick juice collected in a corner of his dinner tray, then lifts the finger to his mouth and inserts it between his lips, sucking off the molasses-like coating.

"Your wife was a fine judge of character," Kinsky says. "She will be missed by all who knew her."

"She left a real gap in the department," Gilrein says. "Not every detective can finesse this part of town."

Kinsky agrees vigorously. "No one knows this better than I, Mr. Gilrein. The idiots your people have sent to barter, I can't tell you—"

"They're not really my people, Mr. Kinsky. I haven't been on the job for several years now."

"Yes, I had heard this. You're in the"—a pause, looking for the word—"transportation service."

Gilrein nods over his mug. "I drive a hack."

"For the red or the black?" referring to the two major fleets in town.

"Neither," Gilrein says. "I'm an independent."

Kinsky's face lights up as if his friend Boz had just discovered some portion of rabbit's *jazyk* in the fridge. Even Weltsch manages to nod his approval.

"A dying breed," Kinsky says.

"There's only a handful of us left in the city," Gilrein says. "The fees are brutal. It's like living in a vise."

"Acht," Kinsky agrees, and their mutual disgust with municipal bureaucracy seems to instantly erase their initial discord. "And they have the nerve to call me a thief. This city would take the coins from the eyes of a corpse."

"And they'd send a clerk to do it," Weltsch puts in from behind his paper, to the delight of his boss.

"So true, Gustav. More true each day, yes?" Then he takes a sip of his drink and says, "Is this why you've come, Mr. Gilrein? You need me to speak to the taxi commissioner?"

Gilrein starts to shake his head, but Kinsky is already saying, "Because I know the man. And though, it is true, this is not the best of times for the family Kinsky, we may be able to work something out. The last I heard this individual was aligned with the black minister—"

"Reverend James," Weltsch puts in, though they're all aware that Kinsky knows the name.

"I'm not here about my hack fees," Gilrein says, letting them have their fun. "I need to talk about August Kroger."

This gets their full attention. Weltsch puts down the paper and adjusts his glasses as he looks across the table at Kinsky.

"What about Kroger?" Hermann asks.

"He tried to take me down yesterday—"

"Without my permission?" with full mock outrage.

"You tell me," Gilrein says and sits back in the booth. "He's one of yours."

Weltsch clears his throat. "Technically, Mr. Kroger has never been in our employ. He is from the old country, but—"

Kinsky thumps the table with one of his enormous fists and bellows, "No Bohemian takes this kind of action without my consent."

"Take a look at my lips, Mr. Kinsky," Gilrein says, matching his volume. "I wasn't getting a goddamn tattoo. So either you want me whacked for reasons I don't understand or your little pal is running loose out there."

"I have no quarrel with you," Kinsky's voice coming back to discussion level. "And I can't see any obvious reason for wanting to do away with a taxi-boy."

Gilrein lets the insult go, tries to decide how much to spill and realizes he doesn't have anything to barter with, that all he can do is tell his story and hope for some response.

"When they were working me over," he says, "they kept asking about a book."

"A book," Kinsky repeats, as if confused, but Gilrein can feel Weltsch tense up next to him.

"The last person I drove before Kroger's animals grabbed me was Leo Tani—"

"The fence from San Remo." Kinsky nods. "Of course, I knew him as Calvino—"

"Leo used a variety of names. The point is he got whacked in a particularly horrible manner shortly after I chauffeured him to some kind of transaction inside Gompers Station."

"We heard of your friend's misfortune. But, as you know, these things happen. It's sometimes a consequence of the business."

Weltsch sniffs out a laugh. Something about Kinsky's word choice amuses him, as if murder were analogous to working late or taking a pay cut.

"That's true," Gilrein says, folding his hands together in front of him and straightening his posture in the booth. "You're absolutely right. These things happen in *the business*," accenting the words into sarcasm. "*The business* is a dicey world. People disappear. Fortunes rise and fall. And a two-bit seamstress like Kroger can even topple the king of the Wing."

Gilrein knows that what Kinsky would like to do, right here and now, is pull his ever-present piano wire from his pocket and turn this guest's jugular into fish bait. But Kinsky has learned over the last few years that impulse is usually not the most valuable way of reacting in the long run.

He looks to his lawyer and they silently exchange counsel with the cast of their eyes.

"Understand something," Kinsky says softly. "August Kroger is an eccentric little worm that I have tolerated only because it has been to my advantage to do so. And the moment it is not to my advantage, the worm will be sent back to hell."

"Then I guess," Gilrein says, "I was mistaken."

"It appears so."

Kinsky pulls his bib napkin free from his collar, swabs at his mouth, and then throws the linen onto his tray. He places his hands on the table and Gilrein feels it tilt as Kinsky pushes himself to standing.

"If you'll excuse me," he says, "I am in need of relief."

He reaches across the table and takes the newspaper from Weltsch, then breaks into a heavy trot in the direction of the lavatory.

Weltsch waits until his boss is out of sight, then turns to Gilrein and says, "I might advise you, for future reference, Mr. Gilrein, that it is not entirely polite, or I might say, wise behavior to come to a man's breakfast table and then make insinuations about his prowess and his status. In the case of Hermann Kinsky, it is less than unwise. It is a form of barbarous suicide."

"I didn't know he was so thin-skinned."

"It is not a matter of sensitivity, Mr. Gilrein. It's a matter of respect and ritual. My client lives by a fairly exacting code. I must say, it's amazing to me that you'll be forgiven for this breach."

"Yeah," Gilrein says, "I guess maybe Hermann is mellowing."

"Our organization has suffered a minor setback. One of our top managers passed away and we lost a good portion of our labor force—"

"Listen, counselor, I don't give a rat's ass one way or the other about the big man's balance sheet. Save it for the auditor, okay? Just tell me why Kroger came after me."

"I don't—"

"For Christ's sake, Gustav, even when he's on the ropes, Hermann knows every Bohemian move in town. Kroger spills some blood, Hermann would know it before the first drop hit the dirt."

Weltsch stares for just a few seconds, then shakes his head in consent and maybe a little relief.

He shrugs his shoulders and says, "You know, if it had been up to me, the two-bit seamstress, as you so beautifully dub him, would have been buried some time ago. Even back in Maisel he was under constant suspicion by the secret police. Say what you want about the Communists, they knew a troublemaker when they saw one."

"So why does Kinsky put up with him?"

"Hermann takes his standard percentage, but mainly it's sentimental reasons. They came out of the same neighborhood."

"That's what everyone says about Hermann," Gilrein nods, "that sentimental old bastard. I'll bet he loves a parade, too."

"Mr. Gilrein, are all the taxi-boys this masochistic?"

"Trust your instincts, Gustav. They'll serve you well."

Weltsch takes a roll of mints from the inside pocket of his suit jacket, peels one free and pops it in his mouth, then turns and offers the roll to Gilrein, who declines.

"My instinct," Weltsch says, "tells me to give you what you want and be rid of you."

"You're a good businessman. Time is money."

Weltsch hunches forward with his elbows on the table and lets his back molars splinter his candy with an unsettling cracking noise.

"The Family," he says, as if there were anyone left beyond himself and his boss, "has virtually nothing to do with Kroger. He falls under our jurisdiction by fault of genetics and geography. Hermann can't stand the toad. We've always felt that sooner or later he'd begin to imagine he could oversee the Bohemian Wing. It's absurd, of course."

"Wouldn't last a week," Gilrein affirms.

"A week?" Weltsch raises his eyebrows and gestures out at the cafeteria. "The man is a little dilettante. Can you even imagine him taking his supper in here?"

Gilrein smiles and says, "I've got to be honest with you, Gustav. You're sitting right here in front of me and I've got trouble imagining you in this place."

Weltsch takes it as a compliment and continues.

"A year ago Kroger began making small comments about his licensing costs. He runs several franchises in the Wing. You must be familiar with his publishing concern—"

"I've been to the home office," Gilrein interrupts.

Weltsch grimaces politely.

"Kroger's yearning for more control began to manifest itself last year. Hermann thought it best to nip the problem in the bud. We'd already decided on a contractor."

"That's when the family Kinsky had their first big setback."

Weltsch nods.

"Jakob, the son, he left the nest and cashed in his stock options on the way out the door. And Felix, the nephew, who was so good on the street . . ."

He breaks off and Gilrein says, "You know the rumor has been that the son whacked the nephew."

Gustav meets his eyes and in a low and suddenly unlawyerly voice, he says, "Rumors are vicious things."

Gilrein drops the subject and steers back to Kroger.

"So Hermann postponed the job on August?"

"It's been a very unstable time. Perhaps more trying than Hermann would like to admit. The Roaches followed Jakob off into the Canal Zone. People are watching and waiting to see how we rebound. We didn't think it was the most appropriate moment. Mr. Kroger's time will come again."

"No doubt," Gilrein says. "But who is Hermann using for street muscle these days?"

Gustav stares at him, expressionless, then finally lets a small smile break at the left side of his lips.

"You are a character, Mr. Gilrein."

"I am?"

"Is this your old friends' way of renegotiating their contract?"

"My old—"

"Because, let me advise you here and now, we won't discuss a revision. Your Mr. Oster agreed to a flat monthly fee and he'll abide by that agreement."

"Oster?" Gilrein says. "Kinsky is using the Magicians for his street crew?"

"You run back to your police friends and tell them we won't even discuss it until their term expires. Tell them their behavior is pathetic and we expected more from professionals."

"Weltsch, I'm telling you, I had no idea."

The distant sound of a toilet flushing reverberates through the walls of the cafeteria and Attorney Weltsch begins to gather his financial journals together into a neat pile.

"But I just—" Gilrein begins, and Weltsch motions him out of the booth.

"Depending on how things went in there," gesturing now toward the men's room, "your life could be in genuine danger if you're still here when Hermann returns."

18

The names you used to call me
Sound so strange and they fill me with fear
But will we ever know if this difference is born
On your tongue or perhaps in my ear . . .

It's "What Is and Isn't Said," a
live version off the *One Night in Wiesbaden* album. The tune was
done with a string section backing and Gilrein finds it greatly
inferior to Imogene's original a cappella rendition, so he asks the
driver to turn off the radio and tries to stop wondering which
interpretation Ceil was partial to, tries instead to focus on the
more pertinent question at hand—why the hell two Bohemian
gangsters might be vying to ice one insignificant ex—bunko cop?

He relays the final directions to Wormland through the safety
partition. He knows he should be humiliated, one of the last of the
independent hacks paying a corporate grunt for a ride home, but
all he feels is tired and jangled, certain only of the fact that it will
probably be a good idea to bring the gun into bed with him

tonight. The smart way to run this mess down is probably to go back to the beginning and start with Leo Tani, to find out what kind of book he was moving and who it belonged to and who has been bidding on it. But the best person to help him answer those questions would be Wylie Brown. And just a few hours ago, she handed him over to Kroger.

Or did she? It's possible, if unlikely, that she had no idea Kroger's animals were coming for him. But in Gilrein's experience, cynicism comes faster and easier than faith and though he doesn't actively want to believe that Wylie set him up, he can't shake the familiar sensation of betrayal that's resting in the hollow of his stomach like a snake with a skin made of diamonds.

So he tries sticking with the few thin facts that he's got and their corollary suppositions.

Leo Tani was whacked because of the sale he brokered at Gompers Station. According to Kroger, the item sold was a book of some sort, which Kroger says belongs to him. Kroger is being dogged by Oster and the Magicians, who are working on contract for Hermann Kinsky. And all of them seem to think that Tani passed this book on to his favorite chauffeur. With both Kroger and Kinsky involved, it seems at least possible that the book in question may either originate in or have some connection to their shared native city, Maisel, the thousand-year capital of Old Bohemia.

Is Gilrein imagining it or did Ceil really mention wanting to visit Maisel some day? Was this an actual statement of his late wife or has he begun to insert her presence into every aspect of his post-Ceil existence?

He refuses to pick at the question. He's too exhausted and maybe too apprehensive about the final answer, the fact that too much of himself died along with Ceil, that the balance of a lifetime this choked and numbed from unrelieved grief isn't a lifetime at all but rather a limbo, a void, a holding cell of paralife, ghost life, where every sense is muted to the point of absurd triviality and ideas of possibility and faith and change are inconceivable.

The black cab's headlights play over the sprawl of the farmhouse and the barn. Gilrein pays the driver and climbs outside,
but instead of heading for the loft, he goes to the main house,
unlocks the front door and makes his way down into the cellar. He
grabs the flashlight from the shelf at the bottom of the stairs and
follows its beam toward the rear of the house, and when the furnace cycles on without warning, he flinches so badly that he
almost drops to the floor.

Some field mice run through the shaft of his light as it plays on
the ground. When he comes to the wooden locker, he takes his keys
from his jacket, finds the smallest one, and opens the padlock. He
rests on one knee and unbolts the manhole cover, pulls the plate
loose and sets it to the side, then climbs down into Subterranea.

It was Wylie who conclusively determined that the original
labyrinth had, in fact, been constructed by E. C. Brockden himself. An earlier Brockden scholar, whom Wylie called, often and
with a kind of glee, "a chronically pissed-off revisionist," had
posited that it was one of the later owners who was responsible for
the book maze. Certainly there were sections of the tunnels that
Brockden couldn't possibly have forged given the materials used
in their construction. But the initial conception, design, and
assembly were all the work of Brockden, the man whom at least
one limerick has memorialized as King of the Worms.

Subterranea was the start of Brockden's final descent into
madness, as Wylie had explained, a little melodramatically,
Gilrein thought, the first time he took her down below. She had,
of course, read deeply in all the specialty works devoted to the
network of veins that comprised the underground library. She'd
studied the photostats of Brockden's original line drawings and
compared them to the most recent computer-generated blueprints commissioned by the Brockden Society. She'd familiarized
herself to the point of memorization with the titles of all the
books found lining the walls of the labyrinth and spent innumer-
able hours at the Southwick reviewing the manifest with a red

pencil and either agreeing or disagreeing with the judgments as to which volumes belonged to Brockden and which had been added by later Wormland owners.

Measured in a straight-ahead, linear fashion, the corridors that comprise the labyrinth run on for close to half a mile, but the layout of the book maze is anything but linear. It turns and twists and wraps back upon itself and so, like human intestines or a wound ball of twine, the eight hundred yards of negotiable space occupy a subsurface cavern that lies beneath a circular plot of earth stretching only to the valley at the edge of the orchards.

There's no reason to believe that he'll find books here on the city of Maisel. Brockden's original stock mainly consisted of obscure theological tracts and fringe science texts. The more recent volumes deposited by the interim owners were a hodge-podge of forgotten novels and manuals of the occult and a sampling of the more notorious, hysterically paranoid political manifestos of the past two hundred years.

The logical course would be to head for the public library and pull everything on rare Bohemian tomes. But that would mean waiting and thinking and remembering, lying in the barn loft, soaking in the now compulsive recollections of how Ceil came into his life and how she departed, culminating always in a vivid skull cinema that can only screen one feature—the Rome Avenue Raid. And the last way Gilrein wants to welcome the dawn is by morbidly pawing over a series of past events that can't be changed by hope or good deeds or even the exchange of one life for another.

So he climbs down into the hole and starts walking randomly, moving through the left tunnel when he comes to the first fork. How many times has Gilrein been through the labyrinth? Fewer than one might think. After Frankie first showed him the tunnels he ventured down alone two or three times, but on each occasion he found the maze more claustrophobic, especially when he'd reach the crawl space sections that could only be traversed on hands and knees.

But then, after the romance with Wylie began, he started to accompany her into the hole and was surprised to find that his phobic reaction had lessened to the point where they could spend hours following passageways to their walled-off conclusions. In fact, it was in the labyrinth that Gilrein and Wylie first consummated their relationship when she tripped on an unseen pile of books left in the walkway and fell backward into Gilrein. He caught her, but lost his own balance and they both went down to the ground, dropping flashlights and landing in an awkward but intimate embrace that, shocking the two of them, took on a life of its own and culminated, somehow, twenty minutes later, with both their jeans loose around their ankles and their legs and asses covered with cold, moist dirt.

"What would Edgar think?" was all Gilrein could come up with between breaths.

Wylie further shocked herself by loving his irreverence and she spent the sleeping hours of the next week in the Checker, keeping him company through all manner of quixotic fares in Bangkok Park and the Canal Zone, lecturing him in a loose and haphazard style on the life, madness, and death of Edgar Carwin Brockden.

Now, he thinks of all she taught him, can hear Wylie's voice as he throws a light across the spines of the thousands of books that line the curving, narrowing, disappearing walls of Subterranea. And he thinks for the first time that though he may never share Wylie's fascination with the life of Brockden, he suddenly understands the frustration she feels at the heart of her research. Because, though Wylie can tell you, in obsessive and intricate detail, what happened to Edgar Brockden, she can't tell you why it happened.

No one can. Gilrein is sure of this. If all of these volumes of print gathered around him, here below the stony ground of Quinsigamond, somehow managed to transmogrify themselves and each grew tongue and larynx and the intellectual mechanics necessary for communication, they'd all fall silent when confronted with the unique components of one man's insanity. Madness is always a singularity. Gilrein knows this no matter how many learned scholars of the mind might demonstrate patterns, systemic consistencies, series of long-proven repetitions. When a man falls away from any trace of rationality, it is a lone, unprecedented descent. And Gilrein's certainty of this fact is a surety born, not of clinical observation and analysis, but of the kind of sharp and pressing and parasitical truth that lives at the bottom of the belly, without known origin or end, like a legendary and eventually doomed redeemer.

He lets himself wander, neither following an established route nor memorizing his current path. Every now and then he stops and faces a wall of books, reads a number of titles—*The Heresy of Jesuit Education*, *The Meretricious Cost of Our Demise*, *The Lair of the Scarlet Filariasis*—their gilt letters wearing toward illegibility. At one point he's forced to duck down to a squat and waddle through a particularly low segment of tunnel. At the end of this segment he stops and shines his beam left and right. On the right hand wall, instead of books, he finds one of those rare notches that Wylie always considered the high point of their underground sojourns. At seven locations throughout the labyrinth, Brockden carved out of the rock face a small indentation or crevice and outfitted each with a ritual altar. To this day, the man's original implements and tools remain displayed upon the altars—skiving knives and stitching needles; paste brushes and dried-up jars of homemade glues; brittle, desiccated pieces of scrap leather and small stacks of marbled paper and wooden screw vises. To Gilrein, the altars resemble temple sites for ancient ritual sacrifice, like places he's seen in documentaries about lost cultures and mystery religions. But Wylie assured him that they were simply workstations where Brockden retreated to calm his fevered mind with lengthy sessions of bookbinding and repair.

"If that's true," Gilrein once challenged her, "his little hobby didn't quite do the trick."

"In the end," she acknowledged, "I don't think anything would have."

In retrospect, it seems to Gilrein that Wylie had some difficulty directly approaching the subject of the Brockden family's final days. But she found ways of chronically, if opaquely, alluding to it in a tone that suggested the clan's horrific demise was somehow, two hundred years after the fact, *her* fault rather than the result of a man whose brain chemistry had become so unbalanced that he committed the most grievous outrage of all.

We rely on texts to tell us the story. Often, there's nothing more to go on. And because there's no alternative, no way to look back and capture our own perception of the truth, we elevate the texts to a level they may not deserve. We venerate them with our study. We consecrate them with the never-ending touch of our saliva-wet thumb. We come, finally, to accept them as more than a representation, a version, one version, of a long-lost reality.

But there were no historians nor anthropologists, psychiatrists nor pathologists present when Edgar Brockden, exhausted from the interminable suspension over his own unique abyss, let go of his ever-weakening hold on rationality and plunged down toward a chasm, a void, toward the mouth of Satan himself. There were no objective observers available to witness the last day. No one to give testament to the progression of facts, to construct a simple time line of fanaticism, delusion, hysteria, terror, and death. And in the absence of an eyewitness, we are left with a succession of theoretical accounts, some better than others and most agreeing on a few basic suppositions, but all of them, in the end, no better than a story. Of which, this is only one more.

We know for certain that on Palm Sunday of 1798, Governor Summer was visiting in Quinsigamond. We know that Governor Summer's guest on his visit was Ambassador Peltzl, Emissary to the Court of St. Gotthard at Bratislava. We know that the Brockden family had been invited to dine with the governor and the ambassador at the Southwick Mansion. And we know that at some point that morning, Edgar Brockden announced to his clan that they would not be taking the carriage into the city to attend the dinner, but instead would celebrate "the new rites" in the family's attic chapel. Lucy, though more concerned than ever about her husband's obvious fatigue, the long nights spent in his chambers below the house, gathered the children without a word and followed the minister up the winding stairways to the top of the tower.

Upon entering the chapel, even the tykes must have been more shocked than amused to find the worship pews, which Brockden had spent weeks sanding and rubbing with oil, now lined with oozy layers of moss and mud, breeding ground for Brockden's latest generation of *vermis*. Lucy's reaction churned from disbelief to a righteous anger when she discovered the altarpiece similarly bedecked with a cover of damp topsoil and writhing with the tumultuous burrowing of countless parasitical *vermicelli*. To the fright of the little ones, she castigated her husband for this blasphemy, begged Brockden to clean up this insult to the bleeding heart of Jesus and pray for forgiveness, then ran back downstairs with Theo and Sophia.

Brockden didn't come down until nightfall. His vestments were filthy with earth, his hair matted as if he'd used the worms' habitat as a kind of pomade. But it was his face that betrayed the news that his condition had worsened rather than improved. His eyes seemed dislocated in their sockets, the muscles around them tight and trembling, the whites shot with branches of red and the pupils dilated into black wells. Lucy tried to pull off his garments, feel his skull for the fever, but he pushed her away. The children watched, holding each other and cowering under the table as their father slapped their mother brutishly across the face, bellowing, "Away from me, demon," calling his wife "King Mab," and launching into a screaming barrage of what sounded like some derivation of Latin, but could just as easily have been the nonsensical gibberish of a mind fallen beyond the community of language.

Lucy fell by the hearth and managed to grab a poker which she brandished against this raving stranger as she instructed the children to run to their rooms and block their doors. Brockden made at least one charge at her. Lucy screamed for God's mercy and stabbed her husband in the area of the groin, slightly piercing a thigh, but causing the madman to retreat into the cellar hole and crawl down among his books and curving tunnelways.

No one has a completely reasonable explanation as to why Mrs. Brockden didn't then retrieve the children, take the horses and flee into Quinsigamond for aid. There is a stodgy group of traditionalists who insist that a woman of faith could not abandon her husband in what was clearly his darkest hour. But a new generation of feminist readers has proposed the theory that it was the homestead Lucy refused to give up, that she had suffered and slaved as much as Brockden for their City of Words and wasn't about to turn it over to a delusional louse with a new enthusiasm for glossolalia and spousal abuse.

Whatever the case, she hovered between the children and the cellar hole, trying to simultaneously calm little Sophia's panic and guard against the return of the monster who resembled her once-loving husband. Brockden did not return to the house proper that night and one can only imagine the long hours Lucy spent seated before the cellar door with, perhaps, her husband's own hunting musket across her lap.

Very likely, it was sometime after dawn that she ventured down into the labyrinth. Though fear and sleeplessness turned her once-beautiful script into a nearly illegible mess, her journal entry for that day seems to describe finding Brockden before one of the bookbinding altars, his lantern long burned dry, working in the dark, attempting, by touch alone, to create a simulacrum of a book made from a combination of worm-mash and random pages from his dream journals. The fury and wrath had vanished from the man, but now he seemed, as his wife phrased it, "a ghost unto himself. He would not answer my calls, would not deem to look my way. I do not believe Edgar heard my voice fill the small space between us. Pray God he is not lost to us again."

Dozens of articles have been written concerning Lucy's use of the word "again." The majority of Brockdenites interpret the usage as a reference to Brockden's attack of the previous day. Others choose to believe something much darker about the nature of everyday life within the Brockden clan. Ultimately, we are left with two final artifacts. There is Lucy's last journal entry from the morning of Good Friday, a single cat-scratch line which reads, "He speaks again, asking us, on this darkest of days, to join him below in prayer to the Redeemer for deliverance from the house of evil."

And there are the bones of the entire Brockden family, found a full year after Lucy wrote those words.

The remains were discovered by a trio of boys who had broken into the farmhouse to explore and scavenge. In the cellar they came upon the open mouth of the labyrinth, crawled into the chambered belly of the earth, and to their horror, stumbled over the skeletal bodies of two children and two adults. Two centuries later, forensic science would be able to precisely demonstrate the hundreds of locations where Edgar Brockden's skiving knives pierced all the way through skin and muscle and fat and cartilage to strike at the bones of his wife and children.

The remains of Brockden himself were found on one of his binding altars, dead by his own hand and swaddled in mounds of the muddy silt he used to incubate his worms.

Gilrein stands in front of the altar, shining his light over the surface, not sure what he's expecting to find. He thinks again about Wylie's story of what happened down here in the book maze, the drama she conveyed about the final days of the Brockden family. And he suddenly wants out of the labyrinth. It was a stupid idea coming down here. All of the claustrophobia he had felt prior to Wylie is returning with the impact of a drowning wave.

Before he can calm himself, take some deep breaths, and reverse his direction, the panic explodes and destroys any chance of simple reason. And he starts to run, to indiscriminately turn corners and break right and left and tumble forward without thought, motivated only by fear, an insidious and primal certainty that the walls of the book maze are literally narrowing, the arched ceilings lowering toward his head and the floors elevating, forming a perfect box, an airless vault, a coffin that will continue to collapse upon itself until it suffocates and crushes its occupant.

He throws himself around corner after corner, running in a crouch, and it's as if his attempt to slow his breathing has exactly the opposite effect, causes his lungs to increase their frantic pace, the exhalations trying to overtake the need for fresh air. If he could only get air, find the path upward, break through, out of the earth. He reaches for the shelving, trying to pull his body along, the sound of his hyperventilation destroying his judgment, obliterating the memory of which path to take, of which path he's already taken.

He falls to his knees and starts to crawl, scurrying like a beetle, like a cockchafer spastically making for its burrow under the threat of an enormous shoe heel. He feels the weight of the ceiling upon his back, pressing down, somehow alive and hateful, wanting to mash him into the ground, make him one with the dirt, obliterate him, grind his flesh back into the silt from which it was made and from which it emerged.

And then he can't move at all, lies motionless on his stomach, the panic finally precluding motion, freezing him in position but for the continued heaving of his lungs inside his chest. He lies this way for an unknown passage of time, awash in the noise of his deafening suffocation, until he shifts his head slightly and sees, at the end of the corridor, the ladder that leads up to the cellar.

It takes some time to get to his feet, but once he's erect he exits the farmhouse and runs for the orchards, just wanting to stand in the openness of the outside world. When his breathing finally returns to normal, he moves to the greenhouse and sits down on the love seat, finds Ceil's notebook and pulls it up to his chest and hugs it against his body, the way you might bind yourself to a sleeping infant.

He doesn't get up again until he realizes the simple reason that Edgar Brockden decimated his family.

Brockden picked up his skiving knives and hacked his family into scrap because, in struggling to receive the divine alphabet, he came to understand the profound ineptitude of the system called language. He came to understand how this inherent, unchangeable deficiency defines each of us, traps us, imprisons us, finally reduces us to a state of absolute isolation. Keeps us forever, uniquely, agonizingly, alone. In Brockden's heart, the slaughter was likely an act of mercy.

Brockden carved his wife and children into nothingness because he could no longer speak to them. And because he came to know, with instantaneous certainty, that this kind of silence, when it descends and becomes a shroud, a cocoon that smothers every sense, is an entombment from which no one will ever awake and arise.

19

On the drive to the Visitation Diner, a news break interrupts a Wedgewood dirge to give an updated body count from a war of ethnic cleansing halfway around the globe, in a country whose name has changed three times in the past decade.

Gilrein turns the radio off. Like most people, he has the ability to sense and instantly suppress the kind of helpless, low-voltage depression that comes from living with the knowledge that actions like these take place every boring day in a variety of locales on this planet. They take place as we eat lunch and watch television, as we read generic myth-stories to our children and stand in line to cash our paychecks and sit in traffic listening to quirky, smack-addicted French-Creole singers bemoan an essential lack of communication in sorrowful, if perfect, pitch. In every moment that we're brushing our teeth or gassing up our cab or rereading Klaus Klamm for the third and, we swear, final time, people are brutalized for the simplest reason of all—because they can be. Because when someone else holds power, they can fuck you over in ways that your imagination has never even considered.

And to Gilrein, the most depressing thing of all is not the fact that these acts of mind-numbing brutality happen. Not even the fact that they happen with a regularity that diminishes them to the mundane. What goes to the core of Gilrein's understanding and mildly lacerates both his heart and his conscience is the fact that he knows, with a childlike, unimpeachable certainty, that the ability to harm someone in so profound and lasting a manner is written forever on our DNA, encoded as unconditionally as our mortality, part of the definition of the word *human*.

Most disciples of rationality would tell you the element that differentiates the human species from the beasts of the plain is not, as our superstition-chained ancestors believed, the soul, but rather the enormity of our intelligence, the capacity of our imaginations, and our ancillary ability to eventually enact those dreams, to find a technology that will allow us to physically realize whatever we can mentally envision. The complexity and speed and flexibility of our brain mechanics propelled us to the top of the animal kingdom.

But Gilrein's take on this is that very likely for every vaccine we've invented, we've concocted two poisons. For every engineering miracle that raised up new modes of transport and expanses of bridge, we've mastered hundreds of systems for the enforcement of isolation. For every method of communication we've devised, we have uncovered thousands of monstrous ways of silencing an individual tongue forever. And by virtue of birth, he shares some unmeasured part in this heinous and expanding brilliance. This is the original sin.

There have absolutely been a few rare times of stress and confusion when, more than anything else, he would have owned death like a birthright, would have moved out of the corral of the acted-upon and into the land of the controllers, where nothing is forbidden. Where the idea that power is just an unmarked gunshot away can instantly escalate to a lifelong, egomanical campaign for dominance at any cost.

But though Gilrein has known the temptation of this worldview, he has never acted on the desire. There is still a gulf between thought and action where free will can opt for either compassion or cruelty. And staying on the right side of that chasm is what separates him from Kroger and Kinsky and the Magicians and all of the neighborhood mayors who believe that imposing their will, their vision of the city and the world beyond, is not only a right, but a destiny.

He swings into a parking space outside the Visitation, gets out of the cab, and is besieged by a half-dozen of the tinker kids dressed in their filthy rags and holding out their scavenged aluminum soup cans for alms. Gilrein reaches around for his wallet, catches the hand of a tiny pickpocket and pushes it away. He pulls out half his cash, divides the rest among the begging children, trying and failing for equal distribution as two of the oldest and fastest among the gang make off with the bulk of his offering. One urchin who comes up empty curses the cabdriver in an unknown language and spits on the door of the Checker.

Gilrein shoves through the line of pilgrims in the entryway, edges by Father Clement as the Jesuit yells, "There is still time, young man," and starts to head for the hacks' booth, but, surprisingly, nobody's there, so he slides onto a stool at the very end of the counter and waves to one of the new waitresses for a mug.

"I haven't seen you in a dog's life."

Gilrein looks next to him to see a guy in an EMT uniform finishing a bowl of chili.

"Shaughnessy," Gilrein remembers. "What the hell are you doing here?"

"We got a call. Turned out to be a headcase. I let Hirsch handle it. He's got a thing for the night nurses up at the 'l'oth."

"And you just had to stay for the chili?"

"Listen, Huie's tomatoes are blessed by the Sisters of Torment and Agony. You can't go wrong."

"And you have access to a stomach pump just in case."

Shaughnessy is about the same age as Gilrein. His mother used to run a rooming house downtown. He's been working the city ambulances at least since Gilrein was on the force. Over the years, they've shared coffee at countless crime and accident scenes, leaning against cruiser and wagon, usually at three A.M., swapping jokes and Bangkok news while a photographer immortalized the victims of car crashes, gang spats, tenement fires, and once even a commuter plane that came down unexpectedly, nose first, into a Little League field. Gilrein always found him pleasant momentary company, a lot less surly than some of the paramedics.

"You believe this place?" Shaughnessy says. "I read about it in the paper. You know, the priest and his followers there. I had to see it myself."

"So what do you think?" Gilrein asks.

"I think Tang's raking it in hand over fist. But how long can it last?"

"Not very. Father Clement is telling the faithful the whole show is over by the weekend."

Shaughnessy reaches for a napkin and raises his eyebrows for clarification.

"The apocalypse," Gilrein says. "You know, the rapture, the last days."

Shaughnessy laughs, wiping his chin. "Shit," he says, "the end is coming and I got two weeks' vacation I didn't use?"

Gilrein nods and says, "How'd you and Hirsch know who was the nutcase in here?"

Shaughnessy shakes his head and looks toward Father Clement standing up in his booth, answering a question from one of his apostles—something about a woman clothed with the sun.

"This is nothing," he says. "We had to mace and cuff the old bastard we pulled out of here. Guy went after the preacher with a knife. Tang was scared he might break a window. Don't you love Huie?"

"A man with priorities."

Shaughnessy pushes his bowl to the inner edge of the counter and lets out a deep breath.

"What the Christ happened to this city, Gilrein?"

Gilrein takes it as a rhetorical question and tries to hear some of Father Clement's diatribe.

"You miss the job at all?" Shaughnessy asks.

Gilrein shakes his head, takes a drink of coffee.

"I hear you're driving a hack now. What fleet?"

"I'm an indie," Gilrein says. "The medallion belonged to my old man."

Shaughnessy shifts his weight on the stool, starts to dig in his pocket for money.

"You ever see any of the guys?" he asks.

"Not too often," Gilrein says. "I'm not big on the donut joints."

Instead of laughing, Shaughnessy says, "I saw Oster and Danny Walden the other night."

And Gilrein freezes in midsip, lowers the mug and swivels to face the ambulance driver.

"That right?" he says, trying for casual and having no idea if he's succeeding. "Where'd you bump into them?"

"We pulled a stiff out of Gompers. Looked like a mob whack. Some broker from down San Remo Ave."

Father Clement is holding a Bible out at his audience like a gun, ranting about "twelve thousand from the tribe of Reuben."

"How come you rolled on it instead of coroner's?" Gilrein asks. "That's against the rules."

Shaughnessy gives him a look like one of them is joking.

He says, "How many times have we hauled stiffs for those dicks? Jesus, Gilrein, you got a short memory. Those guys hate outdoor work. Besides, this was a small fish. Oster called him the 'Shank. He fenced under Pecci protection. You must've kicked his ass a few times back in bunko."

Gilrein stares at him, finally manages to say, "That was a long time ago, Shaughno. I can't remember every fence I slapped."

"Isn't that the goddamn truth."

"And the voice said," Father Clement yells, at the top of his lungs and seemingly in Gilrein's direction, "seal up what the seven thunders have said and do not write it down."

Huie Tang slides in through the swinging doors of the supply room, dressed in a beautifully tailored Armani suit with show hanky in the breast pocket, looking like he's just granted a fat loan, at an exorbitant rate, to a Third World nation. He hammers open the register with the palm of his hand, slides out the bulging cash drawer and inserts a fresh one, then disappears back into the storage room with the newfound grace of a professional dancer.

"If the guy could postpone the apocalypse," Shaughnessy says, "he might start giving his cousin Jimmy a run for Little Asia."

"If the guy could postpone the apocalypse," Gilrein responds, still staring purposefully at Father Clement, "what the hell would he need with Little Asia?"

Shaughnessy says, "Amen, my friend," and slides off his stool. He starts to zip up his leather jacket and says, "It was good seeing you, Gilrein. Hope we bump into each other again."

"Well, Shaughno, it's a small town."

Shaughnessy claps him on the back and heads for the door, stepping over Father C's attendants sprawled in the aisle. Gilrein drains his coffee, wishing he hadn't come to the diner. Before he can even start to replay the conversation with the ambulance driver, Huie Tang pushes back into the galley, now wearing a camel-hair topcoat with a hefty-looking bank bag in the pocket. This time he sees Gilrein and makes his way to the end of the counter, looking a little agitated.

"Bank's closed this time of night," Gilrein says.

"Not the bank I go to," Tang answers, then adds, "Listen, your friends left a message for you," and Gilrein bucks at the word *friends*, not at all sure Huie is referring to the other hacks.

"We had an incident in here earlier," Tang explains while hand-signaling one of his girls to clear a just-vacated booth.

"I heard," Gilrein says. "The EMT told me one of the Jesuit's flunkies went crazy."

Huie shakes his head.

"It wasn't one of the priest's. It was one of your own. Mr. Langer."

Gilrein leans forward and says, "What are you talking about?"

"Jocasta said to tell you he was taken to the Toth Clinic. That you should go up there as soon as you can. She tried to call you—"

"What happened to Otto?"

Tang shakes his head to show his ignorance.

"He'd just come in from a fare. He was sitting in the usual booth. He ordered a cinnamon bun, was listening to the priest with the others. Then he just went crazy. Jumped up and knocked everything off the table. Grabbed some flatware off the floor and charged at the Father. Miss Duval jumped on him before anything happened, but she couldn't calm him down."

Gilrein slides off the stool and says, "Where is Jo now?"

"She went with him in the ambulance. They had to strap the madman down."

Gilrein heads for the exit, stepping on the hands of several of the faithful, whose howls can't distract the priest from his oratory. But as Gilrein pushes open the door of the diner, Huie Tang manages to make himself heard, yelling, "Who's going to pay for this coffee?"

20

The envelope is held out by one of
the tinker children, a young boy, maybe seven, eight years old, filthy
and with sores all over the face from where he's picked at insect
bites. He's sitting cross-legged on the hood of the Checker. Gilrein
passes the child a five-dollar bill slowly, without any jarring moves.
The boy grabs the bill at the same moment he releases the letter and
then jumps off the cab and runs around the back of the diner.

Gilrein slides a finger under the seal of the envelope, pulls out
a sheaf of pages, unfolds them, and reads:

> Langer, the Coward of Maisel
> c/o Booth One
> Independent Cabdrivers' Collective
> Tang's Visitation Diner
> City

Gilrein, the (Faux) Exile of Quinsigamond
c/o Sanctuary, Ltd.
Brockden Farm
City

The Midnight Hour

My Dear Gilrein:

This is the testament of a survivor. I use these particular
words after much deliberation. *Testament. Survivor.* I use
them for my purposes and I use them understanding,
from the beginning, that my purposes may not be your
purposes.

   Shall I tell you a secret—excuse me, I was about to write
"my friend." A force of habit. Do you understand? What
you would call a phraseology. We are not friends, Gilrein.
This is my first confession of the night. Confession, that
is from your tradition. You Catholics. You clear your soul
with each trip to the box, with each transaction. Penance
for absolution. Where I come from there is nothing so
convenient.

   Do you know the story of the Italian Jew? The poet
from Turin? What was the name? Malaban? Something
like this. It was in all the papers several years ago. Even
here, in this bastion of reclusiveness. Only an inch of
print on page twenty-two. Off the international wire. But
you must have seen it. He was a writer of some renown.
Had survived the ordeal at Auschwitz. Spared, apparently, when the Nazis learned of his training as a
chemist. And then, forty years later, he chose to throw
himself down the stairway of the home in which he had
grown up. The general explanation was that he could no
longer tolerate the guilt. The shame of the survivor. The
remorse of the living. It's a sad story, yes, Gilrein? You
would agree? It points out the difference between the
real exile and the imposter. You young men who think
that because you can renounce the state and the church
and the family ties that bind your freedom, you think that
because you can throw off these manacles of history and
conscience and love you are instantly a deportee. The

despised outcast. The hated beast pushed from the village, stones and rotten fruit pelting off his back as he
runs into the serpent's forest.

You know nothing.

And your arrogance is an insult to the true outcast.
You brooding romantics are more dangerous than the
fascists in some ways. Can you even understand what
words like mine mean in a world this hateful and cor-
rupt, this confused as to the real and the illusory? TES-
TAMENT. SURVIVOR. The burden is inescapable. And
unbearable.

You thought we were comrades in our great struggle
against the corporate monsters, yes? You thought we
would fight together, you and I and Miss Jocasta. The last
of the independents. That we were a collective David who
could bring down the Red and Black Goliaths. So pathetic
I do not know whether to laugh or vomit. You lover of stories.

At the Cabaret, I asked the audience a question. Do you
remember, Mister Exile? I asked if anyone present could
submit to the same kind of trial that the girl, Alicia, forced
herself through. I tried to look out at the faces in the
crowd, but with the spotlight, well, you can imagine my
difficulty. So I could only answer for myself.

I could not submit to the test Alicia willingly took.

And I did not.

Do I anticipate you? Are you already asking yourself—
how does he know all that he knows? It is a perceptive
question for a cabdriver. If the girl was the only witness,
how can Langer know these details?

Perhaps I am making the whole thing up. Isn't that the
easiest answer? In any event, you will have to bear with
me, Gilrein. This is the price one must pay for being on
the receiving end of the story. There is profit and loss in
each transaction. And I am forced, by my experience, by

my view of the world at this advanced age, to label storytelling—what others might call an art—simply another
transaction. I would allow that it is a purchase and sale
steeped in tradition, in history, and birthed in the bloody
membrane of our collective, superstitious unconscious.
But it is still NOTHING more than a covenant. Between
the one who has the specific words. And the one who does
not.

Can you guess which category you fall into, Mister
Gilrein?

Are you beginning, finally, to see why I hate you so
much? Can you imagine all those nights I spent at that
miserable table at Tang's Diner, looking across at you, the
loss of your precious wife always barely, badly, concealed
just beneath the skin of your forehead. Like a tumor. A
growth. A parasite that I could see bulging against the
enclosure of your skull, the prison of your bone and flesh.
All your small talk, detailing night after night the fares
that rode in the back of your father's Checker—it will
never be yours, Gilrein—the supposedly funny stories.
The allegedly petty outrages of backseat couplings and
forgotten tips. As you gulped down one more cup of coffee. And all the time the memory of that woman—the wife
you buried along with your meaning—pulsed like the
third eye in the center of your pathetic face. Such a mundane, pitiful Cyclops you made.

And such a horrible and perfect mirror.

No glass could be more polished and true. I hated you
because I saw myself each time I looked in your direction.
Did you ever bother to see the tumor fighting to explode
from my own head? Even now, I would bet my cab that you
have no idea what I am talking about. How did you ever
last on the police force, Gilrein? What does this say about
our city that you not only wore the uniform, but were promoted?

Jocasta always wanted to hear the stories from your days working bunko. Such a funny term, "bunko." And such an inappropriate place for one like you, cabdriver. As if Gilrein could determine the true from the false. As if this taxi-boy could ever, with all the time in this godless universe, find a way to separate, truly and surely, the real from the illusory.

Reach out to the mirror, Gilrein, and take this cup. I move it now from my hands to yours. This is part of your tradition, not mine. I was an Old Testament Jew. You are the New Testament fool. Turn the cheek and drink the sweet wine, taxi-boy. One more transaction you engage in without knowing the value of the goods involved.

Drink deeply.

Alicia kept her eyes open in a way you or I could never manage. She stayed behind the window and she never blinked while below her, they not only killed every single man and woman and child in Schiller Avenue, but insisted on erasing any trace of the Ezzenes' existence. The soldiers actually grew tired from watching the Obliterator, had to work in shifts, take breaks, sit on the ground and smoke cigarettes, call out and point to a specific figure within the mass convulsion, a toddler in blind panic struggling to find its swallowed mother. Critique each course of the machine's endless buffet. And Alicia watched from the attic window, helpless, and let herself be bombarded by images that were instantly transforming her into something else. A horrible and irreversible transformation. She did not blink.

And then, for three days she managed to stay hidden and awake. She gathered together every loose scrap of paper she could find in the attic. She took the pens and pencils from the soup can on her checkout desk and she began to write. She wrote as quickly as her hand could form the symbols on the page. She ignored the muscle

cramp that, toward the end, would cause permanent damage to certain nerves near the base of the wrist and bring
her final pages to the brink of illegibility. But she never
crossed the line into illegibility. Every word, no matter
how smeared and sloppy, proved legible. Completely
readable. You must believe me on this point. Or, depending on the stage of our transaction at this time, you may be
able to look for yourself. But I do not advise this. Remember that you have been warned. Like Lot's wife.

Alicia found words to tell the story of the Erasure.

Now understand, and this may be the most important
thing I have to tell you, Gilrein, she did not write down the
facts. She did not transcribe what she saw through the
window of the library. She did not relate, in words, the
events that took place in Schiller Avenue on that humid
night in July. She did not make a diary nor a journal. She
did not engage in reportage. She wrote, instead, what we
might agree to call a fiction. She told a story. Created a
myth. She transformed what she had seen in the same way
that she had been transformed by what she had seen. If I
had anyone else to rely on, I would. But I have only you—
this New World/New Testament reflection of my own self-
loathing. You MUST understand this, Gilrein. What the
girl wrote was something so far beyond accounting.
Beyond simple journalism. She made her witnessing into
a horrible art. She made a weapon of her epiphany and
her transmutation. She created an evolutionary virus out
of ink and paper. She put air into a trumpet that could
shatter each frozen soul to hear its agonizing music.

I do not mean to be poetic. Poetry is the last thing I
mean to give you. I do not want you to look for multiple
levels of meaning.

I'm lying, Gilrein. Of course I want you to search
between the lines. Of course I do. No act of transcription
is innocent.

And neither is Alicia's Testament. It is a necessary slap
in the form of a story. I realize, as you must, that it is too
late for me. And I have every reason to believe it is also too
late for you. You are already a ghost. You seem one of those
transient spirits that cannot exist in the material world,
yet neither can he find a way into the other world.

The other world. As if such a thing could exist. As if all
the Edens of all our dreams could be anything but a myth
we create to numb the crushing banality of our own
viciousness. As if there were an alternative to the truth
that the whole teeming lot of us is just no damn good.

If you buck against my last statement, then perhaps
there is a hope for you that I have been unable to see. If
you think the existence of Alicia's Testament matters in
the end, then perhaps you are not the perfect mirror I
have imagined you to be. Whatever the case, it is in your
hands now. It feels like a corpse and it smells like
vinegar.

At the end of the third day, Alicia collapsed into sleep.
The pen was still clutched in her hand. The hand was
stained a deep blue. The muscles beneath the skin of the
writing hand were wrenched past cramp and into a kind of
nerve-damaged twitch, jerking and lurching at the end of
the girl's arm, as if manipulated by strings from some
unseen dimension. Even in this kind of comalike sleep,
born of shock-trauma, while the rest of the body lay
prone, the hand continued to move, locked in a loop of its
own particular dream. It played and replayed a Sisyphean
nightmare where it endlessly formed a bottomless well of
blood into signs and symbols and ideograms comprised of
lines and loops and crosses and curves, and though the
hand knew instinctually how to construct these charac-
ters, it could never find illumination as to their meaning,
what the ink lines on the page represented in the scheme
of some other, hidden world.

This is how the Censor's men found her. Teams had
been moving from building to building, stripping anything of value for the State Treasury and dousing what
remained with a generous bath of gasoline. Meyrink had
set his most trusted stooges to secure the attic library of
the Levi and word was given that nothing was to be
touched until the Chief Expurgator himself arrived on the
scene.

When he climbed the stairs and, near the top floor,
came to smell that unmistakable redolence of old paper,
worn and slightly musty pages, beaten leather, that unique
variety of slightly acrid perfume that incenses a room long
filled with used books, the Censor of Maisel stopped and
let it wash over him and felt the excitement of the
addicted in the abundant presence of their opiate. He
stood outside the doorway, eyes closed, the sound of his
nose in full exertion alerting the soldiers within of his
approach. When he stepped through the library entrance
and found his men circled like fascist dwarfs around
Snow White, his anticipatory delight was transformed
instantly from the anarchistic desire of the looter into the
anal responsibility of the authoritarian.

"What in the world do we have here?" he asked the
room in general.

And his youngest attendant, a boy we now believe was
named Moltke, innocently replied, "A survivor, sir."

He gave the boy a look more withering than satisfied
and asked, "How did this happen? I was told every room
was searched."

This time Moltke stayed silent and kept his eyes on the
sleeping body and it was up to another to volunteer, "She
must have been hiding, sir."

But Meyrink wasn't listening. He had spotted the
scraps of paper spread around Alicia and was stooping to
pick up a random sheet. Now, Gilrein, I have gone back

and forth as to whether I am thankful that I will never
know what went through Meyrink's mind in the seconds
that he read some chance run of words from Alicia's Testament or whether, in fact, I am hopelessly regretful that
his thoughts will always be lost to me. I have felt both
ways. There have been days when I remember the warning
of greater minds than my own never to look too long nor
too deeply into the face of a monster. Yet, of course, other
giants of cogitation have insisted that only by inhabiting
the mind of the beast can we demythologize him and deal
with him on our own, earthly terms. It is a debate that you,
too, will soon have to engage in, I would think. But,
though you may or may not wish to follow my lead, I have
finally decided that, in the absence of ever truly knowing
what the Censor thought and felt upon discovering Alicia,
and more important, discovering her gospel, I will imagine what seems most likely.

And I think that Meyrink loved what he found on the
floor. I think he was thrilled with the manner in which his
words and deeds had been elevated to STORY. I believe he
was moved and honored and exhilarated by the idea that
the banal reality of the Erasure had already, almost
instantly, been mutated into a kind of legend, a myth that
made use of all the essential elements—life and death and
language and hatred and power. And within this new
myth, he, Meyrink, the Censor of Maisel, was pulled along
by the force of the story and carried, somehow, to its center, its igniting spark, the initial word that provoked all
that came next. I think Meyrink held a piece of Alicia's
credo between his hands, fingers taut in the margins of
the paper, and I think he was stunned by this new, epiph-
anizing fable of what had been a bloody detail handed to a
faceless bureaucrat. A moment before his mission was set
into motion, Meyrink had been just one more Vice Chancellor of Expurgation occupying a cubicle office in the

basement of the Ministry of Propaganda, Division of Official Indexing, Bureau of Standards and Decorum. And by the end of his chore, once every voice in the Schiller had been silenced, every eye permanently closed, he had been made into a monster of historic proportions, the kind of icon that is needed, every so often, to give the masses a ready, easily accessible definition of undiluted evil.

I think he could have bent down and kissed Alicia. I think he wanted, more than anything else that he'd discovered this far into his small life, to become the prince of eternal darkness in the dreams of the unconscious beauty at his feet.

He got on his knees and began to gather all the disparate papers together, attempting to shuffle them into some kind of order. At one point one of his men tried to bend down and help and the Censor screamed for the soldier to come to attention. He wanted no hands but his own to come in contact with the manuscript. Every few pages that he collected, he would stop for just a second and read a line or two from the topmost sheet, then, flushed and making a slight grunting noise, he would go back to his hunt. When he had found all the pages and double-checked under books and produce crates that there were no stray leaves, he sat on the floor and lay the stack of writing in his lap. There was suddenly a very antsy and nervous air about him, something that combined with his fatigue and exhaustion from working without sleep for too long. He put one hand flat on the manuscript, reached his other into the pocket of his jacket and withdrew a set of keys, which he tossed through the air to Moltke. Then he quietly addressed his men, in a tone that was more request than order, instructing them to wrap the girl in a blanket and take her to his home.

Moltke began to protest with a reminder of the final paragraph in the Orders of Erasure, but the Censor silenced his underling with a hand on the shoulder.

A deputy named Varnbuler quietly, perhaps even chal-
lengingly, asked, "Don't you mean that we should take the
prisoner to your office?"

Meyrink met his stare and even from a sitting position,
willed it down.

"That is not what I said. And that is not what I meant."

No one spoke. Meyrink walked to a bed and stripped it
of a blanket. Alicia stirred momentarily as they rolled her
in it, and then without any further instructions they lifted
her under their arms like a battering ram and exited the
library.

Meyrink sat in the center of the attic and slowly,
methodically began to collate the manuscript into its logical sequence. This accomplished, he began at page one
and read to the end, through the sections where Alicia's
handwriting changes from her normal flowing scroll to a
combined printing and writing and finally into a chaotic
mess of abbreviations, unique shorthand, dropped vow-
els, letters slanting up and down the page, sentences running in counterclockwise circles around the block of main
text, cross-outs, splotches of spilled ink, grievous mis-
spellings, a complete lack of punctuation, and grammar
made eccentric to the brink of unintelligibility.

He read it all and found himself excited to the point of
physical manifestation. He felt empowered in a profound
and virginal way. Alicia had single-handedly rewritten an
image of himself that he had been unable to create in his
entire glacial lifetime. With her eyes and ears and pen, the
sleeping girl had erased everything about the Censor's life
that had come before and forged his entire being anew.

I am forced to confess, my hand grows tired. An honest
man can find the nerve to admit anything.

Do you know what I think insomnia is, my independent
brother? I believe it is a terror so profound that the body

would rather decay, would rather cave in upon itself from exhaustion, than ride one more time into the dreams of the demon.

Do you know what I think a migraine is, Gilrein? I think it is the weight of the victims, the corpses, the bones of the despised, pushing, more pressure each night, upon the skull of the survivor.

Do you know of an antidote for these exquisite trials, taxi-boy? You give it some thought. Perhaps you can help me when we meet again, my twin. In the meantime, I have to silence another old man making promises that can't possibly be kept.

Culpably yours,
Otto Langer

21

Halfway to the Toth Care Facility,
the sound of Imogene Wedgewood insinuating the ballad "Whim-
perative" is interrupted by a staticky bleat from the dispatch radio.
Gilrein grabs the microphone and asks, "Mojo, is that you?"

But instead of an answer comes a muffled voice that may or
may not belong to Bettman the dispatcher.

"Pickup at Gompers Station. Will you respond?"

Gilrein adjusts the squelch, thumbs the mike, and asks,
"Mojo?"

There's a wait of several seconds and then, through even more
static, the voice says, "Fare's name is Brown. Will you respond?"

The cab rolls to the side of the road. Gilrein sits and stares at
the radio, thumbs the mike again, and asks, "Who is this,
please?"

But there's no reply. So, before he can think too much, he
makes a U-turn into a stream of traffic and reverses direction.

He bangs up the curbing and rolls over ash and gravel around the
back of the train station. Gompers has been closed down for

dozens of years and the elements and nonstop vandalism have taken their toll on what was at one time possibly the most beautiful building in the city. These days Gompers is a burned-out shell of marble and granite that serves as communal crib to a transient junkie population as well as a notorious stock exchange for a brand of transactions that will never be reported to the SEC.

The chamber of the .38 is fully loaded and Gilrein sticks it in his jacket pocket, locks up the taxi, and heads for a new entrance that someone has spent a lot of time hacking into the stonework of the south wall. If what's waiting inside is an ambush, the attackers have made an innocent but possibly crucial mistake. For a few years, Gilrein attended a decrepit Catholic grammar school a block from here, an ancient chunk of red brick crammed between a meat-packing distributor and a tiny used-auto lot. To get to and from his bus each day, Gilrein took a shortcut through Gompers, eventually using the extra time this bought to explore the already abandoned rail house. He probed the mysteries of this arc with the bottomless curiosity and expectation of a hyper-dreamy twelve-year-old, always semiterrified of what lay in the shadows of every new tunnelway but unable to walk away with his curiosity unsated.

It was a stupid hobby and a part of him knew it at the time. Some of the Gompers tracks were already being used for the freight lines and there was a known history of more than one rail wanderer losing life and/or limb to four hundred thousand pounds of diesel-driven iron thrown down a track bed at ninety miles an hour. But that might have been part of the allure.

In any event, Gilrein never feared being crushed by the trains as much as he worried about stumbling upon a lair of one of the Gompers tribes, of whom the last-stop drunks who slept with rail-spiked truncheons in their arms were the most serene. Gompers's endless pockets of always shrouded chambers and vaults, utility rooms and lower-level crevices, underground cellars and balcony dining coves offered a wide selection of housing choices for the city's disassociated. In his years as a cop, Gilrein didn't

venture into Gompers territory very often. The station was the
stomping ground for a very specific breed of security. You had to
submit to a fairly grueling psych profile just to apply for metro-
transit. And nobody could tell whether you needed to flunk or
pass the aptitude exams in order to draw assignment. Once in
transit blues, you didn't much associate with the general street
humps. Transit policing was a world unto itself. The rail-yard
gestapo drew its mission and its clout from a different well than
the city's generic force. They were a small and tight-knit outfit.
They ran by their own regs, operated with an autonomy that Chief
Bendix could only envy from afar. The watchword among the train
bulls was *keep your mouth shut*. The fact was that the majority of
transit cops would love nothing better than to spend a single
night scaring the bejesus out of the most street-jaded reporter
The Spy could provide. But the unquestioned word from above—
an amorphous cloud of authority that comprised some conglomerate of the transit commissioner's office, the chamber of
commerce, and an uneasy alignment of rival freight companies—
was that Gompers rumors stayed rumors. No matter what. No one
was more tight-lipped than the cinder bulls about the horrors
they uncovered on a nightly basis. They carried enough hardware
into the tunnels to make the SWAT humps jealous and they never
went anywhere inside the station without full backup, three cops
to a team, and each one knowing that if a pile of rubble suddenly
turned animate, made a run at you instead of away from you, you
emptied the chamber of your Magnum without pausing to yell a
warning. And you didn't bother to question the nature of the rubble until coffee was served at shift's end.

The city's pols had wanted to tear the train station down for
decades, but had been thwarted by federal courts on behalf of a
well-endowed historical society. Even this blue-blood enclave,
however, couldn't lay out the kind of funds needed to restore the
station into anything resembling its former grandeur. Officially,
the mayor's office allowed that, from time to time, an occasional
outpatient from Toth Care might mistakenly wander into Gom-

pers and set up housekeeping for a few hours until discovered and tenderly returned to the Thorazine comfort of their halfway house. No one believed this fairy tale for a second and it may have done more harm than good for the mayor's always dicey reputation for shrouding the truth like a week-old corpse. As if in reaction to this PR fable, the hearsay regarding what actually dwelled in the bowels of Gompers grew to Homeric proportions. Everyone had their favorite monster story—the packs of salivating baby killers who had squatter's rights in the shafts of track 29, the cannibal immigrants of unknown origin who slept in the shadows of the former dining pavilion feasting on rat and wild dog between visits from unsuspecting tourists, the local satanists who celebrated their black masses with orgies and virginal sacrifices in the old porters' locker rooms of the north wing.

As a child, Gilrein never experienced personal contact with any of these supposed denizens of the station, but he did witness a smattering of physical evidence—pentagrams painted on the tile floors of changing rooms and once a pile of unspecified bones next to an old campfire. Mainly he skirted mean drunks and bewildered junkies and a lot of insane and homeless people speaking in languages foreign to everyone but themselves. However, that was over twenty years ago, and if Gompers's devolution even parallels that of the city in general, then it's more than possible, it's pathetically likely, that the majority of train-house rumors are not only true, but just the tip of a heinously cold iceberg.

Gilrein gets down on his knees and crawls inside the station. He can't bring himself to believe that Wylie will be waiting for him within, but he's confident that he knows the layout of Gompers at least as well as any nonresident. And it's likely he knows it better than anyone who might have come to whack him. His first thought is to get up into one of the old smokers' balconies that rim the western face of the building, hanging high, marbled clouds where, a hundred years ago, rich Yankee manufacturers could bathe their lungs in the sweet carcinogens of Europe's best cigars and look down over the rushing ant heap of travelers below and never question for a second whether they were genuinely entitled to the fat bounty of God's grace.

Once secured in a balcony, Gilrein can protect his back and get an overview of the three most likely entrances. The holes in the ceiling will expose him to a cover of moonlight, but that's just as much of a drawback to the opposition and there's nothing to be done about it anyway. His guess is they'll bring at least two shooters, possibly three, and they may decide to separate, find opposing points of vantage and catch the mark in a crossfire. Meatboys like Raban and Blumfeld always want to reduce the odds to a minimum. They'd kill you in your mother's womb if it were possible. At the same time, they yearn to find some margin for the satisfaction of their own sadistic fetishes. They'd love to see the mark twist and shout with new innovations of senseless cruelty, but not if it risks botching the job and drawing the wrath of their handler. Creatures like Oster and his Magicians, on the other hand, are less easy to chart. Their motivations are multiple and sometimes conflicting. They will tell you that at the top of their needs is a profit-driven incentive and an inner motivation to do a job well. Sort of a capitalist/marine ethic. And yet, freelancers like Oster and his boys can't be profiled this easily. There is the issue of their steadfast bachelorhood and their insistent, at times ridiculous machismo posing. There is the confused if passionate amalgam of various nihilistic philosophies, half-digested but completely enactable. And there is a simple and primal bloodlust, the controlled frenzy of an overly trained bloodhound, drives without need of analysis, an uncomplicated desire to put an end to another life and thus manifest a self-evident and absolute power over it. Oster and his creatures enjoy owning death. It's a drug on the level of money and orgasm and belief. It's the epicenter of free will and self-determination. Owning death is God's own impulse, and once it's rolled through the veins of someone like Oster, there's no bringing him back to human. You've got to kill the monster. Burn the body. Salt the ground where it fell.

There's a rapping sound that echoes, metal against denser metal. An even, rhythmic noise, neither too fast nor too slow, a measured beat of metronomic intervals. Gilrein concentrates, decides that it's coming from track 7 and sights in on the mouth of the tunnel. It could be a decoy to turn him in a vulnerable position, but it feels like the real thing. The echo draws nearer. He lifts his gun, works on his breathing.

And a figure emerges from the tunnel, small, possibly a child. It's walking in the rail bed itself, hunched over and using a cane of some kind, tapping the cane against the rail. It's wrapped in a black shawl that both covers the shoulder and weaves into a turbanlike veil over the head. Gilrein gets a bead on the head, tenses to fire, and yells, "Don't take another step."

The figure obeys, comes to a standstill, as if expecting exactly this command.

"Move your hands where I can see them," Gilrein yells, and the figure again complies, stretching the arms out at its sides, parallel with the ground.

Keeping the gun sighted, Gilrein surveys the rest of the chamber and sees nothing. He makes his way down to the main station floor, weapon extended the whole way, until he comes to stand before the veiled child. He lowers the gun, takes hold of one end of the shawl and unwraps it until he's staring into the face of Mrs. Bloch. The blind woman. Oster's tattoo artist from the Houdini Lounge. And Kroger's indentured nanny to all the child artists.

She positions her face as if staring back at him, as if offering up a peeved and challenging expression. But there are the two thick and discolored folds of skin where her eyes should be and the sight of these flaps, these pancake tumors, launches a tremor through Gilrein's body, a quake centered in his stomach, but extending down to his groin.

He tries to think of something to say, but before he can speak, Mrs. Bloch opens her mouth and, in that deep, clipped, guttural, Eastern European accent, she asks, "Ahr du der reeda?"

He's so taken aback, both by the question and the sound of her voice, somehow both ghostly and deeply authoritarian, that he says nothing.

She asks in a louder voice.

"Ahr du der reeda?" the noise of her harsh, croaking words booming through the cavern of the train station as if amplified in far-off corners by some hidden web of microphones and speakers.

Unsure of what to say, but feeling prodded to say something, as if his silence could be an irreversible mistake, Gilrein mutters, "Yes."

Mrs. Bloch turns her head into a shaft of moonlight that cuts across her left ear. And taking this as a sign to repeat himself and speak up, Gilrein says, "Yes, I'm the reader."

Mrs. Bloch doesn't seem to recognize his voice, or if she does she allows no indication of recognition. She steps in close, reaches up, and starts to run her fingers over his face. Then she abruptly stops and nods, reaching into the folds of her ragged trench coat and pulling out a crumpled brown paper bag.

"Dis," she says, "ist fur du."

She places the bag on the ground at his feet, then turns and starts to walk back to the track 7 tunnel, finding the rail with her cane, which, Gilrein sees now, is just a length of lead pipe, and starting a new run of methodically paced clanging.

He waits until she completely dissolves into the shadows, pockets his gun, squats down, and lifts up the bag. He begins to open it and instantly stops himself. This, he knows, is the package. This is the item that Leo Tani died over. This is the book that has caused his beatings, caused his lips to be sewn together. Caused Wylie to betray him. Gilrein has spent the last twenty-four hours trying to convince everyone he's come in contact with that he has no knowledge of this volume. And now, the only thing he can think of is the fastest way out of the station.

He tucks the bag under his arm and runs for the crevice that exits into the rear yard. He tries to ignore what he thinks is the sound of hushed speech from every shadowed notch that he passes. When he reaches the Checker, he pops the trunk and reaches inside, shoves his father's wooden tool chest to the side, finds a pile of oil rags, and selects the largest. He wraps the paper bag inside the rag, then hides it in the hollow beneath the spare tire.

He climbs behind the wheel of the cab, loads the key into the ignition, cranks over the engine, and looks out the windshield to notice, near the roof of Gompers, positioned against one of the half-toppled Ionic columns that rims a section of balcony, what looks to be a child, staring back down at him, hunched over itself, looking feral and skittish even from this distance. Gilrein leans over to the passenger seat to get a better view, but the child vanishes back into the interior of the train station. One more ephemeral tenant of the city's expansive black holes.

22

Wylie climbs out of the red cab, hands money through the front window, ridiculously overtipping the driver. And this after the initial bribe that convinced the fleet-boy to ignore the company regs and take her into Bangkok Park. But he went all the way to the edge of the Vacuum, and for a corporate weasel that's as close to bravery as you're going to get.

Heronvolk Road is deserted, as usual, but tonight the street has somehow managed to outdo itself and evoke an even more desolate atmosphere than is the norm. It's as if the Vacuum in general and Heronvolk in particular were a setting from one of the pirated comic books that Kroger markets, one of those ultra-noir *bandes dessinées* in which doomed schlemiels wander through urban wastelands attempting to impose concepts of logic and ethicality in a hostile place where those ideas no longer have any meaning. And maybe never did.

It's not just the decay, the adamantly worn-out and broken-down milieu that permeates every surface here. Not just the tangible evidence of violence and poverty and isolation, the fire-destroyed buildings or the gutters filled with putrefaction. It's the ethereal sense of omnipresent absurdity, a feeling that there is something in the air itself, some single, guiding impulse that makes the organic want to recede and die, something chronically seeping into one's pores that makes every living organism genetically incapable of hope. This is an environment that radiates its dwellers with the purest nihilism, mutates its inhabitants until they are infertile in the crucial area of faith, barren of any trace, of any type, of belief. The Vacuum is where one comes not to dread annihilation but rather to embrace it like a redeeming lover. And this kind of world will always make people despise themselves just as much as, if not more than, the landscape that perpetually defiles them.

Wylie Brown knows, as she approaches her place of recent employment, that she might always hate herself just a little for coming to work here, for being August Kroger's flunky. For succumbing to the cheap and relentless addiction to the text. The unfortunate are born screwed in this kind of cesspool, but Wylie willed herself into a toxic resident. Made a conscious choice to move here. So how do you forgive a betrayal that turns you into the most cynical monster of all, the breed that can always successfully lie to itself and then take pleasure in the deception?

She stands across the street from the Bardo and looks up at the building, trying to get a fix on how it stays upright, how it prevents itself from cascading earthward into a pile of broken masonry, what ugly architectural magic keeps the mill ensconced on the block while looking every second as if it were about to dissolve into fallen chaos.

As she studies the structure for a clue to its logic, she becomes aware of someone approaching from the opposite end of Heronvolk, a child or a dwarf hobbling slowly forward with a limp, swinging a cane or walking stick as if parting a crowd.

At first, the figure gives no indication that it sees her. Then it begins to move toward Wylie, speed and cadence never changing. And halfway across the street, Wylie realizes it's Kroger's foreperson, the manager of the labor force, the woman August refers to only as *the hag*, but whose name is actually Mrs. Bloch.

Mrs. Bloch comes to a stop directly in front of Wylie, leans forward until their faces are uncomfortably close, the patties of tough skin sealing in Mrs. B's eyes almost grazing Wylie's cheek. They have never spoken before, though Wylie has seen the old woman several times in the corridors. And there was one awkward occasion when they shared the freight elevator, rode up to the penthouse together, both silent through the trip, Wylie pretending to study the cartoon forgeries on the cage walls, Mrs. Bloch imitating the sighted and staring at Wylie the whole time. When they reached Kroger's lair, Wylie got off and Mrs. B rode back down to the sweatshop without explanation.

Now Mrs. Bloch comes up on the sidewalk, stands next to Wylie and asks, "Ahr du der vitnis?"

"I'm the librarian," Wylie says.

Mrs. B's head pivots up and down slowly on the neck, mechanically, as if she can see through her tumors and was appraising Wylie's face for evidence of a lie.

"Teik der ahrm," the hag commands, sounding like an emphysematous prison guard from the Balkans.

Wylie chokes off an impulse to resist and cups the woman's elbow with her hand. And though the request would seem to indicate that Mrs. B wanted assistance crossing the empty street, it is the old woman who takes the lead, pulling Wylie along.

She steers them toward the service alley to the right of the factory's main entrance, and when they swing around the corner and come to a stop in the mouth of the alleyway, Wylie finds it filled with the entire crew of child artists. There must be a dozen or more of them, ranging in age from maybe five years up through the late teens. They've erected a makeshift staging against the side wall of the Bardo, a monstrosity of fruit crates and fence posts, garbage tins and stacking pallets and broken street signs. The kids have fashioned the staging into platforms of varying heights, all of it connected with baling wire to the precarious fire escape.

There are children perched at every level, each equipped with a tin can of paint and some form of brush. They're collaborating on a mural of some sort, an enormous tableau, a picture that when finished will cover the entire side of the building, transforming the sagging red brick into a hyperreal scene that appears to be constantly dripping. The essence of the mural is already roughed out in white and blue chalk lines and Kroger's little slaves have begun filling in the outline with a variety of colors.

Mrs. Bloch turns her head from the building to Wylie.

"Du ahr laikink?" the voice seeming to edge close to threatening.

"Shouldn't they be sleeping?" Wylie says.

Without moving the rest of her squat little body, the crone's left arm comes up and a finger points out accusingly toward the mural in progress.

"Du laik der piktr?" she asks.

Wylie just nods and turns away from the pancake tumors to study the collaboration. And is horrified as it all comes together for her.

"Eet ist der kuvr," Mrs. B says.

"The cover?" Wylie repeats.

"Uf der ferst issu."

"Issue?" as she watches a child of perhaps eight years, kneeling on the top stair of a waggling extension ladder, filling in the pupils of the painting's central figure. "I don't understand."

"Uf der neu buk," Mrs. Bloch tries to explain. "Der neu komik. Der ferst issu. Eet vill bie vert der muni sem dei. Vot ist der verd?" straining, seemingly in pain with the rigors of pronunciation, *"Col-lect-ors i-tem?"*

Though Wylie has no direct involvement in the workings of Kroger's publishing business, she hasn't heard of any new projects being launched.

"There's a new title?" she asks.

Mrs. Bloch nods.

"Another Menlo knockoff?"

"Dis ist aen urij'nul."

Wylie is stunned.

"Mr. Kroger commissioned an original?"

Mrs. Bloch shakes her head *no* furiously. Her voice loudens up and she shouts, "Krueger haez nicht tu du vit dis!" Then she immediately gains back some control, lowers her voice and adds, "Aend Krueger ees naht hiz neim."

The children all stop painting for a second and look down to the alley until Mrs. B makes a hand gesture and they return to work.

"Der piktr bilenks tu der kinder. Der chilten."

Wylie finds this unlikely at best.

"The children did this? On their own?"

"Eet ees beisd an der ould mithus. Bet dei hev meid eet deir oun."

Wylie stares at Mrs. Bloch, then turns and stares at the children working together perfectly like bees, fully synchronized, each concentrated on his or her own small task but conscious of and tied into all the work proceeding around them. She takes a step backward and tries to get a new angle on the mural. The wall is illuminated by the moon and the dim glow of one yellow street-lamp.

The painting is given a strange aura not only by the lighting but also by the children moving here and there in front of it, always some children blocking some section of the picture with their bodies. It's a bit like trying to watch a movie with a swarm of insects hopping along the screen. Adding to the discomfort is the fact that half of the mural is done up in vibrant paint and half of it is still living in the ghost-lines of the chalk marks. As if part of the scene is forever fading even as the rest is being born.

But none of this obscures the subject matter. The mural is a depiction of a heinous act of barbarism, an inventive if sickening display of atrocity. One end of the brick wall sports a machine of some sort. It's a worrisome apparatus, big and bulky and outfitted with engines and tubing and chrome valves. The artists have managed to present the machine as if it were in motion. It's spewing gusts of steam and one gets the impression that it's emit-

ting a loud and grinding noise. But the focal point of the machine
is the aperture at its front end, the mouth of the device. This portal is enormous, stretching out as wide as the body of the entire
monstrosity. And the interior has been intricately rendered with
the precision of an old-world draftsman, showing two huge
rollers, two spinning drums fitted on axles and studded with cutting blades and hooks. The machine resembles a tree shredder,
but a tree shredder as envisioned in the nightmares of a sadistic
and maybe insane engineer.

Spreading out from either side of the shredding machine and
eventually forming a large circle that runs the length of the entire
wall, the children have drawn a net of wire fencing, a combination
of barbed cattle wire and the cyclone webbing used around construction sites. And massed within the fencing the children have
placed themselves. There are thirteen self-portraits, each done in
a different style and yet all of them sharing the same posture—
cowering in a crouch on the ground, squatting in place with arms
raised in terror and attempting, futilely, to ward off an approaching danger.

But the showpiece of the entire mural, the eye magnet, the
point of the piece, is not the shredding machine and not the fencing and not even the children's self-portraits. The thing that
demands the witness's attention is the man shown standing on top
of the shredder, drawn and painted in larger-than-life scale, made
into a superfigure. *Übermensch*. He must be the owner and opera-
tor of the awful machine. Perhaps the designer and manufacturer.

Not quite cartoonish and yet not completely realistic, the
image is drawn out of proportion to the imprisoned and cowering
children. The man's head is made huge beneath a military-like
cap. His body is infinitely muscled beneath a generic but sharply
pressed uniform. And his face is that of August Kroger. The children couldn't have created a more perfect likeness if they'd used a
camera.

But it is Kroger as icon. Kroger as myth figure, elevated to a
status where he is immune to death and the forgetting of history.

It is Kroger depicted in the same manner that Wylie has seen Stalin and Mao and certain fanatical religious leaders depicted, as a kind of semimortal god, part man and part force of nature. Someone who could alter the course of the world a degree or two.

Wylie is looking at a mural in which these prodigies have imagined their own execution by industrial evisceration at the hands of their slaver and boss. And she wants to pull one of them down from their perch and ask why she has done this. Because there is something both more and less than metaphorical about this work of art. Even in its most expressionistic excess, there is something paradoxically mimetic at the heart of this painting. As if the children were working on a billboard rather than a brick canvas, something with a crude and immediate purpose. An advertisement rather than an interpretation of their deepest communal fears and hatreds.

And all at once Wylie is filled with a resentment that's building fast toward a simple anger.

"You told them to paint this, didn't you?" she says to Mrs. Bloch.

"Eet ist deir—"

"Bullshit," Wylie says. "You told them to paint this thing. You're a goddamn pornographer."

"Der laibrerien ist anoit?"—a smile breaking underneath the tumors.

"You kept them up all night to make this thing."

Mrs. B nods, squares back her shoulders and says, "Der bosse vill bei houm sun—"

"I don't work for Kroger anymore."

"Hiz neim ees naht Krueger," yelling again, and again the yell halting the work on the painting. "Hiz neim ees Meyrink. Der Zensor uf Maisel."

Then the voice drops and she adds, "Mai houmlaent."

Wylie looks from Mrs. Bloch up to the mural and then, helplessly, to the artists frozen in place on their roosts. She suddenly realizes that she has no idea what's going on here but that, once again, she's in over her head and the thing to do is retreat.

For some reason she touches Mrs. Bloch on the shoulder and says, "I have to get my things."

But Mrs. B reaches up and grabs the hand, twists it backward into a position that doesn't cause any pain but warns of a terrible consequence if Wylie moves at all.

"Du ahr leavink der Bahrdu?"

Wylie nods for a moment before answering, "Yes."

Mrs. B releases the hand and says, "Den pik vun."

Wylie hesitates and Mrs. B repeats, more loudly, "Pik vun."

"I don't understand."

"Uf der kinder. Pik vun uf der chilten. Tu teik vit du."

"I can't—"

"Teik vun. Dei vill giv du der stury. Uf Meyrink der Zensor."

"I'm sorry but—"

Mrs. Bloch turns away from Wylie and takes a step toward the mural.

"Jiang," she calls and a small Asian boy immediately puts down his paint can and brush and begins to climb down the staging, careful not to look at his fellow artists.

The old woman turns back toward Wylie and says, "Gou paek der tinks. Jiang vill bie veatink."

As if a spell has been cast, Wylie takes a final look at the mural and then runs as fast as she can for the entrance to the Bardo, rushing inside and, unable to wait for the freight elevator, taking the fire stairs up to her room. Where she finds the creature Raban stretched out on her bed reading a comic book that he doesn't understand.

And back outside, Mrs. B, already impatient, squats in place and puts her arms around the little boy, brings her mouth to his ear and begins to whisper her final instructions, maybe a bit too fast, regarding the redemptive methodology of storytelling.

23

The Toth Care Facility is a collection of turn-of-the-century buildings hooked together by a highly imaginative series of eclectically designed additions. It sits on the crest of a hill, originally the bloated estate of Vartan Toth, a notorious local industrialist and land baron whose life story now serves as a kind of archetypal blueprint for success among Quinsigamond's Turkish community.

Originally from the Taurus Mountains region, descendant of a tent-dwelling family of transhumant goat herders, and, occasionally, opium smugglers, Toth came to the States as a teen and flailed away at the national dream of the limitless wealth and independence available to any and all who would will aspiration into currency and power. He made his first investment stash before he was twenty, working the racetrack circuit up and down the East Coast, buying, selling, and betting on horseflesh until he was able to establish a many-tiered bookmaking franchise. But he parlayed this initial wad into a truly grotesque bounty by devising a more efficient way of transforming slaughtered horse bone and muscle into a tremendously binding industrial adhesive. Almost overnight, Toth was elevated from a rough-and-tumble pony banker into a glue magnate worthy of taking brandy with the stuffy and inbred patrons of the Quinsigamond Men's Club. And though the legend that still resounds along Arcadian Way tends to delete the fact, it was at the height of his much-blessed life that Toth plummeted into scandal and tragedy.

A gambler and womanizer during his young manhood, Toth felt the synchronistic sting of karma when, at the ripe age of fifty, he took a beautiful, if high-strung, child bride named Cissy, the daughter of a socially prominent Episcopal minister. During the honeymoon, on Toth's first and last trip back home to his native Turkey, his new wife suffered an irreversible psychotic breakdown and mutilated a ceremonial minstrel in midperformance using the sterling cake knife from her nuptial reception. The herdsmen of the southeastern valleys are well-known for the swiftness and brutality of their justice system and, as the bridegroom watched helplessly, Cissy was torn to shreds by wild boar and rabid jackal.

Unhinged by this tragedy, Toth returned to America and began attempting to reverse a lifetime of avarice and decadence. He devoted himself to funding the burgeoning field of mental health research. Back in Quinsigamond, he moved into a gardener's cottage on his own estate and turned the main houses over to Dr. Renfield Hulbert, a peer and longtime, if one-sided, correspondent of both Freud and Jung whom fate has seen fit to designate to careless footnotes in dense technical histories of the period. Hulbert may well have been a profit- and ego-driven charlatan, but this does not necessarily negate the fact that he was possessed of a complex and highly flexible intelligence. And if it was later proven that the bulk of his medical credentials were either invented or at some point revoked, nevertheless his papers regarding the connections between schizophrenia (then termed *persistent fantasia* by Dr. H) and the mechanics of the brain's language centers (then termed *the alphabetical gears* by Dr. H) were genuinely ahead of their time.

During the Roaring Twenties, while much of the nation's upper crust Charlestoned their way toward the lurking Depression of the decade's end, the hysterical and the delusional and the dangerously unbalanced, the brothers and sisters who roared for less ribald and more torturous reasons, were brought to the Toth Clinic where their concerned but inconvenienced families were given a tour that included the elegantly appointed splendors of the estate but excluded the snake-pit horrors of the basement workrooms, dingy and exceptionally unhygienic laboratories where every manner of fanatical quackery was practiced from hypothermia-producing ice-water therapies to radical and sloppy experimental lobotomies to a veritable smorgasbord of pharmacological remedies not far removed, but likely much deadlier, than those found in medieval witches' breviaries.

Hulbert's favorite innovation, however, was very likely trepanning. The doctor drilled a hole in just about every skull he got his hands on and ultimately it was his undoing. When the wife of Quinsigamond's only impeached mayor sought the help of the Toth Clinic for a series of migraines that coincided with her husband's political downfall, the woman was sent home, over the protests of Hulbert's loyal if equally sadistic staff, with a crater in her forehead the size of a Prussian monocle. The ex-mayor seized on the defacement as a diversionary tool, excoriating the local paper for spreading lies about his finances rather than looking into the medical horrors being perpetrated right under our noses. The wags on the city desk responded that, in fact, it appeared the horrors were just under our hairlines, but *The Spy*'s publisher smelled a good smear story and, with the purchased resources of the accommodating police chief, raided the Toth Clinic pronto.

Some pioneers of the shock school of photojournalism were on hand when a carefully picked team of Q-town's most roguish street bulls kicked open the doors of the asylum. To this day in the files of the Historical Museum one can view sepia testaments to the kind of heart-crushing torture one mad scientist can single-handedly invent—pictures of medical procedures to make a Nazi jealous, brains split open like melons and subjected to humiliations beyond the scope of Sade himself, close-up portraits of strange metal instruments whose purposes could not include anything in the realm of the benign, representations of human beings whose mental illness was only the starting point for a descent into a bottomless hell devised by a first-class maniac with access to money, manpower, and electricity. When the cellars of the Toth Estate were finally aired out, the city was scandalized and mortified by the dirty but not-so-little secrets that Dr. Hulbert, led away in cuffs and sporting two bloody lips, called "my life's work."

The clinic was closed down temporarily. Vartan Toth remained on the estate, a recluse who spent his hours reading the Bible in his shanty home, tending to a garden, lighting icons to his lost but still-beloved Cissy. One rumor proposed that the glue baron himself had been subjected to a few of the doctor's less than delicate treatments. But it was more likely plain grief and regret that did in the Turk. When he eventually lost all his business interests in the crash of '29, he either didn't care or didn't understand the consequences. The city ended up burdened with the estate-cum-asylum and Toth died a few years later, living in a storefront mission, brokenhearted and unhinged right to the end. They say his last words were "My darling, the beasts have finally turned on me."

When a private medical co-op from Toronto purchased and reopened the clinic many years later, they decided, for some determinedly wrongheaded reason, to retain the original name. But the Toth facility has, of late, built a fairly respectable reputation as a rehabilitation center for most of the common modern addictions. Another few years of vacation stays by rock stars and movie princesses and the board of directors is convinced they'll have erased all memory of the hospital's unfortunate history. And if alumni donations keep rolling in at the current rate, the place may throw itself up on the big board, go public, and break ground for a new wing. Every new jones to hit the street is money in the

Keogh plan. As Dr. Raglan said at the most recent management team meeting, "Rest easy, kids. There's no shortage of monkeys on this horizon."

But if the compulsive self-destructiveness of the pampered end of the societal spectrum is the mainstay of Toth, the clinic continues to handle a smattering of more complex and severe pathologies, if only to maintain a standing in the field and earn an infrequent mention in the academic journals. Still, as Gilrein parks the Checker in the visitors' lot and walks the hill to the main hall, he tries to imagine how the Toth's regime of ardent group therapy sessions and mandatory janitorial service could possibly help Otto Langer.

The reception area of the main hall is a showpiece of Victorian gentility. Gilrein finds the front desk and wastes close to ten minutes arguing with a preppy and arrogant intern who continues to repeat that the patient is under sedation and receiving no visitors. Gilrein brooks the refusal politely but when he realizes the futility of manners in this instance, he turns on his cop demeanor, gives a flash of gun, and asks the kid if he'd like to wake Dr. Raglan and inquire if the boss could join them at the pharmacy where a small army of narcotics officers would like to compare the stockroom supply with the dispensing logs.

The intern asks a floor-mopping orderly to watch the front desk, grabs a huge set of keys from a drawer and leads the way to the stairwell. When it becomes apparent that they're headed for the cellar, Gilrein says, "I thought they didn't use this part of the hospital anymore."

"Restraint cases," the intern explains, opening and then resecuring a series of steel fire doors that segment a long, dim corridor permeated with the alcohol stink of some harsh, overused disinfectant. "We try to keep the shriekers here until we can quiet them down. It's very disturbing to the other guests."

"Guests," Gilrein repeats.

The intern ignores him and they turn down a hallway, open another door, and come to a square foyer of concrete walls where

an enormous black man in a brown security outfit is sitting at a
desk reading a tabloid, engrossed in a cover story whose title
informs FLESH-EATING ALIEN MICROBES INFECT ASIA.

"Larry," the intern says to the guard who continues to read,
"give this man clearance to room D."

Larry nods, takes one hand from the paper to reveal a sub-
head—VIRUS HEADED FOR AMERICA—and presses a lock-release
under the lip of the desk. A buzzing noise fills the room. The
intern turns and exits the foyer without a word. Gilrein grabs the
inner door and pulls it open, surprised by its weight. He steps
inside and lets the door swing closed behind him. The sound outside is instantly muffled but the buzzing continues for several
seconds.

He's at the end of another corridor, this one much narrower
and maybe only thirty feet long. One wall is a series of limestone
blocks that give off a faint sparkle from the overhead cone lamps.
The interior, facing wall is a series of four identical, consecutive
cells—simple, tiny squares of limestone enclosed by an iron-bar
wall. They look almost identical to pictures Gilrein has seen of the
cell rooms in Alcatraz. They're outfitted with gray metal cots
topped by thin, roll-out mattresses. In the right-hand corner of
each cell is a seatless toilet. If anything, the disinfectant smell is
even stronger in here, harsh enough to burn your eyes or make
you gag. The first three cells are empty. They're distinguished by
the letters *A*, *B*, and *C* stencil-painted on the floor in front of
their doors.

Gilrein walks the length of the corridor until he gets to cell D
and he looks in on a diorama that could rival anything Dr. Hulbert
created almost a century ago. Otto Langer is naked, his shoulders
covered by a filthy woolen blanket. He's huddled on the floor in
the center of the cell, emitting a kind of whimpering sound, a
noise the runt puppy might make when separated from its mother
for the first time. Langer's face is an abstract expressionist canvas
of blue welts and dried blood and fresh blood and matted hair and
maybe even some fecal matter spread across a cheek. The cot is

turned on its side. The mattress is half-shredded. On the rear wall of the cell, staring out at Gilrein like a minimalist billboard, is a four-letter graffito, painted in what may or may not be Langer's own blood. It's a message that appears to be a word, but is not—*METH*.

And in a rear corner of the cell, suspended in midair, hanging by the neck from a belt secured to a rusted, dripping water pipe, is the ventriloquial dummy, Zwack the golem.

Gilrein goes down on one knee and positions himself in line with Langer's face.

"Otto," he calls out, his voice an intrusion into the rhythm of his friend's keening.

Langer looks up at him, but the eyes seem unfocused, as if he had heard his own name but can't locate the source of the noise.

"It's Gilrein," he says.

Langer lifts his head, cranes it out on the neck, peers out of the cell, suspicious but cut by a drug glaze.

"What the hell happened, Otto?" Gilrein asks. "Where's Jocasta?"

Langer just shakes his head, but then he gets down on all fours and crawls over to the bars. He brings his mouth to an opening, signals with his fingers for Gilrein to come closer. Gilrein leans in and hears Langer whisper, "Go away," then notices the fingers are covered with tiny crisscrossing cuts and scrapes, as if Langer had punched his hands through a window or had them attacked by small kittens or birds.

Gilrein stands up and says, "I'm going to get you out of here."

And immediately, Langer is on his feet as well, screaming, "No, get out, go away, get out," hysterical, clutching at the bars and ramming his forehead into them as he yells.

Gilrein is close to panicking. He doesn't know whether he wants or fears the arrival of Larry the security guard. He steps back from the cell and holds his hands up in a placating gesture, saying, "Okay, all right, I'm going, I'm leaving." He shakes his head at Langer, turns, and starts to move for the exit.

And from the cell he hears, in a clear and focused voice, "This is all your fault, Gilrein."

He stops in front of restraining chamber A, turns around, but doesn't walk back to Langer's cell.

"How is this my fault?" he asks.

"You and your filthy errands," Langer says, not in a yell or a whisper, but at a conversational level. And full of hatred.

"What errands?" but he knows.

There's no response from Langer.

"You're talking about Tani," Gilrein says. "You're talking about me driving Leo Tani around."

A pause and then, "You think you're innocent, don't you, Gilrein? You think you're a victim of God, don't you, you bastard?"

Gilrein walks back to Langer's cage and stares at the old man, leaving a few feet between them.

Langer's accent comes out thick and purposeful.

"There's blood all over your hands, you son of a bitch."

Before Gilrein can think of how to respond, he sees Langer reach down and position his penis through the bars and begin to piss in his visitor's direction. Urine hits the bottom of Gilrein's pant leg and his shoes before he can step back. It's a weak stream and the arc dissipates rapidly, the casualty of restraining drugs or an enlarged prostate.

"Jesus," Gilrein yells, watching the puddle form on the floor. Then the anger comes and he adds, "You can stay here and wallow in your own shit, you crazy bastard."

"I deserve," Langer says, "nothing less."

It's a cryptic enough shift to make Gilrein linger, and he watches as Langer seems to sway under his own weight, sinking to the floor in a half-controlled, slow-motion collapse and dissolving into a melted lotus position. He brings his hands to the bars and pulls his face forward until his mouth and nose poke out of the cell.

"If you stay," he says to Gilrein without looking up, "you will be infected."

Gilrein thinks for a minute that he's referring to St. Leon's Grippe, but Langer has none of the symptoms—no pustules on the tongue, no difficulty speaking.

"Infected with what?" as he gets down on the floor, campfire style, directly opposite Langer's face and carefully avoiding the pool of urine.

"With what?" the voice now aggravatingly low. "With the story."

"Which story?"

"The only one that's left to me."

A pause as they stare at each other. Then Gilrein asks, "Could you tell it to me?"

"Are you sure you want to hear?"

And though he's not at all sure, Gilrein nods his assent.

24

You are here as a convenient pair of ears, Gilrein. Make no mistake, it might as well have been any one of my silent passengers in the rear of my taxi. Or even the orderlies who broke my rib strapping me to the table where they injected me with their controlling fluids. The joke is very likely on them, yes? My liver will not process their chemicals. I am not one of them. I am not like you. I am an exile. A true exile. Not like you, Gilrein. Yes, I know, I've watched and listened. I am aware you fancy yourself the outsider. But it's an act of vanity, mister. For you, it's a pose, a way of killing time, as much as driving the taxi or drinking coffee in the Visitation.

You want a story, Mister Taxi-Boy. Very well then, you listen to me now. As you have never listened before. You listen to the end of my story and you memorize it. You are my receptacle. You are the only form of media left to me. You owe me this act, to become the listener, to give me your ears so that I might fill them like a satchel. You listen, Gilrein. As atonement for your arrogance.

When the Censor emerged from Haus Levi, the manuscript tucked under his coat, crews of latex-clad sanita-
tion workers were sorting through the spoils, the booty of
jewelry and knicknacks and wallets, tossing the better
goods into money sacks imprinted with the Treasury's
seal, tossing photographs and clothing into thriving fire
pits. A secondary crew was hosing the tenements down
with liquid accelerant from tanks strapped to their backs.
A phalanx of heavy machinery waited outside the mouth of
the Schiller, behind the walls of cyclone fencing, cranes
and backhoes idling under their drivers who were
annoyed with the delay but appeased by the overtime
wage. Meyrink called a foreperson over and asked for an
estimated completion time for the entire project. The
young woman consulted a clipboard and guessed it would
be dawn before they could be ready to start burning and
leveling the tenements.

Meyrink was barely listening. He approached a vice-
chancellor who was sipping kava beside the Obliterator
and, mumbling something about exhaustion, relin-
quished command.

Not wanting to take a staff car and aware that all the
taxis had been rerouted for the night, Meyrink walked the
three miles to his home, a nondescript town house in a
bourgeois neighborhood. The walk allowed him time to
think and build the correct degree of relish and expectation he felt the coming days deserved. An evolution of this
magnitude should be acknowledged and embraced,
received by every sensory port available, no matter how
painful.

His deputies were waiting by the curb in a Ministry
jeep. Meyrink stopped by the driver's window and
exchanged with Varnbuler his house keys for the generous
bonus that would buy their discretion.

"Any problems?" Meyrink asked.

Varnbuler shook his head.

"Is she—"

"She's awake," the deputy assured him.

"And you—"

"Just as always," Varnbuler interrupted for the last time.

Meyrink nodded and gestured that they could leave. He waited for the jeep to vanish around the bend of Morgenstern Road, then walked up the stair to his front door, barely able to contain the intensity of some new glandular response that resembled both glee and fury. He let himself into the foyer, made himself stop and pick up the mail that had been pushed through the slot, willed himself to sort and glance at a succession of bills, solicitations, and a letter from his mother on holiday in Matliary. He stopped in the pantry and poured some sherry, inspecting the sideboard to see that the housekeeper had done a thorough dusting. Next, he took his drink upstairs to the bedroom and removed the manuscript, placing it delicately on the bed as he changed out of his uniform, then reattired himself in tennis shoes, work pants, sweater, lab smock, and skiving apron. He studied himself in the mirror, stepped into the bathroom to slick down his hair with a wash of tap water. He dried his hands exhaustively before picking up the papers. Finally, unable to further postpone the culmination of his yearnings, he carried the gospel down to the cellar of the house and into the hobby room.

He threw open the door to find Alicia conscious, naked, and chained to a large brass hook that protruded from the center of the ceiling. Just as his deputy had promised.

A piece of silvery-gray duct tape was bound across the girl's mouth. She stared at Meyrink, silent in terror and confusion. He stepped directly in front of her and though she tried to recoil, she could only bow her body back so far.

Meyrink held the stack of mismatched papers up at chest level and said, "In the beginning was the word, yes?"

Alicia mouthed something that was obscured by the tape.

Three of the room's walls were fitted with oak worktables of differing widths and heights, their surfaces inlaid with ship's linoleum and Formica. Each table was fitted with Anglepoise lamps of higher than normal intensity and two of the tables featured an expensive brand of German magnifying glass on bendable mounts protruding from sockets cut into the wood. Above each table sat a series of pegboards and cupboards and cabinets holding an impressive and long-assembled collection of tools, implements, and utensils including tenson saws, carpenter's squares, band nippers, strops, awls, G-clamps, trindles, blunt-ended shears, back scrapers, sewing keys, rods, riveting sets, light hammers, backing hammers, loaded sticks, gilder's tips, bone folders, chisels, bodkins, backing boards, dog-toothed burnishers, piercers, pins, paring stones, steel rulers, sandpaper blocks, mini-vises, and, perhaps, the most impressive collection of cutlery in central Maisel—knives and scalpels and lancets and razors and blades imported from all over the globe, some antiques and some custom-made, some known mainly to common village cobblers of Old Bohemia, others used solely by research surgeons in clinics unchartered by the republic's Ministry of Health. But all of the metal kept meticulously polished and obsessively honed.

At the wall-head of the central table was a set of three glue pots set in a heated water jacket. On either side of the pots was a line of small cans and glasses containing an assortment of brushes—glue brushes, paste brushes, watercolor flood brushes, sable-hair brushes, hog's-hair brushes, natural thistle brushes.

Beneath each table was a leather-topped tavern stool on rubber-tipped legs. At the far end of the room was a standing iron board cutter with a guillotine arm that could slide through anything reasonable, an antique English standing press, and a smaller, solid iron nipping press mounted atop a matching iron bench. A variety of sewing frames leaned against the roughstone wall, resting on the floor next to a large, black-wood plan chest with narrow drawers. The top drawers were stocked with papers—decorative marbles and Japanese tissues and pricey Ingres. Wrapping papers and blotting papers and art papers and writing papers and drawing papers. All in a spectrum of colors, weights, grains, and pH values. The bottom drawers were stocked with a supply of preskived leathers in various qualities.

Wire drying lines were strung wall-to-wall behind Alicia's head. The floor beneath her bare feet was poured concrete fitted in the center with a grate-covered drain. There were no windows. Adjoining the room, there was a private lavatory which supplied the running water. There was also a walk-in closet from which the doors had been removed and the interior remade with fitted shelving that displayed an impressive assortment of books in pristine and matching bindings. In the middle of the closet area was a wood-and-glass display case filled with two slim books bound in an ugly brownish-purple covering. Their installation inside the hermetic case was the only indication of their status above the shelved volumes.

Meyrink moved to a worktable without taking his eyes off Alicia. He picked up a pair of rubber gloves and made a production of stretching them over his hands.

"Everyone needs a release," he said, contorting his fingers into latex. "A way of calming themselves. Of leaving the pressures of the job. Retreating from the jostling of the outside world in general. That's my feeling, at least."

He moved back to the girl and stood before her, examining her body as if it were a canvas filled with some difficult work of art, some new form that takes effort on the part of the viewer before it will give up its hidden meanings. He stepped back, moved his head from shoulder to shoulder, squinted his eyes. He walked a full circle around Alicia, slowly, stopping for a moment when completely behind her and making a number of snorting and sniffling noises.

When they came face-to-face again, he was nodding, smiling, pleased by something he seemed to have confirmed.

"Very good," he said, probably to himself. "Just fine. Wonderful texture. No major blemishes. Tremendously supple."

He lifted a hand to her cheek for the first time, brushed back to her ear, then adjusted her hair behind the ear.

"You are wonderful," he said to her. "You've taken care of yourself. I can't tell you how pleased that makes me. So many of the young people today, with the cigarettes, the sun worshiping. The alcohol while still in their teens. And then, these days, the body piercing. My God, not just the ears, mind you, but the nose. The tongue. I have even heard they desecrate the nipple."

He walked back to a workbench, shaking his head as he went. He opened some of the cupboards and began to take down tools and place them on the table.

"I consider it a form of self-mutilation," he said. "And I know all the arguments. The talk of expression and rebellion. But I think this is the nonsense of youth. I think we're seeing the herd mentality. I will put a ring through my nose because Ottla down the block put a ring through *her* nose. So much nonsense."

He stared up into a cupboard for a moment, apparently looking for something, then closed the cabinet door and walked back to face the girl.

"I would love to take the tape off. But I have neighbors, of course. And though the house is well insulated, I'm a man who does not enjoy taking chances."

He ran a thumb across her covered lips.

"I know it can be difficult breathing this way. But concentrate and you will find a rhythm. It will begin to feel natural, I promise you."

He took her face by the chin and turned it side to side, inspecting the neck. From here he began to run both his hands around the neck, poking mildly with the thumbs like a doctor checking swollen glands. He moved down her body, over the shoulders, down over the breasts, up under the arms, turning the arms back and forth as wrists rubbed against manacles, all of it very clinical and methodical, in much the same manner that the state nurses inspect the refugees at the border train stations.

"While I'm apologizing, I should also tell you how much I regret these gloves. A problem for both of us, in the tactile sense. So sterile and cold. But in this day and age, what can I say? It's a matter of safety. Of hygiene. You must see that. An intelligent young lady like yourself. You can't take the kind of risks that we would have disregarded in the past."

He spent a good ten minutes inspecting her body, half of that time down on his knees and behind her. From time to time he pinched and poked, pulled skin out from its natural fall over the bones. He even ran a finger in and out between her toes. When he was finally done, he struggled back up to standing and gave her buttocks a playful slap before walking back to the workbench and extracting two or three more implements from the cabinets.

"You look healthy as a horse," he called from across the room, taking a grindstone down from a shelf and climbing onto a stool.

"I mean that, of course, as a compliment," as he selected a midsize skiving knife and began to sharpen its blade against the stone. "Your color is exemplary. No sign of jaundice at all. You have to understand, we, on the outside—outside the Schiller, I mean—we've heard so much about the effects of a poor diet, the results of malnutrition and such. You begin to accept it as fact. But obviously, your environment did no lasting damage to your body."

He stopped sharpening and turned his head to look at her, saying, "Nor your mind."

He put the knife down gingerly and picked up the manuscript, slid off his stool and approached the girl once again.

"It's a stunning achievement," he said, holding the stack of paper up for her to see. "What you have done is simply amazing, my dear. You are a very talented artist. A writer of the first degree. This is my opinion and, certainly, I am not a trained critic. But as they say, I know what I like. I know what I am impressed with. Do you know the shock that would ripple through our city if others saw what you were capable of? A little guttersnipe from the Schiller, barely old enough for the violet passport? I'll tell you this, they wouldn't believe it. There's a very prejudiced mind-set out there, darling. You must trust me on this. I have more experience. I have lived more years and traveled widely through the strata of Maisel society. The bulk of my people could not accept it. This kind of achievement from the vermin of the Schiller. Impossible. This is what they would say. I swear it. I have the proof here in my hands, but it would do no good."

He brought the manuscript back to the workbench and deposited it there, brushing off the top sheet gently, then pausing to reread a few opening lines.

"You have done no less than create—with just ink and scraps of cheap, horrible paper—a totem. Do you know what that is, my child? You may well. I would put nothing past you. Not after reading your art. Think of this. In just three days, without study or planning. Without help or advice or a mentor who might have steered you along your course. Without an aesthetic skeleton. Without an envelope filled with a lifetime of notes. Without the slightest indication that there was a single reason to even *do* so, you have created a bomb. That's what this is, my love. That is exactly what we must call this messy pile of paper. A bomb. A bomb that goes off, again and again, an explosive device whose trigger is the eyes of any and every reader to pick it up and take in the first words. It is an epiphany bomb. Are you familiar with *this* word, child? No? No matter.

"We could talk of an idiot savant. But I know this is not the case. Your extraordinary talent was not given at the expense of normality. This is self-evident to me. You are a beautiful young rose that has grown in the midst of the sewer heap that is the Schiller. You were put here, in all your beauty," his finger pointing out at her, "in all your innocence *and* your wisdom, to make me into an everlasting symbol. Because of you, I will always be here, unadulterated in my darkness.

"I don't mean to be melodramatic, my friend. But surely the moment calls out for it. You have created from nothing a world of written language, ink on paper, a cosmology of symbols, the sum of whose parts is entirely greater than the graphic signs themselves. You have forged the manifestation of reality through your little story. How proud you must be, child. How proud your family and friends, your whole community would be, if only your story had never taken place, yes? It's an awful irony. Even a paradox—if they exist, there is no story to be proud of; if they die, there is no one to be proud.

"But I will be proud for them, young lady. I will do your masterpiece justice. You must trust me on this. I could show you my own best work, but it would pale in comparison to your triumph, believe me. I would be embarrassed just to parade my paltry craftsmanship before the eyes of such genius. And besides, past work does not really ensure success in the future, because each project is a job unto itself. We never know what the result will be like. But we will do our best. This is all we can do. Don't you agree? We give what we have, not what we have not. Our doubt is our passion, as someone once said."

From one cabinet Meyrink took a wide and deep roasting pan, something you might use to cook a holiday turkey. From another cabinet he took a plastic bleach bottle topped with a blue twist cap. The brand label had been peeled off the jug and in its place, printed in black marker, was the word RESTORATIVE. He carried them both to the floor near Alicia's feet, uncapped the jug, and filled the pan about halfway. The basement filled up with a chemical smell, a nauseating cross between dentist's office and reformatory boys' room.

Meyrink moved back to a workbench, took down a small bottle of bluish liquid. He unscrewed the cap, pulled his handkerchief from his pocket. He poured a small amount of liquid onto the rag and quickly recapped the bottle.

He came back to Alicia from behind and forced the wet cloth against her face, covering her nose, holding the back of her head steady.

"It won't be long now," he said.

In a moment, he was back in her line of vision, though

already fading a bit, gauzy, seen through a panel of lightly rippling water. He was holding the manuscript again, placing it inside a plastic bag. His mouth moved.

"In case there's more spray than I anticipate."

The weight of her body seemed to increase, pulling on the wrists bound inside the manacles. The sense of balance began to dissipate. Time moved closer to its state in sleep, a wavering, unfixable condition of varying speed and depth. The sound of his voice appeared almost detached from its port of origin, the mouth moving in a somewhat different pattern of motions than the noise reaching her ears would have implied. And yet, despite this discrepancy, she completely understood the last words she heard. The words were not original. No words are. But this particular grouping had a persistently familiar ring to it. Someone with a clearer perspective might have labeled it a paraphrase.

Though the words were not from Alicia's specific tradition, her native history, or her culture, she was acquainted with them. She had been, after all, in the end, maybe more than anything else, a reader.

"In the beginning," Meyrink said, "was the word, and the word was with the author, and the word was the author . . ."

He pushed the blade of the scalpel into the soft enclave below the neck and opened the body to the exterior world.

For how many hours did he work on the girl? Do we need to be mindful of the passage of time? As in the Bible, where we are told that God made the whole of the universe in a specified interval?

How intense his concentration must have been, cutting sheet after sheet of epidermis. How satisfactory, finally, when he could pull away the entire jacket that covered the torso.

There is no need to dwell on how the body was disposed of. The deputies had handled errands of this nature before, of course. And what was one more body when we consider that this took place at the height of the pogroms collectively known as the July Sweep?

The tanning process you might find somewhat more interesting. The way he dried Alicia's skin and worked it obsessively into a binding material, into a unique hide that would forever gather and house the pages of Alicia's story.

But what I really want to leave you with, Gilrein, at this late date, is the fact that Meyrink's book was stolen from him. At some point in the end, during those frantic and confusing days following the Erasure of the Schiller, when the Censor of Maisel was of no more use to the state. Alicia's book was taken from Meyrink before he fled to America. Or, perhaps, just after he arrived. One more wretched outcast yearning for the new Eden that could give him sanctuary.

There is a myth that the book was taken by a survivor of the Erasure. An Ezzene who was not present on the final night. But I find this hard to believe. How could such a person live with himself? How could he survive a guilt of this magnitude?

Gilrein walks to the Checker carrying the manila envelope given to him by Larry the security guard. The envelope contains Otto Langer's personal belongings. When Gilrein asked, "Don't you want me to sign for it?" the guard just ignored him and went back to reading the mutant virus exposé.

Stopping at the rear of the cab, Gilrein unclasps the package and slides a worn brown goatskin wallet onto the trunk. He opens the wallet, fans through the billfold, counts off thirty-nine dollars. He flips through a series of cellophane photo sleeves that contain business cards, a hack license, a driver's licence, a citizenship card, an expired inoculation card, and a biloquist permit issued by the city of Maisel and valid only during the carnival season.

And a single photograph. It is a picture of an almost-beautiful young girl with deep circles under her eyes. Maybe seventeen years old, she's dressed in a sweater and she has a pencil lodged behind her ear, pushing the hair back on the right side of her head. Carefully, Gilrein slides the photo out of the sleeve and makes himself turn it over in his palm. Makes himself read the inevitable words

> FOR PAPA,
> WITH ALL MY LOVE FOREVER,
> ALICIA

25

The muscle cars are left unattended. This semicircle of obsessively preserved American chrome looks like a secret dealership that caters to a brotherhood of anal-retentive greasers. And sitting out here in the middle of the woods, in the shadow of a half-destroyed factory, it looks like the dealership has been bought out by some pagan with an inexplicable taste for tail fins and spoilers. A red tool chest, standing as tall as a jukebox and filled with an elaborate ratchet set, is open in front of a Daytona. The hood of the Dodge has been left open, as if the mechanic had been called away in the middle of a tune-up.

Gilrein starts to look in on the engine when the sound comes to him. It's muted and slightly distant, but he recognizes it instantly as the specific hum born from the cojoined shrieks of sports fans engorged on someone else's gains and losses. He turns to the Kapernaum and heads for the Houdini Lounge. The panel door is rolled up on its tracks and there's no receptionist at the gun-check table. As he walks down the corridor toward the clubhouse, the noise of the mob gets louder. It's possible they've got the TVs cranked up and are beer-ranting to a satellite trans-

mission of two kick-boxers smashing each other to death in Thai-
land. But when he enters the Lounge, he finds it empty. The bar is
fully covered with discarded bottles of Hunthurst Lager and the
money can is overflowing with damp and crumbled bills. Dumb-
bells have been left on the floor in the weight room. The televisions are on, tuned to a porn channel and a dubbed Hercules
movie, both playing to an empty set of couches. The stripper's
stage is abandoned but for an orange polyester waitress's uniform
left dangling from the lip.

Gilrein climbs the stairs to Oster's office, moves to the exterior window and looks out on the origin of the crowd noise. Down
by the interrogation pit, the place Oster has christened "the penal
colony," rimming the crater left by the Tung's explosion, there
must be over a hundred people. The mob is lit by the halogen spot
on the roof. They're perched on boulders and old tires and quite a
few are balanced on the edge of foldout aluminum-and-mesh
beach chairs. Half a dozen oil barrels are spouting flame, but
they're throwing as much smoke as light into the air. An outdoor
bar has been set up directly opposite the rear of the building—a
trio of kegs dispensing foam to a nonstop line of men holding all
manner of improvised pitchers.

He moves down from the loft and exits the rear of the factory.
The smoke and the noise and the halogen light all hit him at once
and the combined effect is a little dizzying. As he walks toward the
rim of the pit, he begins to recognize faces. And none of them go
together. Retired police sergeants are seated next to a few midlevel
flunkies from various mob houses. A district attorney's deputy is
sharing a picnic bench with one of Jimmy Tang's favorite shooters.
The Tatarka sisters, whose chop shop is known and respected from
San Remo Avenue to Budapest and whose warrants for arrest are
both multiple and active, are passing a bucket of fried chicken legs
back and forth between the Registrar of Motor Vehicles and City
Councilor Frye. It's as if someone designated this Buried Hatchet
Night at the Kapernaum. As if the Magicians have sponsored an
open house as part of a membership drive.

Circulating in the midst of it all are a trio of young women, their long hair uniformly pulled back into impressive ponytails that fall through the rear opening of their kelly green baseball caps. They have matching green aprons tied around their waists and green plastic clipboards clutched in their arms. For a minute, Gilrein thinks they must be waitresses, maybe peanut vendors. Then he follows one, watches her step into a circle of drunks waving money, watches her slide a pencil from behind an ear and point to each man in turn, ordering them with her speed and demeanor, taking their cash, making change, scribbling on her notepad, handing out colored coupons, and all of it with the rote efficiency of a bank teller bucking for management. They're making book on something and Gilrein would like to stop himself from speculating what it might be.

"Hey there, Gilly *boy*," he hears, amplified by bullhorn, and turns to see Oster standing on top of a pile of broken bricks. "Get your ass over here, Gilly."

It comes out in a good-natured, beer-driven roar, a fraternity whoop that draws an immediate share of audience attention down onto Gilrein. People start pointing and waving. Voices come out of the gaps of light.

"We knew you'd be back, G-man."

"We saved a space for you, bro."

"Give the bastard a beer, fer Chrissake."

It's like some horrible performance poem, a kind of ritual vignette fueled by testosterone and camaraderie and alcohol. And he knows he has to walk through it, so he starts to thread his way into a maze of glad-handing hombres who punch his arm and slap his back as if they'd all passed through some hellish foreign war together. He reaches the brick pile and Oster extends a hand and pulls him up to the summit.

"We need to talk," Gilrein says.

Oster shakes his head and squints his disagreement.

"Plenty of time to talk, Gilly," he says. "I'm just so goddamn psyched you made it. I knew—I said to Stewie and Danny—Gilrein's in. Gilly's one of us. You are going to love this shit."

"Oster," Gilrein starts to say, but immediately the crowd drowns him out with a new roar and it climbs to standing as fast as its drunken legs will allow.

Gilrein looks down to the rear of the Kapernaum, to the same exit he's just come through, and sees the source of the cheering. Four men have stepped into the pit spotlight. Two of them he recognizes as Oster's main creatures—Danny Walden and Stewie Green. Boy scouts as trained by Himmler. Rookies born from Satan's anus. They're holding the other two men in full-blown chain restraints, manacles around ankles, waists, and wrists. And an additional touch that, to the best of Gilrein's knowledge, has never been department-sanctioned—choke-chain collars around the prisoners' necks extending to a pull lead that Oster's men are using like a leash, hauling the captive parties toward the center of the pit as if they were zoo stock, wild animals so feared and despised they can't be allowed the decision of when to breathe.

Walden manipulates his choke chain to drive his prisoner down to his knees and when the mob goes loud with the noise of their unbridled pleasure, Green follows suit until both captives are facing each other in what looks like a pray-off.

Gilrein looks down on the spectacle and says, "What's happening here?"

Oster rocks forward and back, a boy so juiced up on anticipation he may lose bladder control.

"You made it in time for the first annual Houdini Lounge Death Bowl," Oster says, shouting over the cheers. "I think you still got time to get some coin down if you want." He leans in close to Gilrein's ear and adds, "the smart percentage is going with the DR. He's small, but he's fast as a bastard." The voice lowers a bit. "And just between you and me, he's going to have a little advantage."

Walden and Green knee their charges in the side until the spotlight illuminates the faces. One prisoner looks small and muscular and Hispanic. The other is older and maybe Middle Eastern. They're both stripped to the waist, their chests sporting what looks like fresh scarring. They're wearing gray sweatpants that have been cut off just above the knee. And they're barefoot.

"They're supposed to fight?" Gilrein asks the obvious.

"They're supposed to beat the absolute crap out of each other, Gilly," Oster says, somehow proud of the event, as if he'd guided the spectacle from initial notion through promotion and finance. "They are going to pound on each other till one of them stops breathing."

"You've got to be shitting me."

"Lounge takes twenty percent of the book," Oster says. "The whole city's been laying down money faster than my beat bulls can pick it up. We're going to use half the proceeds to build some bleachers back here and increase the attendance. You know the old boys down City Hall don't want to be sitting on fruit crates at this stage of their careers."

Gilrein stares at him and Oster says, "Next year I'll save you a place in the owner's box. How's that sound, Gilly"—he pauses and lets his smile fade—"huh? You *will* be attending next year, Gilrein? That is what you're here to tell me, right?"

Gilrein doesn't answer. Down in the pit, Green puts his arm up in the air and swings a big circle as if tossing an invisible lasso.

"Hold that thought," Oster says. "Looks like the festivities are about to begin."

He pulls his piece from his shoulder rig and fires three rounds into the air, which effectively calls the crowd's attention. He picks his bullhorn up from the bricks and brings it to his mouth.

"Gentlemen," his voice amplified into a fuzzy and slightly mechanical echo, bouncing off the wall of the factory and running back out into the woods behind him. "On behalf of the Houdini Lounge social committee, I just want to welcome you all to the first annual Rome Avenue Tournament of Refugees. Now before we begin this evening's feature match, I need to remind you that my boys are passing around a collection hat for the widows and orphans relief fund and I know that you'll all give generously to this worthy cause that benefits the families of our brother officers."

He lowers the bullhorn to chest level and looks out over the crowd, checking to make sure the audience is digging into their deepest pockets. Without looking at Gilrein, he says, "You're going to love this, Gilly. This is going to be better than a gladiator movie."

Gilrein tries to see if he's kidding, but Oster just lifts the bullhorn and says, "Now I know a lot of you have been waiting weeks for tonight's bout and the management genuinely regrets all the rescheduling we've put you through, but I think you're going to find that it's been worth the wait. So let's introduce this evening's fighters."

Without waiting for the crowd's latest drunken cheer to subside, Oster pulls an index card from a pocket and nods to Stewie Green, who holds up the manacled arm of his prisoner and starts to lead him in a display promenade around the periphery of the pit.

"Originally hailing from the Dominican Republic and in town just six short months is Rafael Rojo."

A quick break for both cheers and taunts, then, "Weighing in tonight at a speedy one hundred and forty-three pounds, Rafael was Gunther Berlin's collar . . ." A huge cheer obscures the next few words. ". . . picked up in February on various weapons-possession charges in addition to possession and intent to distribute a class A substance and assault on a police officer with shod foot." A swell of boos as half a dozen beer cans are tossed into the pit.

Oster looks up from his notes and yells, "Excuse me, people, I'll have to ask you to refrain from littering the fight area. Yes, I'm talking to you, Callan. Your debris could affect the outcome of tonight's match."

Someone yells a remark that Gilrein doesn't catch. Oster nods to Danny Walden, who goes into the same circle-trot with his captive.

"And straight out of Karachi, Pakistan, in our fair city for only a fortnight and picked up by Metro Sergeant Horace "He was dead when I found him" Kemp during his rotation with the Office of

Disease Control—that's it, stand up, Kempster, boy"—a huge roar of cheers from the train-yard bulls—"tonight's challenger is Sub-ash Anandi. Awaiting deportation for forged inoculation papers, Subash weighs in this evening at one hundred and sixty-seven pounds of ragin' Muslim muscle."

Walden and Subash come back to center pit and Oster says, "Let's have a big Houdini Lounge welcome for both of our young warriors," and the crowd louds up obligingly one more time, then settles in as Walden and Green unlock all their chains and scram-ble up to their seats on opposite rims of the crater, where they're each handed a twelve-gauge pump Winchester, this tournament's version of the referee's whistle.

"Gentlemen," Oster yells, "whenever you're ready."

Someone lets an air horn blow for several seconds and as soon as it stops Subash leaps forward, going in under Rafael's meatless ribs, driving the teenager to the ground. And then the two of them are rolling around the pit, covering themselves with mud and splintered glass and brick ash. Subash is jabbing at both of Rafael's sides, solid little tags that hurt more than Rafael can believe. Rafael scrambles to get loose, kicks a foot into the Pak-istani's groin hard enough to break off the attack and instantly change the direction of the fight.

Rafael rolls to the side, gets up on a knee and before he can think, he clumsily pounces on top on Subash's back, throwing a thin choke hold around the neck. The Pakistani sinks a skin-breaking bite into Rafael's wrist. Rafael screams, releases his hold, and Subash grabs the bleeding arm with both hands and pulls Rafael over onto his back, then plants a knee on the teen's chest and throws a combination at the kid's face, landing a right below the eye and a left, more solid, full impact, into the jaw.

Gilrein is light-headed but he can't take his eyes off what he knows is very soon going to turn into carnage. Oster chooses this moment to lean to Gilrein's ear and say, "I know you thought I was out of line, bringing you back here, you know, where it all happened."

Gilrein stares at Subash flailing away as if Rafael's head was some speed bag stuffed with bone and meat.

"But I had to make you see, Gilly. I felt honor-bound, you've got to understand this. I needed to make you realize there could be life after Ceil."

The name breaks up the vision and Gilrein turns to look at Oster as Oster drapes an arm over Gilrein's shoulder and squints and smiles and bobs his head a little and says, "This is what Ceil would want. You know that. Deep down, you know it. Ceil would not want her husband driving around Bangkok at night without a badge and a piece."

"I've still got the piece," Gilrein says, confused, but Oster ignores him and continues.

"Ceil would not want Gilrein to spend the rest of his life as some low-rent taxi-boy. Counting out change. Collecting rags. Mopping up the backseat for every scum rat that can whistle. Ceil would be crushed."

"You knew Ceil pretty well, huh, Bobby?"

Rafael can feel skin rip inside his mouth and a jet of warm liquid start to roll over his tongue and gums. He spits a wad of blood and pulp onto his own torso, is pumped up by the sight and instinctively yanks a fistful of Subash's hair and throws the opponent off his chest.

Rafael takes in some air and touches his jaw and gets belted with both a jolt of pain and a burst of adrenaline that has him on his feet and grabbing blindly for Subash, void of thought, absent of ideas about cause and effect, simply wanting to get hold of the bastard who tore up his mouth and go him one better, do some lasting damage, break the man up and stomp on the parts. The kid has never felt this kind of rage. He's crazy with it. He swings a bent elbow, off-balance but with enough force to catch Subash in the throat. Subash starts to bend forward, and Rafael surprises himself by finessing a respectable punch, driving in a fist just above the belt line.

"I'm just saying, Ceil would want you back with family, Gil. Ceil would want you here with us. Ceil would say, 'Go for it.' Ceil would tell you, 'Listen to Bobby Oster.' She was a fine cop. I don't have to tell you that. She was one of the best. Things turned out different, she would have moved past the old priest. I'm telling you, Ceil would want you to be one of us."

"The Magicians?"

"Ceil would say 'Do it in my memory,' " Oster says. "She'd be like, 'You and Bobby O get down to the Park 'n' start kicking some ass. In my name.' "

"Ceil didn't talk that way," Gilrein says.

"The point is," Oster says, "you're home now. And once I talk to my people, we'll have you reinstated in a week. There's a hole in Administrative Vice right now. We're all over AD, Gilly. We own that goddamn department and we're branching out. The boys'll help you move your stuff in here next weekend. You can be on the job by Friday. I got stuff in the pipe for you already. Swear to God."

The air runs from Subash's lungs, empties his body with an awful speed, and sends him down, full weight on both knees. He tries to hold up a flat hand, a panicky stop sign, but his balance is gone and he topples onto all fours, gasping. Rafael is over the edge. He lets a foot kick out, smacking into Subash's side, knocking him over onto shoulder and head.

One of the ponytailed betting agents runs up to Oster and thrusts a wad of bills at him. Bobby crams the stash in a rear pocket, slaps the cashier on the ass as she turns, and calls to her back, "Two more minutes, Dolores, then close it down."

He stands up, waves to Danny Walden, mimes some cryptic body language like a paranoid base coach, then asks over his shoulder, "So, what, is it in the Checker?"

Though expected, the question rocks Gilrein and he asks, "Is what in the Checker?"

Oster turns to look at him and says, "C'mon, Gilly, don't jerk me around tonight. You can see I've got my hands full here."

Rafael's chest is heaving as he circles his downed opponent. Stewie Green has told him to wait at least fifteen minutes before the kill, but Green's Spanish isn't the best and time has a tendency to get distorted in the penal colony. So he stomps down on the Pakistani's stomach with his heel, follows this up with a kick in the face that breaks open a run of blood vessels along the right eye. The crowd's shrieking pushes toward maximum volume and Rafael goes into his act, pretends to suddenly spot something glinting in the spotlight, something metal shining up out of a matted pile of old leaves and blown-up bricks. He grabs hold and picks it up, an old piece of piping, about the size of a small baseball bat, threaded at each end. He wraps both hands around one end, chokes them up an inch and takes a cut through the air that makes a wonderful *whooshing* sound.

A few feet behind him, Subash is moaning and moving, trying to get back on his feet. Rafael turns to see the adversary grabbing hold of a brick. He starts to walk toward Subash, taking warm-up swings with the pipe bat, practice for a swat to the skull that will put the Pakistani down for good.

"I'm not jerking you around," Gilrein says.

Oster waits a long time before replying, seeming to study the fight like a stern dance instructor. He runs a hand over his mouth, then says, "'Course you're jerking me around. You're not stupid enough to come back here without the book—"

"I don't have any book, Oster."

Rafael's chest is heaving and blood is running down his chin nonstop. He brings the pipe back over his right shoulder. Subash forces his way to his feet, lifts his brick back behind his right ear in a pitcher's stance. They start to slowly circle each other, the crowd loving it, screaming down advice or insults at the two fighters in a language that neither one can understand.

Oster stands up slowly, catches Stewie Green's eye, makes some kind of hand gesture that Green confidently nods a response to. Green climbs up on a pile of bricks and starts to call out three equally accented and slightly elongated syllables: *Raf—a—el, Raf—a—el*—and the crowd picks up on it immediately, making it into a group war chant that grows louder in volume with each recitation, a ceremonial egging-on of the kid with the pipe, an aural talisman with the power to turn a desperate refugee with little understanding of how and why he ended up in this moment, into some kind of mythic warrior ready, with the aid of a length of planted lead water pipe, to dispense a messy death to a weaker enemy.

Bobby Oster sits back down and says, "I've always thought you and I were a lot alike, Gilly. Almost like we're brothers. Like one of those old stories, you know? We're separated at birth and we meet up years later . . ."

He trails off, shaking his head.

Gilrein says, "I don't think so. I think it's more like one of those not-so-old stories where one of us has to rip the heart out of the other. And I think both of us know that."

"You really didn't bring the book, did you, you asshole?"

Rafael hesitates, makes a noticeable glance up to Walden. Walden gestures slightly with the Winchester, tipping the barrel down toward the ground. Subash senses something and panics, charges blindly with his brick. But Rafael is too fast. He steps into the charge and bunts Subash in the throat, putting him back down on the ground, choking without sound. Then Rafael straddles the quaking body, a foot on either side of the Pakistani's hips. Rafael chokes up on the pipe, holds it cocked for several seconds like a young Ted Williams posing for what will become an enormously valuable trading card.

"I wish there were some other way we could have resolved this," Oster says, staring, unblinking, down on the pit.

Gilrein listens to the chanting die out in an instant, as if by some unseen signal. He says, "You're going to take me out right here? Some of these people were my friends . . ."

Bobby Oster says, "Don't flatter yourself, okay?"

Subash tries to move, his head rolling on his neck as understanding flows back into the brain. He makes a futile and stuttering attempt to gain balance up on an arm. Rafael is blocking Gilrein's view. Oster moves a few steps to the side, maybe to see if the doomed man's eyes are open or closed.

Gilrein moves up behind him and says, "I'm not going to just roll over, Bobby."

Oster shrugs, intent on watching the finale.

"Doesn't matter what you do, Gilly," he says. "We come after someone, there's nothing they can do."

And then the pipe comes down, flies to the skull with a vicious and simplistic arc, a chop down through the air, fairly graceless but completely effective.

Subash's skull cracks open. Blood explodes. And to make sure the job is done, Rafael hammers home two more blows, leaving no doubt in the mind of the crowd as to who has won money tonight and who has lost.

26

All along the walk back through the factory and out to the Checker, Gilrein keeps waiting to hear the explosion of orgiastic bloodlust that the mob has been building toward since the prisoners were led into the pit. But the air behind him is void of any sound beyond the muted echo of Oster's bullhorn announcing something unintelligible.

As he approaches the cab, Gilrein notices someone in the driver's seat. He takes his gun from his rig and continues to walk, holding the piece down at his side. A few more yards and the face behind the wheel is recognizable. Gilrein leans on the passenger window and waits for an explanation.

When it becomes clear the intruder has no intention of offering the first words, Gilrein says, "I'm sorry, Inspector, I'm off duty."

He gets a throat-clearing noise in response.

"You'll have to find another ride," Gilrein says, more forcefully.

The old priest reaches to the roof and switches on the cab's dome light, then smiles and opens his mouth as wide as it will part to reveal a hole swollen with white, oozing pustules.

"Jesus," Gilrein says, recoiling.

Lacazze lifts his hands in the air like a surgeon, or a monk ready to consecrate a wafer. The hands are covered with similar nodules and swollen to the point where the fingers resemble overstuffed sausages.

Gilrein subdues the impulse to bolt away from the cab.

"I need to speak with you," Lacazze says, the voice phlegmy and choked, as if both his lungs and his larynx were slightly constricted. "It's about Ceil."

"What about her?"

The Inspector shakes his head and says, "Not here."

They stare at each other until, unsure of what else to do, Gilrein takes the keys from his pocket and tosses them through the window, then climbs into the backseat, a passenger in the Checker for the first time since childhood.

Though he left it in the glove box, he finds Ceil's notebook on the seat next to him, a place near the end of the journal bookmarked with the band from a Magdalena cigar.

"I hope you don't mind," Lacazze says into the rearview as he starts the cab and rolls out of the lot. "I marked a passage I thought you might find useful."

The Checker picks up speed down Rome Avenue. And, against what's left of his better judgment, Gilrein begins to decode the last message from his wife.

> Z. Dear Gilrein:
>   You are sleeping, once again, as I write
> this, turned on your side, knees hunched up
> slightly. You've kicked the sheets off and I
> know that in ten minutes you'll be
> shivering. As I wrote that last line you let
> out that noise, that half moan, half sigh
> that signifies the deepest point of your
> dreams. I'll confess now that the noise
> annoyed me slightly when we first slept

together. But lately I've come to find it
reassuring. Don't ask me, yet, what I need
to be reassured about.

This letter is to be an apology, though I
know there is a good chance you will never
come to read it. But letters are created as
much for the benefit of the writer as for
the intended recipient. Maybe more for the
writer. And, in any event, once again, I
cannot sleep.

Husbands and wives are thought to possess
secret knowledge of one another. And in a
manner, of course, they do. But the common
wisdom will never understand what the long-
married know, most viscerally, at times like
now, at four o'clock in the morning, when
life in the perfect bungalow seems somehow
most in jeopardy. And what we know is this:
no matter how much we want to give ourselves
away, some adamant core refuses to yield,
some recalcitrant center will never fully
give. And no matter how much we want to
receive the Other, in no matter how perfect
a totality, our capacity is always wanting.

This has to do with an inherent sense of
personal identity, an essential
individuality. It also has to do with the
inadequacy of human communication. There are
things we simply can never convey.

But I need to go back now and try anyway.
I need to make the attempt in spite of my
knowledge of a predestined failure. I need
to talk about that first night. Our first
extended parcel of time spent together. When
you drove me around this wounded city from

eleven o'clock at night until seven o'clock
the next morning. As if that initial and
unofficial "date" had been a work shift.

On that premier courting, that original
wooing, you told me everything a native
feels it necessary to impart to the blank
émigré. I know it was a two-way
conversation, at least at the start, but I
gave you back nothing of value that I can
recall. You might have thought you were
relaying an informal history of your
hometown, but the history was transparent.
It was a clear laminate. And underneath it I
could see, right there from the start, your
own *personal* history, the checkpoints that
brought you to our maiden night together.

I was impressed, I will admit, not with
the underplayed minutiae you'd accumulated
about this bastion of obsolete industry that
you have always called home. But more with
the unknowing earnestness that was behind
every word, as if instead of delineating for
me the routes of the old P&Q railroad, you
were chanting the sounds that would turn
lead into gold. As if instead of running
down a not-so-brief synopsis of the lineage
of the Quinsigamond Diner, you were
descanting new ways to split the atom.

But what I need to focus on, what I need
to underline, for myself just as much as for
you, is that moment when we made a circuit
on the south side, just as dawn was breaking
and we were cresting over Nipmuck Hill and
you started to point out the spires and
turrets that make up the Gothic wonderland

of the Jesuit Olympus, the College of St.
Ignatius. And you came to tell me, right
then, on our first night—were you convinced
there would be no others?—the story of your
expulsion from the school. What you called,
with a heaping of self-drama that I swore
you were unaware of, "the Transubstantiation
Scandal."

It's a different sensation for Lacazze, being in the front seat
instead of the back, active rather than passive, choosing direction
and speed. He likes driving better than riding, though the silence
is a little discomforting, a reminder that he may never hear the
rest of the old man's story. *Otto's Tale.* In his honor, the Inspector glides the cab through the downtown banking strip and heads
for Gompers Station. Before the night is out, he may even sample
a bearclaw.

He begins the long, slow circle around the train yard, even
imitating Langer's quirk of opening the window a crack as the cab
passes the chronically flaming trash Dumpsters of the east yard.
He looks out on a pack of the more feral tinker kids, huddled
around a Dumpster, basking for a moment in its heat. These are
the ones who've gone fully over to the other side, who've abdi-
cated an integration that was never fully offered. Lacazze wonders
why so many people in this city deny the existence of the feral tinkers, talk of them with the exasperated weariness of the put-upon
scientist denying alien abductions or the flatness of the earth.
Here they are in plain sight. Flesh and blood. How can you call
them a myth? Someone, he decides, should tell their story.

In the backseat, the passenger shifts with the curve of the road.

Not being a Catholic, I had to intuit the
depth of your breach. But as you relayed the
story about those weeks preceding your SIN,
those awful weeks of lying on your back in

the dark, the time that you called (risking
making trite the obviously genuine pain),
your "spiritual torment," I started to wish
I could relate on an emotional level as
well. Because there was just something about
your voice in the telling of this story. It
had changed somehow, taken on a timbre, a
resonance it had not previously had. (Maybe
it was just all that bad coffee you had
poured from a Thermos bottle shaped like a
Menlo cartoon character—I think it was Alice
Watzername.)

And eventually you got to the part where
you made yourself walk to that basement
chapel and attend the Midnight Mass. And I
was as transfixed as if I'd been watching
the most enthralling horror movie ever
lensed. A horror movie played inside the
cortex of your own brain that, at some
unnoticed point, began to incorporate,
exactly and seamlessly, your deepest fears
into the plot line. I was walking with you
down that endless center aisle as the organ
played "Faith of Our Fathers." And I'd never
attended a Mass in my life. I felt you
tremble as you came to a stop in front of
the Jesuit priest—Father Clement, wasn't
it?—and extended your open palm to receive
the wafer. I was sharing your nerve endings
as you tried and failed to respond to the
priest's "Body of Christ," and couldn't
bring yourself to mutter the "Amen." And
your mouth was my mouth when you turned and
brought the Host up and past your lips, over
your tongue, and secreted it in the left—

side gully between the interior cheek and
the gums. I will never forget the coldness
of the early spring air as you made your
way, walking faster with each step, out of
the chapel and across the campus, the fear
as you reached into your pocket to touch the
key to the lab, the key you had gone to
ridiculous lengths to obtain and have copied
weeks before, still not knowing if you'd go
through with it all, and the simultaneous
(but different) fear as the bread began to
dissolve in your mouth, mixing too quickly
with the acidic saliva.

I could hear the terror-making echo of
your boots inside the biology lab, feel the
agony of the short wait as you turned on the
electron microscope and found the glass
slide, extracted the Eucharist from your
mouth, sick to your stomach now with the
finality of your actions, placed the Host
onto the slide and secured the slide under
the clamps of the scope. I could feel the
dry blink of your eyeball as it began making
its way toward the enlarging lens. Could
hear the sound of the door opening behind
you, hear the voice of the security guard,
the "toy cop" as you uncharitably called
her, demanding to know what you were doing.

Had you ignored her even for an instant
you might have gotten a look. Proved to
yourself once and for all the fact or the
absence of fact regarding molecular
conversion and the ways of mystical
transformations. But you stood up, as if
you'd been questioned by the voice of God

itself rather than a minimum-wage security
guard. You stood up and she approached the
table and immediately caught on to what was
happening here. I have to wonder on
occasion, when she took the job, could your
toy cop ever have known that one night her
routine of drunk and disorderlies and
parking violators would be disrupted by, of
all things, a heretical truth seeker?

As your father was neither alumnus nor
contributor to the cause, they managed to
kick your doubting ass out the gates and off
the Hill inside a week.

And now, I would imagine, you realize the
point of this entire diatribe.

There was an awkward pause when you'd
finished the story. Less than ten seconds, I
would guess. We were parked behind the
closed diner at the bottom of the hill and
you were looking up at the crosses that
capped the turrets of the tallest buildings.
I remember your face side-lit by the green
neon that rimmed the diner's marquee. And
that is when I laughed.

I laughed at the story of the
Transubstantiation Scandal.

And I have always hated myself slightly but
consistently for that burst of laughter. That
it ended immediately made it somehow worse.

I have always wondered why, in the wake of
my laugh, in the face of my fierce
insensitivity and disrespect in the moment
after you had just confessed to me the event
that clearly altered your life in a profound
way, you ever wanted to see me again. And

how you ever could have married me. And now,
tonight, sitting here in the bedroom of the
perfect bungalow, the answer comes to me in
an instant, in the way that conversion came
to Saul on the road to Damascus.

As I watch you shift in the bed now, naked
and rolled toward me, as I watch your mouth
fall open, making your face appear so much
younger, appear close to childlike, I
understand everything: You wanted me even
more after I laughed at your story. Because
you wanted to know how someone lives
completely devoid of any kind of faith.
Without that relentless burden that had
chewed at you for so long. Gnawed away, day
and night, at your liver and your soul.

That might not have been much to go on,
but it made you need me in a persistent way.
And at the risk of sounding like a romance
novel, a love grew out of it. We do not
choose our motivations. They choose us.

Except for the occasional sound of a page being turned or the
body shifting slightly, Lacazze could easily forget that Gilrein is in
the backseat.

How did Langer do it? How did the old man focus on his narrative and drive at the same time? How was he able to maneuver
the taxi through its routes while his brain was fully immersed in
another world?

The Inspector knows that the cab must come to a stop in order
for him to finally tell his own story. The distractions of the passing city are just too great. He can't inhabit the past and the present at the same time. The strain would be unbearable. Perhaps
this is another symptom of the Grippe, an effect no one talks
about because there are so many others that are more dramatic.

There is simply so much to see on the street tonight. And all of it appears so vibrant. Almost hyperreal. Even the scrap yards up on Cornell Hill. Even the deserted section of the Vacuum. Everything has a vibration tonight. Everything seems to be calling out for attention, sending a warning that means *I am significant, I am an integral part of the picture.*

But it isn't until he finds himself steering the hack past the Yusupov Garden Room, then cross-cutting alleys until he's passing the Hotel Adrianople, that Lacazze understands there has been an underlying plan to his journey, a system born of his subconscious or the strictures of karma. Either way, he's been taking himself and his passenger on a haphazard, sometimes backward tour, a memorial parade that retraces a historic procession, a trip that once led, in the end, to the Rome Avenue Raid.

```
And now I think, my love, that you were
instinctively correct. My laugh was born
not out of insensitivity to another's
tradition (though, of course, there was
that). Not out of a moment of social
stupidity (though there was certainly a
degree of that). My laugh came for the
exact reason you sensed at the beginning:
because I could not understand the meaning
of your need. I could not understand how a
seemingly intelligent young man could have
so much vested in such an illogical and
obviously symbolic ritual. I could not
understand that it went beyond ritual, that
it was attached to the center of how we
view and then live our lives, of how we
view the reason for our existence. And
ultimately and simply, of how we define and
deal with the agents of good. And maybe
more important, of evil.
```

I was laughing at a young man who had
wanted, more desperately than I could
imagine or understand, to believe that there
was purpose and order and meaning beyond
himself, beyond his own making.

Please try to understand this, Gilrein: I
was laughing because, whether I knew it or
not, I was terrified.

It has taken me the span of our marriage
to realize this. The truth is unalterable. I
laughed out of fear. Tonight's epiphany says
that my intellect could be boundless and it
still would not be enough. I can reject
Mystery, but that will never negate Mystery.
You have converted me with your presence,
Gilrein. I am still an atheist as I know you
to understand that term. But I am less and
less an egotist. By the time you wake up,
I'll be humbled to my core.

Now I find that as a philosopher, I am a
coward. As a linguist, I am made blind and
deaf by my own ego and pride. And as a cop,
I am sinfully envious of the criminal.

I loved you because in the end, you could
not be a monster even when you thought you
needed to be a monster. I have loved you
because you have given me, without a price,
the perfect life in the bungalow, where
Mystery came to live, where improbable and
fragile hope could be born to the sad
accompaniment of a perfect-voiced torch diva.

My mentor believes that language creates
reality.

My mentor now calls his Methodology "The
Final Criticism."

My mentor could not be a bigger asshole if
he practiced on Saturdays.

I have so much to tell you, Gilrein. There
is so much I don't know. But so much that I
suspect. I am tempted to wake you right now.
But I'm already late to meet the Inspector.
Yet another hot tip regarding the Tung. So
I'm off to Hotel Adrianople. You sleep now
and we will talk forever when I return. As
Imogene would say,

> We will talk until
> Every story has been told.

27

The cab bumps up and over the curb and jerks to a stop. The engine dies by way of a stall. Gilrein looks up to find himself in front of the Dunot Precinct House. In the quiet, the shallow and labored breathing from the front seat is more pronounced, the soundtrack to a movie about disease.

"You don't like the noise," Lacazze says.

"Does anyone?"

"Mr. Gilrein, there is a whole breed of people in love with death. This city is lousy with death lovers."

"I wouldn't know about that."

The Inspector tries to clear his throat and fails. "Do you carry a gun?" he asks.

Gilrein pulls his .38, holds it up for Lacazze to see.

"Bring it inside," the Inspector says. "One of us may need it."

Gilrein looks in the mirror and says, "I'm not going inside."

"I think you are, Mr. Gilrein," Lacazze says, without annoyance. "I think you want to come inside."

The old priest climbs out onto the sidewalk, fumbling with the flap on his breast pocket, finally pulling free a Magdalena and launching into a new search for his lighter.

Gilrein watches him through the window and says, "That's just what I want to do," with as much cruelty as he can manage, "spend the rest of the night in a small room with a man in the last phase of the Grippe."

The Inspector comes up with a pack of matches and with a little difficulty ignites the end of the cigar. Gilrein wonders how he can sustain a draw with the trouble he has breathing, but in moments the barrel end of the stogie is glowing and the air is filling up with a heavy, woody smell.

Lacazze holds the Magdalena like some fragile musical instrument and through the smoke he says, "Do you know what I think the Grippe really is, Gilrein? It's a parasite. Genetically manipulated but completely organic. It's a microscopic vermin. Enlarged, I think it would look like a tiny worm. Transferred by the spray of spittle when one has a simple conversation. 'How about this weather?' and you're infected. It crawls through the brain, relatively harmless until it meets the language centers. It lays its eggs as soon as it lands and it immediately starts feeding. Quite insatiable during pregnancy. Gestation is just forty days. The eggs hatch and the offspring join the picnic. *That* is when you know something is horribly wrong. You can't find the correct word. Or you can't find the graphical symbols to represent that word. Any hope of communicating is torn away. Any hope of meaning is devoured. Thank God it's ultimately fatal."

He pauses to take a long draw on the cigar and then adds, "I don't think you could care less about the Grippe, young man. I think you might welcome a chance to contract the Grippe. Such a romantic way to go. Not as dramatic as a shower of bullets, but surely more lingering. A longer period of suffering."

"You have to be a smug prick right to the end?"

Lacazze taps some ash to the sidewalk.

"You mistake insight for arrogance, Mr. Gilrein. But you'll follow me inside anyway. Not really for the contagion, however.

That's just a bonus for you. You'll follow me because I knew Ceil better than you did. And you can't bear that. After all this time. You want to know what I know."

Gilrein throws his door open and goes after the old priest, grabbing him by the lapels and running him up against the bricks of the station house. Lacazze doesn't struggle, just goes limp, lets himself be carried by the force of the attack, eyes open the whole time and staring at Gilrein.

"Why were you waiting in my cab?" Gilrein yells.

"Inside," Lacazze answers. "And bring the gun."

The station house is a definition of chaos. It has evolved beyond its standard of extreme clutter and into the domain of the ruined. File cabinets have been overturned and their contents spread like fertilizer over every square inch of floor space. Some of the piles of paper have been saturated with water. Possibly with urine. Others are covered with perfect black bootprints that, when combined, resemble a set of instructions for an elaborately complicated dance routine. There are trails of vermin droppings here and there. Some graffiti artist has had a party on the walls, spraying can after can of Day-Glo and metallic colors, looping and curving and slashing lines of paint into letters, symbols, pictograms, doodles, everything but intelligible words, then crossing out the bulk of the drawing and starting over again on top of the previous layer, painting over the paint.

There are also dozens, maybe hundreds of bullet holes in the walls. One desk is covered with mud and silt and dried leaves. Another desk has a fire axe protruding from its surface, the blade imbedded in the wood up to the handle. And then, in contrast to this, there is Ceil's desk, left neat as the last night she sat behind it, preserved as a shrine, everything in order, pencils still sitting in a coffee mug that advertises LOFTUS FUNERAL HOMES, reference books lined up along the outer lip, a green blotter occupying the center. And a framed photo of Gilrein, a small candid shot that depicts a content man seated on the edge of his bed in the perfect bungalow. Only someone has altered the photo, defaced it, taken a black marker and drawn onto the picture, making round glasses over the eyes, filling in a pointed goatee on the chin, blacking out the two front teeth. And fixing horns at the top of the skull. Gilrein refrains from touching the picture; instead, he leans down and sniffs at the desktop, smelling the aroma of a recently applied lemon polishing agent.

They move past Ceil's desk, walk to the door of the Inspector's office. The interrogation chamber. The place were the ritual of Methodology was performed. A piece of scrap paper is tacked to the door. It features Ceil's handwriting, or, more likely, a bad imitation of Ceil's handwriting, that reads

ESCHATOLOGY SQUAD COMMANDER
KNOCK BEFORE ENTERING

and beneath this someone has added, with the dry sarcasm that was one signature of Ceil,

THEN ABANDON ALL HOPE.

The Inspector unlocks and opens the door and Gilrein follows him inside. If it's possible, Lacazze's office is even more chaotic than the squad room. It's as if the chamber were trying to transmute itself into a small municipal dumping ground. The interrogation blackboard has been knocked over and its backing mirror is shattered, slivered glass sprayed everywhere like foam on the crest of a frozen wave. Random holes have been gouged into the plaster, each about the size of a fist. One wall displays an abbreviated piece of writing that's illegible and could just be a line of smeared blood. Every one of the paper stacks and file towers has been knocked over, covering the floor with a thicket of yellowed reams. The room smells like a lavatory that has never been properly cleaned. There are also traces of burned gunpowder, alcohol, and a cloying hint of dying vegetation.

They sit on opposite sides of Lacazze's desk, the red chalice in front of Gilrein, the crystal decanter, half-filled, as always, with Spanish sherry, in front of the Inspector. The only other thing on the desktop, spread beneath the chalice like a blotter, is a crumpled and partially wet tabloid-style newspaper.

Lacazze raises the heavy glass bottle to his lips and says, "To your health."

Gilrein picks up the red chalice and brings it to his mouth, then glances inside and sees fat globules of an oozing white substance refusing to mix with what must be the dregs of some sherry.

"Is it consecrated?" Gilrein asks.

Lacazze breaks off his swallow and comes forward in his seat as if he's about to choke. He manages a hard gulp before barking out a laugh, then rubs away the dripping sherry with the back of his newly grotesque hand. Gilrein notices some of the pustules are bubbling slightly.

"Didn't you hear?" Lacazze says, voice weak and raspy, but his tone mildly sarcastic. "I've been stripped of my powers."

"Secular or spiritual?"

"Forgive me," Lacazze says, "but those two always confuse me."

"I'll bet. Ceil used to say that as a cop you made a terrifying priest—"

"She had such a way with the langauge."

"—or maybe it was the other way around."

"I suppose we'll never know," Lacazze says, then takes another drink, more moderate this time, and adds, "but what do you think she meant by that?"

Gilrein crosses his arms and stares at the old man.

"I think she meant you had all the best equipment for either job," he says, "but none of the empathy they both require."

"Empathy," Lacazze repeats, as if only for the sound of the word. "From the Greek *empatheai*, meaning affection or passion."

"If you say so."

"What I say, once again, is that your knowledge of your late wife is lacking."

Gilrein holds back another outburst. What he'd like to do is go over the desk and plant the decanter in the bastard's skull. What he does instead is take a breath, lower his voice and say, "That's why I'm here, right? That's why I followed you inside."

Lacazze seems to study him for a few seconds.

"Drink up, Mr. Gilrein," the Inspector finally says. "Wine loosens the tongue. That's what we need here tonight. Free discourse between rivals."

"Are we rivals, Inspector?"

"We have always been rivals, Mr. Gilrein."

"And what is it we're competing for?"

Lacazze frowns at him as if the answer were beneath them both.

"What all men fight over," he says. "Their own view of the world and the love of a good woman."

Gilrein tenses up in spite of himself.

"The woman in question," he says, "is dead."

"Exactly," Lacazze says. "And since the day she died, you and I have both been living a series of lies. And those lies have been consuming us slowly, haven't they, Gilrein?"

"I don't know, Inspector. I'm not the one with the sores all over my hands and my mouth."

"But it's early yet."

The comment makes Gilrein decide to go on the offensive.

He sits forward on the interrogation stool, leans on his knees and says, "I was a bunko cop for a long time, Inspector. And I never understood why Ceil couldn't see that underneath all your bullshit voodoo you were nothing but a lowlife fucking con man."

This brings another unexpected laugh. Lacazze covers his face with his pus-swollen hands for a moment and leans back in his chair. When he takes his hands away all trace of amusement has disappeared, replaced by a disgusted and maybe pitying look.

"How did Ceil bear it?" he asks. "Taking her brilliance home every night to such an inferior partner. It must be regarded as an act of mercy. On top of everything else, the woman was a saint. Damien to the brain-addled. Mother Teresa to the feeble-minded—"

"Sorry, Inspector, but I find it hard to believe that you can't think of a better way to spend your final hours than insulting a feeble-minded cabdriver."

"—Not a saint, a martyr. Sacrificing herself on this lowbrow cross. Giving up her genius to this Golgotha of stupidity."

"Lacazze."

"Prostituting herself to a pathetic livery boy," the Inspector yells, "who couldn't even make it in bunko. Bunko! My God, what was she thinking?"

It's not that Gilrein can no longer contain himself, it's that he doesn't want to. He kicks out at the desk, knocking over the chalice and spilling the sherry, then he's up off the stool and around the desk, pulling Lacazze out of his chair and backhanding him across the face, hard enough to knock the Inspector to the floor, down onto a bed of ink-infested notepaper. The decanter flies to the back wall and shatters. And then it's that one easy step over the line of the rational, and Gilrein is down on his knees, straddled across Lacazze's stomach, the .38 out and the hammer cocked and the barrel pushed into the swollen left cheek of the old man.

They're both breathing heavily. Gilrein wants to make the Inspector flinch, wants to make him cower under the threat of the gun. But Lacazze just stares up at him, face strained, swollen lips sucking around the mouth of the gun, skim-milk-colored pus oozing down over the chin.

Gilrein immediately withdraws his piece from the face, angles it toward the ceiling.

"Son of a bitch," he says, following out a line of thought that's too late in dawning. "You wanted me to do it."

The Inspector's head falls back and even though it's cushioned by all the paper there's a perceptible thump.

"Jesus Christ," Gilrein says, rocking back on the old man's torso. "You wanted me to pull the trigger. You were hoping you could goad me into doing it for you. You cowardly little asshole. Your own goddamn station house all these years. Such an untouchable hump. And you couldn't even pull your own plug."

He gets up, drags Lacazze back into his seat. It's like lifting a corpse.

"I won't do it for you, Inspector. But don't let me stop you."

And he lifts Lacazze's limp hand and places the Colt in the palm. The hand falls into Lacazze's lap. Gilrein picks it up by the wrist and brings it up to the head until the barrel is resting against the right temple.

"Go ahead," Gilrein says. "You're all set. Just squeeze."

For a moment it seems as if he will. Focus comes into his eyes and the grip on the revolver tightens. But then he thumbs the hammer back gently and settles it into its cradle. He places the gun down on the desk and shoves it next to the toppled chalice.

"I guess," Gilrein says, "intellect is no indication of courage."

Lacazze sits with his head hung back and his eyes closed. Gilrein stares at him, waiting for a reply. When none comes, he picks his piece up from the desk and tucks it in his jacket pocket and walks to the door.

"It's too bad," he says, "you can't use the Methodology on yourself."

The Inspector's eyes come open but don't track to Gilrein, just stare up at the alphabet designs cut into the tin-plated ceiling. In a voice barely audible, he asks, "Why do you think Ceil loved you?"

Gilrein has no idea why he lingers, but he leans against the doorjamb and says, "She just did."

"You're sure of that?"

Gilrein nods, makes Lacazze move his head and look forward.

"From the time we are children," the Inspector says, "we're taught that faith is a gift."

"You're the theologian."

"I am an unbeliever," holding his hands up for Gilrein to look at like some parody of St. Thomas's vision, "and this is proof of my transgression."

"The Grippe?"

"The plague sent down as a response to my pride and my doubt."

"Now that's an enlightened position," Gilrein says, shifting in the doorway, suddenly intrigued.

"The sick man tends to regress."

Gilrein steps back into the room and leans his arms down on the desk.

"The more I know about you, the more I hate you, Inspector."

"You know nothing about me, Mr. Gilrein. You should consider yourself lucky. Your ignorance has protected you."

"From?"

"From doubt, of course," Lacazze says, finally coming forward in his chair, folding his hands on top of the desk like a schoolboy, turning his head to the side and spitting a mouthful of green discharge onto the floor. "Do you know the old saying, Gilrein? 'Act as if you have faith and faith will be given to you'? Are you familiar?"

"I know the saying."

"Then act on it. Take the gun out and execute me. Do the honorable thing."

Gilrein stares at him, not completely sure that he isn't being mocked.

"Ceil would want it this way," Lacazze says.

"You're the second person tonight who's tried to tell me what Ceil would have wanted."

"Ceil understood the value of vengeance."

"Vengeance?"

The Inspector's expression changes to something between disgust and disbelief.

"Are you really this ignorant? Is it possible you haven't suspected any part of the truth?"

In fact, and of course, he has, some part of him has always done just that, up in the barn loft of Wormland as he slept or maybe in the Checker when he thought he was just concentrating on the phrasing as Imogene Wedgewood sang "Chinese Boxes."

He looks down at the Inspector, focuses on the old man's mouth, and makes himself say, "What truth is that?"

Lacazze manages what could be a smile if not for the fact that the musculature of his lips is decaying.

Gilrein steps forward, reaches down, and pulls Lacazze to standing.

"Why am I here?"

The Inspector lowers his voice to show indulgence and says, "Like all neighborhood mayors, the Lord knows the value of his middlemen. You're here to confess me in His absence."

"I don't understand."

"That," the Inspector says, "is because you haven't heard the story yet."

And he reaches down to his desk, grabs hold of the soaked newspaper, pulls it up, and plasters it against Gilrein's chest. Gilrein takes hold of the paper and moves a step backward.

"Did you know," Lacazze says, moving around the desk and taking a seat on the interrogation stool, "that prior to her death your wife had become a very secretive woman?"

Gilrein tries to listen and read at the same time. Droplets of fresh pus have stained the front page of the paper, making it slightly translucent, the words on the next page close to visible, the ink on the title page almost bleeding into the unreadable.

But he can still make out the paper's title:

WORD MADE FLESH: A JOURNAL OF LINGUISTIC COSMOLOGY

And he can still make out the headline of the lead article:

SIX MILLION GRAMMATICAL CONSTRUCTS: THE HOLOCAUST AS
LINGUISTIC ARGUMENT
BY ANONYMOUS

Someone has crossed out "by Anonymous" and below it, written in sloppy block letters, written with a finger, using blood and
pus as a handy ink, are the words

BY BLIND HOMER LACAZZE

"Ceil came to disappoint me in the last week of her life, Gilrein."

Gilrein looks across the desk at the Inspector, all kinds of
meanings suddenly sliding into place.

"You wrote this, didn't you?" holding up the tabloid.

But Lacazze is already locked into monologue.

"Ceil betrayed me. In the way only a lover can. She desecrated
the bond. In time, all things would have been made known to her.
It was impatience that killed Ceil."

Gilrein drops the paper to the floor and stares at the old man.

"She went behind my back. She began to investigate old problems. Without knowing the history. Without understanding how
the Methodology had evolved. Pride is what killed our Ceil."

"You were Blind Homer," Gilrein says softly.

"She gave me no choice. If she had just left Sonia alone—"

"The Tung belonged to you."

"If she had just left Sonia alone, there would have been time—"

"You're Blind fucking Homer."

A pause, and then the smug expression that Lacazze knows
will push his rival over the divide.

"In the—"

But before Lacazze can finish the sentence, Gilrein pulls his
piece and fires twice. The first bullet takes the Inspector in the
groin. The second goes into and through the throat, knocks
Lacazze off the interrogation stool and onto the floor, rolled on
his side.

Gilrein waits for the rush of panic and adrenaline but it doesn't
come. He stares at Lacazze, waits for the Inspector to cry out or
move. But everything remains still. Completely motionless and
almost silent but for the fading echo of the gunshots.

This is the final criticism.

And Gilrein's response is to exit the precinct house. To exit this city as soon as he can. To leave the putrefying body in the chamber. As a sign. A language that is as close to pure as he can possibly imagine.

28

Gilrein parks on the fire road at
the rear border of the Brockden Estate. He reloads the Colt,
gets out of the Checker, walks around the taxi and opens the
trunk. In the moonlight he looks in at this vault of grimy remnants that testifies to his father's life: the mismatched tools,
the burlap sack filled with oil rags and dozens of lengths of
rope, the khaki duffel still loaded with an emergency change of
clothes, and the wooden crate, glossy pine, studded with knot-
holes and packed with brittle, worn-out paperbacks. They are
all western novels, brief adventures in the bloody lives of moral
cowboys. Stories of frontiersmen who dispensed a perfect and
lasting brand of justice.

Shoving the crate to the side, he grabs the paper sack that
contains Alicia's book. There is a density to the bag, a sense of
compressed weight that tells you it holds more than someone's
lunch. He unrolls the top of the bag but does not look inside.
Instead, he eases his hand in, slowly, as if he were blindly reaching for a cobra. And he touches the cover of the book, strokes it
once, feels the buttery coolness of the binding and recoils imme-

diately. He withdraws his hand and closes the bag, tucks it under his arm and eases the trunk back into locking.

He heads for the orchard, cutting through to the rear of the main house, moving in a moderate jog, looking through the line of dead trees, trying to see if there are any lights on inside.

He doesn't have a plan so much as a schedule of movements. A plan implies a progression toward completion and resolution. Gilrein thinks that's just too much to hope for. He'll settle for distance and time to sort through the confusion of the past few days.

He needs to make sure the farm is secure. He needs to leave a short note for Frankie and Anna. Something about moving his life forward. Putting the past away. Some kind of comforting lie that will allow them to forget about a bothersome friend. The idea right now is to simply gain some space. To evacuate the city, leave it to Kroger and Oster, to their creatures and their unique methods for discerning information and disposing of witnesses, techniques that involve blowtorches and pharmaceuticals, customized screwdrivers and tall buildings, steroid-fed guard dogs and all the horrible secrets of human anatomy. Procedures refined by years of studious experimentation, cold and precise observation of the limitless ways the fear response can be prodded, manipulated, turned against a weaker and ultimately helpless victim.

Given the needed abilities—the power, the money, the political sanction, the access to large tracts of private burial ground—Gilrein thinks that what he'd most like to do with the rest of his small life, from tonight forward, from this moment, walking through this barren orchard, is to spend his days methodically eliminating individuals like Kroger and Oster from the planet. To eradicate their existence. To wipe out not just their careers of terror and control, not only their physical presence, but to exterminate any sign that they were ever here, to grind away even the most minute trace of their being from the collective memory of Quinsigamond.

Isn't this both the best and the worst you can do? Somehow
erasing all evidence of a person's existence is so much more
heinous than simply executing her, involving, in some not fully
explainable way, a darker and more hideous human impulse. Who
could hate this much, at this level of energy and expense, with this
breadth of control, wanting to author not just history but reality
itself, wanting to make over the universe in the design of one's
own unique and egomaniacal imagining?

He's at least intelligent enough to know that this would transform him into the kind of monster that even the most ruthless of
the neighborhood mayors only dream of being. But how large a
sacrifice would that be, becoming the killer angel of all things
wicked and cruel? Maybe in the landscape that this city and its
people have arrived at, there's a need for exactly this kind of
definitive monster. A beast not just of destruction, but of obliter-
ation. It's not a new argument. He's had it before with Ceil and
maybe he played devil's advocate just a second too long, even after
she'd spoken the forced cliché that should have changed the
course of their discussion.

You'd be turning into the thing you despise most.

You would become them.

It isn't completely true and Gilrein had said so at the time.
Ceil countered that it was true enough to be the only point that
mattered at the end. But Gilrein couldn't stop himself from arguing that there is a distinct difference of motivation. Kroger and
Oster kill for money and power and ideas and the rush of sadism
that comes from slaughtering the weak and the different and the
innocent. But the monster who went after the killers was acting
on another impulse, was responding from a sense of retribution
and righteousness, of cold, Old Testament justice. The monster
was trying to end the slaughter, not perpetuate it.

But the problem with monsters, Ceil had said, in a voice that
still, in memory, sounds both disappointed and resigned, *is that
they always come to love the process and forget the reasons for
their actions.*

He comes to the clearing at the end of the orchard and looks up at the farmhouse. And again he calls up his dead wife's voice. Ceil had once said that the best place to hide a book, any book, would be among other books. Gilrein can no longer remember the context of the discussion in which this was spoken. He can't even think of why they would have been worrying the question in the first place. But his instinct says that Ceil was right and immediately his plan is to jam Alicia's story on some shelf of Brockden's library, then get on a highway before Kroger and Oster can make their moves. Because he knows that he just doesn't have the abilities he would need to become the eradicating monster. That he'll never have those abilities and that he should be thankful for that deficiency.

He enters the house and stands in the kitchen trying to calm himself, trying not to telescope, not to think beyond the next few actions: plant the book, grab a few belongings, and drive away. Everything else can be sorted out later. He walks under an archway and into the first-floor library, heads for the stairwell in the center of the room, feels around until he grabs a banister and starts up the spiral. He has no idea why he wants to hide the book up in the chapel.

When he gets to the top, he heads for the stacks opposite the stairwell. He lifts his free arm, lets his hand run along the spines that rest on a shelf set at eye level. At some point he simply stops and forces two volumes apart, creates a tight space, a gap in the line of leather bricks. Then he begins to insert Alicia's story into the gap.

It's a tight squeeze and it gives him a vague but uneasy feeling. And that's when the lights go on and he turns to see August Kroger. Kroger is standing at the mouth of the aisle. And Wylie Brown is gathered in his arms, tape across her mouth and around her wrists and the huge, glinting blade of a buck knife pressed against her throat.

"Bring it here," Kroger says.

Gilrein stands still, Alicia's book hovering in the air.

Kroger lifts the knife from Wylie's throat to her cheek and runs it along the surface of the skin as if brushing dust from a fragile artifact.

"Stop it," Gilrein says, trying to keep his voice even. "You can have it."

He takes a step forward and both Raban and Blumfeld swing into sight from the left and right side walls of the book stacks. Raban has an automatic in each hand. Blumfeld is leveling a Calico machine pistol, which he now rests on his shoulder as he extends a free hand to accept the book.

"Let her go," Gilrein says, looking past the meatboys to Kroger.

"You," Kroger says, "do not use this tone of voice with me, taxi-boy."

"I've got your book—"

"Exactly, Mr. Gilrein, *my* book. My property."

Blumfeld takes a step forward, but Gilrein doesn't release the book.

"Take the knife away, let her go, and I'll hand it over."

Kroger looks to Blumfeld with raised eyebrows. He moves the tip of the blade back to Wylie's neck as he stares down the aisle and says, "Mr. Gilrein, you are embarrassing yourself and you are annoying me. There are two guns pointed at your head and I have a knife at the woman's throat. Now you give me my property or I will slice her open. And then we will deal with you."

"It's just a goddamn book," Gilrein says.

"You did not read it, did you?" Kroger asks and it sounds like a genuine question. "All the time it was in your possession and you never opened it?"

Kroger shakes his head like someone's disappointed father.

"You *are* a banal people," he says in a lowered voice. "You did not even look inside. Do you know what that says about you?"

Gilrein tries to focus on Wylie's eyes. He says, "You know you're not the only one looking for it. You think you can really beat Hermann Kinsky on this?"

"Kinsky is an old man in dirty pajamas. His glory days are over. And this book means nothing to him."

Gilrein makes himself say it.

"What does it mean to you, Kroger?"

"It's a scrapbook," the voice unfazed, maybe even amused, "of my former career."

Everyone stays silent as the words take hold and when Kroger is satisfied with the impact of his announcement, he says, "Now give me my book."

"And then you'll let us go?"

Raban and Blumfeld actually turn and smile at each other, then the Censor of Maisel says, "No, Mr. Gilrein, then I kill you for being the weak and illiterate worm that you are."

And as Gilrein starts to respond, Stewie Green steps into the aisle behind him and fires half a dozen rounds into Raban before Blumfeld can even raise the Calico. Then Green jumps back around the corner of the stacks, but Blumfeld begins returning fire anyway and Gilrein throws himself on the floor as the books on either side of him start to pop and burst and the echo of the assault takes on a ridiculous volume. Gilrein starts a spastic elbow-crawl to the end of the aisle. Blumfeld finally releases his trigger and flails backward until his spine is pressed against the end of the shelving. Kroger is squatting with his back against the far wall with Wylie pulled in front of him as a shield against a sus-pected blitz.

Gilrein pulls his Colt. Blumfeld repositions and tilts the gun down at him. Gilrein rolls around the corner into the next aisle as a crater is blown into the floor. He gets to his feet, starts to run for the end of the aisle when Danny Walden appears in front of him with a sawed-off extended, braced low for firing.

Gilrein goes back to the floor.

The sawed-off explodes, misses Blumfeld at the opposite mouth of the stacks. Blumfeld returns the fire and blows up Walden's chest, then sights down on Gilrein. Gilrein gets off a single round, which goes high. He escapes the aisle just before it's sprayed with assault fire, runs toward the stairwell, breaking into the open to try and get to the opposite bend of the room, buy himself a margin of distance and time to figure out just how many people are in the library and where they're positioned.

But halfway across the floor, Stewie Green pokes out of a stack aisle and lets two blasts fly in Gilrein's direction. Both charges burrow into century-old vellum and leather. Instead of diving for cover, this time Gilrein stops, extends arms and fires the last four rounds in his cylinder. One of them catches Green in the face and throws him over onto his back. An arm jerks upward, the hand quivers as if reaching for something, then falls back onto the chest.

Running for the nearest aisleway, Gilrein instinctively reaches into his pocket to reload and comes up empty. He thinks about going back for one of Raban's automatics, but he hears movement along the outer rim of the wall, someone coming at him from the right side.

He stays low, walks to the edge of the aisle, sticks his head out and immediately back as a short blast of artillery pop ignites. Blumfeld wants to play with him for a few seconds before ending it.

"Mr. Gilrein," Kroger's voice, echoing from an indeterminate position, "step into the center of the room this instant or I am going to cut the woman's throat."

He does what he's been ordered to do. He steps into the center of the room and stands still and waits. Blumfeld appears first with the Calico held high, up at shoulder level. Kroger follows, pulling Wylie along, an arm wrapped around her waist and the buck knife pointing in toward her navel. They position themselves across from one another, separated by the open mouth of the stairwell.

"The book?" Kroger asks.

Gilrein gestures back toward the aisle where the shooting began.

"I dropped it," he says.

"Put the gun down," Blumfeld says and Gilrein lets the Colt fall to the floor.

Kroger releases Wylie and walks to the aisle where his servant Raban has bled to death. He steps over the body, bends down to retrieve and inspect the book. And Bobby Oster steps from the shade of the exterior wall, his Smith and Wesson already extended and sighted, and shoots Kroger twice in the head.

Blumfeld panics and runs to his master and Oster, ready for the meatboy, now down on one knee and sighted on the mouth of the aisle, opens fire as soon as he appears. Blumfeld takes the assault in the chest and then the head, goes down backward, firing the whole time, the Calico blasting another shelf-load of books, tearing down the line of their spines, shredding binding and paper until at last falling silent.

Wylie crumbles to the floor and Gilrein runs to her. In a second, Oster appears in front of them with Alicia's book in his hand. Gilrein ignores him, begins peeling the tape from Wylie's mouth, expecting the echo of artillery to be replaced with hysteria. Instead, Wylie tips into his arms and he feels the noiseless sobbing, the quake of her body as it slides toward shock.

He goes to work on the tape wrapped around her wrists, ripping out tiny hairs as he frees the skin from the adhesive. Oster comes to stand in front of him, gun in one hand, Alicia's book in the other. Gilrein sees that several bullets have passed through the volume.

"Hermann Kinsky," Oster says, "is going to be pissed."

Gilrein pulls Wylie into him, hugs her as tight as he can, and asks, "Now you kill us, Bobby?"

Oster shrugs, draws some air through his nose. The noise makes Gilrein look away.

"People disappear, Gilly," Oster says, closing one eye, lining Gilrein's head up along the barrel of the .38 and cocking the hammer.

Then he eases the trigger back into the cradle and lowers the gun. Gilrein stares up at him, still unsure of what's about to happen.

"I've got the product," Oster says, wagging the book. "My job's all done, I guess."

He moves for the stairwell and adds, "And nobody paid me to whack a brother officer."

Sweating, his breathing labored, Oster kisses his own fingers and brings them to the lips of his comrades before rolling the bodies of Walden and Green into their makeshift grave. The boys shared everything in life, Oster reasons, so this interment shouldn't trouble them. It's a natural thing to do. As organic as these fat, red worms swarming in the bottom of this hole, waiting to help decompose the bodies back to the bone, to devour the flesh, transform it into energy.

Gilrein and the woman are long gone by the time Oster finishes filling the trench in the deepest part of the orchard. Oster knows he should be leaving too, getting down to that cafeteria in the Wing and delivering the book to Kinsky. Begging off the assorted innards in the glazed pear sauce and trying to save his bonus. Then maybe heading back to the Houdini and putting in a few hours with the needle if Mrs. Bloch is feeling inspired. Maybe Mrs. B can work Walden and Green into her map of the city. Some kind of representation. A symbol of his fallen brothers etched right into the skin. Something fitting.

He knows he should be going and yet he lingers in Wormland. Tamping down the already smooth grave with his boots. Toeing the pocked ground, the hundreds, maybe thousands of worm holes. And then Bobby Oster finds himself doing something wildly uncharacteristic. He feels his own forehead and wonders if he might be ill.

He sits down, gingerly, in front of the grave, his back against the base of one of the desiccated trees. And he opens Alicia's book. He opens it randomly, somewhere in the middle, and brings a finger to a crumpled page. He's shocked to find it's not even a real book. The paper is cheap and thin, like notebook paper you might buy at the corner store. And there's no fancy printing, just this terrible handwriting. Some of the lines are practically illegible. The letters don't look familiar. But even if they did, getting the whole story would probably be impossible. All those bullet holes.

Oster is in the process of pushing his finger through one of the holes when Mrs. Bloch approaches from behind and pulls the blade of Kroger's knife across his throat until the jugular is severed. It's like slicing soft bread and she knows this is exactly how she will describe the act at some later date. She'll turn slightly on her stool as one of the prodigies colors in some background. She will study the face of the child she has chosen and say, "Laik der vei du kaht entu frisch bred, gest oot uf der ufen, steel ahl meizt aend stemink."

The spurt of blood paints Alicia's page. Obliterates a long passage that might describe the death of Rabbi Gruen or the young mother and infant who dissolved within the bottom of the Ezzene mob. The blood hides the words that took those events and transformed them into something else, into a language that could hold the meaning of the Erasure and convey it across space and time and culture, across the gulf that separates primary from secondary experience, being from the lack of being. A language that could manage to keep the event pure and whole enough to make the child quake, even if only for a moment, with the immensity of the loss.

Though her job is to give the story to everyone who needs it, Mrs. Bloch is unconcerned as she pulls the dripping book out of Oster's spastic hands and listens to the Magician thrash toward death.

She's aware that she can never fill in what has been covered over or expunged. There's just too much she doesn't know. But she can hold on to whatever is left. She can become a constant and creative reader, even without her vision. And if her inherent ignorance of the author's final intentions will always prevent her from delivering the complete narrative, still she possesses accounts of her own. Details which can be bound and spliced and grafted to Alicia's tale. She can make a hybrid myth. A mutant legend. And in this manner, she'll rebuild the book. In the end, that might be sufficient.

Because, if you want to badly enough, there are probably many ways to tell a story.

Relax. They will not bother you. These are simply a group of local fanatics. They follow the old whiskey priest. They are waiting to see if his prophecies of Armageddon come true. These are not the ones you need to fear. Calm yourself, please. This kind of stress will kill you, most certainly. I've seen it happen again and again. You should be happy we were able to get a booth. Drink your coffee. Try some of the food. Mr. Tang serves only the freshest of wares.

You owe yourself one final meal in the city. Can you walk away without so much as a last dinner? Reward yourself. You have been watchful and you have been patient. What you have done has required dedication and intelligence and I compliment you. Seriously now, not everyone would have persisted as you did. To be honest, I, myself, did not expect you to last so long.

And now we come to the end, the terminal moments of our time together. Do I embarrass you if I say that after what we have been through I feel entitled to call you friend? Embarrassment or not, this is the case. Who else have I been so close to? I do not mean to turn this into a confession of any sort, don't get the wrong idea, as they say, but I think you will understand when I tell you that I am not what one would call an extrovert. I do not make friends easily. My days are spent much like yours—watching, waiting, trying to make sense of it all. I simply don't know what else we can do. I am always open to ideas on the subject, but I have racked my brain for years and I can see no alternative. It is a lonely burden, yes? A difficult path to walk.

We are all plagued to one degree or another, I would think. Look at Gilrein there, on the pay phone. He is speaking to Mr. Willy Loftus. Yes, the Mortician. Very good, you catch on quickly. He is asking Mr. Loftus for assistance, requesting some aides be sent to the son's farmhouse, some janitors to straighten up the place before the owners return home. Look at his face as he speaks. Watch the tension around the mouth, the biting of the lip as he listens to the Mortician's instructions. Is he not the definition of the troubled man? And in this way is he not the mirror that each of us resists?

Did you see that? The way he shoved the disciples on his walk back to the hacks' booth? Was there not just a bit more force than was necessary? Yes, they are blocking the aisle, swarming around the radio, but was this mundane aggression really necessary? Study the body language. Notice the rage in the musculature itself. If I'm not mistaken we'll next see him reach into his pocket—

Yes, but allow me to confess. I'm not quite the psychic you believe. I noticed him out the window when he pulled into the parking lot. While you were praying, I saw him using a pry-bar to detach the medallion from the hood of the Checker. We should not treat this action lightly, however. Do you know how much livery medallions cost these days? And after all, this was his father's medallion. The father's legacy to Gilrein. The only thing of substance left to him but for the cab itself. Which, if I'm not mistaken—

Forgive me, I am not trying to show off or exhibit a skill that I do not possess. I saw him take the registration from the glove compartment and sign on the rear. And logic would ask what good is the medallion without the cab to go with it?

I want you to observe the woman, Wylie Brown, as he hands them both to her, medallion and registration. Try to notice the trembling. Perhaps a single shudder. Did you catch it?

She is not an intuitive creature by nature. But she is trying. Already she suspects the value of the things she has been given. She has been made witness by Gilrein's gift. Baptized, if you will forgive the dramatic pronouncement. The medallion is the holy water and the registration is the balm.

The keys?

Well, my friend, sometimes a key is just a key.

But were I clairvoyant, there are certain predictions I might make.

Wylie will never finish her book. Does the world need another book about worms and madmen? I see her seeking asylum at the gates of Brockden Farm with her new charge. After a time, she might come to offer assistance to the owners. Reading to the children. Perhaps tending a garden of some sort.

But I could be wrong. She has the Checker now. What more does she need? This will be her livelihood and her mission. There is a beautiful convenience in the duality, I think. Once a day she might bring pastry to the old man, Langer, up at the Toth Facility. Otherwise, she will drive Gilrein's old routes, collecting the new stories. Maybe telling some of her own. What else does one do with a functional tongue?

And Gilrein?

Well, remember, he made a promise years ago to his wife. Can there really be peace until he pays his debt to Ceil? He said he would build the Church of Imogene Wedgewood. I think at the time they imagined a smoldering lounge, a dark torch club full of passion and mystery. If I recall, there was an ongoing debate as to location. One favored Paris and the other wanted something more tropical. But after all that has happened, can we blame Gilrein if he cannot sustain this kind of romance any longer?

No, no—do not misunderstand me. I still believe he will build the Church. It is simply the location that is in question.

Very soon now, Wylie will drive him to the bus station. Her first fare. He will tip her magnanimously.

Yes, I have some ideas about where Gilrein might be going. He could be heading north, eventually finding the last freighter—I believe it is the *Jhain Gei*—that will take him to the Palmer Peninsula and a lonely parish in desperate need of entertainment. Or perhaps he is traveling east. In the general direction of Old Bohemia. I am told there is a vacant parcel of land available. In the city of Maisel. The government owns the property and has been trying for some time to sell it. They would listen to any offer.

Oddly enough, I have no problem seeing Gilrein as the first priest in his new church. Ministering to the faithful, hearing their unique myths, and absolving them with the arrogant conceit that sooner or later we will all speak the same language.

Excuse?

I'm sorry, I'm having trouble understanding you. Is that a sore on your tongue?

Ah, yes—the priest is climbing up onto the counter. Look at Mr. Tang grimace as the preacher's muddy sandals muck up the Formica. Look at how the cleric manages to silence the crowd. They hang on his every move. They all flinch as he leans forward to turn up the radio. This must be the big moment.

Perhaps the Rapture does indeed approach.

Take my hand, friend.

I can think of no one I would rather be with.